I0768518

The Four-Bar Progression

A Neil Ames, PI Mystery

Swinton Woolfe

Swinton Woolfe Books

Book Cover by Stuart Bache Designs

Print ISBN: 979-8-218-47046-3

Dedication

For Mike, Joe, Garry, Dan, and Dale

Acknowledgements

Writers spend hours of each day with our words and characters, but self-doubt often whispers in our ear. What keeps us going? Friends and family who give words of encouragement. Our critique partners. The copy editor who takes care of our newborn words. The cover designer who makes our books an irresistible treasure to take home. Here are the people who have helped and inspired me: Natalia Leigh, Enchanted Ink Publishing; Stuart Bache Designs; Sarra Cannon, Publish & Thrive; my critique partner, Julie Ciccarelli, for her indispensable feedback; Cathy Steiner, whose friendship is a treasure beyond words; Sherlock, my constant companion and muse, and my greatest inspirations: Arthur Conan Doyle, Robert Galbraith, Patricia Highwater, and Tana French.

CHAPTER 1

"**N**eil Ames, where the hell are you?"

Octavia Clarke's finger hovered over the send button. She took a breath, hit it and watched as the message was sent off into the digital void.

A minute passed, then five—ten. No reply. She set her phone on the tray table and fixed her gaze out the window of the Yuu International Holdings corporate jet. She felt an intense mix of dread and anticipation. Forty-eight hours earlier, she had received a text.

Mom passed away. Come to New Orleans.

The message from her brother, Michael, had not been unexpected. Her mother had been placed in hospice three weeks ago. Their mother-daughter relationship had been tenuous for years. Now she was heading to New Orleans to plan a memorial service.

I have to be there for Mikey.

Flying anywhere was difficult given the global viruses, international conflicts, and forest fires. Getting out of Japan was more difficult than getting into the States. As the Yuu International Holdings jet was about to take off from refueling in Honolulu, Octavia received a puzzling email originating from Beaudine, Cachemaille & Bleu, a law firm in Montreal.

Dear Ms. Clarke,

Beaudine, Cachemaille, & Bleu are saddened to learn of the passing of your mother and I extend our heartfelt

CONDOLENCES TO YOU AND YOUR FAMILY DURING THIS DIFFICULT TIME.

IT IS WITH DEEP SADNESS, THAT I WRITE TO INFORM YOU OF THE UNTIMELY DEATH OF YOUR FATHER, WHOSE PASSING IS CURRENTLY THE SUBJECT OF A MURDER INVESTIGATION.

Before reading the rest of the message, Octavia texted her brother.

WHY DIDN'T YOU TELL ME WHAT HAPPENED TO DAD? WHAT WAS HE DOING IN MONTREAL?

She got a quick reply.

DAD IS FINE. HE ISN'T IN MONTREAL. IT WAS MOM WHO DIED. ARE YOU OKAY?

Octavia blew out the breath she had been holding and took in three more slow breaths to calm her pounding heart then looked back at the email from Montreal.

DR. BASTIEN BEAULIEU LEFT EXPLICIT INSTRUCTIONS WITH OUR FIRM TO SHARE A PERSONAL REVELATION WITH YOU: HE WAS, IN FACT, YOUR BIOLOGICAL FATHER. ADDITIONALLY, YOU HAVE BEEN RECOGNIZED AS AN HEIR IN HIS WILL, ALONG WITH A SISTER YOU MAY NOT HAVE KNOWN ABOUT, DR. CADENZA BEAULIEU.

TO HONOR DR. BEAULIEU'S WISHES, THE WILL READING WILL OCCUR UPON YOUR ARRIVAL IN MONTREAL.

I RECOGNIZE THAT THIS INFORMATION MAY BE BOTH SHOCKING AND DISTRESSING. OUR FIRM IS HERE TO PROVIDE YOU WITH ANY SUPPORT YOU MIGHT NEED, WHETHER IT BE LEGAL GUIDANCE OR ASSISTANCE WITH TRAVEL ARRANGEMENTS.

ON A PERSONAL NOTE, BASTIEN WAS MY LONG-TIME FRIEND AND CLIENT. HE WAS A GOOD MAN AND I SHALL MISS HIM.

PLEASE REACH OUT TO ME AT YOUR EARLIEST CONVENIENCE TO COORDINATE YOUR VISIT. I AM HERE TO ASSIST WITH ANY QUESTIONS OR CONCERNS YOU MAY HAVE DURING THIS CHALLENGING TIME.

My deepest condolences are with you.
Bernard Cachemaille
Beaudine, Cachemaille & Bleu

Octavia called the Yuu corporate headquarters to request a layover in Seattle and inform them that unforeseen circumstances might require her to travel to Montreal. Fuji Yuu, who had recently become the director of cultural technology development, approved her request and offered the corporate jet and the substantial Yuu International Holdings influence to ease issues of travel between the United States and Canada.

More than two years had passed, yet Octavia could still feel the weight of guilt emanating from Fuji, a constant reminder of his sister's failed scheme to kill her.

To think I almost died because of a tree.

Octavia, who owned one of the two existing bonsai trees known for their rejuvenating and healing properties, commanded respect at Yuu International. When Fuji personally asked her to join as creative director of their fashion and shoe design division, Octavia immediately accepted the offer.

She uncapped her Namiki Yukari fountain pen, one from the $33,000 Seven Gods Limited Edition set presented to her at the press conference announcing her new role at Yuu International Holdings. Her intent was to jot talking points for an upcoming meeting, but instead, she absentmindedly began to doodle, a habit she had acquired from Neil, who always seemed to have a pencil in his hand, when he wasn't scrolling on his phone.

Her phone began to vibrate. She snatched it up only to find a meeting notification. "Damn it, Neil, sometimes you can be so frustrating," she hissed under her breath. "Just call me." Disappointed, she clenched the pen in her hand and looked down at the image she had just doodled—the sacred bonsai tree her grandfather had left to her—a reminder of the faith he had placed in her.

I am strong and independent. I can handle whatever comes my way.

She let the steady drone of the jet engines carry her thoughts away. She gently twirled her glistening straight, shoulder-length pale blonde hair around her long fingers as she searched for solace in the tranquil environment, but the knots in her stomach persisted.

Octavia reread the email message.

Bastien Beaulieu. I know that name. But from where? Someone murdered him. Why? Why would he even put me in his will? She shook her head and put the pen down. *Dealing with this is the last thing I want to do right now.*

She forced herself to focus as she opened her laptop. Thirty minutes later, the video conference meeting with her staff began. She listened intently to their reports, scribbling notes as they spoke, and then delegated a series of assignments for the upcoming days. Later on, she had another video meeting with Kozo Sato, her trusted employee at Yuu International. He had recently been promoted to cybersecurity specialist and had been immensely helpful in assisting Neil with the Sterling murder investigation.

"Just one more thing," said Octavia as the meeting was about to end, "I need your help with a private matter."

Kozo swallowed hard. His facial muscles tensed. "What kind of help? I still have nightmares about helping your friend, Mr. Ames."

"And look how that turned out. You got a major promotion," Octavia smiled at his nervous face on the screen.

"What do you need me to do?" he asked.

"I need you to dig into a Canadian law firm, Beaudine, Cachemaille, & Bleu. They're based out of Montreal. They are handling the sensitive business affairs of a friend of mine. I need to know if they are on the up and up."

Kozo's face relaxed. "I see. I can do that."

Octavia smiled broadly. "Good, thank you. I knew I could count on you."

The call ended and she motioned the steward over. He brought a bottle of Jameson and poured a two-finger shot into a glass.

"Is there anything else you require, Ms. Clarke?"

"You know me too well, Kimji. I'm fine, thank you."

As he turned to leave, she stopped him.

"Leave the bottle, please." She savored the drink and sat back.

Her phone pinged.

Neil!

She looked at the phone.

I will be at the airfield when you arrive, madam.

It wasn't Neil. It was her driver, James. She texted back.

It's good to know I can rely on someone.

She pressed her fingers to her temples and took a deep breath. The rising sun was shining brightly above the reddish-brown smoke-infused clouds over the Pacific Northwest.

It's like I'm in heaven looking down at the gates of hell.

Her phone pinged. She braced herself for disappointment, but found relief in the message.

"At last," she whispered to herself.

Back from Kazakhstan. Leaving New York. In Seattle by 3.

Octavia poured another shot into her glass. She took a sip, leaned back, and stared out the window. She was tempted to down another shot, but instead, checked the time.

Seattle in an hour. I need to do my stretches.

After a half an hour of stretches, Octavia took out her travel mirror and reapplied her Rouge Dior lipstick. She checked her eye make-up and looked into her piercing sapphire blue eyes.

I look tired, maybe I should use an eye mask to take down some of this puffiness.

She continued to stare at herself in the mirror. *What am I thinking? My mother just died, of course I'm going to have puffy eyes.* She slipped her mirror and lipstick into her travel case.

The cabin speakers chimed and the pilot announced they were approaching Seattle. The steward whisked away the bottle and glass. Octavia, stashed her laptop, pulled her cane next to her, and buckled up.

It's good to be coming home.

———

There was a thick yellow legal-size envelope waiting for her at The Pinnacle.

She glanced at the postmark—Montreal—and tossed her coat over it. She didn't want to think about Montreal or New Orleans. It was time to be with her true family—the people who kept her baby, the Pinnacle, alive.

Claudia, who had been managing the club for the past two years, came out of the back office. Once they had been more than friends—now they were sisters. She embraced Octavia warmly. "I'm so sorry about your mom," she whispered in her ear. "It's good to have you back."

But there was no warmer greeting than that of the sleek black miniature pinscher who greeted Octavia with such enthusiasm that he nearly knocked her down.

"Sherlock! Stop!" she commanded as she steadied herself with her cane.

The dog sat and drooped his head, looking like his heart was broken. She scratched his ears and smiled. "High five, Sherlock!"

The dog obeyed and raised his delicate paw to her. She laughed, and they high-fived.

"Good boy!"

He looked at her adoringly and spun around in circles at her feet.

"He sure is happy to see you."

Octavia turned to see Aidan Sterling, his arms splattered with white paint. He looked much happier than the last time she had seen him. Aidan began working at the club after Neil solved his mother's murder. His eyes carried a hint of sadness, but his posture was straight and his smile genuine.

Claudia poured two glasses of wine for herself and Octavia and a root beer for Aidan. They sat down and filled Octavia in on the current state of the club, which had been closed for seven months for remodeling. The club had been thriving before that until the global virus and the lockdown.

Octavia had taken advantage of the opportunity and negotiated permits from the city, and meticulously researched and designed a complete renovation of The Pinnacle during the mandated closures; all while she was in Japan. As she stood in the splendor of the nearly completed venue, she could already envision the awe on people's faces as they walked through the stunning new entrance and explored the modern interior, their spirits lifted and energy restored by experiencing her labor of love. The same lift she would have felt, if it weren't for that yellow envelope peeking out from under her coat. It was stealing her attention. It was stealing her energy and her joy.

Octavia bit her lip and looked at her watch. "It's four. Neil should be here anytime now; unless there's a back-up on I-5."

"So, you two are still in touch?" Claudia asked.

"He texts me and we chat from time to time."

"You've been living in Japan for quite a while."

"Two years," said Octavia.

"Since the club has closed we haven't seen too much of anybody," said Claudia. "What's Neil been up to?"

"He's been globetrotting: Korea, Thailand, Singapore, and god knows where else, on the hunt for answers. Looking for Emily's murderer." Octavia sipped her wine and shook her head. "I want him to find justice for his murdered fiancée, but I'm also scared of what painful truth might come with it. I don't know what it is, something just bothers me. I wonder if she was the saint he thinks she was." She sighed. "Most recently, he's been in Kazakhstan. "

"Kazakhstan, where's that?" Aidan asked.

"A world away from here." She fell into a thoughtful silence, gazing wistfully at the contents of her glass.

"Octavia, are you all right?" Aidan asked.

"Yes, I'm fine. I think I'm hungry. Once I eat, I'll be fine."

"The truth is, the club is not the same now that you're not here," said Claudia. "You're the spark that lights up this place. Our numbers were declining even before the virus."

Octavia reached out and covered Claudia's hand.

"But the numbers were still good and I'm optimistic. I'm working on a strategy to rebrand The Pinnacle, and this much I know: people who are extroverts will always want to gather with other people. To make it happen, we need to create the most stimulating environment possible. The Pinnacle has to be the star, not a person. I'll come up with a spectacular plan to launch us into the stratosphere! We'll do it together—the three of us."

They laughed. Sherlock jumped onto Aidan's lap, wanting to be a part of the excitement.

"Now, let's order some food. There has to be someplace with decent food open."

"Wait!" Claudia stood up. "I have an idea. I'll call Tony, the most bored chef in town, and ask if he will cook one of his fabulous meals. We'll all sit together and celebrate your return. What do you think? Come on, girl! Let's eat and drink and turn on some rockin' music." She winked at Aidan. "I might drink one of those root beers you like. Are you okay with that?"

Aidan grinned. "As long as there's a bone for Sherlock, I'm game."

There was a ping and the elevator doors whooshed open. A man stepped out, his footsteps echoing in the empty club. His hair was a wild mess of graying ginger strands, and he wore a dark blue overcoat. There was a backpack slung over his shoulder and a phone in his hand. He boldly stepped into the club's center.

"Is there room for one more at this party? And will cookies be involved?"

"Neil, I've been waiting for you!" With her rock star swagger and cane tapping, Octavia made her way over to him, dropping the cane and wrapping her arms around him. "My mom died."

"I know, that's why I'm here," he whispered in her ear.

"And my dad died, only I don't know if he was my real dad or if it's all a terrible mistake. And I have a sister, only I don't know if she's really my sister or if this is a twisted game. And, he was murdered. At least that's what the attorney said in the email, and he said I should go to Montreal because I've inherited something, but I don't know what that means."

She gasped for air, her grip on Neil like that of a drowning person holding onto a lifeguard for dear life. Neil dropped his backpack and wrapped his arms around Octavia, holding her close to his chest. She calmed down.

He whispered in her ear, "Octavia, do you know what I think it means?"

She looked up at him, loosening her grip. She stepped back and said, "No. What does it mean?" Neil took her by the shoulders and gave her a little shake as he looked into her eyes. "It means you need to eat."

CHAPTER 2

The large yellow envelope lay forgotten all evening.

Octavia and Neil relaxed in her cozy loft, the sound of Ryuichi Sakamoto's music adding to the ambiance as they enjoyed their wine.

She sat back and sighed. "His music is like a balm for the soul." She leaned back and closed her eyes, savoring the music as much as the wine. "His compositions are minimal, yet complex; it lets your mind breathe."

"Do you miss being in the music business?" Neil asked.

"I miss producing music. Working with the musicians. That's why I love The Pinnacle. It keeps me connected." She poured more wine in her glass and offered to do the same for Neil. He nodded.

"Are you feeling better?" he asked.

"I don't know quite what to feel," she said. "I don't think it's grief—I think it's—" she paused.

"What?" Neil asked.

"Anxiety."

With a gentle clink, she set her glass down on the coffee table. She spoke while keeping her eyes fixed on the glass. "Over the past few hours, I've spent all my energy trying to calm myself, to stop the overwhelming sense of being crushed. Somehow, I've lost my compass and balance in the world. It's unsettling."

"Your world has been turned upside down," said Neil. "It might be triggering—"

"Memories...no...sensations of my accident? Possibly." Octavia leaned forward, grasped her wineglass, and pressed it against her cheek while she pondered. "Your presence has a calming effect on me, which is surprising considering the danger we always face when working together." She grinned. "I guess I thrive on adventure and danger," her grin turned into a frown, "which was why I'm so confused by my current state of mind."

She finished her wine.

"Enough about me," she said, her voice a mere whisper, the weariness evident in her tone. "Tell me about Kazakhstan."

Neil lifted his glass to his lips, staring into the wine as if searching for words at the bottom. He took a slow sip, but remained silent.

"What happened?" she asked.

He shook his head, the movement slow and heavy. "I'm too jet lagged to talk about it," he muttered, his voice thick with exhaustion. "I should go home, I need to sleep."

"Stay here," she said, her own fatigue making her eyes droop.

Without another word, Neil's body gave in, sinking into the sofa. Octavia moved quietly, retrieving a spare pillow and blanket. She gently roused him enough to slip the pillow under his head and drape the blanket over him. He barely stirred as she removed his shoes,

Standing back, she gazed at him, the lines of weariness etched deeply into his face.

He looks so fragile, so burdened with guilt, grief, and rage, and yet, here he is, his breath already deep and even. He feels safe with me, just as I feel safe with him.

She turned off the lights and went to bed.

Octavia slept fitfully, her mind a chaotic storm of surrealist horrors. Her dreams twisted and turned, faces from her past mingling with faceless beings who seemed to stretch and distort like shadows under a flickering light. They pressed against her, their mouths opened wide as if they wanted to consume her.

She was under attack, but her limbs were leaden, unresponsive. She found herself trapped in an out-of-control car, the steering wheel spinning wildly. The car veered off an overpass, the world outside slowing to a sickening crawl. She could see the pavement and a speeding truck below, their collision inevitable. Her heart pounded, trying to escape her chest.

Her body froze, paralyzed with fear. She tried to scream, but the words choked her, strangling her voice before it could escape her lips. The faceless beings closed in, their presence suffocating, pressing the life out of her body.

Suddenly, a sharp voice pierced her eardrums, slicing through the cacophony of her nightmare. It was a voice she knew all too well, her grandmother's voice from beyond the grave.

"Racheal! Get up!" The words cut through her like a knife, searing from one ear to the other.

"No, I'm not Racheal!" she screamed, her voice finally breaking free.

She woke with a start, gasping for breath. She found herself crouching by her bed, drenched in sweat. The remnants of her nightmare lingering in the shadows of her bedroom.

CHAPTER 3

Neil stood in the doorway, his hair in a wild, chaotic mess.

"Octavia, are you okay?" he asked.

"Who are you?" Octavia cried out.

She grabbed her cane at the bedside and brandished it menacingly at him. "Get back! Get away from me!"

"Octavia, it's me, Neil. I'm Neil. I'm not going to hurt you." Slowly, he walked towards her, his arms outstretched, offering protection and safety.

Her knuckles turned white as she tightened her grip on the cane, holding it in front of her defensively while staring back at him.

"Octavia," he said calmly, "You had a dream. It's alright. You're all right."

She shuddered and took a deep breath. "No, I'm not."

Neil helped her up. She sat on the edge of her bed, staring off into space. "What time is it?"

"It's 8:10."

"In the morning?"

"Yes."

"It's so dark." She rubbed her face and ran her fingers through her hair. "I need a shower and lots of coffee." She stood up and leaned on her cane.

"I'll make coffee," said Neil.

She nodded and made her way to the bathroom. He looked for coffee in the kitchen, but found none. He slipped on his shoes and was on the verge of stepping out when he remembered Octavia's security system.

"I'm going downstairs to get a bag of coffee. You'll have to let me back in."

"Take my bracelet," Octavia called out from the shower. "It's on the counter, in here."

Neil cracked open the bathroom door. Steam rolled out. Through the frosted glass on the shower door reflected in the bathroom mirror, he could see the outline of Octavia's body as she leaned against the shower wall, allowing the water to pulsate against her skin from all angles.

"I'll be right back," he said as he grabbed the bracelet and closed the bathroom door.

Neil examined the bronze-colored bracelet he held in his hand. Etched onto the smooth metal surface were symbols resembling archaic pictograms–or perhaps–mathematical equations–that her home security system was designed around.

He entered the club and switched on the lights. When he visited Octavia at night, the club was always loud and filled with partiers. Now the room felt like it was holding its breath and waiting.

Neil found a half-empty bag of coffee and, as he turned to leave, he noticed Octavia's coat and tote on one of the barstools. He put the coat over his arm and spotted the large yellow envelope. It was heavy and appeared to be stuffed with papers of varying sizes. He placed it on top of the coat, grabbed the tote, and headed upstairs.

After scanning the pad, Neil deposited the bracelet and package on the kitchen island. He put water in the teapot and prepped the French press. As the kettle began to heat, Octavia emerged from the bathroom, wrapped in her bathrobe, and made her way slowly to the kitchen island.

Neil noticed her pallor, the slight sheen of sweat still on her brow, and the way she clutched her cane for support, her knuckles white. Her eyes were transfixed on the yellow envelope, a look of deep unease etched across her face. She seemed to shrink in on herself, the strength he so admired in her momentarily eclipsed by the shadows of her dread of the yellow envelope. He didn't understand why it troubled her so deeply. It was just a package, an object that, in his mind, should not evoke such fear. He wanted to ask, to understand. Instead, he stepped closer, and put his hand on her shoulder.

"I found that in the club under your coat. Are you ready for coffee?"

Octavia's tired eyes lit up as Neil carefully handed her a piping hot cup of coffee, the rich scent instantly awakening her senses. As she wrapped her hand around the comforting warmth of the mug, she turned towards the window. There was no view of the mountain or the bay—the city was invisible. The thick red-brown smoke hid all. It shaded a round, bright light in the distance. It was the sun.

"I don't want to go outside."

"You don't have to go outside."

She turned and looked at the envelope. "I don't want to open that envelope."

"You don't have to open the envelope."

"If I open that envelope, I think it will change my whole life." She shivered. "Christ, what's wrong with me? Why is this scaring me so much?"

"Drink your coffee, and then we will assess and act." Neil pulled out the chair next to him. "Sit with me."

They drank coffee as they stared out the window at the hazy world beyond. When the cups were empty, Octavia refilled her mug.

"Let me get dressed and put on my makeup, and then we'll open it." She limped into her room. The old injury had reawakened.

The yellow envelope lay deflated on the kitchen island.

Neil methodically sorted through the sheets of paper and placed them in concentric circles on the floor. "The package was sent by a journalist, Michelle Perusse," he said, "She included this letter." He carefully retrieved the letter from the center of the circle and held it out to Octavia.

She shook her head and pushed it back toward him. "You read it," she said. "Please."

Neil scanned the pages. "Interesting."

"Out loud," she said, "read it out loud."

He paused for a moment, taking a final glance before beginning.

Ms. Clarke,

My name is Michelle Perusse. I am an investigative journalist.

I understand how shocking it must have been to learn about the murder of Bastien Beaulieu, who was revealed to be your biological father. How do I know this? It is my job to know these things. You must have questions. I am also full of questions, so I am sending what information I have to you, hoping we may find answers together. Enclosed is my article on Bastien Beaulieu and The Four-Bar Progression, the jazz band he founded.

"The Four-Bar Progression?" exclaimed Octavia, "I know that band."

"How do you know them?" Neil asked.

"What else does she say?"

I'm sure your friend, the private investigator Neil Ames, will do a background check on me.

Octavia's eyes narrowed. "How does she know about you? What do we know about her?"

"I did a quick background check on her," said Neil, "and based on her past articles, she seems to prefer world in crisis journalism."

"World in crisis journalism?"

"War crimes, epidemics, and political upheaval in developing countries. She's published in credible newspapers and foreign affairs journals around the world."

"War crimes? What's her interest in the band?"

"She says she's a big fan," said Neil as he looked back at the letter. "She wrote a proposal to a jazz magazine and was hired to write the definitive story on the band, with the primary focus on Bastien Beaulieu. Evidently this is the twenty-fifth anniversary of their landmark release—"

"The Four-Bar Progression," Octavia whispered.

"So, do you remember him?"

"I remember the music and the album. It was a long time ago." She sat on the couch.

"At least twenty-five years," said Neil.

She leaned back and sighed. "It was the first album I ever produced."

"That has to be memorable," said Neil.

"I produced albums for five indie bands," she said with a soft, faint smile, "the only jazz band I produced was The Four-Bar Progression." Her smile faded. "Then I had my accident and my life changed." Her mouth tightened. "Go on, what else does she say?"

Neil scanned the page.

I HAD THE PLEASURE OF INTERVIEWING BASTIEN AND THE OTHER BAND MEMBERS THREE TIMES. HIS MUSIC MOVED ME DEEPLY—SUCH PASSION AND EMOTION COULD BE FELT IN EVERY NOTE.

I ASKED WHY THE BAND NEVER RELEASED ANOTHER ALBUM AND WHY THEY ONLY PERFORMED OCCASIONALLY, HERE IN MONTREAL

AND IN NEW ORLEANS. BASTIEN SAID FAMILY WAS MORE IMPOR-
TANT THAN BEING ON THE ROAD. BUT LATER, I LEARNED THAT
BASTIEN WAS ALSO A MATHEMATICIAN AND RESEARCHER AT ELROD
NANOTECHNOLOGY CENTER.

"Wait," said Octavia, "I think I knew—never mind, continue."

AT FIRST I COULDN'T BELIEVE IT, A JAZZ MUSICIAN AND A SCIEN-
TIST? BUT IT WAS THE FACT THAT HE WAS DOING RESEARCH AT A
CENTER SUPPORTED BY LODER INTERNATIONAL THAT REALLY GOT
MY ATTENTION.

"Why is that significant?" Octavia asked.

"A good question," said Neil. "I've heard whispers of dubious activities linked to them and conflicts in Africa. She possibly heard those same
rumors."

Neil held up the letter in his hand. "Let's keep our attention on this."

I ATTENDED ONE OF THEIR REHEARSALS SIX WEEKS AGO FOR MY
FINAL BAND INTERVIEW. I NOTICED SOMETHING STRANGE ABOUT
BASTIEN. THERE WAS A PALPABLE AURA OF MELANCHOLY SUR-
ROUNDING HIM. AFTER I BOUGHT HIM DRINKS, HE TOLD ME MORE
ABOUT HIS WORK AT ELROD NANOTECHNOLOGY CENTER. HE
STARTED SPEAKING OPENLY, REVEALING THAT HE HAD CONDUCTED
HIS OWN BACKGROUND CHECK ON ME.

HE WAS TROUBLED ABOUT THE PROJECT HE WAS WORKING ON,
BUT HE CONTINUED BECAUSE HE KNEW IT HAD THE POTENTIAL TO
CURE A VARIETY OF NEUROLOGICAL DISORDERS, INCLUDING THE
ONE THAT CLAIMED HIS WIFE'S LIFE. BASTIEN CONFESSED THAT
HE QUESTIONED WHETHER THE FINDINGS OF HIS WORK WOULD BE
USED FOR GOOD INTENTIONS AFTER LEARNING ABOUT COMMUNI-
CATIONS BETWEEN THE CENTER AND A CLASSIFIED INTELLIGENCE
GROUP ABOUT SECURITY ENHANCEMENTS USING HIS RESEARCH.

"Security enhancements? What does she mean by that?" Octavia
asked.

"It's bureaucratic speak for anything questionable or deadly," Neil replied and continued reading aloud.

I TOLD HIM HE HAD A RIGHT TO BE CONCERNED AND THAT I HAD BEEN INVESTIGATING LODER INTERNATIONAL AND THEIR FUNDED STUDIES AT THE CENTER. WE AGREED TO STAY IN TOUCH AND MEET UP REGULARLY, AND WITH EACH MEETING, BASTIEN DIVULGED MORE SUSPICIOUS INCIDENTS AT THE CENTER. THREE WEEKS BEFORE HE DIED, WE MET FOR THE LAST TIME.

THE BAND WAS PERFORMING AT A PRIVATE PARTY HOSTED BY A LAW FIRM. I CAME AS A GUEST OF THE BAND. HE TOLD ME HE HAD CONTACTED THE DIRECTOR OF THE CENTER TO GATHER FURTHER INFORMATION. THE DIRECTOR REASSURED HIM THAT THESE TYPES OF INQUIRIES BY SECURITY AGENCIES ARE COMMON DURING THE DEVELOPMENT OF INNOVATIVE TECHNOLOGIES.

BASTIEN WAS NOT REASSURED AND INFORMED ME OF HIS INTENTION TO SUBMIT HIS RESIGNATION. BEFORE OUR CONVERSATION COULD COME TO A CLOSE, HE RETURNED TO THE STAGE FOR THEIR FINAL SET.

"Oh my god, do I really want to know all of this?" Octavia pressed her palms against her eyes.

"I don't know, do you?"

"I need to eat." Octavia headed for the kitchen.

Neil followed her. "Do you want to eat, or do you want to finish this?" he asked.

"I want to eat—and finish this." She turned back. "Let's just do it."

"What? Eat or finish?"

"Let's get it over with." Octavia's phone buzzed. "Damn it."

Her brother was texting again.

SIS, ARE YOU OKAY? WE NEED TO GO OVER MOM'S FUNERAL ARRANGEMENTS.

"One more thing to deal with," she groaned.

"Here, drink this, you'll feel better." Neil handed her a glass of water.

Octavia gulped down the water without stopping to breathe, then wiped her mouth with the back of her hand.

Neil took the glass from her. "Ready?"

"Yes." Octavia leaned against the kitchen island, staring down at the empty yellow envelope.

Neil poured coffee into a mug, added half & half and took a sip before finding his place on the page.

THEY PLAYED THE EXPERIMENTAL COMPOSITION 'FOUR-BAR PROGRESSION'. IT WAS HAUNTINGLY BEAUTIFUL, YET DISTURBING. I ASKED HIM ABOUT THE PIECE WHEN HE RETURNED TO THE TABLE. HE EXPLAINED THAT HIS DAUGHTER HAD INSPIRED THE SONG, WHICH I HAD MISTAKENLY ASSUMED WAS AN ANTHEM FOR THE BAND. THE DAUGHTER HE WAS TALKING ABOUT WAS YOU. HE SAID HE'D CREATED A DESIGN OF HIS COMPOSITION AND HAD IT CRAFTED INTO A BRACELET. HE SAID HE'D FOUND A CLANDESTINE WAY OF GETTING IT TO YOU.

"My bracelet—was from him?" Octavia's hand hovered over her wrist, missing the comforting feeling of the bracelet. "I inherited that bracelet. It was supposed to go to my grandmother, but she had just passed away and my grandfather gave it to me. At least, that's what he said—Oh my god, my grandfather knew. He knew."

"Do you want me to go on?" Neil asked.

She nodded.

BASTIEN DRANK HEAVILY AND TALKED NONSTOP. HE DESCRIBED HOW YOU HAD BEEN INVOLVED IN A SERIOUS ACCIDENT ONLY WEEKS AFTER RECEIVING THE BRACELET. HE KEPT REPEATING THAT IT WAS ALL HIS FAULT. HE TOLD ME THAT YEARS AGO HE WAS APPROACHED BY AN ORGANIZATION THAT TRIED TO LURE HIM INTO JOINING THEM WITH FULL FUNDING FOR HIS RESEARCH, BUT HE SENSED SOMETHING WASN'T RIGHT AND TURNED THEM

DOWN–SEVERAL TIMES. THE PRESSURE BECAME 'SINISTER,' THAT'S THE WORD HE USED. HE COULDN'T PROVE IT, BUT HE WAS SURE THAT YOU WERE TARGETED IN RETALIATION.

"What does she mean, I was targeted?" Octavia demanded. "That doesn't make any sense. We had no connection."

"It sounds like Bastian thought they knew about you and—"

"They caused my accident?" Her voice rose with each word. "This happened to me because of him?"

"We don't know that," said Neil. "It's merely speculation, but this letter implies it was more than an unfortunate mishap."

"An unfortunate mishap? Neil, I nearly lost my leg—I almost died." Fury flashed in her sapphire eyes. "Are there any more details in this letter?"

"There's just a few more sentences left," Neil said calmly. "Are you ready?"

"Finish it."

HE SAID THEY WERE BACK AND PRESSURING HIM AGAIN, 'SAME GROUP—DIFFERENT CLOTHES' WAS HOW HE PUT IT. I URGED HIM TO RECONSIDER RESIGNING AND HELP WITH MY INVESTIGA-TION. HE SAID HE HAD TO THINK ABOUT IT, THAT THERE WERE OTHERS TO CONSIDER.

"Others to consider," Octavia retorted. "How *considerate* of him."

Neil didn't reply, but continued reading.

BASTIEN CALLED ME TWO WEEKS LATER AND SAID HE HAD THE PROOF I NEEDED. NOW HE IS DEAD, AND HERE I AM WITH NO OTHER CHOICE BUT TO CONTACT YOU TO ISSUE A WARNING THAT YOUR LIFE MAY BE IN DANGER.

READ MY ARTICLE ON THE BAND AND THE ENCLOSED NEWSPAPER CLIPPINGS ABOUT YOUR ACCIDENT. BASTIEN SUPPLIED THEM TO ME IN THE HOPES I COULD UNCOVER EVIDENCE OF THE ORGANIZAtion's involvement, though, so far, nothing has been concretely uncovered. Still, I'm continuing my investigation.

If you come to Montreal—be careful. And if you do come, I would like to meet with you. I am listing my contact information below.

My deepest condolences,

Michelle Perusse

Silence hung in the air. Octavia's phone pinged. An email notification from Yuu International.

"I'm going upstairs to work," she said, "I can't think with all —this." Octavia pointed at the papers on the floor. "Work goes on. Life goes on. And there is wine up there. Lots and lots of wine."

"Coffee. Lots and lots of coffee first," Neil said as he circled the rings of paper on the floor. "And breakfast."

Octavia grabbed her tote and went out the door, leaving the bracelet behind for the first time in years. Moments later, there was a knock.

Neil grabbed the bracelet and opened the door.

"I forgot something." She pushed by Neil and grabbed her cane. "My leg is killing me." She turned back to the door.

"And this," said Neil as he dangled the bracelet from his fingers.

Octavia took the bracelet. The object, once cherished, now seemed to repulse her as she handled it gingerly. She slipped by Neil without saying a word.

CHAPTER 4

Neil sorted through the information Bastien had sent to Michelle Perusse.

There was a photocopy of a 1990s article from the British magazine NME about the release of The Four-Bar Progression, which featured two pictures. The first image depicted the band, fully immersed in their music, while the second image focused on Octavia mingling in a club setting with the caption: *"The coltish Octavia Clarke, innovative music producer credited for blending a chic sensibility with the soulful roots of New Orleans jazz."*

Neil placed Michelle Perusse's letter in the center of the floor and began sorting the additional information.

Circling the letter was newspaper articles about the accident and Octavia, whom they described as an indie music producer who had established herself in London before moving to the Pacific Northwest.

The pictures showed the crumpled wreckage of Octavia's car and the semi-truck that had collided with it. The reports indicated that her car had tumbled over the viaduct railing and ended up in front of the truck. Cellphones were a rarity, but a reporter stuck in traffic managed to capture the accident aftermath using a disposable camera.

Octavia was lying on the pavement, her body broken and battered. Blood dripped from every wound and pooled around her. The paramedics were crouched beside her. Her clothing was ripped open in places to reveal the flesh sliced off down to the bone of her right leg, splayed open from ankle to thigh, the shattered bones and severed muscles shining white against the dark red that stained her flesh. Her eyes were swollen shut, her face unrecognizable. As Neil's eyes landed on the limp arm by her side, he noticed the glint of the bronze-colored bracelet on her wrist.

The next circle was the police report about Octavia's accident.

He moved on to the insurance company reports that were data based and written with dollar sign eyes. They presented Octavia with a choice: complete coverage for amputation and rehabilitation or partial coverage for a limited number of surgeries and rehab. She chose the latter, a decision sure to deplete her inheritance, but an anonymous donor had paid for all the surgeries.

So, there you are, Bastien Beaulieu, hidden in the shadows.

Neil pulled out his sketchbook from his backpack and began sketching, capturing every detail of her injuries and the people and cars that had been around the accident.

I will find the person who did this to Octavia, and my retribution will be swift and unforgiving.

In his mind, Emily's voice playfully whispered with a mischievous tone, "You're channeling your inner Sherlock Holmes again."

He turned his attention to the last circle around the letter, an article Perusse had written about the Elrod Nanotechnology Center and its connection to Loder International. Neil had heard whispers about Loder when he was in Kazakhstan. There were rumors they were part of a network of private and government-controlled corporations. An armaments developer had created the network to develop new weapons systems in the wake of the breakup of the Soviet Union.

Advanced tactical nuclear weapons were not the only arms that were rumored to be in research and development. The development of AI enhanced bio-weaponry and stealth technology could render thermal imaging systems obsolete and protect even small terrorist cells from detection.

According to Perusse's article, the prototypes had been tested during conflicts in Africa, but they'd been more experimental than practical. Loder's name had become synonymous with the murky world of human trafficking, according to some. It was one of the companies Emily had focused on for her research for Katherine Sterling's investigative articles and book, nearly twenty years ago.

But Emily and Katherine were dead. Both had been murdered. Loder was just one company mentioned in Katherine's book, but now there was a connection to Octavia and to a man who had claimed to be her father. A connection to Emily's murder.

Neil heard the electronic lock on the door click. Octavia was standing in the doorway. With a confident swagger and a swing of her cane, she entered the room, exuding the air of the rocker queen she was.

"All right, I've had enough of this." She tossed the tote on the couch. "We're going to New Orleans the day after tomorrow. My brother and I have confirmed the details of Mom's funeral. She's going to have a good send-off."

Octavia looked at the empty French press and spoke as she took it to the sink to wash. "And then, after many drinks and lots of food, I'm going to find out the truth and what my brother knows." She wiped her hands and stood above Neil, looking at the circle of papers. "Have you made any sense out of this?"

"Yes." Neil gathered the papers, put them in order, and placed them back into the yellow envelope. "I think Bastien was right. The bracelet was the reason for your accident."

CHAPTER 5

Neil left Octavia's loft an hour later.

The Uber driver dropped him off at the entrance of the apartment building where he had resided for the past seventeen years. Without hesitation, he headed straight to Athena Sailto's apartment. When she didn't answer the door, Neil sent her a text message.

As he walked into his apartment, located two floors below Athena's, he dropped his backpack to the floor with a thud, kicked off his shoes, and let out a deep sigh of relief. He unpacked his backpack, then grabbed his phone, ordered takeout, and after taking a long, hot shower, put on a pair of dark blue flannel pajamas.

He walked over to the large picture window, taking up an entire wall of his studio apartment. The air quality was poor, the worst Neil had seen in this port city. A breeze usually blew over the bay, clearing the air. But there was no breeze. The massive forest fires had changed the wind and stilled it. There would be no walk to clear his mind.

Neil turned to his record collection. He had a habit of listening to a select few vinyl recordings that he curated, with a handful of them being rare jazz recordings. He pulled out a 1961 pressing of Curtis Fuller's *Soul Trombone*. It was a highly praised album that Emily had found in a vintage record shop and given to him for his birthday. Neil's inclination was towards jazz pianists such as Alfred "McCoy" Tyner's style as part of John Coltrane's legendary quartet in the 1960s, Bill Evans with the Miles

Davis Sextet, and the Dave Brubeck Quartet. He read the *Soul Trombone* back album notes, searching for clues.

What makes the trombone special? Beaulieu composed for the trombone. I should have paid more attention to this album. I should have realized why this album was important to Emily—why she gave me this for my birthday. Well, I'm listening now.

Neil placed the record on the turntable and gently dropped the needle onto the opening track. The warm, vibrant trombone tone filled the room as he opened his phone and started deleting the redundant photos. Then, a single image caught his eye that he found himself unable to delete. He kept going back to it, yet hesitating.

What is it about this picture? Not much of a photo—just the backs of heads. Why can't I delete it?

Neil put his phone down and went to his drafting table. He began sketching the details of his trip to Kazakhstan. He'd learned long ago—while he was in elementary school—that if he sketched, he could process answers to questions, analyze stories, or solve math problems. Of course, his math teachers had been perplexed. "Show your work, not your sketches," they'd told him. "If you don't, I will have to give you a D. Your answers are correct, but the important part is showing how you arrived at the answer. The process is more important than the answer."

Neil smiled at the memory of his reply. "This is my process. I am showing you my process. This is how I came to the correct conclusion."

He sent his final Kazakhstan report. Neil's client was a major medical supplies manufacturer. They had been hacked, and armed bandits were hi-jacking their vital shipments to Central Asia and Eastern Europe, the primary target being humanitarian aid to Ukraine. His client arranged to have Neil included in a Red Cross delegation delivering medical equipment.

Neil had slipped through the dimly lit alleyways of Almaty with a practiced ease, the familiar feel of danger brushing against his skin like an old, unwelcome friend. Memories of Afghanistan surged back, the oppressive heat, the constant tension, the ever-present threat. Kazakhstan was different, yet eerily the same—a corruption hotspot masquerading as a burgeoning hub on the new Silk Road. The air hummed with clandestine deals and shadowy figures.

Neil's clients were playing a high-stakes game, venturing into the treacherous terrain of corruption and criminal ties. They were relying on him, a seasoned navigator of these murky waters, to locate the elusive intermediaries whose network of hijackers was bleeding their shipments dry.

Neil charged them five times his usual fee for international cases plus expenses. They signed the contract without hesitation.

He picked up his pencil. What he really wanted was coffee, but he had already consumed too much. He was dealing with jet lag, so he decided on water instead. He downed the first glass.

Dehydrated. That explains why my mind is drifting.

There was a knock. He turned down the music and opened the door.

CHAPTER 6

"Welcome back!"

Athena Sailto wore an Arts Connect When We Can't mask, but her eyes telegraphed her smile.

"I got your text while I was picking up my takeout from the bakery." She held up a brown paper bag. Neil opened the door wider as she stepped in and took off her mask.

"This thing actually helps with the terrible air outside. I got you a dozen of your favorite cookies. Don't worry, they're not vegan. They deliver, by the way." Athena handed him the bag. "Still jet lagged, I see."

"Bless you." Neil opened it and sniffed the still-warm chocolate chip cookies. "These require coffee. Would you like a cup? I'm looking for an excuse to make a pot."

"Yes, please!" Athena sat on the chair at the drafting table and glanced at his sketches. "So, how was it ?"

"It had an intriguing...vibe." Neil filled the teapot with water and scooped ground coffee into the French press. "We safely delivered the donated medical equipment. There was never any danger of our delivery being hijacked—it was too public. Thanks for the help, by the way. Your intelligence connections over there were useful."

"You're welcome," she replied

Neil put the cookies on a plate and placed them on a side table beside his overstuffed chair. He knew she wouldn't eat any. Athena was a proud vegan. The water began to boil and Neil poured it over the grounds.

"I like your music. It's something I don't hear often," she said.

Neil poured the coffee into two mugs and handed one to her. "You want something to cool that down?"

"No, this is fine."

He watched her blow on her coffee. Athena looked at him as she took a sip.

"You look tired."

Neil grunted and munched a cookie.

She looked out the window. "It looks like the world is burning down." She took another sip of coffee. "Were there many people at the delivery ceremony?" Athena tossed her long, dark braid over her shoulder. The silver-gray strands, which had become more prominent, sparkled as they caught what little light was coming from the window.

"No one from the American embassy showed up. They declined because of Kazakhstan's latest suppression of dissent."

"We're still negotiating oil and mineral deals." Athena wrapped her fingers around her mug. "We'll stamp our feet and not show up for events, but we're not going to do anything that could weaken our economic relations, especially with China investing billions in the region's infrastructure."

"The Ukrainian delegation was sizable." Neil sipped his coffee and bit into another cookie.

"They need all the friends they can get. Did you do the grip and grin? Find anybody interesting?"

Neil shook his head as he chewed. "I was the outlier of the delegation, so they didn't notice I was missing from the group pictures of nodding and elbow bumps."

Athena chuckled. "Always pay attention to the people on the fringes."

Neil nodded as he put the rest of the cookie in his mouth and took a sip of coffee. "I took pictures of the attendees on the fringes of the receiving delegation. Most kept their backs turned. I had the feeling they didn't want their faces showing up on any of the cameras in the room."

"Why show up at a publicity event?" Athena paused. "Ooh. They wanted to make officials aware of their presence. There were probably meetings going on in the hallway."

"That's why I wandered around. It gave me a chance to take more pictures. I connected with Wismer. He was buddying up with a couple of characters there. He didn't appear pleased to see me."

"I told him to behave. Also, Wismer's justified in his dislike of you. He didn't enjoy being publicly humiliated, especially by you." Athena looked pointedly over her cup at Neil. "Was he helpful?"

"If he hadn't been so bad at strategy, I wouldn't have had to point out to the colonel that his plan would force an entire village into a minefield. Anyway, yes, he was helpful, but only because he said he owed you."

"How was he helpful?"

Neil went into the kitchen and poured more half & half into his cup. "He works for a private security corporation providing transport for high-level executives from metal manufacturing and distribution companies who are doing business in the region."

"In other words, arms dealers."

"Correct."

Athena finished her coffee and went to the sink to wash her cup.

"You don't have to do that," said Neil.

"I know how cranky you get if someone leaves a dirty cup for you to wash, that is, if anyone should show up." She grinned.

"They don't usually bring cookies," said Neil as he took the mug from her.

Athena wiped her hands on a dish towel. "So Wismer—"

"Wismer has connections with those who have *connections,*" said Neil as he finished washing the mug and took the dish towel from her. "The evening after the ceremony, he came to my hotel room and handed me a flash drive. It was more like a family tree than exact information, but it contained the names and reports on, let's say, the enemies of our enemies."

"You spotted a weakness in the group that was doing the hijacking."

"Of course."

She shook her head and smiled.

"I know what you're thinking." Neil rinsed out his cup.

"Really? What am I thinking?"

"You're thinking, 'How does he do it?' "

"I stopped asking that question a long time ago," she replied. "So cut to the chase."

"As you probably guessed, those hijacked medical supplies were being funneled to the conflict zone."

"To the Russians."

Neil nodded. "But the Ukrainian government hasn't been able or isn't willing to stop them because the criminal network has connections with corporations who are also supplying Ukraine."

"Cut them some slack. They're taking on the real bad guys, right now."

"The entire world is taking on bad guys," said Neil.

"Let me get this straight," she said, "these corporations are supplying equipment they know will be hijacked? They're double dipping?"

Neil nodded. "They get paid no matter which side gets the goods. They look like a victim and can claim losses while rolling in twice the money, if not more."

"And they're just getting away with it?"

"There's been no actual proof—until now."

"You found something?"

"Oh, I found a lot."

"And that's the bargaining chip?"

"If my client's shipments continue to be hijacked, they'll release the evidence to the UN, WTO, Europol, and Interpol."

"Ouch. Are they up for that? Or are they not the nice guys we think they are?"

"That's what my client decided." Neil rinsed out the French press. "I sent the information to them, and they sent me instructions to contact someone who could pass along the—"

"Threat?" Athena interjected.

"Opening gambit in a negotiation."

"And did you?"

"Wismer set up a meeting with a coffee distribution dealer."

"Coffee will get you anywhere. How did it go?"

"I laid out the—"

"Threat?"

Neil gave her a look. "Potential difficulty for anyone he may work with. He was poker-faced and noncommittal. Clearly, he'd had this type of conversation before."

"Then what?"

"I waited and then a couple of days later I got a 'message received' knock on the door."

"Was that all?" Athena asked.

"Nothing I couldn't handle," he grinned. Negotiations were initiated and I returned to New York with the delegation. We went into quarantine, because there's some kind of virus making its rounds in Central Asia, and I got back here last night. It's up to my client's negotiation team from now on."

"Don't you want to continue on with the case?" Athena asked.

"No. I have something much more important to deal with. Octavia's mother died, and apparently, a father she didn't know she had was murdered. She needs my help."

"Poor Octavia!"

"Besides, I found what I went there for."

"What was that?"

"The network is a link to Emily's murderer."

"You found that out in South Korea, so . . . ?"

"So, based on the last report I got, he left South Korea heading for Singapore, but ended up in Eastern Europe. He's also changed his name, but I now have a connection who can help me locate him."

"The coffee guy?"

"The coffee guy."

"And how are you going to get him to cooperate?"

"Well, I do buy a lot of coffee."

Athena chuckled and shortly after, she left. Neil turned the music up and went back to work.

CHAPTER 7

N eil's food arrived, but he was too full of cookies to eat it.

I need to move, but I don't want to do yoga. I want to walk and breathe fresh air. I hate being trapped inside. He put the food in the refrigerator and walked to the window. There was nothing to see. Neil's hand brushed the surface of the antique drafting table as he closed his laptop.

"You're suffocating too, aren't you?"

Neil lovingly rubbed wood oil onto the surface and wiped it clean. There were only two possessions that Neil prized: the antique drafting table, which had been used by one of the city's early entrepreneurs and benefactors, and his Sherlock Holmes book collection. He used the same cloth to wipe down the walnut bookcases that held the collection and ran his fingers along the spines. He pulled out an anthology of Sherlock Holmes short stories. It was an exquisite leather-bound book published as a limited edition in 1921—a gift from Emily.

She had bid on a batch of books from a private collection for the library. The catalog had listed six books with titles; however, when she opened the small oak trunk containing the books, she found there were seven books. The Sherlock Holmes anthology was missing from the inventory list. She registered the six books for the library collection. The seventh she put aside for Neil. He had only read the copyright and title pages, along with the introduction. With great care, he meticulously wiped away the dust from the aged leather cover of the treasure.

"Hello, my friend," he said, "I shall read you tonight." Neil put the book on the side table, picked up his phone, and scrolled to the photo of the four men. *This picture is triggering something. What is it?*

As Neil scoured his memory, his eyes darted back and forth, searching for any trace of recollection. Now and then, a faint sense of familiarity would brush against him, but he couldn't quite grasp it. Despite his fatigue, he couldn't shake the restless energy coursing through him. With a flick of the switch, the room was bathed in a warm, inviting glow. With a yawn escaping his lips, he stretched his tired muscles, feeling the satisfying release of tension. His body cried out for more. Neil responded by unrolling his yoga rug onto the wooden floor. Slowly and continuously, he moved through the Sun Salutation sequence, feeling his body awaken and his mind clear with each repetition.

He decided to heat up his meal and poured wine into a crystal glass. He took a swallow and walked over to his record collection.

He chose one of Emily's favorites. He carefully slipped Curtis Fuller's *Soul Trombone* into its album cover and placed *Tapestry* on the turntable. In the evenings, during dinner, he played one of three albums in rotation: Carole King's *Tapestry*, Neil Young's *After the Gold Rush*, or Elton John's *Madman Across the Water*. They'd been Emily's favorite albums.

Only after the Katherine Sterling murder case, two years ago, was he able to find solace in the melodic tones of Carole King's voice. With closed eyes, Emily would harmonize her voice with the music. Now, Neil's mind was filled with a swirling blend of the two voices. As he ate, the music's warmth enveloped him, making him feel relaxed and content.

After Neil finished his meal, he meticulously washed the dishes. He poured another glass of wine and turned off the kitchen lights. The music was off. There was an eerie stillness in the air; the exterior smoke buffering any outside sound.

He settled into the overstuffed chair and picked up the anthology, admiring the leather cover. He carefully thumbed through the book, caressing and inhaling the scent of ink on paper. Then he noticed something inserted between the pages near the middle of the book and opened it. Tucked into the book as a bookmark for the story "A Scandal in Bohemia" was a picture of Emily.

Was it in here when she gave it to me? Why did she put it in front of this story?

Neil had never cared for "A Scandal in Bohemia." He'd never understood how Sherlock Holmes could have dismissed "the woman." Like Watson, Neil had thought it was impossible for Holmes to fail at assessing the target of his investigations until Scandal.

He closed the book and stared at Emily's picture.

No, her hair is different. It looks like she cut it. She's wearing a T-shirt. She never wore T-shirts. I wonder who took this picture. She looks worried. That's not like her at all. I'm looking at a stranger. I don't know who she is in this picture. It's Emily, but it's not. Who is the woman I'm looking at?

He put the book on the side table and placed the picture on top. As he filled his glass with wine once more, he slowly drank himself into a fitful sleep, his dreams filled with leering figures and a sense of impending doom.

He found himself disembodied, an observer floating above a snow-laden train yard in Kazakhstan. The cold was biting, cutting through him like a thousand needles. The stench of death and destruction clung to the air, heavy and suffocating.

Below, he saw himself standing amidst the chaos, frantic eyes scanning for a woman whose name eluded him. Orders were shouted in a cacophony of languages, blending into the deafening rumble of an idling train. Crates, dark and full of death, were being loaded with precision— each one a Pandora's box of weapons and toxins. He knew he had to stop the shipment, but his feet were mired in a nightmarish quicksand, dragging him down as he struggled to reach the last boxcar.

Then, a voice cut through the chaos—Emily's voice. Sweet, angelic, it rose above the din, pulling him like a siren's call. He saw himself lunge towards the sound, desperation etched in every movement. The air grew thick with toxic fumes, searing his lungs. Just as his fingertips brushed the boxcar's cold metal, a blinding explosion erupted, throwing him backwards with violent force.

Disoriented, he floated above his own prone form. Ears ringing, vision blurred, he saw four men standing around a canister. One of them turned, his face twisting into a cruel smile—the man from the picture. The scene shifted, disjointed, like pieces of a shattered mirror. The man's fist connected with his gut, the pain radiating in surreal waves. Neil watched himself double over, gasping, the nightmare gripping tighter.

"You're too late—again," the man sneered, standing over him. The words echoed, each syllable a dagger of guilt and helplessness. In the haze of smoke and confusion, Neil saw Emily—a specter—blown into a red fog, her angelic voice silenced forever.

The scene warped and twisted, the train yard dissolving into an abyss of darkness. He floated aimlessly, the sense of loss and failure an anchor dragging him deeper.

Neil woke howling in agony. Gasping for air. He leaped up, struggling to get out of the dream. The wineglass was still in his hand. It crashed to the floor and shattered, sending splatters of wine across the book cover and Emily's picture. He took a step to regain his balance. Sharp pain shot from the bottom of his left foot as it landed on jagged glass.

"Damn it! Damn it!"

Neil sat back into the chair, still gasping from the dream. It took a minute to focus his eyes so that he could pull the glass from his bloody foot. He put the pieces on the side table and picked up Emily's picture. The red wine looked like blood splatter across her face.

He limped to the kitchen and carefully dabbed at the wine stains on the picture then hobbled to the phone on the charger. He scrolled to the photo with the four men with their backs turned to the camera. His heart pounded as he focused on the image.

Who am I looking at? Who am I drawn to?

Neil closed his eyes and took in deep, cleansing breaths to calm himself.

What do I see?

He opened his eyes slowly, and his gaze went directly to one man in the picture—a man with gray hair and glasses, his face turned slightly. The realization of the person's identity struck Neil.

Is it possible? Is it him, the man who murdered Emily?

Adrenaline sent his heart pounding. He needed to move. He grabbed the first aid kit from the bathroom and tended his wounded foot, then swept the floor to remove the tiny fragments of glass, and picked up the larger pieces from the side table. He picked up Emily's wine-stained photo after emptying the dustpan in the sink's trash can.

He stood with his eyes fixed upon the photograph until daybreak. The air was still smoky, and his foot hurt. He got dressed, put on his coat and mask, and left the building in search of relief.

CHAPTER 8

The Yuu corporate jet lifted above the wrathful smoky clouds into blue sunny skies.

Octavia reviewed her notes for a video conference scheduled to occur during the flight.

The purpose of the meeting was to complete negotiations for approvals and tax waivers by the provinces of Quebec and British Columbia, along with the Canadian federal government, for real estate and commercial development of two major fashion design centers for both the Sacred Tree clothing collections and high-tech artisan sneakers by Yuu International Holdings. Her strong business acumen quickly decimated any hesitancy she encountered.

They completed the deal within twenty minutes, and the call ended with Yuu gaining everything it required as long as they arranged safety and quarantine measures. Octavia reassured the Canadian officials that Yuu International Holdings already had safety and quarantine measures in place that superseded government requirements.

She video conferenced Fuji Yuu to let him know the good news.

"You are the most amazing woman."

"Why limit it to 'woman'? I can out-negotiate anyone, whatever gender they ascribe to."

"This is true." Fuji smiled. "We are very pleased with your success, and you will be rewarded."

Octavia knew that a large bonus was coming her way, but she wanted more than money. "I hope that means a place on the board."

Fuji hesitated. "You have only been with Yuu International for two years. You are very impatient."

"I'm also of great value, and you know it."

"It isn't me who needs to be convinced. But I can tell you that a sizable bonus package is being prepared for you as we speak, and I am going to authorize use of the jet for any needs you may have. I know how hard it is to deal with the death of immediate family members, especially the loss of a mother."

Octavia paused before replying.

"Thank you. I have another personal matter to take care of, and I don't know how long it will take. I need to spend a few days in Montreal."

"We have a state-of-the-art music production studio complex, in Montreal. I'll have my assistant arrange for a guest house in that location, ensuring it meets all your needs during your stay."

"That's very generous of you. I didn't realize that Yuu International had interests in the music industry."

"We have interests in every aspect of global enterprise," Fuji replied. "I believe you have a background in producing music; perhaps you would like to tour the complex while you are there?"

"Perhaps." Octavia sighed. "Thank you, Fuji."

***

"Welcome back Mr. Ames," said the head steward.

The memory of Neil's last flight on this jet—the return journey fraught with peril, as Sherlock Holmes would say, left a powerful impression on the flight staff. Taking down a hitman who's targeting a witness, all while being airborne, will do that.

The steward brought him an Americano and a small pitcher of half & half. Neil began going over the papers in the yellow envelope and doing research on Bastien Beaulieu.

While completing his PhD, Beaulieu had been considered a shooting star. His writing illuminated the nanotechnology field, but his periods of silence gave him the reputation of being a rebel. His charm made him popular with mainstream media, which created friction with and jealousy from others in the field. Some questioned his conclusions, but none questioned his methods. One researcher called his equations musical and the mind behind it improvisational.

There were articles about his band and his original jazz compositions. His mastery of the trombone was lauded in reviews. The trombone was not usually thought of as sexy, but something about the way Bastien handled the large brass wind instrument made his fans swoon.

The Four-Bar Progression jazz quartet live performances mesmerized audiences. One improvisational piece, which had been based on a four-bar progression, received glowing reviews from jazz critics and music journalists.

Neil took out his sketchbook and pencils. He drew, and as he drew, he mused.

Octavia's bracelet and the symbols. Musical notes. What do they mean? Why did Bastien compose these notes for his daughter, and why did he mix math notations with the musical notes?

He began another sketch.

Octavia's vehicle tumbling over an overpass. The crumpled car. Octavia, with her clothes shredded. Octavia's leg ripped open. Her hand and arm exposed, and the bracelet glinting in the sun.

I need to draw the vehicle that witnesses reported hitting Octavia's car, forcing it over the viaduct. What was it? It was a black SUV. Was it the same black SUV that passed by the scene in a picture the reporter took? What was the model of the SUV? Escalade. Partial license. What is on that plate? Washington State 553. I'll put in a request for a license plate search. Black 2000 Cadillac Escalade.

Neil's sketching came to a halt as he reached for his phone, his focus shifting to composing and sending a series of texts. He was on the last sip of his cold coffee when the steward arrived with a hot replacement. Neil's eyes lingered on Octavia as he savored his drink.

She didn't look his way. Her gaze was inward, while her eyes focused on the patchwork landscape below them.

What is she thinking?

CHAPTER 9

Octavia steeled herself for what was ahead: her mother's funeral, a confrontation with her brother, and the man she had always thought was her father.

The jet hit turbulence, buffeted by a powerful storm leaving Louisiana. Three hurricanes had hit New Orleans in quick succession over the season. The next one would batter the city harder than the last three and was scheduled to strike New Orleans within the next forty-eight hours. Octavia had every intention of leaving before then.

How much do they know?

She wondered how much she herself knew without realizing it. She glanced at Neil. He was scrolling slowly on his phone.

There's something going on with him. He looks like he hasn't slept for the last couple days. Maybe it's jet lag. Maybe something from Kazakhstan is haunting him.

Octavia turned her attention back to the window. They were flying through a sea of thick clouds and she couldn't see anything, mirroring the haze of uncertainty clouding her mind. She closed her eyes and tried to recall the stories she had been told about her young life and the family that had led her to this very moment.

She'd loved hearing the stories her grandmother told of her adventurous life with Octavia's grandfather, a handsome "bad boy."

He'd been a dashing rumrunner who made his deliveries on an Indian motorcycle during prohibition. He climbed the ladder of a successful criminal organization, specializing in what was now called white-collar crime. Her grandmother was very much her own woman, and they lived well. They traveled the world while people around them lost all during the Great Depression. Crime paid, especially during tough times.

But becoming pregnant was the one thing her grandmother could not do, so they adopted three daughters. The first was an infant girl, and four years later they adopted three-year-old twin girls who did not look alike. One was dark, and the other was fair.

Octavia realized it had been almost a year since she last spoke to her aunts. Guilt prickled at her conscience.

I should have called them about Mom's arrangements. I wonder if they will be at her funeral. It would be good to see them. They were always there for me. I knew them better than my own mother.

With children to raise, Octavia's grandfather went legit with his business affairs and remained successful, especially during World War II. He was completely devoted to his daughters. The beautiful and gifted eldest daughter, Racheal, was his pride and joy.

But Racheal lacked innate wisdom. She could be foolish and impetuous. Because of this, they sent her to a private religious academy for not only an excellent education but for strict guidance. At seventeen, she rebelled, ran away from school, and married a mechanic she thought looked like the young Cary Grant.

Eighteen months later, she had a son, Michael. Her young mechanic husband went over a cliff six months later while driving a dump truck down a treacherous logging road. He was in a coma for months. The doctors said he wouldn't live, but he did. They said he would never walk. He did, but it took months of self-determination to achieve it.

Racheal was not up to the task of dealing with months of recovery, but when she discovered she was once again pregnant, she remained in the marriage and tried to reignite the passion they had once had when they were first married. The marriage continued to be troubled. They separated on Octavia's first birthday and divorced six months later.

Racheal asked for help from her parents to start over. Her father gave her money. She left and took Michael with her, declaring she could not live without her little boy. She seemed to have forgotten about the daughter, or she was too tired to fight with the grandmother, who was determined to keep the girl and make sure that she would not be exposed to her mother's ill-advised behavior, which continued through four more marriages.

This was the story Octavia had been told throughout the years she lived with her grandparents. Her grandfather had shown her great affection, but her grandmother had consistently called her Racheal.

Octavia rubbed her temples. It was only now that she felt regret—not about her mother or father, but about Michael, her brother. Memories of a time they shared together flooded her mind. Her mother was making a rare visit.

Michael was laughing and making revved-up car noises while riding his brand-new bike with training wheels. He had a big red cinnamon sucker in his mouth, and his lips and hands were all sticky and red. He looked like he was having the best time ever.

And then there's me, sitting on the back steps in my yellow dress, crying my eyes out, watching from the sidelines while Michael was having all the fun. Everything felt so mixed up inside me.

I remember pounding on the door calling out, "I want to see my mommy."

Mom finally opened the door. "Stop knocking on the door!" she said, "Stay outside and play with your brother." And then she slammed the door.

I couldn't stop the tears. I sat and cried. Mikey came over and put his arm around my neck and said, "It's okay, sissy. I love you." I pushed him away. I didn't want my sundress to get sticky. That's not true. I was jealous because he got to live with mommy.

A tear ran down Octavia's cheek, and she wiped it away when the steward collected her glass and untouched cheese plate. He informed Octavia that they would land soon and went over to Neil to collect his coffee cup. Octavia smiled at Neil.

"Are you okay?" she asked.

Neil nodded.

"It's true," she said. "I believe Bastien Beaulieu is my real father."

"Okay," he said, "Now we have to find out what happened to him."

Octavia let out a deep, weary sigh. *But first, my mom's funeral.*

CHAPTER 10

They sent Racheal off in glorious New Orleans style. Her jazz funeral sealed her soul to New Orleans.

She had loved the city and been as multifaceted as the city itself. The procession opened with a brass band performing solemn marches and dirges as Octavia, Michael, and Racheal's two sisters, three ex-husbands, and friends accompanied Racheal's ashes to her bar, The Storm Bar & Jazz Club, which she co-owned with her son. Eventually, the band broke out into upbeat and swinging numbers, allowing mourners a cathartic release in music and dance. It was raining, and the wind was blowing, but no one minded.

Racheal's urn sat surrounded by flowers on the bar. Her fifth and final husband played clarinet in a band, Joe's Red Blood Trio. They played jazz standards—her favorite music. Food and drink flowed for hours.

Octavia was happy to see her aunts. She loved her gentle Aunt Caroline and her exacting Aunt Patricia. They'd challenged and advocated for Octavia as she grew into a young woman. Now their hair was gray, and their deeply etched laugh lines crinkled above their face masks. They were the only women wearing masks in a sea of faces. Octavia hugged them and caught up on their lives.

They invited her to spend the Christmas holiday with them, but she declined.

"I would love to, but, as you know, it's so hard to travel anywhere these days. I was lucky to get here. Once I'm back in Japan, I doubt I'll have a chance to get back to the States this year. It's not a happy time, but I am so pleased to see you, and if you need anything, let me know."

"The only thing we need is to see you more often," said Aunt Caroline. Aunt Patricia nodded in agreement.

Octavia grabbed a glass of wine from a tray and downed it. She hated funerals. There were too many memories, too many unresolved issues, and too many secrets. Friends and bar regulars surrounded her brother, Michael, so she had to wait to talk to him. She scanned the room.

Neil was standing in the corner. Next to him was Warren Clarke, the man she had thought was her father all these years. She had not understood why he had ignored her. Now she understood. More memories poured over her with each glass of wine.

An arm wrapped around Octavia. She realized she was weeping.

"C'mon, sis. Let's go to the office."

Neil watched Octavia walk into the office with her brother. The confrontation was about to begin.

<hr>

Neil listened to Warren reminisce about his dead ex-wife.

He told Neil that he had come for "my boy" but said nothing about Octavia. Neil wandered around with the pretense of going to the bar for another drink or to the spread of food, which circled the edges of the entire space. He liked funeral receptions and wakes.

Stand with a drink in your hand, and people start talking.

He took pictures and overheard snippets of stories about Racheal as the crowd clustered into small tribes close to the food tables. Her last husband, who'd been with her to the end, announced the songs his band was performing. His introduction included a story about Racheal and why she loved the song. She had a room full of friends who loved her.

Neil realized Emily never had this. No memorial, no wake, no room full of people who loved her telling stories. He'd been in Afghanistan. Her parents flew in from Europe, arranged for cremation, and flew back with her ashes, leaving all her possessions in Neil's studio.

I never got to say goodbye. They never attempted to contact me.

Neil downed his drink.

But why should they? No, that's not quite right. They left her engagement ring with the police. The message was loud and clear.

He got a plate of food to counter the alcohol he had consumed and found a space facing Michael's door.

I've got to keep a clear head.

A short gray-haired woman with a pink face mask moved through the crowd toward him. Aunt Caroline had her sights on Neil. Her sister, Aunt Patricia, also masked, followed behind her, but stopped to survey the food table. Aunt Caroline conveyed an air of compassion and sweetness like a light perfume. Her aging eyes were a honey brown but direct, and they were looking at him. She pulled down the mask and gave him a warm smile.

"You're Octavia's friend, aren't you? She's quite fond of you. Thank you for being here to help her." She put her hand on Neil's arm. "She's going to need your support more than ever. I imagine you understand what I'm saying."

"You knew Bastien Beaulieu?" Neil asked.

"I know about him. I never met him." She looked across the room at Warren. "I didn't approve of what my sister did. Warren loved her with all his heart, and he was still recovering from his accident." She turned back to Neil. "But I love Octavia. She's probably going to meet him, Bastien, isn't she?"

"Actually, she has met him, but she didn't know he was her father," replied Neil. "But she will never talk to her real father. He was recently murdered."

"What?" Aunt Caroline gasped. "Why would someone want to murder him?"

"That's what we're going to find out." Neil took a bite of spicy shrimp. "Do you know anyone in this group?"

"Other than Warren and Michael, no. But I had a strange conversation with a man. He didn't really fit in here. He watched everybody, especially Octavia, but it seemed he was watching you too. He came over to me to offer condolences."

"Really? What did he say?"

"Not much. I asked if he was a friend of Racheal's. He said no, but that he knew Octavia and wanted to offer his condolences to her. I told him she went into the office with her brother. I pointed to the door, but when I turned back to him, he wasn't there. Then I spotted you and came over."

"Is he still here? What does he look like?"

"You are taller than him. He's older. He was too formal for this crowd. He wore a mask, standing out like Pat and me." Aunt Caroline playfully nudged Neil in the ribs.

"Do you remember anything else about him?"

"Gray hair, black-framed glasses." She glanced around. "Look, there he is! He's leaving."

"Excuse me!" Neil handed her his plate and pushed through the crowd to the door. When he stepped outside, the man was already gone. Neil scrolled through his phone as he reentered.

"Oh, good," said Aunt Caroline. "I was about to eat your food. Did you find him?"

Neil shook his head and showed her the picture of the four men in Kazakhstan.

"Did he look like any of the men in this picture?"

She adjusted her glasses and squinted at the screen. "All of their backs are turned." She looked closer. "I wish it were a bigger picture."

Neil zoomed in the photo.

"You know, I didn't get a look at his face because of the mask, so I can't be sure. But when I saw him heading to the door, he had a haircut and posture like this man."

She pointed to the man of Neil's nightmares.

Chapter 11

Mikey has replaced his sticky red face with a handsome one. He looks like Dad—his dad. I don't look like my mom or my brother. I have a stranger's face.

As Octavia embraced her brother, she buried her face in his chest, tears streaming down her cheeks. In a tender gesture, he enveloped her in his arms, their rhythmic rocking creating a sense of comfort and understanding without the need for words. After a couple of minutes, Octavia stepped back.

"You're a mess, sis." He handed her a box of tissues.

They sat on the red sofa opposite Michael's desk, and he spoke as she wiped her face.

"I have something for you. It's something Mom told me to give to you. She'd been sick for a few weeks. She got the cancer diagnosis, and bam! She was gone. But she had a little time to put some things together, and there's a box for you. It's not much, but there is a letter in there, and she said it might really upset you when you read it."

Michael opened a drawer in his desk and took out a key. He unlocked a cabinet and took out an antique hatbox covered in drawings of the French Quarter and handed it to Octavia. It was light, as if there were nothing in it, but as she tilted it, something shifted inside.

"You know what's in here, don't you?" she asked.

He nodded and shoved the key into his pocket. He scrunched his face up like he was about to crash into a wall. He was feeling the pain he knew his sister would feel. She reached out and touched his arm.

"So do I."

She opened the box to find a small pink vintage photo album and a vinyl record that was slid into a faded brown paper sleeve with The Four-Bar Progression and The Bllack Market Studio logo stamped on the label.

Octavia caught her breath. "I used to work for The Bllack Market Studio."

The last item was a sealed envelope with *To My Daughter* written on the front.

Octavia opened the envelope and read the two-page letter.

My Dearest Girl,

When you read this, I will be gone, and you will think I am a coward. You're right, I am a coward. I didn't have the courage or the strength to care for you, my greatest treasure.

You are my greatest treasure because you come from my greatest love. Not the man you knew as your father, but another man. A beautiful and brilliant man who is a scientist and a musician. We were together only a short while.

Some things are just too painful to tell, and I can't blame anyone but myself, but you are the jewel of that time.

He didn't know about you until after you were born. I sent him a picture of you. He called me and wanted to see you. I had to arrange a secret meeting because I was still with Warren, and I thought I could still make a go of the marriage, but I was wrong.

He spent a day with you. He adored you! He asked what I had named you. I told him I called you my baby girl. Officially, you were still Baby Girl Clarke. He said he would like to name you. He looked at you and said, "Her name is Octavia. It is a musical name. A name for a queen." So, you became Octavia Clarke. I am leaving you the album of the pictures that were taken that day.

You are the mirror image of him. It was hard for me because whenever I looked at you, I saw him, and unfortunately, every time Warren looked at you, he saw him, too. It was too hard for me to deal with it all, and I began drinking.

I became a drunk. Warren sent Mike to his parents, and my dad, your grandfather, took over care of you. My mom disowned me, but she took loving care of you. Your grandfather hired your father as a consultant on a government project contracted by Envoy Ventures and kept him informed about you. He gave him one of your school pictures every year.

I wrote to Bastien—that's his name, Bastien Beaulieu. He is a researcher at the Elrod Nanotechnology Center in Montreal.

I told him I am dying and that I am going to tell you everything. I am sure he will welcome you with open arms. He has a family. His wife died over four years ago, and he has a daughter, your sister.

I had to beg forgiveness from your brother, and I was fortunate that he forgave me. I am asking for your forgiveness. I know I don't deserve it. Remember that your brother loves you and always will.

Love, Mom

Octavia folded the letter and put it back into the envelope. She hugged her brother.

"I love you," he said.

"I love you too. I have to go now."

He nodded, and she tucked the pink photo album and the vinyl record under her arm. He handed her cane and opened the door. Neil was standing outside the door, holding her coat and tote bag. Aunt Caroline and Aunt Patricia were standing beside him. They both hugged Octavia.

"You take care of yourself, and remember that we'd love to see you at Christmas," said Aunt Patricia. "I plan on baking up a storm."

Octavia kissed her on the cheek.

Aunt Caroline took Octavia's hand. "We love you, baby girl. Come see us soon."

Neil helped Octavia with her coat. She put the envelope and the photo album in her tote bag, along with the record, and headed toward the door. She paused and went over to Warren, the man she had always thought was her father—the father who had abandoned her. She gave him a warm hug and whispered in his ear, "Take care of yourself."

She walked out of the bar with Neil close behind her. As he was about to step out the door, Neil turned and shouted, "Laissez les bons temps rouler!"

The room went silent. Michael laughed. He laughed so hard tears ran down his face.

"My mom said the same thing at one of her friend's funerals. She got the same reaction."

The rest of the room burst into laughter. Neil grabbed an umbrella from a stand by the door and stepped out. Octavia smiled as he popped it open and took his arm.

"You sure know how to make an impression."

"Are you ready to go to Montreal?" he asked.

"Yes," she said as she put her sunglasses on in the pouring rain.

CHAPTER 12

The jet took off just moments before the hurricane descended on New Orleans. Almost immediately, the jet hit turbulence. Octavia and Neil sat apart, their bodies jolting in sync with the turbulence, but their minds were preoccupied with the uncertainty that lay ahead in Montreal. Octavia contacted Fuji Yuu, sharing the details of their intended destination and the reason for their visit. Taking the initiative, Fuji covered all bases during the call, going beyond to offer support in any way needed.

Neil used the flight to write notes on the information he had gathered at the funeral. He sketched the bar and the clusters of individuals, noting the conversations in each group. Some had talked only of Racheal. Some had talked about the free-flowing food and alcohol. There were others who gossiped about Octavia. She stood out in the crowd. She was an outsider. No one remembered ever having seen her before.

Racheal had told friends she had a beautiful, brilliant daughter who was an executive in a major Japanese corporation, and because of this, the gossipers said they thought she would look more Japanese.

While sketching Warren Clarke, Neil focused on the subtle way he would steal glances at Octavia while sipping his drink. When he made his way over to Racheal's urn, his hand trembled as he reached out to touch it. Michael had given him a hug and patted his back. Neil sketched the two of them together. He paused the sketch as his mind went to the one image he hadn't captured: the gray-haired man with a mask. The one who'd gotten away.

"I'd like to have that one." Octavia gestured toward the drawing of Michael and Warren.

"Of course." He handed the sketch to her.

With the turbulence finally subsiding, Octavia shifted her position and settled herself in front of Neil. She motioned to the steward, catching his attention with a slight wave of her hand.

"Yes, madam?"

"I'm starving, Kimji. I need protein. Would it be possible to have a ribeye steak with mashed potatoes and gravy? Also, a small Caesar salad."

"Of course, madam. Would you like your steak medium rare?"

She nodded.

"Anything for you, sir?"

Neil asked for coffee and a plate of cookies, which the steward promptly brought after placing Octavia's order in the galley.

Octavia employed one of Neil's preferred questions. "So, what do you know?"

"No one at the funeral, other than your brother, your aunts, and Warren, who was silent on the subject, knew anything about Bastien Beaulieu. You were the big question in the room. So, what did you learn?"

"Everything I did and didn't want to know," she said. Octavia pulled her mother's letter out of her tote bag and handed it to Neil. "Read it; you'll know as much as I do."

The steward brought her a Caesar salad and a glass of white wine. She took a bite and continued to eat as Neil read the letter. He examined the paper, then folded the letter and put it back in the envelope. "Is it her handwriting?" he asked.

She paused mid-chew and swallowed. "Yes, as far as I remember. Would someone forge something like that?"

"If they had something to gain from it."

"Who would gain from it?"

"Your mother was the co-owner of the bar. Maybe your brother wanted to divert your attention somewhere else so that you wouldn't try to claim your share of the business. You are a successful club owner. Maybe he thought you'd like to start up in New Orleans."

"He wouldn't do that. Besides, there's too much—it's too personal. I don't think he's that great at writing. Talking, yes. Writing, no." She took the last bite of salad and pushed the plate away. Kimji took the plate and returned with her steak. Octavia took a big bite of her mashed potatoes and gravy. "Oh my god! These are the best mashed potatoes I've ever had."

"At last, you're coming back to life." Neil finished the last cookie and held his coffee cup up to signal for more. After savoring every bite of her steak, Octavia pushed her plate away with a contented sigh and sat back with her glass of wine.

"I feel like we are out of balance," she said, her words tinged with concern, "and I find this feeling quite unsettling."

Kimji refilled Neil's coffee and collected the plate and silverware. "Was the steak to your liking, madam?"

"Yes, it was exactly what I needed."

"Would you like some dessert?"

"No, I don't believe so."

"And you, sir? Would you like anything? A dessert, perhaps?"

"Just coffee and cookies."

"Kimji, He'll have a chef's salad with that coffee and a pitcher of water. He's dehydrated."

"Yes, madam. What dressing would you like with the salad, sir?"

"Ask her. She seems to know what I want before I do."

Octavia gave Neil a look. She asked the steward to bring a couple different dressings for Neil to choose from. After he left, Octavia leaned forward.

"Neil, could you please tell me what is bothering you?"

"I've been jet lagged, and I haven't slept well."

"I noticed you were limping the whole time we were in New Orleans. Are you hurt?"

"I stepped on some broken glass. I'm fine. In a day or two, I won't feel a thing."

"I think it's more than that."

The steward arrived with Neil's salad and water.

Neil drizzled dressing on his salad and ate without speaking to or looking at Octavia. She poured a glass of water for him.

"Let's start over." She smiled brightly at him. "Tell me about the case."

"What?"

"The case. The case you're working on now."

Neil took a drink out of the glass. "Well, for one thing, I'm not getting paid."

Octavia choked on her wine and laughed loudly. She grabbed a napkin and continued to laugh and cough into it. Finally, she took a deep breath and another swallow of wine. With a slight cough, she tapped on her cellphone; the screen illuminating with a soft glow as her fingers danced across it.

"I just transferred five thousand dollars into your business account as a retainer. So, tell me, what do you know about the murder of Dr. Bastien Beaulieu?"

"He was a handsome and brilliant researcher who everyone liked until someone didn't."

"Well, I could have come to that conclusion." Octavia grabbed her glass of wine and sat back. "What else do you know?"

"His wife died of a neurological disorder five years ago. Lately, he has been dedicated to studying the application of medical nanotechnology, specifically in the field of neurological disorder treatment. As the disorder had a genetic connection, his daughter is routinely tested for it as a precaution. Cadenza Beaulieu is a researcher on genetic disorders and a bioengineer specializing in nanotechnology. She is at the forefront of exploring ways to repair genetic codes."

"So, she's brilliant. Anything else?"

Neil finished his coffee. "You will not like what you're going to hear next."

"What is it? Hold on." Octavia motioned to the steward. "More wine and leave the bottle." Grinning mischievously, she locked eyes with Neil. "What is it? Is she an evil scientist?"

Neil patiently waited as the steward slowly poured him a glass of wine, relishing Octavia's anticipation of the answer. Once the steward had left, Neil leaned in and revealed, "They use research animals."

Despite Octavia's love for steak, he knew she passionately opposed any form of animal testing in the medical and product industries, and that she made substantial financial contributions to various animal rights organizations.

"They test on *animals?*" She took a large swallow of wine.

Neil imagined he could see fumes rising above her head.

"Not that it matters," she said, "but what *kind* of animals?"

"The testing initially involved rats and mice, and later expanded to include dogs, cats, and monkeys."

Octavia looked like she was going to be sick. "Oh my god. Those poor creatures." She closed her eyes and took a deep breath. "Okay, what else?"

"Wallace got the police records on your accident. There was little evidence left. I asked him to search for a black Cadillac Escalade. At that time, there were only a few of them available, and they were mainly used by government and private security forces."

"You're working with Detective Sergeant John Wallace?" she asked, her voice filled with curiosity. "Have you and he reached a peace agreement since collaborating on the Katherine Sterling case?"

Neil took another bite of salad.

Octavia chewed on her lower lip. "So, it wasn't an accident."

Neil put his fork down and leaned in. "I want you to listen to me, and I want you to take this seriously. You are still in danger."

"After all this time? But it was so long ago."

"It never stopped. They kept your father—Bastien—and his work under surveillance all these years. His work was revolutionary, and now it's even more advanced. They approached him and wanted him to work directly for them. He turned them down. He hid his work from them, and they killed him."

"Why would they be after me? I don't have his research. I didn't know this bracelet was from him until a couple days ago."

"I think your bracelet is the key."

"The key? To what?"

"To whatever he has put in your possession through his estate."

Neil reached for his wineglass. Octavia slapped his hand.

"Water—you need to drink more water." She refilled his water glass and pushed it toward him. "Why wouldn't he give it to his daughter? She's been working with him."

"I think he is giving it to his daughter—you."

They both sat quietly, thinking. Octavia drank her wine.

Neil finished his glass of water.

"When I left the apartment before our flight to New Orleans, I stopped by Athena Sailto's loft and asked for her help. She still has friends from her intelligence days. And one more thing . . ."

"What?"

"I'd like to get a look at that pink picture album that's in your tote."

"I haven't looked through it yet. I peeked at it, they're baby pictures."

"I can wait until you're ready to share it."

Octavia sighed. "Everything feels so tangled and intricate."

Neil leaned forward. "But that's what makes it so much fun."

"It isn't *fun*, Neil." She stood up and winced after taking a step. "I've been sitting too long."

Neil reached out and steadied her. His touch was gentle as he held her arm in his hand, "I promise," he said, his voice filled with determination, "I will protect you no matter what."

CHAPTER 13

"Apologies for the delay, ladies and gentlemen," announced the pilot, "we are now beginning our final approach."

"It's strange that I'm looking forward to returning here, considering the circumstances." Octavia looked out over the city as the jet flew over the St. Lawrence river. "I've been here several times for the Montreal International Jazz Festival," she said, "I remember the summers in Montreal as being a little too hot."

As she reminisced, a bittersweet expression washed over her face. "I was in a relationship with a musician," she said, "It ended during a cold, snowy winter here." She smiled, "But autumn was always magical. The leaves on the trees begin to wither and fade, but in their last moments, they create a breathtaking tapestry of colors. The symphony of death is the crackle of their dried veins as they are crushed underfoot."

"That sounds very poetic," said Neil.

"Musicians," she sighed, "they have a way of creating a beautiful mess of chaos and poetic expressions in your life." With a thoughtful expression, she paused and gazed out the window. "I wonder if that's how mom felt."

The jet landed and the flight crew opened the door.

Octavia's signature aviator sunglasses were in place, and she wore a transparent Yuu International face mask, a requirement upon entry into Canada. She regally proceeded down to the tarmac using her multifaceted cane, which Neil had dubbed her scepter.

Yuu International fashion visionaries had meticulously crafted Octavia's modern take on a 'seventies rocker-inspired emerald, green pantsuit, featuring form-fitting trousers made from a futuristic fabric that dynamically shifted hues according to its surroundings. Complemented by a tailored jacket and a low-cut vest that changed patterns as she moved; the ensemble embodied Octavia's avant-garde style, highlighting her statuesque silhouette and blonde hair with every step she took.

Neil exited behind her with his own signature look. His curly medium-length ginger-gray hair gave him a cool academic vibe. His unbranded matte black sunglasses hid his eyes. There was a flash of a platinum watch just under the sleeve of his jacket. He wore a disposable black medical mask.

Standing on the tarmac was a fit man with close-cropped hair, a stubble beard, and a wide dimpled smile.

"Welcome to Montreal, madam."

"Thank you, James. What are you doing here?"

"Your assistant contacted me."

"I'm lucky to have such good people around me."

James nodded at Neil. "Hello, sir. Was your flight pleasant?"

"Yes, it was," Neil responded, "the cookies were delicious."

James opened the rear passenger door for Octavia, then he rounded the car to open the door for Neil, who was reading a text. One of the jet stewards approached with a cart carrying their luggage, which James loaded into the trunk.

"Would you like to be driven directly to your guest townhouse, madam?" James asked as he entered the luxury Audi.

"Yes, I need to relax."

Neil's phone pinged. He glanced at the text and grunted.

Octavia looked at him. "What is it?"

"I got a message from Athena's contact. He'll connect with me after we arrive at the townhouse."

"How does he know about the townhouse?"

"He's with the Royal Canadian Mounted Police. I'm sure they are aware of the negotiations with Yuu International Holdings." Neil cleared his throat, and James looked up in the rearview mirror. "I may need your help later, James."

"I'm at your service for any needs, sir, as long as they're acceptable to madam and comply with Canadian government regulations." James glanced at Octavia, who was gazing out the window without response.

"Why would the government be keeping tabs on us?" Neil inquired.

"I'm not privy to all the details, but it could be due to your recent travels, sir," James responded. "Apologies if it's too forward, but officials here are quite strict about global health regulations. There's been a viral outbreak in Central Asia, and authorities are vigilant about cases among foreign travelers from that region."

"I understand," Neil acknowledged.

"My employer has arranged special accommodations," James explained. "Your customs clearance has been expedited...with certain conditions."

"I might need your assistance to leave discreetly," Neil mentioned.

"Your movements will be limited. I can drive you anywhere, but we'll have to be...prudent," James cautioned.

Octavia sighed. "Neil, I'm stressed enough without dealing with upset officials. They could kick us out of the country."

"You forget I was an intelligence agent and have slipped in and out of a variety of war-torn and tense situations."

"Please, Neil."

As promised, they breezed through customs and arrived at the townhouse located within the AZZ Musique Studios complex, a subsidiary of Yuu International Holding. James stopped the vehicle and opened the door for Octavia. Neil got out on his own and stood by the trunk of the car until James came to retrieve the luggage. "Do we have an understanding?" Neil asked.

"Indeed, we do, sir. Just message me whenever you need me."

"I can hear you," Octavia said, her voice laced with disapproval.

James and Neil brought the luggage to the townhouse doorway, where masked medical personnel met them. They swabbed Neil, Octavia, and James. Staff from the AZZ campus, suited up with protective clothing and masks, sprayed the interior of the Audi.

James's diplomatic status had made him one of the few people to receive an experimental vaccine against the global virus. He was required to be tested daily, but not quarantined.

Upon their arrival, they were met by a man, conservatively dressed in a fitted navy-blue suit, a light blue dress shirt, and a meticulously knotted navy silk tie in a Windsor style. Beside him was a woman clad in a disposable medical gown, wearing a mask and gloves.

"Mae is an infection control technician," said the man, who was also wearing a mask. "She will come daily to change bedding, refresh towels, sanitize the kitchen and bathroom, and remove trash."

"So, she's a maid," said Neil.

"Every morning, she will take samples from you to be tested for any sign of viral infection," continued the man in a steady voice. "Your movements outside the house will be monitored."

Octavia's eyes crinkled above her mask. "At least I won't have to worry about tipping you." Her phone pinged. "Bastien's attorney just sent me an email."

"Let me assist you in setting up the computer for your secure call." The man gestured toward a door. "Your office is in the bedroom suite."

Octavia followed him, leaving the door slightly ajar.

Neil took off his mask and walked out onto the balcony to survey potential escape routes.

With quarantine in place, it was going to be a challenge. He could simply jump over the balcony, but there were cameras pointed in the immediate area.

I can disable two of the cameras easily, but I would have to wait until tonight. If I could divert their attention, I could do it sooner. Octavia could create a diversion.

Neil felt a rising sensation of being smothered, imprisoned.

I need to clear my head. Focus. Breathe in and focus. What does the air feel like? Clean. Fresh. Warm for September. I've got to shake New Orleans off. Shake off the funeral. Shake off Kazakhstan. I was close enough to Emily's murderer to—stop. Focus. What was he doing there? The question remains: was his presence linked to the murder of Beaulieu?

Neil took another cleansing breath and opened his eyes. A handful of AZZ staffers were walking the paths of a park about five hundred feet from the townhouse. On park benches, a few individuals sat alone, intently scribbling on their tablets, while others filled the air with the sweet melodies of violins and guitars. In the distance, behind the vibrant copper-colored leaves of the maple trees that dominated the landscape, he could hear a brass jazz band.

"You're wasting your time."

A slight Scottish accent growled the words behind Neil. He turned to find the masked man standing in the doorway.

"Excuse me?"

"You're wasting your time trying to find a way to go AWOL. That's why I'm here."

"To monitor our every move?"

"I'm here at the request of Athena Sailto, who asked me to help you with a murder investigation."

"You are . . . ?"

The man presented his badge and identification. "Chief Superintendent Matthew McGregor, Royal Canadian Mounted Police."

"And the infection control technician?"

"Is an infection control technician—part of the deal struck by Yuu International."

"You mean she's also part of their security team."

McGregor nodded. "I'm here in an official capacity. Making sure that Yuu International Holdings is following the rules. I got myself assigned so that we could meet. Yuu seems to be very practiced in security techniques."

"Yes," said Neil. "They're quite good at surveillance."

"You've dealt with them before?"

Neil nodded.

"But you don't trust them?"

Neil shrugged his shoulders. "My trust card is full," he answered.

McGregor grunted. "I think I'm going to keep a closer eye on them from now on." He motioned for Neil to enter the townhouse. "I'd like to show you some of the *conveniences* available inside."

He pointed out the subtle presence of built-in cameras and listening devices lining the walls of the townhouse. "I didn't detect anything in the bedrooms or bathrooms. While Ms. Clarke's computer may seem secure from external eyes, it's not necessarily impervious to Yuu Security." McGregor ushered Neil into the master bath and firmly closed the door behind them.

He removed his mask, revealing his rugged, chiseled look with well-defined cheekbones and a square jawline. McGregor's intense hazel eyes darted around the room as if he were constantly scanning for potential threats. "Now, tell me, why is Ms. Clarke under such intense scrutiny by underworld crime organizations?"

"What do you mean?" Neil asked. "Are you saying Yuu International?"

"No, not yet," replied McGregor, "but there has been chatter, and it's connected to Bastien Beaulieu."

"Is the RMCP involved in the investigation?"

"Not officially, it's a Montreal police matter."

"But you're aware of the kind of research he was doing?"

"Yes. So why is there so much interest in Ms. Clarke?" McGregor repeated.

"I think we'll have a clearer understanding after Octavia's meeting with the attorney overseeing her father's will," Neil replied.

"Her father?"

"Yes, she just found out that Bastien Beaulieu was her father a few days ago."

The doorbell rang, and Neil headed towards it. McGregor stopped him. "I'll get that," he said as he strode towards the door and unlocked it. James was standing there, holding a box filled with sandwiches, a bag of coffee, and a small jug of cream.

"What are you doing here?" McGregor asked, barring James from entering.

"Ms. Clarke called me and asked me to find the best deli in Montreal and pick up a few items."

Neil stood behind McGregor. "I will gladly take those from you."

James handed the sandwiches and coffee to Neil. McGregor started to shut the door. James stuck his foot in the way.

"Excuse me, sir." He looked past McGregor to Neil. "There is a receipt in the bag for your records."

"Thank you, James." Neil put the bag and coffees on the entry table and pulled out the receipt. There was writing on the back. Neil glanced at it and pulled out his wallet. He pulled out two American twenty-dollar bills and handed them to James.

"Not necessary, sir. It went on the corporate credit card. Will you be needing anything else?" James locked eyes with Neil.

"No, he won't," McGregor answered. "He has everything he needs."

Neil gave McGregor a look and smiled at James.

"I'm sure Octavia will be in touch with you soon. We won't be in Montreal long."

CHAPTER 14

"**N**eil, come here. I need you."

Neil walked briskly towards the office, with McGregor close behind.

Octavia cocked her head to one side and frowned. "Just Neil," she said. "You can go." She waved McGregor away.

Neil walked McGregor to the door. McGregor smiled, before putting on his mask. "I don't think I've been dismissed since I got out of the navy. You know how to contact me."

"I'll be in touch," said Neil. "By the way, she'll be very apologetic when she finds out who you are." McGregor left and Neil returned to Octavia.

"The meeting has begun," she whispered.

"What? So soon?" he asked.

"The daughter asked for it to be moved up." She muted the call. Four video feeds were up on her monitor. "Screen one is the attorney, Cachemaille, handling Beaulieu's will, screen two is the attorney from Yuu International representing me, and the third is Cadenza Beaulieu and her attorney, and of course, the fourth one is mine. The attorneys are doing lawyer things, but it's happening soon. Could you bring me coffee? I'm going to need a clear head."

Neil left the room. The enticing aroma of freshly ground coffee filled the room as he carefully measured it into the French press and turned on the kettle to heat the water. His phone pinged. A text from Octavia. Attached was Kozo Sato's report on Beaudine, Cachemaille, & Bleu, which provided detailed information about their backgrounds and accomplishments.

The firm had been established in Montreal during the mid-1800s and had gained a reputation as one of the most esteemed law firms in all thirty countries it operated in, with a focus on legal contracts and litigation related to global tech innovation.

That's sweet talk for ruthless legal juggernaut that crushed competitors and left them in the dust. As he poured the hot water over the grounds, Neil pondered Bastien's choice of attorney. *This is not just any law firm. It's all about power and financial prowess, and operates on a global scale. Why would he choose this firm to execute his last will and testament?*

When Neil returned with the coffee, Cachemaille was offering Octavia his condolences.

"Bastien and I had a friendship based on trust and mutual understanding. I greatly admired his mind and his music." Cachemaille paused and took a breath, "I shall miss him."

Following that, he embarked on a detailed overview of Canadian inheritance laws. The lawyers took nearly an hour making clarifications. Octavia calmly sipped her coffee as her Yuu-assigned lawyer asked for points of clarification.

They took a brief break while Cachemaille prepared the actual reading of the will.

Neil occupied a corner seat, nursing his own cup of coffee, keen on observing Cadenza Beaulieu. Her seat was empty. He could see shadows on the wall behind her chair. He pulled out his phone and popped up the images of Cadenza from the Google search he had done.

She is the polar opposite of Octavia. Where Octavia's sapphire eyes are accented by her pale hair and skin; Cadenza is a study in dark. Olive skin, brown eyes, and brown hair pulled back into a bun with gray highlights. Round, black-rimmed glasses. Her lips are full, but she presses them tightly together—stifling any hint of a smile.

In one photo, she wore a white lab coat. In another, she wore a black pantsuit and white button-down shirt with black one-inch heels. She held a plaque for the group, recognizing their outstanding work in genetic nanotechnology. Another picture identified her as one of three researchers wearing hazmat suits to protect the nanotechnology creations on which they were working.

While on the flight to Montreal, Neil found a handful of articles and studies she had cowritten on medical nanotechnology advancements, particularly its potential for mechanical engineering of medical delivery systems. There was one anomaly in the articles she'd published. It was an excerpt from an article she had submitted to a journal of offshore energy technologies.

Whenever she was mentioned in a review of her work, she was always listed as Dr. Cadenza Beaulieu, daughter of world-renowned nano science researcher Dr. Bastien Beaulieu. In one news article, it identified a picture as "Doctor Bastien Beaulieu congratulating his daughter and her award-winning nano science research team."

Octavia finished her coffee as she asked questions of her attorney. Cachemaille returned to his seat, as did Cadenza.

Bernard Cachemaille had a distinguished appearance with his thick, salt and pepper hair, neatly trimmed in a sophisticated business style. His choice of attire was impeccable, from the gray pinstripe suit to the bright white cuffed shirt and the tastefully patterned silver-gray tie. His cuff links bore his initials. Although he had a French accent, his English was flawless. He seamlessly navigated the digital conference system, displaying a remarkable comfort with virtual business transactions. Behind his timeless titanium framed glasses, his pale blue eyes seemed to radiate warmth and understanding, complemented by his soothing, compassionate speaking style.

"Ms. Clarke, I acknowledge that this sudden disclosure has unquestionably taken you by surprise and I anticipate that you will have many questions. Cadenza Beaulieu, has also joined this digital conference for the reading of Bastien Beaulieu's last will and testament. I would ask you both to hold any questions you may have until the reading is complete. Do you understand?"

"Yes," Octavia responded.

Cadenza's attorney answered in the affirmative. Neil kept his eyes on Octavia's sister. She glared at the camera, her arms folded. She sat perfectly still, and her posture was almost military in its rigor. There was no jewelry, and her lips were untouched, with the possible exception of a touch of nude lip balm. Her nails were clipped neatly with no polish.

The reading of the last will and testament of Bastien Beaulieu began. Cachemaille had been named as the executor to the will and would handle all the business of administering the wishes as outlined.

There was a letter for Cadenza. Bastien bequeathed to her all her mother's belongings, personal items, picture albums, paintings, and the furniture that remained in the house except for the furniture and contents of the home music room and private study. She was the beneficiary of a million-dollar life insurance policy.

Octavia inherited the Montreal house, the summer home in the south of France, and all her father's belongings, particularly those items in the music room, to do with as she wished. He also bequeathed to her the rights to all his compositions, his music collection, his original recordings, and his trombone and case. But the last wish astonished both Octavia and Cadenza. They both gasped when they heard he left all his nanotechnology research papers and any patents he had obtained to Octavia.

Startled, Cadenza leaped out of her chair. Neil and Octavia strained to see her head and shoulders, but the stationary camera only captured her wild gestures with her hands and arms as she spoke incredulously.

"Why? *Why?* She knows nothing about our work. That belongs to me, not her!"

"We have not concluded the reading," Cachemaille reminded Cadenza calmly. "When the reading reaches its conclusion, you can seek guidance from your attorney on the actions you can pursue. However, if you wish to contest the will, it will be my duty to assure that Bastien Beaulieu's wishes are fulfilled. It may take months, perhaps years, before it could be resolved."

"*Years?* We can't wait years for my father's papers to be released!"

Octavia spoke up. "I do not wish to inherit anything, but since Dr. Beaulieu—"

Neil softly cleared his throat and shook his head when she glanced his way. Octavia closed her mouth and looked at Cachemaille.

"I apologize. Please continue."

Cachemaille responded to her apology. "Ms. Clarke, as I reminded Ms. Beaulieu—"

"Doctor! I am *Doctor* Beaulieu, like my father!" Cadenza retorted.

Her attorney touched her on the arm and muted their microphone. One didn't need to lip-read to understand that he was advising her to sit down and not say anything that might jeopardize her case if it should go to court. She sat back in her chair, glaring at the screen with her arms tightly crossed. The attorney turned on the mic.

Cachemaille asked, "Shall we continue?"

Her attorney answered, "Yes, I apologize on behalf of my client."

The remainder of the will included funding scholarships for university art students, and support for a handful of charities his wife had passionately backed throughout the years.

"We have reached the conclusion of the reading of the will." Cachemaille paused, and his expression softened toward Cadenza. "Your attorney can handle the arrangements to acquire the physical items listed in the will. Do you have any questions?"

Cadenza sat pouting like a petulant child and said nothing.

"I understand this must be difficult for you," he said, "and I am terribly sorry for your loss, Doctor Beaulieu."

Cadenza stood and walked out of the picture. Her screen went dark.

Cachemaille shuffled through a stack of papers.

"Ms. Clarke, there are legal issues that will need to be addressed regarding this last request. The Elrod Nanotechnology Center claims they own any proprietary research and patents developed during the time of your father's tenure with the organization."

Octavia sighed deeply. Neil began typing notes on his phone.

That's why Beaulieu hired Cachemaille to handle his will. He knew there would be a fight with Loder International. I suspect that Yuu International Holdings was aware of Beaulieu's patents, so they have a vested interest in helping Octavia.

Cachemaille continued. "Do you have questions for me?"

Octavia glanced at her attorney and shook her head.

"Ms. Clarke, would you like a break, or do you want to continue?"

"There's more?" she asked.

"Yes, something Bastien wanted to share only with you."

"I think I would like to get this over with."

"There is one more thing to review. The video your father sent to me. It was his wish that you alone view this, so I did not open the attachment. I will send it via email on this secure server."

"Thank you. Is that all?"

"There is paperwork to sign, and there will be taxes to pay. Your father asked that I handle that for you. You can, of course, have your own attorney handle it."

"Excuse me for a moment." She muted Cachemaille's connection. "What do you advise?" she asked her attorney.

"I think we can get an extension on the payment of taxes because of the circumstances of your father's death. I believe it would be best to allow me to advise you on tax issues. My immediate advice is that you should take a few days during this emotional time to think things through before signing anything."

"Thank you. I know that your counsel to Yuu International on tax issues is quite adept, and I value your advice. However, I must insist that everything you discover throughout this matter not be shared with Yuu International."

"Of course," she assured Octavia. "I am your attorney. All that I see or hear is confidential."

"Thank you." She unmuted Cachemaille. "Mr. Cachemaille, please send all the paperwork to my attorney. I need time to think before we conclude this business."

"Whatever you wish, Ms. Clarke." He began clicking on a keyboard. "I am in the process of sending you the video by Dr. Beaulieu."

A notification chimed on Octavia's computer.

"I will send a messenger with the paperwork that will require your signature. You can do it digitally, but an actual signature is always best."

"Please send it to my attorney."

"One more thing I should mention. Your sister—Cadenza Beaulieu, may fight the will because she does not believe you are Dr. Beaulieu's daughter. He discussed this possibility with me and had a variety of samples for DNA testing at a secure medical lab not connected to the Center. I am sending the information you need if the occasion should arise. I can say, as a casual observer, that you have Bastien's face. I am in no doubt that you are, indeed, his daughter."

Octavia took a deep breath. "I'd like a moment with my attorney." She muted Cachemaille and spoke briefly to her attorney, who then signed off. She returned to Cachemaille.

"Please send all that information to my attorney as well. I do have a couple of questions. First, are there any other family members?"

"Bastien was an only child; when his parents died, he inherited everything, including the home in France. That's where the family originated."

"I see," Octavia said.

"You said you had a second question?" Cachemaille prompted.

"Yes, I want to go to the house as soon as possible. Do I need to sign anything before I get access?"

"I can take care of that. Would the day after tomorrow work?"

"Yes, thank you." Octavia sighed. "I'm exhausted. Have we covered everything?"

"Yes, for now. If there is anything I can do, please contact me."

"I will, thank you. Goodbye."

"Goodbye."

Cachemaille's screen went blank.

Octavia sat silently with her face pressed into her hands. Neil said nothing.

Octavia looked up. "Will you sit with me while I watch this?"

"Of course."

Octavia placed her fingers on the keyboard, poised to click the attachment, then pushed back from the desk. "Will you please get the pink album out of my tote?"

Neil retrieved the photo album and handed it to her.

"I'd like to look at the album first."

Neil sat in the chair next to her.

"By myself. I have to see it by myself first. I'll show it to you later."

The doorbell rang.

"I understand," said Neil.

The doorbell rang again.

"Where's that butler?" Octavia asked crossly.

CHAPTER 15

Neil opened the door to two masked men. One was Chief Superintendent Matthew McGregor, who was carrying a file. The other man was wearing a transparent mask and holding a badge and an identification card: Inspector Serge Aumont, Section Des Crimes Majeures.

Inspector Aumont looked to be in his late thirties. He was shorter than McGregor, small and compact. He exuded a nervous energy. His wavy hair and intense eyes were deep brown. His skin was fair, and his full lips surrounded his perfect white teeth. He looked like an actor who portrayed a detective in a TV cop series and the look of disdain so French and so stereotypical that Neil found it amusing. However, when Inspector Aumont spoke, his tone was filled with a deadly seriousness. He spoke in French, which Neil understood perfectly.

"Je suis l'inspecteur Serge Aumont. Je fais partie de la section des crimes majeurs de la police de Montréal. J'ai un mandat de perquisition pour le dernier testament de Bastien Beaulieu."

Neil's mouth twisted into a bemused smirk.

I am Inspector Serge Aumont. I am part of the major crimes section of the Montreal police force. I am in charge of the investigation of the murder of Bastien Beaulieu. I get it. You're more French than the French.

"May we come in?" McGregor asked.

Neil opened the door wider. McGregor entered. Aumont remained on the steps.

"Il est obligatoire que vous portiez un masque en tour temps lorsque vous êtes en presence d'autrui."

Mandatory to wear a mask. So, he wants to play a game. Okay, I'll play.

Neil stepped outside on the top step of the entrance into the townhouse. He towered over Aumont.

"Je mettrai mon masque lorsque vous arrêterez de prétendre que vous ne parlez pas anglais," Neil replied.

"Gentlemen,"—McGregor stepped between them—"let's stop playing who has the biggest . . . ego. Mr. Ames, please put on your mask. Aumont, I know you think French is the superior language, but please speak English."

"Je devrais l'arrêter pour ne pas être conforme," retorted Aumont.

As Neil pulled his mask from his pocket. He glanced at McGregor, their eyes meeting for a brief moment, before he shut the door, intentionally leaving Aumont on the other side.

"That is unwise," said McGregor. "He has an attitude, but he is a highly skilled detective, who can provide you invaluable assistance if you show him respect. You should really check your ego."

Aumont pounded on the door. Octavia came out of the office and leaned on her cane.

"What is going on?"

"It's the police."

"The police? Well, let them in. Never mind, I'll let them in."

She went to the door and opened it as Aumont was in mid-swing to pound on the door and narrowly missed Octavia's face. She instinctively shielded her face using her cane. The movement caught him off balance, and he tumbled down the steps onto the ground.

"I'm so sorry!" Octavia recovered her balance. "I wasn't expecting a slug to the face."

Aumont stood up and brushed himself off.

"I apologize, madam." He looked at her. "Where is your mask? Vous Américains

n'avez aucune considération pour la sécurité des autres."

Octavia planted her cane, and the power of the rocker queen poured forth.

That's my girl. Sic him! Neil stood back and enjoyed the show.

"Je ne suis pas venu ici pour être harcelé par la police. Je suis ici parce que mon père a été assassiné. And you *do* speak English, *oui*?" She said firmly, "I didn't come here to be a punching bag for the police. Now, if you're done being unbearable, I'll put on my mask, and you can come in."

Octavia walked up to Neil. Her eyes were on fire. "Really? You get into a childish argument with a police officer? We have enough to worry about without alienating the Canadian authorities." Her cane struck the floor with resounding thuds as she confidently strode toward her office. She stopped long enough to address McGregor. "You call yourself a butler?"

"Well, actually I—"

Octavia slammed her door. McGregor looked at Neil and motioned to the bathroom. "You're a mess, Aumont, clean-up your act," he said, handing Aumont a towel. After closing the door, McGregor and Neil exchanged a knowing grin. "Perhaps it would have been wise to inform her about our plan," he suggested.

"She's got a lot on her mind," Neil said. "But her reactions were spot-on for the situation."

"She is a force." Aumont wiped the remnants of soil and leaves off his trousers.

Neil gestured toward the file in McGregor's hand. "What's in there?" he asked.

"Aumont let me review the police and evidence reports from the Beaulieu case as a courtesy to another law enforcement agency. I brought copies, but you can't keep them." McGregor opened the door. "I'm going to introduce myself to Ms. Clarke. Play nice, you two. I'll be back soon."

"Maybe," said Neil with a grin. "Octavia took down a professional killer with that cane."

"Really?" McGregor grinned back. "Sounds like my kind of woman."

Neil opened the file.

"The notes are written in French. Do you need to have them translated?" asked Aumont.

"No, that won't be necessary. Things can get lost in translation."

Neil began laying sections of the reports on the countertops. He spread out the crime scene photos on the floor.

"I can brief you on our findings at the scene," Aumont offered.

"No, not yet," Neil replied. "I don't see the medical examiner's report."

"We're still waiting on that."

Neil examined the photos taken of Bastien's face, which had captivated so many people over the years, now bloated, the facial muscles were distorted and his teeth clenched as if his last sound had been a growl.

"Any preliminary opinions about the cause of death?"

"Nothing definitive," said Aumont.

"It looks like he was hit on the back of the head," said Neil.

"His wallet was missing," said Aumont. "We found it tossed in the garbage a couple of blocks away. The killer hit him on the back of the head, grabbed his wallet. It looks like a robbery gone bad."

Neil continued to examine the photos. "What do you see in these pictures?"

Aumont looked at them. "This is a close-up of the left hand, and this one is a close-up of the right hand. There is a wedding ring on the left hand, and . . . it looks like the fingers are broken on the right hand. He was fighting back."

"His watch is gone. No, not a watch...some kind of bracelet, did you notice?" Neil asked. "His skin is much paler compared to his hands. Now look at this one." Neil indicated another photo of the face. "There is a lot of vomit." He paused and reexamined one shot of the doorway close to the body. He selected another of the same area at the entrance of the alley where the body had been found. "This is the jazz club, yes?"

"Yes," confirmed Aumont. "It's one of the clubs where he used to play. It closed two months ago."

"Why would he go to the club if it was closed?" Neil asked.

"There are four clubs that are closed but would open up on rotation weekly so that the band could come together and rehearse. He was supposed to go to a rehearsal the night he was murdered."

"You said four clubs. Why were they closed?"

"The pandemic resulted in the demise of many businesses," said Aumont.

Neil went through the pictures, pulled five pictures from the collection, and put the rest in the envelope. Neil handed the photos to Aumont.

"He was going to a rehearsal?"

"Yes," said Aumont.

"If he was going to a rehearsal, where were the other band members?"

"One of the band members got sick and the rehearsal was canceled."

"But, he came anyway?"

"They tried to call him and sent texts, but he didn't answer them."

"Who found the body?"

"The club owner. He's also a band member. He waited to see if Beaulieu would show up and was locking up when he discovered the body."

"Hmm," said Neil, "Where's his instrument?"

"What instrument?"

"Beaulieu was going to a rehearsal, where's his trombone?"

"It's possible his fingers were broken, because he wouldn't let it go," Aumont remarked.

"You need to search the area for the trombone."

"We searched—"

"You need to broaden the search area, and one more thing—"

"What?"

"His fingers weren't broken, they were contorted like he was in extreme pain or having a seizure, and he was vomiting. You see it around his mouth and over by the door to the club. And there's something else, there was redness and subtle bruising around his wrists, his neck, and temples. The wound on the back of the head. It's an odd angle. Barely broke the skin. Not much blood for a head wound. Were you at the crime scene?" Neil asked.

"No, the case was reassigned to me yesterday, at McGregor's request."

"So you didn't actually see the body at the crime scene? Pity."

"No, but I did see it at the morgue, just after the autopsy was done," said Aumont defensively.

"Then we have to rely on the photos," said Neil. "Despite the circumstances, I have seen what was necessary."

"And what is that?" ask Aumont.

"The bruising and redness came from attacks from within."

"Within? What are you talking about?"

"Bruce Lee," said Neil.

"Bruce Lee? Je le savais, vous êtes fou, n'est-ce pas ?" Aumont stuffed photos in the file.

"You need to find the trombone, he may have hid it on the way to the meeting."

"You mean rehearsal," said Aumont. "I think you're jet lagged."

"I think he was meeting someone, someone he didn't trust."

"Who? The club owner? And why hide the trombone?" asked Aumont.

"I don't know," said Neil, "but we need to find it quickly, because Octavia inherited it, and if Bastien was killed because of it, her life is in danger."

CHAPTER 16

"I would appreciate it if you would fill me in on what the hell is going on?"

Octavia stood firmly in the doorway, with McGregor standing close behind her.

"This man," she nodded her head toward McGregor, "tells me he is not a butler." Neil and Aumont exchanged uneasy looks as Octavia's narrowed eyes and irritated frown bore down on them. "And, how shall I say this to make myself perfectly clear to both of you?" She paused. "Ah. Pardon moi, but why are you rendezvousing with a police officer in the toilette?"

"Inspector," said Aumont.

Octavia's icy look could've chilled champagne. "What?"

"I'm an inspector."

She shot Neil a look. "You're keeping things from me, and I don't like it."

Leaning in, Neil spoke in a conciliatory tone. "This is a Yuu building. Do you remember what security was like on the campus in Japan? We were under constant surveillance. Remember? If we are to have a private conversation, it has to be in the bathroom or a bedroom."

"Oh, good grief!" Octavia rolled her eyes. "There are things I want only you to see and hear. Does that mean we're going to be spending all our time in the bathroom?" She pushed past McGregor. "I'm going to have a glass of wine. No, a brandy sounds better." She glared at Aumont, "and I'm way past worrying about putting on my mask."

She walked into the dining area, where a well-appointed bar stood at the ready. There were a dozen Canadian whiskies to choose from. She stood looking at them. Aumont approached her carefully, as one does a skittish cat.

"May I help you select one? We Canadians are proud of our whisky." He looked over the selection. "These are the best we offer. I suggest you try the Forty Creek Confederation Oak."

He took it out of the cabinet and offered to pour it for her. She nodded. He handed the glass to her. "Look for notes of praline, honey, and dark fruits on the palate."

Octavia took a sip and then another, this time letting it swirl around her tongue. "Excellent selection. Thank you." She took a long look at this Montreal police inspector. She took another sip and asked, "Who are you, really?"

McGregor and Neil whispered as they came out of the bathroom. Neil nodded. "Octavia, let's go into your bedroom."

McGregor and Aumont entered Octavia's bedroom suite, which was meticulously designed to serve as both an office space and a haven of relaxation. Perched in her desk chair, Octavia swirled her glass thoughtfully, casting a glance at McGregor and Aumont, who were seated in two plush emerald-green velvet armchairs. Neil lingered, standing. Octavia took a measured sip of whisky, reclining slightly.

"I'm all ears. Who are these guys, and why are they here?"

"This is Chief Superintendent Matthew McGregor. He is with the Royal Canadian Mounted Police. McGregor knows Athena Sailto. She contacted him, and he has agreed to help us."

McGregor spoke up. "I'm interested in what happened to your father because of his connection with Elrod, the foundation created by Loder International. I've been investigating them and there have been questionable activities that might connect them to a major international crime syndicate."

"So, why haven't you closed them down?" asked Octavia.

"Loder International's presence in the business world is formidable and has powerful allies. We need concrete evidence and brave individuals willing to testify. When your father contacted us, he described being coerced to work for them in great detail. We thought we had our shot. It is crucial that his research remains secure and does not end up in the wrong possession. We arranged a meeting with him. However, prior to providing further details, he emphasized the need for assurances regarding your safety."

"What about Cadenza? Wouldn't she be in danger as well?" Octavia asked.

Neil spoke up. "Cadenza could be the one who is the go-between for the criminal organization."

"Criminal organization? I thought we were dealing with Loder International."

"That's why we are investigating them. There have been rumors," said McGregor.

"So I've been told," said Octavia. "But, why would she be involved?"

"Your father expressed concern because she had gotten involved with some bad people. That's all he revealed," said McGregor.

Octavia looked at Aumont. "And are you part of this charade?"

"I'm afraid I am," admitted Aumont. "I am in charge of the investigation of your father's murder."

McGregor stood. "Serge is here because I requested his assistance." He glanced at Neil. "We will be working intelligence during the murder investigation. It was mentioned by Athena that Ames had a previous background as a highly capable intelligence operative. I worked with her before joining the RCMP.

"Serge led a police unit that supported the Canadian military and the RCMP in the Middle East. I trust his instincts, and I trust him. Given the complexity of this case, it is vital that we all cooperate. Isn't that correct, Ames?"

Neil was scrolling through his phone.

"Ames?"

Neil looked up. "Yes."

"I'd like to see my father's house." Octavia stood up and finished her drink. She handed her glass to Aumont. "His attorney said he would arrange for access. Can you coordinate that for me, Serge?" She smiled at him.

"Yes, Cachemaille has influence in high places," said Aumont, "but we are still investigating a murder. No one should go into the house until it's been properly processed."

"What if you went with us?" she asked. "You could investigate while you're there."

Aumont expressed his intention to explore its feasibility. Neil took pictures of the police report and returned the hard copies to him. Octavia had one more request for Aumont.

"I'd like to see the pictures of my father's . . . murder scene."

"I think that is inadvisable, Ms. Clarke," he replied gravely.

"That's all right. I have my own sources," Octavia replied.

"Ms. Clarke, I implore you, with the utmost urgency, to refrain from entangling yourself in the investigation," Aumont warned solemnly.

Neil and Octavia exchanged glances.

CHAPTER 17

They were alone, and Octavia sat on the white couch with the pink photo album.

Neil sat next to Octavia with two sandwiches and two bottles of water.

"I want more whisky," she said.

"We should eat first. You're facing intense and sensitive revelations, and it's going to be a demanding and exhausting process. You need to hydrate to think straight."

"I don't want to hydrate. I want to get drunk. I want to wipe all of this away."

Neil uncapped a bottle of water and handed it to her. She took a drink and another. Then she reached for the roast beef sandwich and began eating.

"You're right," she said, "I do need to relax for a little while. I'm going to take a shower and change into my pajamas. But we need to go through the pictures, the letter he wrote me, and the video message attached to the will."

Neil nodded, and Octavia left the room. He ate his sandwich and downed a bottle of water. He took the plates to the kitchen then gazed out the balcony door toward the park. The sun was setting, and the sky was a coppery gold. Soon it would be dark, and the day would end.

Neil took off his shoes and brought his laptop and sketchpad to the couch. Relaxed, hydrated, and nourished, he began his work—typing everything he had noted and a follow-up plan. After stretching his body, he grabbed the sketch pad and pencil, eager to capture the day's events on paper.

Meeting McGregor and the house cleaner. Escape routes from the townhouse. Locations of the surveillance cameras. The expressions of Octavia's sister. Reveal of RCMP Chief Superintendent Matthew McGregor and Inspector Serge Aumont. The argument. Octavia defending herself and knocking Aumont down. Pictures of the victim. Contortions, vomit, the white strip of skin on the victim's wrist.

He organized them, circles within circles on the floor. He rubbed his eyes and went into his room to put on sweatpants and a T-shirt. There was a yoga mat in the closet. He unrolled it onto the bedroom floor. The yoga stretches felt good, and the deep breathing calmed him, but releasing the tensions of Octavia's case opened other thoughts he had put away. Neil's mind went to Kazakhstan and to the trail of clues that had led him there—to Emily Granger's murderer. The murderer with a new name.

His modus operandi is glaringly evident, yet the man himself remains an enigma. His counterfeit identification and fabricated background records were meticulously crafted. Trying to grasp his true identity is like chasing a fleeting mirage, always just out of reach.

Neil brought his thoughts back to his breath. He achieved stillness for a few moments, but his mind quickly shifted from one thought to another.

I hunted him down through his twisted web of victims scattered across the globe. The network rewards him for acting as a serial killer, and he takes delight in his job. He stalks women like prey. His attacks are brutal. He likes to see the terror on their faces. With men, it's all business, a quick puncture of poison in the dark or a deadly accident in broad daylight. The men never see him. He has no interest in watching them die.

Neil opened his eyes.

I found him, and I didn't know it. Fool! You fool! My target was right in front of me, but I failed to notice it.

"May I join you?"

Octavia stood in the doorway of his bedroom. Her hair was still damp, and she smelled of fresh soap. She had her yoga mat under her arm.

Neil looked at her. He took a breath. His mind cleared. "Of course."

She rolled out her yoga mat, and together they proceeded through poses and breathing exercises.

Octavia gingerly navigated through the positions. Neil could see she felt the ache in her injured leg and hip. Still, she persisted in her movements and he noticed her body gradually loosened up and flexibility began to emerge. Their movements became as one, and they moved in rhythm like dancers waltzing across a ballroom floor. They fell asleep on the floor during the last rotation of relaxation and breathing.

Midnight came, and at that same moment, both woke up, refreshed but hungry. Neil helped Octavia up and rolled the yoga mats. He took a shower as Octavia checked out what was available in the kitchen. She whipped up omelets and made toast. She brewed a pot of ginger tea. Neil came out in a bathrobe and slippers. They went out into the cold, clear autumn night and ate by candlelight on the balcony, staring at the stars and planets.

"Do you want to do it now, or wait until the morning?" Neil asked.

"Now," she said. They went inside, to the office, and sat on the couch. She picked up the pink album and opened it. Inscribed on the inside cover was one line: *My Two Treasures. Forever Cherished. Forever Summoned to My Heart.*

CHAPTER 18

Octavia turned the page to find a faded photo of two people cradling a baby, their arms wrapped around each other.

The man was looking at the small bundle, and the woman was gazing up at the man.

Octavia put her hand over her mouth and struggled to keep her tears from rolling down her face. Her mother was young and beautiful, with long reddish-brown hair, and her father was equally beautiful, with sunlit blond hair. His eyes were sapphire blue, and his lips were full, surrounding a generous smile. He had hands with long fingers—an artist's hands.

"So, this is my father and mother when they were in love. I wonder who took the picture. A passerby, I imagine." She turned to the next page. It was a photo of the same man, this time alone with a baby in his arms. He looked so adoringly at the child. It looked like he was stroking its cheek.

She turned another page and then another. She held her breath as she looked at each new photo. There were a dozen in total. She closed the album and sat quietly.

Neil took it gently out of her hands and scrutinized each picture. It was in stark contrast to the pictures of a much older man lying dead in an alley. He shut the album, placed it on the table, and patiently sat in silence.

"Let's see what my father has to say." Octavia rose from the couch and sat at the computer. She clicked the mouse, opening the link to the video recording the attorney had sent.

Neil pulled up a chair next to her. The video sprang to life, and the face of Bastien Beaulieu appeared on the monitor as he spoke to his daughter for the first time in nearly two decades.

He smiled. "Hello, my beautiful, brilliant girl."

His face bore deep laugh lines, and the skin sagged a little. His hair was duller. His eyes were no longer the bright flashing sapphire lights of youth, but there was still a twinkle. His smile was the same as the one in the photos.

He sighed and looked directly into the camera.

"There is so much I want to say, but I don't know if you want to hear it. I know this has come as a shock, and I'm sorry for that. All these years, I wanted to reach out to you, to tell you how much I love you. I'm so proud of you, though I have no right to be. You have turned out to be such an amazing woman. Strong and independent. Beautiful and successful. And you love music! You are the daughter every man hopes to have."

Octavia bowed her head as her breathing changed. Her shoulders shook. She paused the video.

"Why am I crying? I remember him from when we worked on the album, but I don't know him. But looking at him and hearing his voice—I feel such loss." She wiped the tears from her face and continued the video.

"I met you once when you were a baby and we worked together when my band was recording at The Bllack Market Studio in London. You were our producer. It was the first time you had produced an album. You were so full of ideas. You charmed the guys. We had fun. I have a picture of you standing with the band. I arranged for you to come to Montreal to the jazz festival to promote our album… just so I could watch you and occasionally talk to you. Do you still have the album?"

He choked up and took a moment to compose himself.

"I am so sorry I wasn't there for you. But you have always been with me in my heart. I'm leaving my house to you and entrusting my trombone and music to your care. This is especially important, because if you are watching this, I have come to a terrible end."

His face changed. His expression became deadly serious.

"The trombone and the music carry secrets. Do you remember the composition I wrote called 'Four-Bar Progression'? People thought it was about the band, but it is about far more important things. Many years ago, you received a bracelet with symbols. If you still have that bracelet, and I hope you do, the symbols are the key to everything.

"I'm afraid I've put your life in jeopardy. When I sent it to you years ago, it was a symbol of hope and connection. But there are bad people who want that bracelet and the secrets that my trombone and music hold. I am entrusting them to you. I am foisting a heavy responsibility on you, and I fear for you. But I heard you have a friend named Neil Ames, and I think he will be of great help to you.

"One last thing, and it pains me to say it, but don't trust your sister. She is ambitious, and that has led her down a path that is treacherous. If you can protect her, well, that is asking too much. I love her, and I loved her mother, just as I loved your mother so many years ago.

"Your mother wrote to tell me she was dying—she may have passed away by the time you see this. I want you to know I loved her and I'm sorry for the pain she went through. I'm sorry the three of us won't be able to sit and have coffee or a meal together." He grinned. "Maybe someday in a future life. I love you and always will, my precious girl. Even though I have departed this earthly realm, when you see this, I will always love and watch over you."

The screen went black. Octavia got up and walked to the window. She remained in that spot, gazing out, but her vision was inward.

"Do you mind if I check something?" Neil asked.

She turned away from the window. "No, go ahead."

Neil tapped away on the keyboard, then sat back as a low growl came from his throat.

Octavia moved toward Neil, putting her hand on his shoulder. "What is it?"

He concentrated on the screen.

"Neil, what is it?"

"Do you mind if I watch the video again?" he asked.

"Of course, but I'd rather not watch it again, right now."

"I understand that this is challenging for you, but I must do what I do to solve it. I fear for your life; to protect you, I must find a solution. I must remain detached during my investigation. Trusting me is imperative, regardless of the choices I make or the words I speak."

"You just turned on your Sherlock Holmes voice, didn't you?" A slight smile crossed Octavia's lips, then disappeared. "I do trust you. Do what you do. Find out who murdered my father."

"All right, the first thing I need to tell you is that you are to trust no one else."

"Why are you saying that?" she asked.

"Cachemaille said your father sent this video to him and that he didn't open it, per Bastien's request that it be for your eyes only."

"Yes."

"This video has been opened before you, from two unique IP addresses. I found the first one, it's attached to the Nanotechnology Center, but the second one is using advanced encryption methods or proxy servers to hide. An experienced hacker might be employing a myriad of clandestine techniques to cover their tracks."

Octavia sat on her bed, the plush pillows tenderly cradled her fatigued form. "I'm tired," she said, her voice filled with exhaustion. "Shut off the lights on your way out."

CHAPTER 19

Octavia pulled off her sunglasses as the police vehicle came to a halt in front of the Beaulieu home. "Neil, look at the meticulous craftsmanship, the unmistakable French influences, and the breathtaking details that were painstakingly integrated into the design. It's absolutely stunning."

Aumont and a uniformed officer ushered them into the enclosed yard with its elegant wrought-iron fence and two towering maple trees covering the walkway with copper-toned leaves. A grand entrance featured a wide stone staircase that led up to the house's expansive covered front porch.

Musical notes etched into a stained-glass window highlighted the prominent front door. Aumont entered first, then held it open for Octavia and Neil. The uniformed officer handed them latex gloves and remained outside.

The foyer was modest. A Persian rug, worn with time but still retaining its vibrant blue hues, stretched across the hardwood floor. A mahogany coat rack, its handcrafted wrought-iron hooks fashioned into musical notes, stood close to the entry.

Neil pulled down his mask and sniffed the house, detecting a combination of vanilla and oil-based paint, giving the air an undisturbed quality. However, there was an undeniable fragrance of femininity that permeated the surroundings.

"Mr. Ames, you are still under quarantine precautions," said Aumont. "Please keep your mask on."

Neil pulled his mask up without comment and continued wandering about the room, taking shots with his phone. It was tidy, with not a speck of dust in sight. Neil typed a note: Check on housekeeping service.

Octavia gazed at a series of framed photographs that adorned the wall to the right: Cadenza with her mother and father. Cadenza as a baby, a toddler, and entering first grade. She was waving at the camera, a broad smile on her face; her prom pictures, graduation pictures with her BS diploma, her master's diploma in nanotechnology, and a picture of her receiving her PhD.

Nestled beneath paintings signed by Adrienne Beaulieu, Bastien's late wife, a small wooden bench invited visitors to linger and admire the artistic masterpieces.

Neil took pictures of the paintings. "So, his wife was an artist. Clearly, this floor was solely the wife's domain."

"Yes, she was quite good," replied Octavia. "This is all going to Cadenza. This isn't my home."

"It is now," replied Neil.

"It's my house; this will never be my home." Octavia walked toward the kitchen. A pan, a plain white plate and bowl, two spoons, a fork, and a knife were on the dish rack. "This reminds me of someone I know." Octavia glanced at Neil.

He opened the refrigerator, which contained eggs, a variety of cheeses, a bowl of grapes, and two bottles of Sancerre, a white wine from the French Loire Valley.

"And this brings to mind someone I know," Neil commented, his gaze briefly shifting towards Octavia.

They went into the bathroom. It was neat and clean. There were basic white towels and shirts in a laundry hamper. They passed the laundry room and stepped out onto the enclosed back porch, where they discovered a tray of kitty litter.

"He has a cat. Where is it?" Octavia asked as she stepped back into the kitchen. A lonely cat bowl sat untouched, waiting to be filled with kibble.

"There is a lavender-gray tuxedo cat featured in some paintings," said Neil. "That's probably the one we are looking for."

Octavia went back to the living room, scanning the room for any sign of the elusive cat. Neil went outside and surveyed the beautifully landscaped backyard featuring rose bushes, a pebbled path leading to a garage, and a covered seating area. A single strand of rope that had once supported a swing hung limply on one of the larger limbs of a magnificent maple tree. Above his head, Neil heard the loud plaintive meows of a cat. He searched among the remaining leaves on the tree and located the lavender-gray cat looking down at him.

"I suppose you'll be wanting some help down from there, cat."

The cat meowed loudly in response. Neil took a picture and headed into the house.

"I found the cat," he called out.

Octavia came back to the porch. "Where is it?"

"It's up there." He pointed at the tree.

"Oh, poor kitty. It must be cold and hungry. I'll have to find out if Cadenza can take it."

"You can keep the damn cat. I have no use for it." Cadenza entered through the back gate.

Aumont, who had been silently following their every move, spoke with authority. "You should not be here," he warned.

"I have every right to be here. This is *my* home." She glowered at Octavia. "This is not *your* home. You should not be here."

"Do not come any closer," Aumont ordered. "Who are you?"

"I'm Doctor Cadenza Beaulieu. I came to collect my father's research papers. We were working together on a project, and we are at a critical juncture. We're—I'm on a deadline, and I need the papers to complete the work."

"There is no chance of that occurring." With determination in his eyes, Aumont stepped forward. "This house part of a murder investigation, and removal of any evidence that might lead us to the one who murdered your father is reason for arrest."

"I don't see any notice or tape to indicate that," Cadenza shot back.

Octavia stepped forward. "I want to talk to Cadenza." She turned to Aumont. "I know you have the authority to do as you please and order all of us out. But I think you can appreciate the complexity of this... dynamic." Octavia turned to Cadenza. "Are you agreeable to a short civil conversation? No attorneys, no police, and no,"—she glanced toward Neil—"interference from others."

"Ms. Clarke, you are boldly pushing the boundaries to their absolute limit." Aumont's annoyed tone relaying his intensifying impatience that was brewing inside.

"Octavia, don't trust her," Neil whispered, his voice filled with concern. He locked eyes with Cadenza. "You need to leave now. I think you know why."

"And who are you to tell me what to do?" Cadenza frowned at Neil.

"I'm a private investigator, hired by your sister."

"A private investigator?" Cadenza's face contorted with a smirk that gradually morphed into a menacing snarl. "I'll leave. I don't want to waste my breath talking to this bastard child."

She turned and headed toward the back gate, shouting over her shoulder, "You'll be hearing from my attorney." Then she disappeared behind the gate.

Octavia turned and headed toward the staircase leading to the second floor. Neil followed her up the stairs. With each forceful strike of her cane on the steps and her brisk pace, it was clear that she was upset.

She opened the door to the first bedroom, Cadenza's childhood sanctuary. A pink canopy bed, posters of Marie Curry and Albert Einstein, and science fair awards she had won in high school.

The second room had a clinical vibe. The room was dark, illuminated with a little daylight around the edge of the closed blinds. Octavia shivered. "This was probably the room where Cadenza's mother spent her last days."

They moved on to the next bedroom. Octavia stepped through the doorway. "It feels like it's waiting for Bastien."

Neil surveyed the room. One of the walls had been meticulously stripped down to the brick, giving the space an industrial and raw aesthetic. A black shade covered the window, blocking any view of the backyard. A large skylight created a striking contrast between the bright beam of light and the rest of the room. The walls, except for the brick one, were beautifully lined with aged oak paneling.

Octavia flipped on a light switch. Blue lights illuminated the edges of the walls, immersing the space in a jazz club ambiance.

"This room looks like a slice of New Orleans dropped into Montreal," Octavia remarked, "a musical oasis."

Octavia walked over to a cabinet filled with vintage vinyl jazz records, including original pressings of the two albums by The Four-Bar Progression. She examined the state-of-the-art turntable and sound system.

Neil joined her and took pictures of a rack of suits that stood along the wall beside the cabinet. Octavia looked through the suits, checking the labels.

"These are for live performances. I recognize the designer. He's an old guy with a little shop in New Orleans."

Neil's attention was drawn to the center of the room, where there was a worn brown leather couch with a blanket and a pillow. It faced a small stage area with one spotlight.

"This is sad, he must have slept on the couch." Octavia stepped up on the stage, using Neil's shoulder to balance. "Performing was his passion, I remember...he said he felt most alive under the heat of the spotlight."

In the corner by the door was a vintage maple desk and half a dozen beige and gray metal file cabinets. Sheets of composition paper covered the desk. Octavia stepped off the stage and shuffled through them.

"He was in the process of composing something new." She examined them closely. "These are quite good."

She went to one of the filing cabinets and pulled on one of the drawers. "Locked." She tried the next cabinet and the next. "They're all locked. This is probably where he stored all his compositions and music contracts."

Neil looked at the sheets of music on the desk. He checked one page and then another.

"Look at this." Neil pointed around the desk. "In the left-hand corner of each of the marked-out compositions is a symbol, like the ones etched into your bracelet."

"There's still one more room to look into." Aumont was standing in the doorway.

Neil agreed with him. "He must have worked from a home office during the global virus restrictions. Let's go, Octavia."

"You look. My father and I connected through music. I want to spend more time here."

"We'll be leaving in a few minutes, Ms. Clarke," said Aumont. "Please don't remove anything."

She flashed him a mischievous smile and said, "Feel free to frisk me before I leave."

Aumont cleared his throat and left the room. Neil shook his head and followed him.

CHAPTER 20

O ctavia went to work, meticulously arranging the compositions according to the symbols on her bracelet.

She scrutinized the sheets of paper multiple times, searching in vain for any clues or explanations behind Bastien's cryptic symbols. Frustrated, she sat back, crossing her arms.

This has to be a message from Bastien. He said my bracelet was the key to the code. The key! This is a map to the key!

As she shuffled through the papers, her hand slid against the top sheet of paper. It shifted, exposing the second symbol on the next sheet. She looked down, hanging her head.

I don't understand! Give me a clue.

She squeezed her eyes and opened them. *It's a design.*

She moved the second sheet over the third and the third over the fourth until she got to the last sheet. She pulled out her phone and took a picture of the reconfigured composition. Then she saw it.

It's the Four-Bar Progression, but he's crossed out sections of the original and inserted variations. She took more pictures as she moved the connecting symbols and variations, then stood back and looked at the big picture.

The lines of correction match across the pages with the last marks ending in a horizontal V. An arrow pointing—

She looked to the left. In the corner was an old traveling trunk turned on one end. She walked over to it and tried to move it into the light. It wouldn't budge, and it had a padlock securing the latch. She sat on the trunk to catch her breath.

She looked up at the ceiling and silently cried out, "What is this? Some kind of test? Enough already. What do you—?"

She stopped mid-question and looked more closely at the ceiling. There was a tiny symbol—a shape under the paint on the ceiling. She used her cane to steady herself as she climbed up and balanced as best she could on the trunk while poking the symbol with the tip of her cane.

A piece of paint chipped off and landed in her eye. She worked out the paint, causing her eye to water and making her vision blurry. She balanced for a moment with her cane, steadying herself on the trunk. When her vision cleared, she looked up at the ceiling. It wasn't a symbol. It was a key. An actual key.

She reached up with her cane and poked at it just as she heard the others coming down the hallway, heading toward the music room. Neil called out, "Octavia, we're leaving now!"

"So soon?" The tone of her voice was infused with the innocent disappointment of a child. "I was hoping for more time."

"Actually, I would like to take a crack at the password on his computer. Serge, can we go back for one more look? I'll try a couple of times." Neil headed back to the office.

"We've been here long enough. It's time to leave," Aumont insisted.

A loud bang came out of the music room, and Octavia let out a scream. Aumont and Neil rushed in. They found Octavia precariously teetering on the trunk, frantically trying to get out of her shirt. Her coat and cane were on the floor, and the papers on the desk were scattered around.

"Oh my god! A spider! A huge black spider! It was crawling on the ceiling, coming toward me. It had its eyes on me! I tried to crush it with my cane, but I just made a hole in the ceiling, and it fell down my shirt. Oh my god! I hate spiders!"

"Octavia, come down from there." Neil lifted her off the trunk.

When she got down, she shrieked again and pointed at the floor close to Neil's feet.

"There it is! There it is! Kill it! Kill it!" Octavia grabbed Aumont and, still with her shirt undone, spun him around as she clung to him for dear life.

Neil stomped on the floor close to where Octavia had pointed.

"I've got it. It's okay. It's dead. Do you want to see?" he asked.

"No! I do not. I want to get out of here. There might be more in all those papers."

"It's gone now. You're safe. I have you." Aumont held her close to soothe her.

"Thank you. Thank you for saving me."

"You're going to be fine."

"Excuse me, but I'm the one who killed the spider," said Neil.

Octavia pulled away from Aumont. "This is inappropriate and unprofessional behavior."

She straightened and buttoned her shirt. Neil passed her the cane and draped her coat over her shoulders. Stepping back, he couldn't help but be entertained by Aumont's obvious embarrassment, who seemed to be at a loss when it came to deciding what to do with his blunder and his hands. "Really, Aumont," he chided him, "you need to control yourself." Neil's eyes twinkled, hinting at a smile hidden behind his mask.

Octavia left the room and headed down the stairs. Aumont followed her.

"I apologize—I meant no disrespect or intrusion of your personal space," he sputtered. "I only meant to calm you."

Octavia walked past him through the front door. Neil followed, and Aumont locked up.

"Wait." She abruptly stopped on the top step. "What about the cat? We can't abandon it in the tree—no food, no water, and no human to come home to."

"I'll have the officer call animal control." Aumont walked past her and headed toward the police vehicle. Octavia followed him.

"No. You can't do that. Isn't there a way we can find a home for it? I'll pay someone to care for it. Maybe a neighbor will take it temporarily."

"I'll take care of it for you."

The voice came from behind a white picket fence adjoining the property line of the two homes. The head and face of an elderly woman peered over it. She held a rake in her hand and wore a broad straw hat on her head and a red bandana covering her nose and mouth.

"That cat has been coming over to my house for years. She has practically lived here for the past few months. I've gotten attached to her. Her name is Lavender."

Octavia crossed the yard. "Thank you for your generous offer. I would be happy to send you a stipend to pay for her food and pet insurance to cover any vet bills she might have. My name is Octavia Clarke. What is your name?"

"Agnes Abercrombie. It's nice to meet you." Agnes pulled her bandana down. She looked like a cross between a hobbit and a bandit. "Allergies, Ah, c'est toujours quelque chose, hein?" she said in the flavor of French-Canadian Montreal, but with the hint of a Scottish brogue.

"Yes," Octavia grinned, "It seems I'm finding new things to be allergic to, as well."

"You're American, aren't you?" asked Agnes. "I can tell from your accent. Are you related to the family next door? I don't think I've seen you before." Agnes chuckled. "I'm sorry. I'm naturally nosy. That's what happens when you get old. The world gets smaller, and little things seem important."

Octavia smiled back at Agnes. She liked the old lady.

"Ms. Clarke, it is time for us to depart," Aumont declared while standing next to the police vehicle.

"You must be important to have a police escort." Agnes squinted at Aumont. "And it looks like you have a handsome man waiting on you, too."

"I'm not as important as it looks," said Octavia.

"It's such a shame about Dr. Beaulieu's passing. Is it true he was murdered?"

"I only recently arrived and I'm still getting my head around his passing. But I'm worried about the cat, I want to make sure it's taken care of."

"Oh, don't worry about it." Agnes grinned, then took a moment to think. "Granted, vets can be expensive, so if you could handle the pet insurance, that would be very generous of you."

"Not at all. I'll make arrangements. Could I get your contact information? I'll probably need it for the insurance company."

"I don't have a pen on me. Hold on!" Agnes leaned her rake against the fence and did a slow jog to her house.

"I could put your information on my phone," Octavia called out after her.

Agnes waved and went into the house.

"Ms. Clarke, it is imperative that we depart," Aumont summoned.

Octavia waved him off, as Agnes had done to her.

Neil walked over to Octavia. "I think I'd like to meet your new friend."

Agnes carefully walked down the steps of her porch and jogged toward them. She had a business card, which she handed to Octavia.

"Thank you." Octavia smiled at Agnes and put the card in her pocket.

"Well, look at it." Agnes looked a little disappointed.

"Oh, of course. I'm sorry. This is my friend, Neil. Neil, this is Agnes Abercrombie."

Agnes grinned at Neil. "I bet you are a very interesting man." She winked.

Octavia laughed when she looked at the card. It had the street address, an email, and a phone number, but what tickled Octavia was the name and profession at the center of the card: Agnes Abercrombie. Professional Nosy Neighbor.

Octavia showed it to Neil. He laughed. "I think you're my kind of girl."

Agnes's deep laugh lines curled around her smiling eyes. "You shouldn't flirt with me—my husband will get jealous."

"I think you will be very valuable to the investigation," said Neil.

"Investigation? I like the sound of that." She grinned and pointed at his mask. "You have allergies, too?"

Octavia pulled out her phone. "Agnes, I'm going to call your phone, so you will have my number."

"Mr. Ames and Ms. Clarke!" Aumont called out.

"He's getting cranky," Neil muttered to Octavia. "Goodbye, Agnes." He headed back to the police vehicle.

Agnes's phone buzzed in one of her pockets in her overalls. She pulled it out. "How do I spell your name, dear?"

Octavia spelled it out for her.

"Octavia, that's an unusual name. Reminds me of Dr. Beaulieu's daughter, Cadenza."

"Okay, I have to go. Thank you so much, Agnes. I hope to see you again."

"You be safe now, dear. Oh my, did you know you have paint chips in your hair?"

Octavia waved as she headed toward the vehicle.

"She seems like an amiable lady," said Neil once they settled back into the vehicle. "I bet she was a good neighbor."

Octavia agreed. Neil continued. "I hope we'll have time to see her again before we leave."

"Oh, I think we will." Octavia reached over and slipped something small and cold in his hand. He glanced down and casually slipped the ornate key into his pocket.

"I hope you are feeling better after your encounter with that spider," he said. "It was rather large."

Octavia shuddered. "The first thing I'm going to do is hire an exterminator." She winked at Neil and slipped on her sunglasses.

CHAPTER 21

"I'm off," Neil called out to Octavia.

He had woke up at sunrise and spent the morning doing his yoga and meditation practice, allowing for a peaceful start to the day. After downing a liter of water, he slipped on his running shoes and a navy windbreaker.

"Where are you going?" she asked.

"Out for a run," Neil answered as he went out the door. He jogged around the AZZ Music Production Complex for 45 minutes. After checking out the area and locating the security cameras, he climbed a tree up to the balcony.

Octavia didn't look up when Neil stepped through the balcony door. She handed him a mug of hot coffee and poured two glasses of blueberry smoothies, then placed them on the table and pulled out a tablet, while Neil took his phone off the charger. They sat at the table, scrolling their devices in silence. No words were necessary. The rest of the day would be dedicated to devising and strategizing, but this morning, they were content.

An hour later, Octavia received a call from Aumont. Bastien's body was being released. She spent the next hour on the phone with Cachemaille arranging her father's cremation. Bastien hadn't wanted a funeral and there was a family plot. And then there was the question of what to do about Cadenza. Cachemaille said he would handle all communication with her.

After the call, Octavia added one more thing on her to-do list: Have lunch with Neil. Learn full details of Bastien's murder. She went into the living room. Neil looked distracted.

"I'm going to order takeout. What sounds good to you?" she asked.

"Anything. I'm hungry, so anything you order is fine."

She sent a text with their order.

Neil printed out the police report and crime scene photos. Next, he set about sketching the position and condition of the body. He made a sketch of the victim's clothing: An overcoat for warmth, a blue sweater, dark wash jeans. Black walking shoes that were scuffed at the toes. He studied his sketch of Cadenza Beaulieu.

She's studious. Serious. Focused. Determined to prove herself. She feels unappreciated, underrated. There was hatred in her eyes when she looked at Octavia. Did she think she could never compete against the golden girl? She feels second best. Is that why Bastien told Octavia not to trust her? Or is there something more? He said she's involved with bad people. She's dedicated to her work. Did they flatter her? Did they play on her need for approval and admiration for her mind? Was she going to sell out her father and his work? Would she kill her own father?

Neil looked at his sketch of Octavia and compared the two sisters side by side. They were both beautiful in their own way, two sides of the same coin. The key distinction between the two was that one attracted people while the other pushed people away.

He scrolled through the pictures he took of the paintings and photographs throughout the Beaulieu home.

How was Bastien portrayed by the family? What's the dynamic in the formal family portraits? His wife included Cadenza in her paintings, but there were none including her husband.

I see Cadenza in these landscapes. Her head down, reading a book. The cat prominently featured in the landscapes and as a solo subject. The formal family portraits are almost identical. The wife is standing behind her husband, her hand on his shoulder and Cadenza on his lap.

Cadenza's position changed through the years. Three of the family portraits had Cadenza sitting next to her father. In the last three portraits, she stood beside her mother with her hands by her sides and her mother declining, becoming thinner and thinner.

Neil zoomed in on Bastien's left wrist. The first ten portraits revealed a glimpse of a gold watch, but in the next three portraits there was nothing on his wrist. In the fifteenth portrait, Neil could see a glimpse of something that looked like a leather strap. It was in the sixteenth portrait that Neil spotted what he was looking for.

He zoomed in on the photo he had taken. It was a bracelet identical to Octavia's in design, but the symbols were in a different configuration. He sketched it.

He looked at a photo of The Four-Bar Progression band members and began sketching.

Bastien glows like Octavia. The same sapphire eyes. The others are like set pieces. Average-looking guys. The piano player has a mustache and a friendly smile. The drummer has wire-framed glasses and thinning hair. There's an intensity about him. His attention is on the drums, not the camera. This last member is tall with caramel-colored skin and thick, dark eyebrows and hazel eyes. He's holding the upright bass like a lover.

Neil looked at the finished sketch. He could read the group dynamic. Though they'd posed the photo, the nuances found through the sketching process had exposed every feeling, every conflict, and every resentment.

We have to get access to the band members. There's a reason Bastien was using The Four-Bar Progression as a method of developing a code.

He stopped sketching, arranged the sketches in a circle, and walked around them.. He was looking for a pattern. Octavia approached and followed him. Her eyes lingered on the crime scene and victim sketches.

"I have photographs of Bastien's revised composition," she said as she turned away, "and I think they capture intricate details that could be significant clues."

The food order arrived. Octavia dished out the chef salads and sandwiches as gusty winds blew clouds across the sky. Neil opened a bottle of wine and poured the deep red liquid into their glasses.

"It's time you tell me everything you know," she said.

As Neil recounted the known events leading to her father's death, Octavia picked at her salad and finished her wine.

Neil poured more wine into her glass. "McGregor found out something interesting."

"What?"

"He interviewed Bastien's assistants at the Center. According to them, the day before Bastien was killed, he went to Cadenza's office and downloaded something from her computer. Cadenza was furious when she found out and when she tried to log in, she couldn't because he had changed her password. She grabbed files and left the lab."

Neil sipped his wine. Octavia said nothing. He continued. "And then there is Bastien's trombone."

"What about it?" she asked.

"The trombone case belonging to Bastien was found concealed behind a dumpster at a jazz club where he was a regular performer. The police are holding it as evidence."

"The case? Was the trombone in it?"

"It's locked and they haven't opened it...yet. Somehow, Cachemaille got wind of it and slowed the process by producing instructions from Bastien that no one was to open it except you."

"I remember that was in the will," she said. "So he hid it before—"

"Yes."

"He was meeting someone, that he didn't trust."

"Or, he realized he was being followed and stashed it." Neil took a sip of wine.

"Why would he have his trombone with him?" she asked.

"Sources indicate that he was on his way to a rehearsal."

Octavia said nothing until her wineglass was empty. She pushed it toward Neil. "Pour."

"Do you want me to go on?" Neil asked as he poured. "If I do, I will be direct and pragmatic."

Octavia folded her hands on the table and nodded. "I saw your sketches."

Neil methodically went through a description of the crime scene and the condition of her father's body. She sat with her poker face firmly in place.

"Then why did they break his fingers?" she whispered.

Neil seized the wine bottle and got to his feet. Bending closer, he whispered, "Let's go in the bedroom."

She took a sip of wine and trailed behind him. He shut the door.

"We've been talking openly at the table," she said, "Why the secrecy now?"

"Everything I've told you, Yuu International probably already knows."

"You still don't trust them?"

"No, I don't."

"So, what does Yuu have to do with Bastien's broken fingers?"

"His fingers may have broken of their own accord—or rather, the result of actions within his own body. The medical examiner is going to conclude that he died of heart failure, which is true, but I believe that it was triggered by an invasive device or devices."

"What the hell are you talking about?"

"I'm basing my assumption on the unusual bruising found on his body. The bruising came from pressure points inside his body."

Octavia swirled her wine glass. "Pressure points within his body? What has that got to do with Yuu International?"

"Yuu doesn't care about Bastien's murder, only the methodology behind it. Do you know what kind of research Bastien was doing?" Neil asked.

"Something to do with nanotechnology."

"Loder International poses a significant challenge to Yuu International. Bastien's research has piqued Yuu's interest, particularly regarding the applications that Loder is considering. Do you really believe their generosity is purely driven by their kind-heartedness?"

Octavia finished her wine. "Nothing about this case is going to be straightforward, is it?"

"No, I'm afraid not," he replied. "I told you, you would need to trust me. Do you?"

She paused and sat back in her chair. "So," she smiled, "the game is afoot."

"Indeed," Neil replied.

CHAPTER 22

Late the next morning, Neil dialed Michelle Perusse's number; it went straight to voicemail. He hung up and sent a text.

NEIL AMES HERE. WE'RE IN MONTREAL. CALL THIS NUMBER.

Two hours later, his phone chimed. He looked at it. *McGregor*

At the same time, Octavia's cell phone rang.

"Hello?"

"Hello, dear, his is Agnes Abercrombie."

"Agnes! I was going to call you. I have the insurance policy for Lavender, and I thought I would have my driver bring it over to you today."

"I'm calling to tell you that Cadenza went into the house, and I saw her take out one of those boxes you put files in out the back door. I'm fixing my husband lunch, and I thought she left, but I saw her going back inside. I overheard the conversation you and your friend had with her the other day. I suppose you gave her permission. I'm probably sticking my nose where it doesn't belong."

"No, Agnes, you did the right thing by calling me. I'll send someone over right away."

"No problem, dear. Maybe I should go over there."

"No, absolutely not! I'm calling the police right now. I'll call you back. Thank you. Goodbye." She hung up. "Neil!"

"What?"

"Agnes called. Cadenza is at the house. She took a box of files out and went back in. Call Aumont and tell him to get someone to the house now!"

"I've got—hold on—McGregor, Cadenza Beaulieu is in the house taking files out...It's too late for that," Neil growled. "Get Aumont over there now to stop her." He prowled around the room as he listened, then looked at the phone and threw it on the couch. "Damn it!"

He pointed at Octavia. "Call Agnes now and have her find out if Cadenza's car is still there."

"Should we really get her involved? It could be dangerous."

"She's known as a nosy neighbor. All she needs to do is take a quick look and see if Cadenza's car is still around."

Octavia called the elderly woman on speakerphone.

"Hello, Agnes. We called the police, but could you please check to see if Cadenza's car is still there?"

"I'm ahead of you, dear. I sent my husband out to throw out the trash and take a peek. He didn't want to be bothered, but I can be pretty persuasive. So he put his shoes on and took the trash out. He told me that her car is still there and there's a black van parked in the alley."

Octavia glanced at Neil, who anxiously paced back and forth in the room. "Thank you, Agnes. I really appreciate everything you've done."

"You're welcome, dear. This is fun. You know when you get old, things can get routine, and—oh my! There's smoke billowing from the house!"

"Wait, are you telling me that your house is on fire?" exclaimed Octavia.

"No, not this house," said Agnes, "Your house."

"*My* house is on fire?" Octavia cried out in disbelief.

"Tell her to call 911. Now."

"Call 911, Agnes. I'm going to hang up now. Goodbye."

"Call James," said Neil. "We're going to the house. Quarantine be damned."

CHAPTER 23

Ten minutes later, James arrived.

They sped through the city. Smoke could be seen billowing in the sky blocks away from the scene and they arrived to find the street barricaded. James put the car in reverse and navigated the car back down the street, and found a parking spot three blocks away from the house.

Neil jumped out of the car and was met with the sight of intense flames devouring the corner section of the second floor. "That's Beaulieu's office," he said. "That's exactly what I feared."

James opened the door for Octavia and followed as she and Neil hurried toward the burning house. They were blocked by the police officers at the barricade, but Octavia gained their entry when she identified herself as the house owner.

As they watched the fire department work, a figure appeared in the upstairs window, a face contorted in the mask of horror and covered in blood was pressed against the pane when slid out of sight.

"Oh, my god," Octavia cried out, "there's someone in there."

The fire team hurried to bring their ladders to the window, but the window suddenly exploded, sending glass flying as flames and smoke billowed out the broken window.

Although masked, Neil noticed a strange smell permeating the smoke. It was a chemical odor, different from the typical smell of a house fire. "Someone has used an accelerant," he said to Octavia. "This is arson."

He countered across the street and scanned the group of people watching the fire, looking for someone staring at the house with a gleam in their eye or a look of satisfaction. Neil scrutinized the faces, noting anyone whose gaze lingered too long on the destruction, as though they were committing it to memory.

Arsonists like to admire their handiwork. Is there someone trying too hard to blend in?

He pulled out his phone and took pictures of the two groups that had gathered: one group was standing across the street and the other was standing in the Abercrombie's yard. Octavia was there, along with James, standing next to Agnes.

His attention was drawn to a particular face, one that he recognized from her online photographs—Michelle Perusse. Neil approached and stood by her as she jotted down notes.

"You didn't start this fire so you could meet with me, did you?" he asked.

Michelle looked at the stranger beside her. She arched an eyebrow in recognition. "Mr. Ames. No, this is a chance meeting. We'd better talk while we can."

"Where can we meet later?" Neil asked.

"Oh, look at who just showed up," Michelle said.

McGregor rolled onto the scene in an RCMP vehicle. Aumont followed close behind.

"Do you know them?' Neil asked.

"Oui," she replied. "Intimately."

McGregor and Aumont spoke with the fire captain. Aumont frowned when he saw Neil approaching.

"What the hell are you doing here?" he demanded, his voice laced with anger. "You're blatantly disregarding quarantine protocols."

"I've got my mask on," Neil retorted. "If you'd bothered to secure the house properly after we encountered Cadenza Beaulieu, maybe this blaze wouldn't be devouring Bastien's office."

McGregor's jaw tightened. "You entered the house with Ames?" His eyes narrowed. "Without a search warrant?"

"Ms. Clarke wanted to see the house she inherited and I escorted them," Aumont admitted.

The tension in McGregor's face melted away, replaced by a cool and collected calm. "I should've insisted the RCMP oversee this investigation."

Aumont was about to protest when Neil interrupted.

"We saw someone in that window," he gestured toward the charred room on the second floor.

McGregor's expression darkened. "The fire captain confirmed they found a woman's body. The arson team and medical examiner are en route."

"Is it Cadenza Beaulieu?" Neil asked.

"We won't know until an identification has been made," McGregor said grimly. "When you called, you said she parked her car in the back?"

"Yes, and there was a black van behind it."

Aumont got on his radio and sent more officers to the back of the house. Neil sprinted across the street toward Octavia.

"We need to check to see if Cadenza's car is still out back," said Neil as he got closer.

"This way," said Agnes, her elderly frame moving with the speed and agility of a twenty-year-old. Neil ran alongside her, gesturing for Michelle to come along.

"What's going on?" Octavia called out as she picked up her pace with James by her side.

From Agnes's backyard, there was a clear view of Cadenza's car, but the black van was nowhere in sight. Neil ran out the gate to the car.

The trunk was partially open. He cautiously peeked inside and quickly retreated before the police arrived.

"No sign of the box of files Agnes saw her carrying out."

"Where is she?" Octavia asked.

Neil took her aside. "A body was found in the office."

Octavia gasped. "Is it Cadenza?"

"I don't know," said Neil, "and we probably won't know for a few hours, depending on…"

"How badly she's…" Octavia's words faded as she looked back at the house.

"Honey, I think you should come into my house and sit," said Agnes. "And I think you need a shot of bourbon."

Octavia continued to stare at the house.

"Octavia?" Neil said gently.

She raised her hand to silence him. "James, would you walk me to the car, please?"

"I'll bring the car to you, madam," said James. Minutes later, he pulled up beside the Abercrombie's garage and Neil walked her to the car with a protective arm around her.

"Octavia," he said softly, "I promise to keep you informed as soon as I have any updates."

She didn't acknowledge him and James drove off with Octavia, leaving Neil behind.

"Do you believe that Cadenza is the woman they found in the house?" Agnes hung her head. "Oh, that poor girl! I should have done something. I should have gone over there. Pounded on the door. Talked to her. Maybe she wouldn't be dead."

Michelle Perusse was recording with her cellphone.

Neil leaned in and whispered, "Not now."

She saw the look on his face and turned it off. Neil returned his attention to Agnes.

"You did exactly the right thing. If you had gone over there, you might be dead, and I think Mr. Abercrombie would have been deeply sorry about that."

"I sure would be."

Agnes turned around to see her husband standing behind them.

"You should go inside," said Neil. "The police will want to talk to you. It might be best if you didn't mention this last part."

"Don't worry about it. We nosy people have to stick together." Agnes walked back with her husband's arm around her waist.

"She's right, you know." Michelle stood next to Neil. "We nosy people should stick together. It looks like you need a ride. My car is down the street."

Chapter 24

Michelle Perusse drove Canada's car, a reliable Honda Civic. It was so ordinary that it seamlessly blended into its surroundings. Handy for an investigative journalist.

Its blue exterior was polished to a high gloss, but the gray interior told a different story. She'd covered the back seat with boxes of files, pens, and a pile of notebooks, all labeled and dated. Wedged between the boxes was an older Dell laptop. This was her mobile office.

She moved a steering wheel tray, two books on nanotechnology, and a variety of snack food wrappers off the front seat so that Neil could sit. He had to tilt back and adjust the seat as far as possible to fit in the car. She slid the tray between the seats, put the two books on the floor by Neil's feet, and jammed the wrappers into a paper shopping bag, which she stuffed behind her seat. She pulled out her phone and uploaded the pictures she had taken into the cloud.

Michelle made no apologies for the state of her car. She started it without saying a word, then removed a hair tie from around the gearshift and pulled her long, frizzy reddish-brown hair into a ponytail. She flipped on the blinker and pulled out onto the street.

"Do you know where you're going?" Neil asked.

"Yes," she replied.

"Of course. You probably got the address where we are staying."

"No," she replied as she flipped the blinker to go right, "I'm going to a cafe one of my friends owns. I'll call ahead for takeout. They make the best burgers. Je pensais que vous me donneriez les indications pour votre emplacement."

"Oh, so now you're going to test my French?" Neil shook his head. "Getting food sounds good. I'm hungry."

"Excellent," she said, "because you're paying."

After getting the food, they parked alongside Parc Outremont, a quiet park where the air smelled like bagels and benches looked out on a pond. They got out of the car and walked in the brisk air with their bag of burgers and cups of coffee to a bench.

"You're probably in a lot of trouble," Michelle said as she took a sip of steaming black coffee. "Jumping quarantine is a serious offense here."

"We get tested every morning. I would probably be in more trouble if I had tested positive." Neil stuffed his mask in his pocket and sipped his creamy coffee. "Let's talk about why I'm here."

Before answering, Michelle's eyes closed briefly as she took a bite of her burger. She chewed slowly and deliberately, a soft moan of pleasure escaping as she savored the flavors, then swallowed and grabbed a paper napkin to dab at her mouth. "I can tell you what I know for sure and what I feel in my gut, and I'd like to know the same from you."

"Agreed."

Michelle reached into the bag and handed Neil a burger. "Here, eat while I talk." She sipped her coffee, looked out over the pond, and began.

"I've been investigating the Nanotechnology Center and their funding from the Elrod Foundation, aka Loder International, for over a year. The name kept showing up while I was writing an article on neurotoxins found in food distributed to remote villages amid regions of civil unrest in Africa. There are rumors that the same neurotoxins were attached to an experimental project by a center funded by the Elrod Foundation."

She took another sip of coffee and looked out over the pond. "I saw you talking to Matthew McGregor. I crossed paths with him in Africa when Royal Canadian Mounted Police assigned him to probe how an entire village was wiped out because of neurotoxins found in food sup-plied by a Canadian charity."

"I take it they found nothing solid to go after Loder," said Neil.

"Oh, they did." Michelle paused and watched a couple laugh and smile at each other as they walked on the path by the water. "But, I did something stupid. I wanted to expose those arrogant corporate tyrants who thought they could get away with anything. I revealed a source to McGregor. We were . . . having a fling, I guess you could say. It was the biggest mistake I ever made and will never make again."

"What happened?" Neil asked.

"McGregor interviewed my source, and the next night the rebels de-capitated the man and burned the home to the ground with the entire family trapped inside." Michelle coughed after sipping her coffee, but managed to finish it before crushing the cup.

"At the time, I was on assignment for a German foreign policy journal, so I wrote an article based on the information I'd gathered and submitted it. Three weeks later, I got a message that they'd killed the article. They gave no reason for burying it, but they paid me the amount I was to receive upon publishing."

Neil finished his burger and wiped his mouth with a napkin. "Why do you think they refused to publish?"

"I know why. I met the editor for coffee, and he told me."

"So, why didn't they publish it?

"Because Loder International said they would sue if it went to print. One of the head editors had sent a copy of my story to Loder and asked for a comment."

"You named Loder specifically? What did you say about them?"

"I found evidence that they had funded scientific projects that were used in the development of neurotoxins. There were hints they had also provided the ships for transporting the neurotoxins to the areas of unrest. The witnesses I spoke to were too frightened to back up their statements after what had happened to my source. That's the excuse that the journal used to not print my article. Because the evidence wouldn't hold up."

"Do you think McGregor had something to do with the death of your source?"

She shrugged.

"But because of what you found out in Africa, you suspect Loder was funding Bastien's research projects at the Center to be used for nefarious events?"

"Nefarious events?" she chuckled, "That's a fancy way of saying it. Yes, I believe the project Bastien was working on, which he intended to be a method for treating neurological disorders, was being turned into a mechanism for bio-attacks via nanotechnology. No one would know because it's too hard to trace."

"Bastien told you this?"

"He alluded to it. He went to the Royal Canadian Mounted Police with his suspicions. But the bad guys found out. He received multiple threats. He hinted his daughter, Cadenza, may have alerted them."

"Why would she do that?" Neil asked.

"If she's the one who's dead; we may never know. But we've got to get the goods on these guys. That's why I'm hoping we can work together on this."

"Anything I find out will be to help Octavia and to protect her." Neil shoved the burger wrapper into the bag. "I've checked you out, and you have a reputation that—how did one editor put it? That once you get the bit between your teeth, you don't stop until you've got the story. It's a cliché, but I suspect it's accurate. I rarely ask for help, but it's difficult to get anything done under the current conditions. So, if we are to work together, there's something I need from you."

"What is that?"

"I'm not just investigating Bastien's death—I'm also investigating Octavia's accident. You mentioned in your letter that Bastien thought it wasn't an accident, that there's a larger organization—a criminal network—involved. But there is another connection. My fiancée was murdered nearly twenty years ago by someone I believe has an affiliation with the same network. This line of inquiry is steep and dangerous. It could be your career maker or your death."

Michelle stuffed the remaining napkins into the bag. "I can promise you I will work with you on the Bastien Beaulieu story. I can't guarantee that I can help you with the murder of your fiancée. But if we get in deep and find evidence that this organization has been working in the United States and Canada for the last two decades, there's no way I'm stepping away."

The light was changing. Neil got up to signal that it was time to go.

"I want the man who killed my fiancée arrested and charged. He's already been let go once because of mishandling of evidence, and now I'm wondering if that mishandling was intentional. But let's find out what happened to Bastien and what the connection is with Loder International, if there is one. And maybe investigate Cadenza's murder as well."

Michelle nodded in agreement. "It's all very convoluted. The pieces are all there. We have to put them together and find the patterns." She stood up and breathed in deeply, then exhaled slowly. I've done my part by sharing what I know, now it's your turn."

Neil told her about the police report and the pictures at the crime scene."

"Hmm," said Michelle.

"Did you notice," said Neil, "that Bastien had a fondness for the number four? He formed a band called The Four-Bar Progression, he wrote a composition called 'Four-Bar Progression,' and he routinely played at four bars in the same progression throughout the years."

"Interesting pattern. We need to talk to the other band members," she said.

"I'd like Octavia involved with that," said Neil. "She's very good at charming information out of people. She's not in a very good frame of mind right now, but she wants to find out what happened. She will get things out of them that nobody else can."

Michelle nodded in agreement.

"The other thing we need to do," continued Neil, "is find out exactly how Cadenza died, if it is Cadenza's body found in the fire."

Michelle nodded. "You know, we could let the police handle the heavy lifting on that. Of course, whoever arranged for her death probably money to line people's pockets. We have to be careful about who we talk to. We also can't trust anybody. That could include McGregor. I don't trust Matthew McGregor. I've found no evidence that he's dirty, but ever since my source was killed, I've been uneasy about him. We can't be too careful."

"Someone I trust contacted him, and I trust her with my life," said Neil. The lights popped on in the park. "But in the meantime, there are certain things we should keep between ourselves and Octavia."

"Don't get yourself kicked out of the country," said Michelle, "and don't avoid quarantine again. Let me do the footwork. I'll arrange meetings with the band members and talk to the owners of the four bars."

"Let's go," said Neil, "I need to get back."

They headed toward the car. "Where am I going?" Michelle asked.

Neil pulled out his phone. "I'm texting you the address, but I want you to let me off on the other side of the park near there. I don't want you to be involved in any kind of dustup that will happen when I get back. They also won't have a picture of your car."

"Who's they?

"Yuu International."

"Here, take this," she said as she handed him a burner phone. "The only contact on it is my burner number."

Michelle started the car, and they drove off as the streetlights popped on.

CHAPTER 25

As Neil walked down the dark, leaf covered pathway through the park forest, he spotted two figures in the distance.

Their body language told him everything he needed to know - he was in for it. He casually pulled his mask out of his pocket and slid it on. With his hands nonchalantly tucked in his pockets, he continued to saunter towards them.

"Where the hell have you been?" asked McGregor.

"Sans McGregor, vous seriez arrêté sur-le-champ et placé dans un quartier d'isolement." Aumont's jaw tightened, his face set in a hard, unyielding expression as he stepped closer to Neil.

"I had to give myself some time and space to process and think things through," said Neil.

McGregor said nothing, but his stony face did.

"I acknowledge that I have been defying your protocols," Neil confessed, "but, the only way to crack this case is by conducting this investigation outside the customary parameters, where the truth lies hidden."

Aumont opened his mouth to protest. Neil raised his hands to stop him.

"Let me finish. There is a sinister plot afoot. Bastien's research could enable the replication and lethal delivery of neurotoxins using nanotechnology. I suspect it was used on Bastien."

"I can't believe this—" Aumont sputtered, "Sci Fi fantasy!"

"McGregor, you know better, don't you?" said Neil. "You started out helping me because Athena asked you to, but now you are taking charge of the case and bringing in the RMCP. You know what the stakes are and that it calls for more than just following police protocols."

McGregor leaned forward. "Your assessment may have some merit," he said, his voice low and serious. "But if this is indeed a covert operation, which I strongly suspect it is, you must follow the rules of the game. You can't make a move without first disclosing your objective to me beforehand."

McGregor's piercing hazel eyes locked onto Neil's, his voice commanding and unwavering. "Listen closely," he said. "I am now the chief investigator on this case. The RMCP has assumed jurisdiction in collaboration with the Montreal police. Aumont has worked with me before—you have not. You are the unknown entity, and you need to prove yourself to us." McGregor stepped back, studying Neil with a calculated gaze.

"You have an impressive military record, however, you are a rogue operator. It got you in trouble with your superior officers in the marines and, though Athena trusts you, there are others who mistrust you. Enough with the arrogant loner nonsense. Let's work together. We can bring justice for Beaulieu and prevent further harm by catching the real culprits—ones capable of causing mass destruction."

Neil's eyes narrowed as he studied the man standing in front of him. He couldn't shake the words of warning from Michelle, who claimed McGregor was untrustworthy.

"Has the victim in the house fire been ID'd yet?" Neil asked Aumont.

"No," said Aumont, "but it all points to Cadenza Beaulieu. We questioned the next-door neighbor and searched Cadenza's car. We were about to leave when the husband asked if we wanted the license plate number to a black van that had been parked behind her car. His wife got after him for not telling her. We're running it. I haven't heard the result yet."

Neil looked down at the ground, amused at the thought of Agnes getting after her husband. He looked up and sighed. "I have a request to make."

"Of course you do," said Aumont.

"What is it?" asked McGregor.

"We need to get back into the house."

"What?"

"We need to get into the house because the files she took weren't what she thought."

"What do you mean?" asked Aumont.

"McGregor, you know Loder International has connections with terrorist groups and foreign governments, even if you can't prove it yet. Beaulieu thought his innovative research would be used for harm. He hid his work using a code. The files Cadenza was looking for wasn't in his office. We need access to one of the other rooms in the house."

"The music room," said Aumont.

"Yes, the music room."

"That's what that whole spider thing was about, wasn't it?" Aumont fumed.

"Octavia is terrified of spiders. The way she screamed? There was a spider."

"What's in the music room?" asked McGregor.

"I will have an answer to that," said Neil, "as soon as we get in there. There are indications he was using music to code information. There is only one person who can decipher that code if there is one."

"Ms. Clarke," said McGregor.

"How do you know she can decipher it if there is a code?" asked Aumont.

Neil didn't answer, but continued to direct his remarks to McGregor.

"We also need access to the trombone. Beaulieu gave instructions to his attorney that she was the only one to open it. She needs to see what is inside."

"The trombone has been taken in for evidence," said Aumont, "in a murder investigation," he stressed.

"We need to know what we're looking at," said McGregor. "We'll bring Ms. Clarke in to view it."

"Bringing it here would be the better option," Neil advised.

"Under no circumstances will I permit the trombone to be removed from the evidence room," Aumont adamantly declared.

"Just hear me out," Neil insisted. "The trombone may contain coded information, and Octavia might be the only one who can decipher it. Bringing the trombone to the townhouse ensures that only we have access to it. We don't know who is on Loder's payroll and...Octavia's been through hell this week," he said, trying to convey his friend's trauma. "Every dimension of her life has undergone a profound change, and she's... overwhelmed."

McGregor nodded to Aumont.

"I will bring the trombone here tomorrow afternoon," said Aumont.

"Thank you," said Neil and extended his hand.

Not saying a word, Aumont turned and walked away.

"Nice try," said McGregor, "too bad it wasn't genuine." He started to walk away. "Here comes the quarantine agent. Good luck." He continued walking. "Hopefully, we'll have an ID on the victim tomorrow," he called out.

CHAPTER 26

Octavia was oblivious to Neil's arrival at the townhouse. She was in her pajamas and halfway through her third bottle of wine.

The volume on "Four-Bar Progression" was cranked up and her eyes were closed as she moved to the music. She was in her own world.

"Octavia." Neil raised his voice. "Octavia." Neil shouted. "Can we turn down the music? Octavia! Can we turn down the music?"

She didn't respond. She kept moving to the sound of the music. He went over to the turntable and turned down the volume. She glared at him.

"Turn it back up," she said. "I'm listening to the sound of my father. This is the only way I know him. How dare you interrupt me while I'm listening to my father?"

She went to the turntable and cranked up the music.

"Octavia."

"Quiet!" she said. "I don't want to hear you. I need to listen to the music."

Neil was stunned. The tone in which she spoke to him was completely unfamiliar.

She is so angry. Why is she angry at me? I'm trying to help her. I'm trying to keep her safe.

He filled a glass with water and rummaged through the kitchen until he found a bag of maple leaf shaped cookies. He took them to his room and closed the door behind him.

With his noise reduction headphones in place, Neil tuned out the music and focused on sketching individuals in the group photos, trying to see if anyone looked out of place.

I'm sure the arsonist was there, watching.

He sketched Michelle Perusse. He sketched her car and the interior. He sketched the park and the dark pathway through the naked trees with McGregor and Aumont standing in the distance. Seeking a new perspective, Neil channeled his energy into sketching McGregor's face. He was determined to depict McGregor's true essence on paper.

He sketched non-stop for an hour, then pulled down his headphones to listen to the jazz composition by Bastien Beaulieu pounding at the closed door.

Such artistry and complexity within four bars of music. It mutates and refreshes each bar. There must be a pattern. Is the pattern repeated on Octavia's bracelet? Was the pattern there on Bastien's bracelet? What about the variations on his original composition at the house?

Before long, his thoughts overpowered the music.

What is in the trombone case? We'll find out tomorrow. What shape will Octavia be in?

The music stopped. He put his phone on the charger, got undressed, and went to bed.

He tossed and turned, unable to fall asleep. The woman in "A Scandal in Bohemia" playfully poked at his mind. He got up and grabbed his phone to reread the story. He fell into a troubled sleep, dissolving into the darkness.

CHAPTER 27

Octavia's voice was raspy as she eased out of her bedroom. "Any news on Cadenza?"

She was nursing a killer hangover and was still wearing the same clothes she had worn the previous day; her mascara and eyeliner smeared under her eyes and her hair disheveled.

It was 1pm and Neil had just told her to prepare for a visitor when Aumont arrived with Bastien Beaulieu's trombone case securely gripped in his hand.

Neil greeted him at the door. "I know. Where's my mask? Disregard for rules...blah blah blah."

"Not at all," said Aumont as he entered. "McGregor has arranged for your release from quarantine; given your tests have remained negative, and you were in quarantine when you returned to New York."

"Really?" Neil replied, his voice tinged with a subtle disappointment. "Although I'll miss your taunts, I'm confident that you'll discover a fresh way to assert your superiority."

Octavia didn't acknowledge Aumont. Cautiously, she made her way to the kitchen, carefully steadying herself every few steps. She grabbed a handful of aspirin, tossing them back with a gulp of water. Then poured herself a cup of coffee and took a seat at the opposite end of the table, distancing herself from where he had placed the case. She stared at it.

Neil broke the silence.

"Octavia, you need to open it to see what's in there."

She sipped her coffee, her eyes fixated on the case as if it were a venomous serpent. Aumont glanced at Neil, who extended a steaming cup of coffee towards him and gestured for him to take a seat at the table.

Aumont spoke in a hushed tone. "Ms. Clarke?"

Her gaze remained locked on the case.

With a touch of intensity, Aumont raised his voice. "Ms. Clarke?"

Neil raised his hand to silence him.

Octavia shifted uncomfortably in her chair, her gaze darting away from the case and back again as she took occasional sips from her coffee.

"I don't want to open it," she said. "I don't think I want anything to do with Bastien Beaulieu." Octavia winced and closed her bloodshot eyes for a moment. "I want nothing to do with his music...I want nothing to do with his house,... and... I want nothing to do with his research." She took another sip of coffee. "His daughter hates me and I don't blame her...if she's even alive." She took a gulp of air. "Why am I being pulled into this nightmare?"

Neil sipped his coffee. Aumont sat with his hands folded on the table, his eyes darting between Neil and Octavia.

"Octavia," Neil spoke in a firm and no-nonsense tone, "you possess great strength and power. You are the queen of every room you walk into. You're a pro at dealing with tough negotiations. Your comprehension of music is unparalleled. Time to get it together and stop feeling sorry for yourself. Open that trombone case, it could be the key to answering all your questions and solving Bastien's murder."

Octavia narrowed her eyes. "You're making my head hurt."

"No, you did that to yourself," Neil said firmly. "You need to take a shower and wash away the despair, brush your teeth until they sparkle again, comb you hair back off your face so you can see what's ahead of you and get dressed as if you were ready for battle. You're going to open this case and face whatever it holds head on. We're going to find out who killed Bastien then you're going to go home, to the club, to the Pinnacle."

"I want to go home," she whispered.

"You're going to be with people who love you, in a city that adores you. And then you're going to go back to Japan, where you're going to relax and be happy, and you're going to smile. And you have to smile, Octavia, because that smile pulled me from the deepest chasm of despair."

"I want that."

"Soon this will all be over. I will be with you every step of the way. I will always be by your side when you need me. Just as you have always been beside me when I needed you." Neil stood up. "So get out of that chair and go kick some ass!"

Her bloodshot eyes stared at him as she swallowed more coffee. She groaned as she stood up and moved slowly into the bathroom, then closed the door, and turned on the shower.

"What do we do?" Aumont asked.

"We drink our coffee," said Neil.

Octavia came out of the bathroom wearing a towel.

She walked into her room and the next time she came out; she was wearing an ivory cable-knit sweater, a pair of designer blue jeans, simple silver hoop earrings, and red lipstick.

Her eyes did not sparkle as they usually did, but she looked determined. Octavia walked over to the table and took a deep breath, then reached out to stroke the textured trombone case with her fingers.

"Wait," said Aumont as he handed her a pair of latex gloves. "You'll need to wear these while handling evidence." He handed Neil a pair of gloves and then slipped on a pair for himself.

"We haven't found a key for the case, so it will need to be forced open," he said.

"No," said Octavia. She examined the lock. "I have a hunch." She looked at Neil. "Do you have the key I gave you?"

He nodded and retrieved it from his bedroom. Octavia squinted at the key's ornate design, then began twisting and bending it into a completely different configuration. She smiled and slid it into the lock. The center latch flipped open, and with a counter-clockwise turn of the key, the remaining two latches clicked open.

"I am constantly amazed by your skill-set," said Neil. "Go ahead, open it."

"When there was downtime, during the recording sessions, Bastien would compose a line of music and then turn the notes into a design. I recognized one of the designs on the key when I got a closer look at it. I thought it was to the file cabinets."

"You found this in the music room, didn't you?" Aumont accused her.

"Be quiet," she hissed. "Bastien said you should never open the case on a table or a chair. You put it on the floor, handle and latches facing you. The logo should be facing the ceiling to open it correctly without pieces falling out when you lift the cover."

She nodded at Neil who slid his hands under the case and gently placed it on the floor. There wasn't a logo, but there were initials. Using Neil for support, Octavia leaned down and gently ran her fingers across the two engraved letters, *BB*, and carefully opened the case.

Inside was a bright blue velvet lining and a spectacularly polished trombone. She felt the trombone's weight and cool smoothness as she lifted the pieces out of the case and began to assemble it.

"I remember Bastien showing me this." A sad smile came to Octavia's face. "I was hungry to learn everything."

"That's where the mouthpiece goes," she demonstrated. "And with your thumb, push the slide out, and with your two fingers, pull it back. So, as you go out, the thumb pushes it, and the fingers catch it, and then the fingers bring it back, so you're almost throwing it and catching it, throwing it and catching it."

Neil examined the scrollwork and the symbols on the keys, methodically recording each inch of the trombone with his phone; then closely examined the etchings on the instrument. The slide was adorned with intricate designs, including scrolled lettering and symbols.

Octavia disassembled the trombone before delicately returning each piece to its case. She then carefully opened the small compartment nestled inside. It contained a mouthpiece. She ran her fingers along the velvet lining and found an area where the lining was loose. She lifted it up, and it pulled away from the case. Inside, were two envelopes: the first one she opened contained photographs.

She looked at the pictures. There were two distinct sets. One was a series that had been taken at The Bllack Market Studio during the time of the recording, and shots of her in the studio, her fingers on the soundboard. Another set was taken at a separate location. In each photo, she was standing with one of the band members. The last, a photograph featuring her alongside the trombone player, both with captivating sapphire eyes, both adorned with matching smiles.

Neil looked over her shoulder. "Do you remember when those pictures were taken?"

Octavia nodded. "I was so proud to be the producer of the album. Now I realize it was my father who had requested me. He listened to all my suggestions and agreed to all of them, except one."

"What was that?" Neil asked.

"I found one of the trombone solos oddly discordant. There was one section that sounded . . . *painful*. That's the only way I can describe it. I stopped the recording session and told the band that discordance could cost them sales. The other band members were willing to rework it, but Bastien refused to change his composition. He said, 'This section is the whole point of the piece.'

"It was so odd because he looked like he was pleased about my reaction to it. The band and the production crew took an hour for lunch. I went to my desk, and Bastien followed me. He said, 'I want to explain why that section is so important. I love music. It's part of me, part of my soul and spirit. But I am a research scientist too, and it is also a big part of who I am.'

A grin spread across Octavia's face as she recalled the memory.

"I told him he looked too cool to be a scientist. He laughed and said, 'Being a research scientist is cool. The world is at the precipice of transformative progress, with imminent advancements that hold the power to completely alter the course of humanity.'"

Octavia cocked her head to the side, studying Neil with a perplexed expression. "In hindsight, he sounded a lot like you."

"I remember he stopped smiling, and just for a moment he looked...you know those pictures of Oppenheimer? The ones where it looks like he's looking into the abyss?"

"Yes," said Neil. "He realized he was a destroyer of worlds."

"That's what Bastien looked like. I just realized that. But it was a brief...a flutter across his face. He went on to say, 'It's progressing swiftly, presenting me with a predicament that I am grappling with. I infuse my music with that struggle, allowing it to resonate through every note. It is a representation of what we will all be struggling with soon, so it is imperative that the composition remains exactly as I composed.'

"I was so in awe of the thought that had gone into the music, but I still didn't think it would sell. The music business is a business. He said he was willing to take the chance; that ardent jazz fans would get it. So we recorded it as composed."

She opened an envelope. Inside was a typed note. She read it and handed it to Neil.

GIVE US WHAT WE WANT, OR SOMEONE YOU LOVE WILL SUFFER.

"High-quality printer paper, matte finish, fairly new." Neil sniffed it. "There's still a slight scent of the toner. He got this recently." He handed it to Aumont.

Aumont's narrowed eyes radiating intensity. "I'm taking custody of this," he declared. "We now have proof that Bastien Beaulieu was threatened with physical harm."

"He received it," Neil said, his voice filled with concern, "but the person he loves is the one in danger."

CHAPTER 28

"May I please keep these photos?" Octavia asked, as she slid them back into the envelope.

"I'm sorry, I cannot allow that," said Aumont, "I must place them in evidence, along with the threatening note."

Octavia lowered her head and slid the pictures back into the envelope, extending it towards Aumont.

"Please don't look like that, Ms. Clarke," said Aumont.

"Like what?" she asked.

"Like a sad Madona." He hesitated. "You may take pictures of them first, if you like."

"Thank you, Serge," she whispered.

Octavia took pictures of the photos and was about to latch the case when Neil stopped her.

"Hold on."

"Now what?" asked Aumont.

"Open the case, the compartment with the mouthpiece."

"What are we looking for?" Aumont asked.

"The musician places the mouthpiece against their lips, and they blow air through it. The sound of the trombone can be modified through the technique of tonguing. It would be the perfect place to apply a neurotoxin or slow acting poison. Remember, he had his trombone with him, and he stashed it."

Aumont lifted the lid of the case and opened the small compartment. "Wouldn't he have cleaned it after he used it? And why use a neurotoxin as a poison? And what kind of delivery system?"

"Would your medical examiner consider testing for a neurotoxin or searching for a nano delivery system? If we're lucky, maybe Bastien did a quick clean and left something behind."

"He might, but ...a neurotoxin ?"

"All medicine with the wrong dosage is poison. Beaulieu's research delved into the potential of medical nanotechnology to effectively treat neurological disorders."

"You think someone poisoned him with his own delivery system?"

"I think there is a strong possibility."

Aumont took an evidence bag out of his pocket and placed the mouthpiece inside. He placed his gloves in a disposal bag and had Neil and Octavia do the same. "Better safe than sorry."

His mobile phone started to ring. He responded to it. "Aumont. Oui? What? Envoyez le rapport sur mon téléphone et la photo du fourgon utilitaire également." With a click, he ended the call. Two notifications popped up on his screen.

"They found the van?" asked Neil.

"We have a photo of a black van taken when it ran a red light, yesterday afternoon, and a clear image of the driver's face."

"Cadenza Beaulieu," said Neil.

"What?" Octavia grabbed the phone and stared at the image. She let out a deep, tired sigh. "Thank god she's alive," she whispered with relief. She handed the phone back to Aumont as she sat at the table and pressed her fingers against her temples.

"Then who is the victim in the fire?" asked Neil.

"I just received that information." Aumont scrolled through the report. "We have tentatively identified the victim as Michelle Perusse, an investigative journalist."

"That's not possible," said Neil. "She was standing with a group of people watching the fire. I spoke to her." He omitted the part about burgers in the park.

"How do you know her?" Aumont demanded.

"Before we came to Montreal," Octavia explained, "she sent me a packet of information about my father and his work."

"What? Have you been withholding information on this case?" Aumont asked, his voice tinged with suspicion and a hint of skepticism.

Octavia winced and squinted. "Could you please find a more gentle way to express your frustration?" she implored.

"You have a habit of making me raise my voice," Aumont replied.

"Octavia pressed her fingers to her temples. "She was a fan of his music. She has a hunch that Loder International was behind his murder, and she intends to prove it."

"How was she identified?" Neil asked.

"First, answer my question," said Aumont. "Did you release information to her when you spoke to her?"

"Seriously, how could I?" Neil's comeback was dripping with irony. "You said she's dead."

"Yet, you insist she's alive, so answer my question."

"At the house fire?" Neil responded. "No. As Octavia told you, Ms. Perusse had sent articles about Loder International, and she had interviewed Bastien about his work. And no, I don't believe that Michelle Perusse is dead," said Neil.

"There must be some evidence," Aumont insisted, "otherwise her name wouldn't come up as the victim."

"Exactly, so what is the evidence?"

"A business card was found on the body. There was no other ID."

"That doesn't mean the victim was Michelle. Let me prove to you that the identification of this body is wrong."

"Oui, no one knows more than you," Aumont fired back.

"Listen to me," said Neil. "The real Michelle Perusse is not dead. I have her phone number. If you let me call her, I can prove she is alive."

"You talked to her long enough to get her number?"

Octavia intervened. "She sent us her contact information when she sent the articles. Neil may appear arrogant, but there's a rationale behind it. He is annoyingly... perpetually right, and he's not the only one that saw her. I did, too."

Neil raised his eyebrow and glanced at her, then redirected his attention to Aumont.

"If it turns out the woman I talked to is an imposter, I can arrange a rendezvous and you can apprehend her. But I'm sure she's who I believe her to be and could be of assistance. You'd win either way."

"We're calling the shots on this case, not you," Aumont insisted.

"Someone brutally murdered Bastien," Octavia declared, "then set his house on fire, killing a woman. My sister may be involved, or maybe, she's fleeing to save her own life. Stop the pointless arguing."

There was a sudden, forceful knock. Aumont moved to open the door. It was McGregor.

"What's going on here?" McGregor asked.

Aumont explained the situation. Neil told his side of the story. McGregor sat listening. After hearing both sides, he proceeded outdoors with his phone in hand. Octavia, Aumont, and Neil waited, glancing at one another. Five minutes later, McGregor returned.

"Serge, I know this is going to...upset you, but you do not have the facilities to handle the scientific and medical components of this case, and neither does your medical examiner. My team is coming and we will find out who the actual victim is." He paused and, as he stood in deep thought, wrinkles etched themselves onto his forehead. "Allowing Ames and Ms. Clarke to have some leeway in their movement is of utmost importance."

Aumont snorted.

McGregor turned to Neil. "I know Michelle and I'm sure that this would intrigue her. Call her on speakerphone. I will be able to tell whether it's her. We—collaborated in a war zone five years ago. She had been quick to make connections that could have compromised our security operations, but her instincts were right. If she's investigating Loder International and its foundation, there's justification for us to broaden our investigation."

Then McGregor turned to Octavia.

"Ames told me you would be the right person to talk to the band members. You worked with them in the past?"

"Yes," said Octavia, "a lifetime ago."

McGregor grunted and nodded. "All right. Make it a personal visit. Ask about your father and his music. Warm them up. If they give any intimation that they know something, notify me at once. Neither you nor Ames are to take direct action."

"Your detectives have interviewed the band members, yes Aumont?" McGregor asked.

"Oui," Aumont replied, "they said they tried to contact Beaulieu when the rehearsal was canceled, but were unable to contact him. We are still looking for the drummer. The other band members said he often travels between the United States and Canada."

"Maybe he'll show up if I ask the others to meet me," Octavia suggested.

"My detectives will find him," Aumont declared, bristling with anger. He squared up to McGregor. "You can't leave me out of this investigation. Two people have been murdered in my city, et je ne le supporterai pas."

McGregor nodded and pulled Aumont aside. "Serge, I'm counting on your instincts, and we will be collaborating with you on those murders, which includes anything Ames and Ms. Clarke uncover. However, national security is at risk and if Loder is involved in developing a delivery system for nano toxins, they may orchestrate a covert handoff within their network to transport it to other entities. There's no time to waste; we have to stop it now."

Aumont picked up the trombone case. "I have evidence to turn in. If you want it, do the paperwork. Goodbye, Ms. Clarke. Please take care. Don't do something just because your friend wants you to." He opened the door, but before stepping out, he turned. "Please take precautions to protect yourself."

"I will," Octavia said. "Thank you for your concern."

McGregor's attention shifted to Neil. "Make the call. Let's find out if Michelle Perusse is dead or alive."

CHAPTER 29

Michelle answered Neil's call with a flirty, "Calling so soon? You're a little needy, aren't you?"

"You have no idea," replied Neil. "I'm curious as to whom I spent some time with yesterday."

"What?"

"There's a report that you died in the house fire. So, I thought I would call and find out who you really are."

"I've been wondering that for years," she replied. "I've realized that I am a fervent journalist, on a quest to uncover the secrets that lie beneath the surface. I'm prepared to spend countless hours in my car, watching and talking to people I don't know. Then I write the story and sell it to whomever will publish it. I write books that no one reads, but the facts are there for anyone interested enough to find them. I am a loner, and I like that just fine."

"We're a lot alike," said Neil, "except I don't own a car and I don't write books."

"By the way," Michelle continued, "I thought it was Cadenza Beaulieu who was dead. Where is she?"

"We don't know. She was spotted driving a black van. The one behind the house. Just so you know, I'm on speaker phone and Matthew Mc-Gregor is here with me."

"I thought as much. I'm sure it was exciting for you to learn of my demise, Matthew. Sorry to disappoint."

"Hello, Michelle. I'm relieved you are alive," Matthew answered. "I wonder who wants you dead, or at least wants us to believe you are."

"You mean besides you? I told Neil not to trust you, and I'm sticking by that warning."

"We need to meet." Neil took over the conversation. "You two may have reasons to distrust each other, but for now, we need to work together. First, we need to find out how the medical examiner concluded you were the victim. I have an idea who the victim is and why she was at the house."

"Okay, I'm curious," said Michelle. "Who do you think it is?"

"The housekeeper. The house was immaculate. You knew there was a housekeeper didn't you?"

"Stop feeding her information." McGregor took over. "Michelle, what have you been up to? Who have you been talking to?"

"I hope it's not her," said Michelle. "She was very upset about Bastien's death. I asked her to meet me at the house. I gave her my card. We were supposed to meet."

"That's why you were there at the fire," said Neil.

"I arrived at the same time as the fire department. I didn't know she..."

"What is her name?" McGregor asked.

"Molly Obote."

"Why were you nosing around the house?" McGregor asked.

"I've been investigating the Elrod Nanotechnology Center for months, but more intensely, since Bastien Beaulieu contacted me. He had been providing me with information and he said he had something definitive, and after he died, I wanted to see if it was at the house."

"Michelle, you should have come forward with this information," said McGregor.

"That would be a grand idea if the RCMP could guarantee me they won't have my story censored."

"This is a matter of national security," said McGregor

"Here we go again!" Michelle retorted.

"That is more important than your selfish need to be published. I am not willing to give you carte blanche with all the intricacies of intelligence gathering."

"Let me talk to her." Octavia took over the conversation. "Michelle, this is Octavia Clarke. I neglected to thank you for the information you sent me about Bastien. It gave me a heads-up before walking into all this. Have you talked to any of the band members?"

"Yes, I've left messages, and I'm meeting one of them at 4 o'clock this afternoon."

"I'd like to talk to them face to face and the club owners as well."

"Two of the band members own clubs and one of them is who I'm meeting later."

"So, may I join you?" asked Octavia.

Michelle agreed to meet her at the club.

"What's the name and the address?" asked Neil.

"You're not invited," said Michelle.

"I have no intention of being a part of the conversation," said Neil. "Octavia can handle that without help from me or you. She has a driver who will make sure she gets there and back again safely."

"The name of the club is Bass Frequencies. The band's bass player is the owner, or at least he was. Everything is up in the air for everyone. It's in the basement of a building close to Dièse Onze on St. Denis between Duluth and Rachel. I'll be on the street waiting for you."

"I'll meet you there at 4." Octavia stepped away to call James.

"Don't worry about me, I'm not dead yet," said Michelle. The call ended with a beep.

"I'm going to follow up on the real identity of the fire victim," said McGregor, "What are you going to do?"

"I'm going to think," said Neil.

CHAPTER 30

After McGregor left, Neil made coffee, grabbed more cookies, and headed for the couch, where he sat with his sketchbook.

He stared at the blank page. Nothing was coming. His thoughts felt congested. He closed his eyes and allowed his pencil to move across the page. His fingers swirled around the paper, page after page. The pencil flew out of his hand. He opened his eyes and looked at his doodles. Spirals covered the page, with question marks dangling from the spirals.

"Look at the pictures," a voice whispered.

Neil startled and shifted his attention to the area behind him. No one was there. It was a voice in his head, one he had heard before, but it wasn't his.

Emily. Emily's voice. Why am I hearing it again?

Neil stepped outside onto the balcony, clutching his sketchbook, and gazed over the park. The chatter of birds filled his ears as he watched the graceful blackbirds dance in the sky, their wings catching the fading rays of the sun. Storm clouds were rolling in and a sudden chill filled the air.

He looked at the doodles in his sketchbook. The doodles had turned into chains, which had turned into stones. The stones had turned into a wall that held the chains in place.

He shook his head vigorously, repeating, "No, no, no."

Neil realized the restricting quarantine, Octavia's trauma, Kazakhstan, and the encounter in New Orleans had triggered his PTSD and memories he had long kept locked away—memories of Afghanistan, where he had been held captive in a dark cave, chained to a cold stone wall. The sound of buzzing flies echoed in his mind, making him shudder with disgust.

Flies...crawling around my head wound...sticking to the blood on my face, their incessant buzzing roaring in my ears. My eyes swollen and on fire...and the rats.

Neil unconsciously wiped his face and arms, brushing the phantom rats away with his sketchbook.

Crawling all over me, licking my blood, biting my flesh, taking a sample of the feast they wanted. Waiting for me to die.

The fresh autumn air turned to filth. His mind filled him with the smell of human sweat and excrement, his own. It all washed over him, murmurs of voices and laughter, the smell of campfire smoke, coffee, and his captors...the one.

I never saw him. His face was covered, his stench was suffocating, the gun he held against my temple promised death. He poured a trickle of water past my cracked lips, just enough to keep me alive, but not enough to soothe my parched throat. Why did they bother keeping me alive? Was it just the torture of seeing and smelling Arash's decaying body chained to the wall across from me, while rats and flies feasted on him? I wanted to die. I wanted it to end. But then I heard the voice, Emily's voice saying, "Stay alive! Come home. You must stay alive!"

Neil returned to the kitchen. He splashed cold water on his face, trying to snap out of the nightmare he had buried for years. But the memories just kept coming.

It was my fault Arash died. He was my informant. They followed him and captured both of us. I promised him I would find a way for us to escape. But I failed him. I failed Emily.

Neil heard their laughter. One more torment he couldn't escape.

The man came with a cup of water. He let me drink it all. I choked. I opened my eyes a crack. He pointed his gun at me and took aim. This is it,

I thought. I closed my eyes and heard shots. My ears were ringing, but then I heard laughter. I squinted. He was laughing at me as he dangled dead rats in front of my face. "You thought they would feast on you tonight, but you'll be feasting on them."

Neil chugged a glass of water and gasped for air.

I never had that feast. I survived. He didn't. Athena arrived with the unit. She slit his throat as he roasted the rats. Silenced, he fell into the firepit before he could warn the others. The unit took a prisoner; the rest were dead. She had come looking for me because she had news—Emily was dead.

He breathed in and out until his mind was calmed.

Octavia came out of her bedroom. She was back in her rocker uniform: a black leather jacket, black jeans, and artisan sneakers. Her straight medium-length blond hair hung perfectly. Her red lipstick was the one pop of color, and her transition lens sunglasses hid her eyes. Octavia was ready for battle. Her royal stance as she posed with her cane projected her intention. She was ready to go in and take no prisoners.

"Are you all right?" she asked. "You look shaken."

"Not stirred," replied Neil.

Her phone buzzed. She looked at it. "It's James."

CHAPTER 31

The moment James and Octavia rolled into The Plateau district, they were immersed in a world of vibrant colors, eclectic shops, and the energetic buzz of the local artists and jazz.

Trees lining the streets were shedding their mesmerizing canopy of fiery red, burnt orange and golden yellows. Colorful murals adorned the sides of buildings. The air carried a blend of earthy scents, hints of wood smoke wafting from chimneys and food from cafes offering diverse culinary delights, but predominately French pastries: panin au chocolat, eclairs, and rich espresso.

James parked close to a pedestrian-only area where locals embraced the cooler temperature, wearing stylish scarves and jackets as they strolled and street performers provided entertainment. "I'll escort you, madam."

"Thank you, but that won't be necessary," said Octavia. "I might be awhile."

James opened her car door, and Octavia got out. As Michelle approached them, she smiled and arched an eyebrow. "That's not your everyday Uber driver. He's damn fine."

"He's not an Uber driver, and yes, he's damn fine."

The two women grinned at each other. "Did we just offend you, James? I apologize if we did," said Octavia.

"Not at all, madam, I'm happy to hear you approve of my driving skills."

"Are you ready for this?" asked Michelle.

"Locked and loaded," said Octavia. "Let's go."

James' eyes lingered on the two women as they walked along the street—Octavia, exuding sophistication and allure, and Michelle, embracing her distinctiveness with her tousled locks and captivating presence.

They approached a lit sign pointing to the basement entrance of Bass Frequencies.

After a buzz and two quick clicks, Cliff Squire greeted them.

"Michelle! Come in."

The club was dark. The chairs were upside down on the tables, and the shadowy stage at the far end looked forlorn. The only lights were over the bar area.

"Too bad you're here when we're closed," said Cliff as he pulled a couple of chairs off a table and set them on the floor. He motioned for them to sit. "So, you're Bastien's kid."

"How did you hear about that?" Octavia asked.

"Word gets around." He smiled. "I remember you from a long time ago when we were recording our second album. Course, we didn't know who you were. Well, Bastien knew who you were, but the rest of us didn't. I can't believe he's gone. He was a good friend. Great musician. A genius composer." Cliff walked toward the bar. "Would you like a drink?"

"Sure, you got any whisky open?" asked Michelle.

He grinned. "Honey, there is always whisky open here. How about you, Octavia? Or is something else to your liking?"

"I'll take whisky and branch, please."

Cliff brought the drinks to the table. "I think Bastien would appreciate the three of us having a shot of his favorite whisky in his honor. How about a toast to Bastien?" He lifted a glass. "Rose-lipped maidens, light-foot lads."

"Rose-lipped maidens." Michelle downed her shot.

"Light-foot lads." Octavia paused, knocked back her drink, and followed it with water.

Michelle and Cliff reminisced about the last time Bastien had played the room. Octavia's attention was on the arrangement of the jazz club. It was a cozy, intimate space. Signed photos of jazz artists who had played there—some were legendary, most weren't, but their photos were displayed on the walls side by side.

"This is a nice place," said Octavia. "I own a club."

"Where?" he asked.

"Destiny Point, it's a port city in Washington State."

Cliff made his way back to the bar and brought the bottle of whisky to the table.

"So, you still play the bass?" she asked, "I remember you were very good."

"I don't play it as much as I used to," he sighed. "For more than a decade, I have been the proud owner and operator of this club. Getting the band together was always a blast, playing the classics and improvising Bastien's new compositions. But, we've become old men, our hair gray and our bodies tired...and now Bastien is dead." He sipped his whisky.

"I love coming to this place." Michelle sipped her whisky. "I love the music. I hope you'll be reopening soon. It looks like the streets are coming alive."

"The locals are coming back, but it's a fraction of what it used to be. Tourists and the jazz festival keep the doors open." Cliff leaned back in his chair and looked around the place. "I've got a little money put aside. I might be able to keep it open, but I have a gut feeling that will not happen."

"What will you do?" Michelle asked.

"I'm not really sure."

"You said Bastien had new compositions, was he coming up with a fresh sound?" Octavia asked.

Cliff chuckled. "Back in the day we used to say, 'Far out' but this new stuff was literally 'far out'."

"Maybe he was struggling to find a balance between his research...science mind and his soul...jazz brain," said Octavia.

Cliff sipped his whisky and looked down at the table. "We laughed about it the last time he was here. He said, 'I'm writing jazz for the future when listeners will be living with AI.'"

Cliff looked up. "You know...artificial intelligence? He said, 'Their life will be written in code. Jazz can show them the way to navigate the complexity of the future and still keep the soul of humanity."

"It sounds like he was a philosopher as well as a musician and scientist," said Michelle.

"He used to play here routinely, didn't he?" Octavia asked.

"Yeah, we would play on a Friday or Saturday once a month and go to three other places on the other weekends, but lately, we'd just rehearse."

"When was the last time he was here?" Michelle asked.

"It was the day he died. He stopped by at about four in the afternoon. He wasn't supposed to show up until 7: 30." Cliff emptied his glass and set it on the table. He spun it slowly as he spoke.

"What was his mood like?" Octavia asked.

"He was a little antsy. Something wasn't right, but he didn't say what it was. I asked him if he'd like a drink. He said he was tired and a drink might do him good, and we just sat and talked about old times. He asked me to play the Four-Bar Progression album, the one you produced. It was a damn good album."

"Yes, and it still holds up," Octavia agreed. "Each of you left your unique mark on the sound, made it legendary."

"We're not quite legendary, but thank you for saying that," said Cliff.

Octavia nodded. "It will be, I'll make sure it does."

Cliff's lips tightened and his forehead furrowed. Octavia sensed an underlying anxiety he was trying to conceal.

"It seems like the concept of a four-bar progression obsessed Bastien—the name of the band, the music he composed," she said.

"Now that you mention it, he would only play it on a four-bar rotation. That composition was like our calling card." Cliff poured another round of whiskies and took a drink.

"It's like he wanted a physical manifestation of Four-Bar Progression," said Octavia. "So, I'm wondering, was the progression or rotation of the band always the same? Your club on the first weekend of the month and another the second weekend and then to the third one—you get what I'm saying, right?" she asked. "And did he play the four-bar composition differently at each gig?"

"It's jazz. There is always a fresh way of playing a piece. We'd all do a riff on it. And, yeah, we had a fixed rotation; the first weekend here and the other three clubs in succession throughout the month, but this month was to be our last for a while. The owner of Blue Jazz Club retired and shut its doors; it was the first club we played when we were starting out. Charlie is in poor health, and Bastien was going to a conference."

"Charlie—the piano player?" Michelle asked. "Doesn't he own a club too?"

"Yeah, well, he recently had to sell half of the club to another party. Times are hard, and like I said, his health isn't good. Hell, we're all getting old. The last time Bastien came in, he said everything in his life was ending. That just came to me. Do you think he had a premonition?" Cliff grabbed the bottle of whisky and poured another shot. "Anyway, he said he was going to go to the Deep Red Club after he left here. That's as much as I can tell you."

"I thought the band was supposed to rehearse here that night," said Octavia, "Why was he going to the Deep Red Club?"

"I don't know," said Cliff, "He didn't tell me and it didn't occur to me to ask him."

"Huh," said Octavia, "I heard the rehearsal for that night was can-celed."

"Yeah, it was…about a half an hour after he left. Charlie wasn't feeling good. I tried calling Bastien, but he didn't answer so I sent him a text."

"Isn't the Deep Red Charlie's club? Why didn't he tell Bastien when he was there?" asked Michelle.

Cliff shrugged. "I don't know."

"But then he came back here?" Octavia asked.

"No, I didn't see him," said Cliff, "Would you like another round? I'll open another bottle."

"No, thank you." Octavia leaned forward. "I was told that a band member found him and called the police. Was that you?"

"No, it wasn't me. A band member found him? Who?" Cliff asked.

"I thought maybe it was you," she said.

"Do you know who it could have been?" asked Michelle.

Cliff blinked and shook his head.

"Sorry for asking all these questions," said Octavia, "it's just…I'm trying to wrap my head around it all. I'm sorry, I'm sure this is hard on you." She placed her hand on his. "You were his friend for a long time."

"Yeah," he uttered.

"I should go." Octavia drew her hand away. "I…but… his body was found in the alley behind this bar, right?"

"Yeah, but I didn't see him. I headed home after Charlie called."

"So you didn't leave through the back door into the alley?" Michelle asked.

"No, I always go through the front door. I enjoy walking home, hearing music, watching people."

Octavia and Michelle exchanged glances and stood up.

"I'm wondering, did he have his trombone with him when he was here?" Octavia asked.

Cliff's forehead wrinkled as he thought. "Yes, I remember him going out the door with it. Why are you asking?"

"Thank you so much, Cliff. It's been really nice to see you again after all these years. I hope your club reopens soon. It would be such a loss to not have this place." Octavia smiled and gave him a hug.

Cliff hugged her tight and whispered in her ear, "Sometimes people just need to see a beautiful smile."

Michelle and Octavia said their goodbyes and were about to go out the door when Octavia turned back and asked, "You said he was going to a conference this month. What conference?"

"I'm sorry, I don't know. I think it had something to do with his work. I think it was in California? Yeah, I think he said California."

"Let's check out the alley," said Octavia.

Michelle pulled out a pack of cigarettes and lit one up, blowing a cloud of smoke into the evening sky. "I feel like we're on the trail of something. You did a superb job of finding out information."

"That's because I've hung around with Neil for years," said Octavia, looking up at the waning crescent moon. "I've learned what to ask and how to ask. I'm the one who asks the questions a little more—how should I put it?...I don't know. Let's just say Neil is a little blunt with his questions. I found that a little charm and showing interest in the person will get you a lot more information. So, I take his lead. He asks his blunt question, and I soften it. I get the answer that Neil wants. That's how we've always worked together."

Michelle took another drag on her cigarette, then tossed it on the sidewalk and crushed it with the toe of her boot. "Very fond of him, aren't you?"

"Yes, I am. He can be difficult. But yeah, we work well together. He treats me with respect, and I do the same for him. We allow each other to be who we are."

"Were you two ever an item?" Michelle asked.

"No. God no. That would ruin the relationship completely." Octavia leaned on her cane and shivered. "We care about each other, but I think we're more like brother and sister. He can be protective, but sometimes he goes off and does his own thing. He always leaves me out whenever he goes on the hunt."

"The hunt? That's an interesting way to put it. Tell me about Emily's murder." Michelle leaned in, eager to hear the story.

"How do you know about Emily?"

"Neil mentioned her."

Dark clouds hid the moon. The evening became darker and colder. The alley was lit by two street lamps. Octavia lifted her sunglasses and placed them on top of her head, There was no trace of Bastien left behind. She recognized the back door to Bass Frequencies and the placement of Bastien's body from Neil's sketches. She stood on the spot and looked down the street. "So this is the last thing he saw and felt." She stared into the distance.

"Let's go," said Michelle. "How would you feel about going to the Deep Red?"

They began walking.

"I think that's a good idea," Octavia said.

"I'll call the Charlie, see if we can get in to talk to him."

Michelle turned and stepped away. Octavia watched her, recalling how many times she had seen Neil do the same thing. She continued walking toward the front of the building. James jumped out of the car and caught up to Octavia.

"Where are we going, madam?"

"Michelle and I are going to the Deep Red Jazz Club—if we can meet with the owner."

They could hear jazz coming from a building down the street. The music fit the rhythm of her thoughts, sometimes synchronous, sometimes discordant. Michelle returned.

"I got hold of Charlie Allen, he was the piano player with the band."

"Yes, I remember Charlie, he was pretty lively back in the day."

"Unfortunately, he isn't seeing anyone. Like Cliff said, his health isn't good. I asked if his new partner would allow us inside. I told him I was doing an article on the continuing impact of the lockdown on jazz clubs and we wanted to get pictures to go along with the story."

"Clever. What did he say?"

"He said he'd talk to his partner."

"So, we won't be able to meet with Charlie?"

Michelle shook her head. "Not in person and he won't do a video call, but he will do a phone conversation if he has a good day."

The music stopped.

"Thank you for doing this, Michelle."

Michelle nodded. "I'll see you tomorrow. You too, handsome!" She laughed and walked down the street in the opposite direction.

Octavia and James walked to the car. Just as he opened the door, her phone rang.

"Hello?"

There was breathing on the other end.

"Hello, who is this?"

"Is this Octavia?"

"Yes," said Octavia.

No response, only the faint sound of cars passing by.

"Who is this?"

"This is Cadenza. I need to talk to you."

Octavia said nothing.

"Are you there?" Cadenza asked.

"Why did you call me?"

"Because you're the only person I can call. I'm in deep trouble, and I'm afraid it's all my fault. I don't know what to do. And I have no one else to turn to."

"Where are you?" Octavia asked.

"I don't know if I should tell you or not." Cadenza coughed and took a breath. "I'm afraid you're going to call the police on me. But I'm more afraid of—I need to talk to you about what happened yesterday. I know you have no reason to trust me. I hate...don't even like you. But you're the only one I can turn to."

"Hold on." Octavia muted her phone. "James—"

"Whatever you need, madam."

She unmuted her phone. "I'll meet with you. But I am going to have someone with me. He won't listen to our conversation. But he'll be there if you do anything stupid."

"As long as the police aren't involved."

"So, where can I meet you?"

Cadenza gave her an address to a park. Octavia repeated the address to James. He looked it up on the GPS.

"It's about fifteen minutes from here."

"Don't make me regret this," warned Octavia. "We'll be there in a few minutes." She hung up before Cadenza responded. "Let's go, James."

Octavia reached into her pocket and pulled out the envelope that had been in the trombone case. *For your eyes only* was written on the front. She had slipped it out with the photos without Neil or Aumont noticing. Inside was a folded piece of paper. It was a variation on the "Four-Bar Progression" composition. A smaller piece of paper fell out.

Written on it was one line. *You'll know what you are looking for—once you learn how to listen.* She looked at the music again, but she saw nothing she could decipher.

I hope I'm doing the right thing.

CHAPTER 32

The arrival of winter was sudden, extinguishing the lingering warmth of autumn and replacing it with a bone-chilling wetness.

James drove slowly into the dimly lit parking lot. Octavia spotted a shadowy figure standing in the rain under a pool of light.

"That's Cadenza. You stay here," she said. "But keep the engine running."

James opened her door and handed her an umbrella. Octavia took a deep breath. She hadn't noticed how tense her body was until she stepped out of the car. She steadied herself on her cane and scanned the area. No van was visible.

Remember, she can't be trusted.

She came to a stop in front of Cadenza. They sized each other up. Tension charged the air between them.

"Hello, Cadenza."

"Hello, Octavia."

Cadenza wore straight leg jeans, their medium blue indigo shade growing darker as rainwater seeped into the denim. The downpour turned her once pristine white tennis shoes into waterlogged messes. The hood of her black hoodie obscured her face, and the gleam of the parking lot light reflected off her glasses, creating an enigmatic effect.

In the business sphere, Octavia often demonstrated her adeptness in handling hostile negotiation situations. She read this stranger's body language and saw a wall of defiance and animosity.

"You called, and I came." He removed all of them from the shelf and examined each one.

Cadenza scoffed. She began pacing back and forth. The shuffle of Cadenza's feet and the vibration of her aggressive energy gave Octavia the sense that she was being advanced upon by a boxer in a ring.

"I never wanted to meet you. I want nothing to do with you. I didn't want you to exist, and yet you were always there—in my house, at school. Everywhere my father was, you were there."

"What do you mean?" asked Octavia. "How was I there?"

"You were there because my father carried you in his heart long before I was born. You were the shiny golden child. I was the dull penny in his pocket. I always knew there was something standing between me and him. I tried so hard to get his attention—to get his acknowledgment. I tried music. I even tried composition as a form of mathematical writing. But it just didn't click in my brain. He carried the music within him, and I didn't have music in me. There was nothing for us to have in common except for his work as a neuro-technology researcher."

Cadenza confronted Octavia face-to-face, her eyes hidden behind the fog that had formed on her glasses from the rapidly changing temperature.

"That's why I worked so hard in school. I wanted to get good grades. I wanted to excel at math and science, and I did! I won science fair awards. I won math competitions. I wanted him to just say, 'Well done, my daughter.'

"He came to the science fairs. He came to my award ceremonies and my graduations all the way through my PhD. I was awarded research fellowships to Cambridge and Harvard. You would think a father would be proud of that, wouldn't you? He said nothing to acknowledge my accomplishments. All he did was question my methods."

Octavia realized she was a sounding board for all the frustration and grief her sister was feeling. She opened her mouth to speak, but Cadenza continued as if no pause had occurred.

"I came home on Canada Day three summers ago. While I was there I checked out dad's library, and I was so excited to find—an entire shelf that proudly displayed the scientific journals featuring my research papers and articles."

"Doesn't that prove something to you?" Octavia reached out to touch her, but Cadenza pulled back out of reach. Octavia withdrew her gesture, but continued to talk to her sister.

"Just listen."

Cadenza opened her mouth to lash out, but Octavia interrupted her.

"Bastien thought the world of you from the moment you were born."

"How would you know? You don't have a clue what our relationship was like."

"Yes, I do. I have a clue. It's your name."

"My name?" Cadenza sneered. "Don't use that 'I'm superior to you' tone with me."

"That's not what I'm doing. I am a stranger to you. Hell, I'm an outsider. But that is exactly why I'm able to look at your relationship from a neutral perspective. Bastien named me, and he named you, Cadenza. You say you had no connection to his music, but that is untrue. He knew what you were from the moment he first saw you. Cadenza is a jazz concept. It's improvisation, a showpiece. It is an unaccompanied passage. He saw the strong, independent woman that you would become. He wanted you to find your own path, and he was confident that you would."

Cadenza nervously watched a car entering the parking lot, ready to run. It circled the parking lot and left. She watched it turn onto the street and speed away. She turned to Octavia.

"*If* he was proud of me,"—she shook her head—"he had a funny way of showing it. On that same day, he questioned me about every article or paper that I had written. He took all of them off the shelf and opened each one up.

He had meticulously marked up my articles with annotations and proceeded to dismantle all my work, pointing out what he said were the errors in my thinking and critiquing the approaches I had taken. Influential scientists and professors had praised me for that work. I received accolades for my contributions to current research, as they created new avenues for future exploration. I had done thorough and precise research, but all afternoon he dissected every single one of my theories and conclusions apart."

In the time they had been talking, the air had grown colder. The rain transformed into freezing rain and began to coat everything it touched. James got out of the car and headed toward them with a blanket, an umbrella over his head.

"You should get in the car, madam," said James as he draped the blanket around Octavia's shoulders.

"Madam? What are you, her lapdog?"

"Let's get warm in the car. James is right—we need to get out of this weather."

But Cadenza was not ready to trust her.

"Thank you, James. I'm fine," said Octavia.

"Yes, madam." He ran back to the car.

Cadenza shivered and continued her story.

"How he did it was so odd. Along with the notations, he had written some kind of weird symbols that were—I don't know how to explain them. They looked like the runes on an ancient manuscript. He had translated my findings along with his analysis and turned them into some kind of mystical language. That's the only way I can put it.

"I thought it was just his thinking process. I thought it was part of his beautiful mind, how he could see things. He said I needed to see through the deceptive and misleading reasoning that is accepted as truth instead of trying to fit my thinking into those fallacies. I should break free and see for myself, see truly.

"It humiliated me. My father was so disappointed in me—after I had worked so hard to be like him, to be a scientist. I left, and I didn't see him for over a year. My mother—my beautiful mother . . ."

Cadenza's eyes filled with tears. She struggled to hold them back. She took off her glasses and wiped her eyes with the sleeve of her hoodie. She took a couple of deep breaths and cleared her throat.

"She put up with his ways. She knew she would never see him on a Friday or Saturday night. Those were his holy nights—the nights he spent with his true love: music. He cared about us. But we could tell there was someone else in his heart."

Cadenza became calm, almost matter-of-fact.

"It wasn't until Mother got sick that I learned about you—no, it was before that. I was ten or eleven. Dad got a phone call. He became frantic. He was packing a bag. My mother walked into the bedroom and closed the door. I could hear raised voices, but all I could make out was, 'No, you can't go. There is nothing you can do for her.' I caught another scrap of the conversation. 'I know she's your daughter, but you've not a part of her life.'

"My father raised his voice. He said, 'It's my fault. It's my fault that she got hurt. It's all my fault.'

"That conversation rolled around in my head for years. Shortly after I graduated from college, my mother got sick. I spent hours with her in her room, and we talked about our memories and my plans for the future. She wanted to offer advice while she could. As time passed, she got quieter and quieter until she faded away.

"One day she said to me, 'There's something you need to know. You have a sister. She's older than you—she was born before your father and I married—but you will probably meet her one day. She's in the music business. She has that in common with your father. He showed me a picture of her, and she's beautiful—a female version of your father. She met him years ago, but she didn't know who she was meeting. Your father's heart is with her. He cares for you, but she's the one he carries in his heart."

Cadenza hung her head. Her soaked hoodie was coated in an icy glaze and clung to her head and body. Octavia stayed dry under her umbrella, but she was swimming in emotion. Compassion filled her as she looked at the woman in front of her. She wanted to reach out and put her arms around her.

"I'm so sorry. I'm so sorry you experienced that."

"When my mother died, I felt the one person in the world who truly loved me was gone forever. I was alone." A growl rumbled from Cadenza's throat and she roared at Octavia. "I hate you! I never wanted to meet you! I wanted you to disappear!"

She hugged herself, to calm her trembling.

"Where is your vehicle?" Octavia asked.

"It's not here. I hid it and took an Uber."

"Let's go to my car. It's warm and dry. You will be safe."

Cadenza hesitated. Octavia motioned to James.

"You called me. You wanted to talk. But what you need is help." Octavia spoke calmly. "Bastien was murdered, and I have one question. Did you murder him?"

James drove up and jumped out to open the door. When Octavia climbed in, he took the umbrella and held it above her. She glanced back. "Actually, I have another question. Did you start the fire?"

Cadenza stood motionless—an ice sculpture standing in the freezing rain under a pool of light. Steam rolled out of her nose and mouth.

James shut the door and got in. The headlights flashed across Cadenza as James turned the car around to leave. As he was about to pull onto the street, there was a loud pounding on the trunk of the car.

He stopped. Cadenza pounded on Octavia's window, her face wet with tears and icy rain. Octavia cracked the window open. Cadenza's fingers grasped the opening.

"Please let me in! I need your help!"

Cadenza initially resisted, but with James's assistance, she climbed into the trunk of the Audi. She pulled out her phone and he wrapped Octavia's blanket around her, then shut the trunk.

The streets were treacherous as James maneuvered through the city. His eyes darted between the two side mirrors and the rearview camera. Octavia was in the back seat, her phone pressed to her ear, listening to and reassuring Cadenza.

"I hate closed spaces! I can't breathe" Cadenza gasped. "Let me out!"

"You're going to be fine, Octavia assured her. "We need to take extra precautions to make sure no one sees you. Just close your eyes and take a deep breath...now let it out slowly. You have plenty of air."

James pushed a button on the dash screen. "This is driver 7154. We need an exception at unit one."

"What's going on?" Cadenza asked.

Octavia tried to calm her. "We're entering the complex."

"Complex? What complex?"

Headlights flashed in the rearview mirror and were speeding toward them.

"Make sure your seat belt is secure, madam."

James tapped the dash screen and sped up toward the gates of the complex.

A digital voice answered the call. "Play?"

"Double deuce double down," James said. His eyes darted to the left. Headlights lit up James's face on the driver's side.

"Watch out!" Octavia cried out as a large Cadillac Escalade careened across the green landscaped grounds toward them.

A masked man extended an arm out of the passenger window with a gun pointed at the driver's side window. With lightning-fast reflexes, James slammed on the brake pedal, deftly rotating the steering wheel a full 360 degrees to the right. Their car spun in a daring move, narrowly avoiding a collision with both the Escalade and the car rapidly closing in from behind. Skidding down the icy street, James headed towards the gate of the complex.

Cadenza pounded on the trunk.

Octavia's voice carried a soothing, tranquil tone. "Calm down. We're almost there, Cadenza. Right, James?"

"Yes, madam. Not to worry. I will safely deliver your package." The gate slid open, the tires gripped the road as he accelerated and sped into the complex.

"So, I'm a package?" asked Cadenza.

CHAPTER 33

Neil had Bastien's entire home office on the floor of the townhouse living room. Clear-headed, he pieced together the intricate details of each sketch and photo in front of him, meticulously positioned in concentric circles.

The room is sterile, but that's not surprising. He wanted no distractions to analyze his research. But this . . .

Neil retrieved his magnifying glass, sketchbook, and graphite pencils. He examined the anomaly and began sketching.

Why is this in the office? Why is it sitting on top of this—

His head snapped up abruptly. Of course!

He put a kettle on to boil and scooped coffee into a French press. His phone pinged—a text from McGregor.

Need to see you. Will arrive in an hour.

Neil poured the hot water over the grounds and took the steaming cup out to the balcony. Fixated on the pathway lights, he became mesmerized on the stark contrast they created against the bare branches of the park trees. Then they underwent a transformation and dissolved into Bastien's office.

Neil sipped his coffee. He remembered looking out the office window and seeing the police vehicle and officer sitting in front of the house. A memory, sharp and distinct, surfaced.

Someone was parked across the street. A Mercedes? Someone was inside. Who was it?

Neil took another sip of coffee. A chilly breeze wafted across the balcony. He shivered.

I can't see through the tinted windows, and I can't see the license plate.

Neil stepped inside and began sketching the Mercedes, but his thoughts returned to Bastien's office. He recalled that Aumont was looking at the bookcases, running his gloved fingers over the spines and reading the titles silently.

There were three bookcases, handcrafted walnut bookcases with scrollwork along the top and the base, filled with books on spiritual exploration: four different editions of the Holy Bible, books on the apostles and on the gnostic scrolls. One shelf was devoted to the works of Joseph Campbell and collected writings of Emerson. The bookcases surrounded a leather chair and a small square table with a stack of books by Thomas Merton.

Neil's head snapped up.

The book on Bastien's desk. A collection of works by Thomas Merton. It was open and lying face down on the desk.

Neil sat with his hands clasped behind his head, his eyes focused on the wall in front of him. He was in Bastien's office, picking up the book. He turned it over to look at what Bastien had been reading. The words appeared before him, and Neil saw into Bastien's soul.

So, this was what was driving him.

Neil remembered the book for one of his university classes twenty-five years ago. He recalled the substance of the Thomas Merton collection. Technology. The role of technology and the role of man. Technology as an inexpensive, complicated way of cultural disintegration.

Man becomes a biophysical link between machines. Instead of Mother Nature, we'd depend on technology's artificial nature to sustain us. Bastien was declaring war on the forces of technology; that's what got him killed.

Neil stood up, rubbing his forehead, and made his way back to the balcony. He breathed in the chilly, moist air. It was dark. The weather had changed. He had just turned to go inside when he heard multiple vehicles approaching. A crash. A vehicle sliding to a stop and then the lights went out.

As Octavia burst through the door, the lights flashed on and the room was instantly illuminated, casting a spotlight on her confident stance with the cane. A fierce gust of wind and rain followed her through the doorway, causing a chaotic dance of Neil's sketches and photos throughout the room. Amidst the swirling chaos, Octavia looked like a superhero—empowered and unstoppable.

"I have Cadenza. We need to help her."

Neil rushed outside. Two figures approached—the driver and a figure wrapped in a blanket. When they reached the steps, Cadenza hesitated.

Neil opened the door wider. "Come inside."

James returned to the car, which was still running. Neil called to him. "Nice job blinding the cameras with your lights."

"We had a bit of company on the way. Sometimes it's hard to tell who your friends are. Better safe than sorry, sir," James replied with a grin. With a firm hand, he closed the car door and drove away.

CHAPTER 34

Cadenza was still shivering and wet. "Come with me." Octavia motioned to the master bath. "I'll get you a robe. Take a soak in a warm tub and we'll talk after that."

Cadenza was in the tub when Octavia returned with a glass of wine, a fluffy white robe, and slippers. "The towels are here, and use any soap, shampoo, or lotion you would like."

Octavia grabbed the wet clothes, closed the door and sighed deeply. Neil poured a glass of wine and handed it to her. She told him about the evening's events as she helped him collect the pictures and sketches that had blown around the floor. She looked at the sketches from Bastien's office.

"This is his office? It's so . . . sterile."

"Yes." Neil pointed at one of his sketches. "Until you see this wall. Look at the bookcases."

"Thomas Merton? There's nothing like that in the music room."

"Exactly. Now look at what was on his desk."

"It's a collection of Merton's work."

"Look at the file under it. See the symbols?"

"Speaking of symbols, there were four jazz bars that my father played at routinely."

"A four-bar progression."

"That's what I'm thinking. Two of them are owned by former band members. There is one member who has fallen on hard times, according to Michelle—whom I like very much. We're meeting up again tomorrow."

"We've got to decode these symbols and arrange the sequence. It begins with the original musical composition, then your bracelet. My presumption is that the trombone is next, and it ends with the four jazz bars."

"Maybe Cadenza can decipher the symbols."

"I don't think you should trust her," cautioned Neil, "but I am interested in what she has to say."

"She's very emotional." I don't want to be heartless, but I want to know what happened... who murdered my father. I guess I should say *our* father. I'm still rolling that phrase around in my mouth. It doesn't come naturally. It sounds like a prayer, doesn't it? Our Father who..." Octavia took a drink of her wine. "I'm starved. What do we have to eat?"

Octavia made soup from vegetables and chicken bone broth. Neil made sandwiches. They heard the water draining from the bathtub and steadied themselves for the conversation that was about to come.

———

"Please, join us at the table," Octavia beckoned, her voice warm and inviting.

"We've crossed paths before, but let me formally introduce myself," Neil said as he opened a bottle of pinot noir.

"I know who you are," said Cadenza coolly.

"Neil possesses a remarkable ability to unravel complex and perplexing situations," said Octavia, "I have complete faith in him."

Cadenza reached for her wineglass, saying, "That doesn't mean I should."

Neil took a bite of his sandwich. He watched Cadenza as he chewed. Her hand trembled as she sipped her wine. He savored the soup as he ate without saying a word. Octavia did the same. Cadenza sat looking at her soup.

"You should eat it while it's hot. It'll warm you up," said Octavia. "It's quite good, if I say so myself."

"I don't think I can eat it. I have a nervous stomach."

"Just have a taste," Octavia encouraged her.

"You sound like my mother."

There was an uncomfortable silence, and then Cadenza reached for her spoon, hesitantly dipping it into the soup and taking a taste. The bowl was soon empty.

As Neil picked up the pinot noir, he raised an eyebrow and gestured toward Octavia. She nodded and lifted her glass toward him. He gestured towards Cadenza. She nodded. As he poured, he asked, "How did you become involved with your father's work?"

"That's none of your business."

"I've already told him everything you told me at the park. Neil and I have no secrets between each other." Octavia sat back and sipped her wine. "He knows how messed up the whole situation is, and he is here to help, but we need to know more."

"I don't need or want his help," Cadenza said, her tone brimming with disdain.

Neil pulled out his phone and pushed a number. Cadenza could hear a phone ringing on the other end.

"Who are you calling?" she demanded, her tone sharp and anxious.

Neil's response was quick and clipped. "The police."

"No! Stop, please."

The call was directed to voicemail.

"Voici l'inspecteur Serge Aumont. Je ne suis pas disponible pour le moment. Veuillez laisser un message, et je vous le retournerai dès que possible. S'il s'agit d'une urgence, veuillez appeler le 911."

There was a beep.

"Aumont, call me." Neil hung up.

Octavia picked up her sandwich and took a bite.

"Why didn't you stop him?" Cadenza pushed back her chair and stood up. "I have to get out of here. I knew you couldn't be trusted!"

"Sit down," said Neil. "You are embarrassing yourself. I thought you were a scientist. I expected a more logical way of thinking. I can see why your father was so disappointed in you."

Cadenza's mouth dropped open, but no words came out.

"Sit down and steady yourself," Octavia said.

"I have to get out of here. He's called the police. They'll arrest me! I have to get out of here and back to the van. You don't understand!"

"Of course we don't understand, and of course you can't trust us. We can't trust you," said Octavia. "Trust is a two-way street. If we are to help you, tell us everything." She leaned in. "Sit down and talk."

Cadenza sat and downed her wine in a single gulp. Neil refilled her glass.

"Now," he said, "how did you come to work with your father?"

Cadenza looked at the wall beyond Neil.

"After my mother died, I didn't speak to my father. I was busy doing my research, making a name for myself. I didn't need him. There were others who encouraged me, who appreciated me and my work.

"I was offered a research position at the Elrod Nanotechnology Center heading the nano engineering department. The first day on the job, and who do I run into? My father. I don't think he knew they had recruited me."

"What happened?" Octavia asked.

"He seemed genuinely delighted to see me and invited me to lunch. I thought, well, he is the head of one of the departments here, and it would be good to talk to him as a colleague. So, we met at the cafe for lunch."

"What happened at lunch?" Octavia took another bit of her sandwich.

"I told him I was going to be the project leader on an innovative nano robot design and that I had become well-known for my work in nanotechnology engineering—despite the condescending bosses and a former team member who had tried to take credit for my work."

She drank more wine and looked at Octavia.

"He listened and watched me with those sapphire eyes, only two percent of the world's population has eyes that color, the same eyes you have. You have the same look, like you can look at somebody and see through them." She leaned back with her arms folded. "He told me congratulations and that I should be very proud of myself for all I had accomplished."

Neil's phone buzzed. He looked at it. "I've got to take this." He stood up. "What have you found out?" he asked as he walked into his bedroom. He shut the door.

Octavia grabbed the bottle of pinot and refilled her wineglass. She returned it to the center of the table and fixed her eyes on Cadenza. "I honestly don't know what to think of you," she admitted, her voice tinged with skepticism." I don't trust you, and there's a reason for that. I hesitate to tell you, but..." She sipped her wine.

"But what?" asked Cadenza.

"Bastien left me a video. He warned me not to trust you."

Octavia leaned back in her chair.

"He said that he loved you, but that you had gone down a treacherous path and become entangled with dangerous characters. So, with him being murdered, the house being set on fire, and a woman's body being found in his office, well, you can understand my hesitation."

"You've got the same judgmental look Dad had the day before he died," Cadenza said, her words laced with a touch of bitterness and grief.

Octavia leaned forward. Her eyes were fixed on Cadenza like laser beams. "There's something else our father said in that video."

"What else did he say?" asked Cadenza.

"He asked me to protect you."

"That would be unwise," said Neil as he reentered the room. He sat in the chair directly in front of Cadenza and placed his phone on the center of the table.

"Octavia told me we should help you because she believed your story. What story is that?

All I've heard is a never-ending stream of self-pity and complaints about your daddy issues, 'My daddy didn't love me,' blah, blah, blah. It sounds like you're working on the sob story for the jury to take pity on you before they find you guilty of murdering your father."

"I didn't murder him! I loved him. I would never—never—" Cadenza sobbed.

Neil continued to pressure Cadenza.

"When's the last time you spoke to your father?"

She swallowed and dropped her head.

"We know he didn't approve of your actions or who you were hanging out with. So, fess up, sis. Let's see if the story you come up with falls in line with what I already know. And make it quick because time is running out."

"What do you mean, time is running out?"

"I mean that RCMP Chief Superintendent Matthew McGregor is on his way here, and unless I hear something to change my mind, I'm turning you over to him."

Cadenza jumped up. "I have to get out of here! Where are my clothes?"

A pained expression crossed Octavia's face. She shifted in her chair and winced. Neil knew that tension had built up over the past few days and found a weak spot to nest...her injured leg... the leg that had taken years to heal from the life-threatening incident, a premonition of this very moment. And it hurt like a bitch.

Octavia slammed her glass on the table, shattering it. "Enough! I've had enough. This ends now. If you don't talk to us, you can talk to McGregor. Maybe the best thing to do is to turn you in and wash my hands of you."

Cadenza sat down. Neil watched her squirm.

"I know you want to run, but that is a dangerous move," he said. "You saw what they did to him, and I think you know how they did it."

Cadenza struggled to breathe.

Neil and Octavia made no move to comfort her or relieve her anxiety.

This is it. This is when we will hear the truth.

CHAPTER 35

"It never crossed my mind that they might kill him."

"Who?" asked Neil.

Cadenza pressed the heels of her hands against her eyes. "Vaccineops."

"Vaccineops? Who the hell is that?" Octavia exclaimed. "Elrod Foundation, Loder International and now Vaccineops?"

"They are working with the foundation to expand the possibilities of nano robotics as delivery systems," Cadenza replied. "It's all very complicated, you wouldn't understand."

Octavia leaned in. "Yuu International has divisions working on nano structural materials for health, energy, and environmental applications using naturally occurring nanomaterials like volcanic ash or soot from a fire—nanotechnology that is being used for the Sacred Tree Project."

"Yes, I am aware of Yuu International's research," snarled Cadenza, "or what little there is beyond marketing hype. Dad had the financial magazine with you on the cover. He proudly displayed it on the wall behind his desk. None of my scientific articles ever made the cut to be featured in his office."

"You're getting off track," said Neil. "Continue with your story—the one that actually interests me."

Cadenza glared at him. "Have you ever heard of DNA origami?"

"I've come across articles on the topic. It's supposed to be promising for cancer treatment—perhaps a cure."

"They tout everything as a potential cure for cancer. That's where the money is. DNA origami has potential for so much more."

"What is DNA origami?" Octavia asked.

"It's a method to manufacture on a nanoscale."

"Hold on, I want to make sure I understand. You're saying you possess the talent to make your own flea circus?" A mischievous grin spread across Neil's face.

"I can design an entire universe." Cadenza glowered at Neil's bemused face. "Given enough research and money."

Neil placed his elbows on the table, folding his fingers under his chin. "We can call it the Supercilious Universe."

"Okay, you two," Octavia interceded. "Like you said, Neil, we're going off track. Now, how can you manufacture on a nanoscale? How is it like origami?"

"We fold DNA materials like pieces of paper. My designs create the robots for delivery systems. Dad's research focused on receptors that would attract the deviant cells and cut off signals or starve them so they would die. His project was on neurological disorders, far more complicated and difficult to detect and treat than cancer. My latest design will direct and deliver the receptors more precisely."

"How are these delivery robots designed?" Neil asked. "How does DNA become material for the origami to occur?"

"Most people don't understand that DNA is material that holds information provided by genes. Dad used to tell me that DNA is the record and the music is the genes."

"The record holds the music, which is created with symbols."

"Yes, that's one way of putting it," said Cadenza.

"Do you manipulate genes to create the robots?" asked Octavia.

"No, we use DNA. Weren't you listening?" Cadenza sighed. "It's called manufacturing, but it's really designing. The DNA designs the origami."

"How is that possible?" asked Octavia.

"I create the design by drawing the engineering plan and downloading it into an app that was designed by another researcher on my team."

"Go on," said Octavia, "explain to me how it works."

Cadenza rhythmically tapped her fingers on the table, as if typing.

"You mix human DNA with unique properties and heat it. After several hours, we cool it."

"Then what?" Octavia asked.

"That's it.

"We check the results under the microscope, and if our design was executed correctly, we will have several viable representations."

Octavia walked to the kitchen and came back with a towel and trash can to clear away the shattered wineglass. Nobody said a word as the shards were wiped away, making a distinct clinking sound as they landed in the trash.

"How is that workable?" Neil asked when Octavia returned to the kitchen.

"DNA has four compounds, or bases—G, A, T, and C. When they're copied, A is always attracted to T, and C is always attracted to G. It self-assembles. We take advantage of that. We combine DNA of different lengths. The long DNA is a template and artificially synthesized short DNA combines the long DNA and folds it into the designed shape. I design where and how the shape will form."

Neil sat in silence, giving Cadenza the captive audience she longed for.

"Our structures make it possible to move small atoms and molecules around. They can be containment devices to protect cells. To do that, it has to have holes large enough to let, say, a vaccine flow out but small enough to keep the body's attack cells from getting in. It's precision design."

Neil stood up with his phone and scrolled as he walked to the couch. Cadenza followed him.

"Vaccineops emphasized the need for urgency in completing my work, explaining that their projections pointed to a higher frequency of major pandemics across the globe, and to effectively administer the distinct vaccines, nano delivery systems had to be developed."

"And how much did they offer you to undertake this...project? What was your price tag?"

"It wasn't like that. They would fund any amount of money I needed to complete my work. They said that if I could succeed at this project, I would surely be named director and perhaps even have my own center."

Neil continued to read. Octavia returned to the room and Cadenza turned to her.

"Imagine having a mechanism in place to manufacture and transport special vaccines. It could save millions of lives. My life's work could lead to unbelievable possibilities."

"How long ago was this?" Neil asked.

"They first approached me about two years ago."

"And you just went along with their savior scenario?"

"No, of course not. They showed me the basic design of a virus they had found. It was unlike anything I had seen before. That's when they mentioned Dad's work. They said they had been following his work for years. He was the key to the project's success."

"How did they find this virus?" Neil asked.

"They told me that an international security group investigating crimes that lead to genocide gave them the inside scoop on a secret report about a deadly experimental virus."

"When did you tell Bastien about your project?" Octavia asked.

Cadenza sat down at the table. She closed her eyes and rubbed the back of her neck. "I received an award for my ground-breaking work on DNA origami. Dad said he wanted to celebrate my success."

"I'm confused," said Octavia. "I thought your project was a secret. How did you get an award?"

"The purpose for the project is secret, but not the containment system I designed."

"And funding would start flowing in to cover R & D costs," said Neil.

"Anyway," Cadenza continued, "This was my chance to convince Dad to work with me and Vaccineops. I was so proud of my accolades."

"But you didn't get the response you hoped for." Neil came back to the table.

"No. He told me I was very foolish for getting involved with them."

"Why did he say that?" asked Octavia.

"Loder International funded Vaccineops through the foundation. They would have the patent and could do with it as they pleased. He warned me not to trust them."

"He had more to say, didn't he?" Neil asked.

Cadenza looked down at the table and nodded. "He said that to create the delivery system I would have to work with the live virus. In doing so, I may actually contribute to their knowledge of how to make the virus more efficient."

"Had you considered that?" asked Neil.

She glanced at him and quickly looked down at the table.

"What else did he say?"

She swallowed and took a deep breath. "He said Loder International had been involved with biowarfare for years. That they had been trying to coerce him into working for them for decades."

Octavia shook her head. "There are countless conspiracy theories swirling around about global viruses, suggesting contagions have been deliberately created and unleashed by foreign governments."

"All conspiracy theories start with a grain of truth." Neil's attention returned to Cadenza. "Was there anything else that disturbed Bastien?"

"Isn't that enough?" asked Octavia.

Cadenza took a sip of her wine. "Dad was concerned about bio-hack-ing. He contended that a clever hacker could find backdoor access—using a computer, laptop, or a smartphone—to control nanorobots. He speculated that by hacking a single nanorobot, a network could be built within the body, and they could command a person to do their bidding or turn your body against you."

Neil pushed his chair back and stretched out his legs. He rubbed his face vigorously, which ended when he pushed his hair back and left his hands on top of his head.

"Are you saying people could become robots?" Octavia asked. "This just becomes increasingly bizarre. I feel like we've entered some kind of dystopian nightmare."

"I think there is a far greater potential for ransomware attacks," said Neil, "nano attacks on their competitors and domestic security, targeting key individuals. I wonder . . . Did he talk to you about what security measures should be taken?"

"No, he didn't say anything to me. But he talked about a presentation recorded at a conference in Japan. I don't remember how the subject came up, but he said—what was it? He, the presenter...I don't remember his name, wanted to regulate types and strengths of security needed on nano–medical devices. He said any new advance in biological technology and medical devices is a target for hacking."

Cadenza's fingers once again began rhythmically tapping on the table. "I need some paper and a pencil," she said.

"What?" asked Octavia.

"Don't talk, just give me paper and pencil. Quickly, before I lose it."

"Lose what?"

"Paper and pencil!"

Octavia handed her a pen. Cadenza frowned but got up and went into the kitchen, where she began writing on a paper towel, her focus totally on the numerical equations and markings of an engineer. Octavia knew that look. Neil would often have the same look when he was sketching. It was the same way Bastien had looked when he played jazz.

Cadenza worked quietly for a quarter of an hour, then stopped and stared at her work. She folded the towel and said, "I need to put this somewhere safe."

"What is it?" Octavia asked.

"I need to drink some water." Cadenza grabbed a glass from the cupboard and watched the water flow from the faucet and fill the glass to overflowing. She gulped down her glass of water, crumpled the paper towel in her hand, and threw it into the trash. "I have to go to the bathroom."

"Go. You don't have to ask permission," said Octavia.

Cadenza left the room.

Neil went to the trash can and pulled out the paper towel. He straightened it out and took a picture. "Curious."

"Why?"

"Did you hear it?" Neil whispered.

"What?"

"The rhythm of her tapping on the table."

"The rhythm?" Octavia thought for a moment, then her eyes shot up to Neil's face. "It's the rhythm and cadence of the Four-Bar Progression."

"Exactly. Now look at this." Neil showed her the paper towel.

"They look like equations, some of the symbols look like..."

"The symbols on your bracelet and the trombone," said Neil, "and I bet on the bracelet that Bastien used to wear."

"So what does it mean?"

"It means she has half of Bastien's code, but you have the key code. The math is the rhythm and perhaps the composition is as well. But she doesn't have what you have."

"What's that?" Octavia asked.

"The soul. The music. The composition is always subject to interpretation. It's like Shakespeare, where reading the text only scratches the surface, but the true impact comes from watching the plays unfold or, in this case, immersing yourself in the jazz performance. She doesn't understand that. You do."

"So she's..."

"She's playing you so that she can get her hands on the other half of the code."

"But why did she write this and then toss it away?"

"Her brain is consumed by this formula, churning with calculations. Just now, an idea struck her, and she scrambled to find something to write with before it slipped away. But once it was written, she didn't need the paper anymore. She retains it once she sees it in physical form."

Neil crumpled the towel and tossed it back into the trash. "I also asked Kozo to do a forensic analysis on the Center's server. He has the perfect mind-set for a cybersecurity expert, he's suspicious of everything. He seems to think I'm always trying to get him in trouble. I told him it was to protect you."

"I have to say, he has reasons to feel that way."

"Kozo emailed me a few minutes ago," said Neil. "He discovered a fascinating anomaly."

Cadenza came out of the bathroom. "Now what? What do you plan to do with me?"

"I plan to continue questioning you," said Neil, "so sit."

Octavia and Neil sat on the couch while Cadenza settled into a mid-century modern armchair. Her body was no longer on alert, but her fingers were fidgety.

"I've told you everything I know," she said.

"You told us that your father had concerns about security, but he had more esoteric reasons for objecting to the work."

Cadenza looked down at her hands. His concerns were far more pro-found than I initially realized."

"I know he was immersing himself in the writings of Thomas Merton."

"How do you know that?"

"I saw several books in his home office when we went through the house."

"He was obsessed with the writings of Thomas Merton. He wasn't thinking like a scientist anymore. He seemed to become more radical as he prepared for a conference scheduled for the first week of November. I was afraid he would destroy the data and research papers—or something worse."

"Make it open source," Neil said.

"Why would he do that?" Octavia asked. "He was against using it."

"Because those who could use it for good, which was Bastien's original intent, would have access, and those who had evil intentions would lose billions. Antidotes could be developed to counter it."

Neil typed on his phone. "Is that the international conference to be hosted in San Francisco by the University of California?"

"Yes, it will be livestreamed. Dad was scheduled to give a presentation on our work. But he was more interested in another forum."

"He's not the only one to be concerned," said Neil. "Was it the preconference ethics symposium?"

"I believe so."

"Some in the scientific community are concerned that the rapid advancement of nano robots could get out of control—that they could replicate themselves, take over the world and destroy humanity."

Octavia cocked an eyebrow. "It sounds like a science fiction horror movie to me."

"What we once thought to be science fiction is now possible," said Neil. "If Bastien was being influenced by Merton's writings, it was more likely that he was concerned about humanity's acceptance of becoming hosts for these nano parasites, essentially allowing themselves to be programmed."

"That's the kind of nonsense that's perpetuated every time we develop revolutionary technology," Cadenza argued. "Nano robots are not dangerous in and of themselves. They are amazing. Soon they will be part of everything that we do or create."

"It's not the technology that's evil," said Neil as he leaned forward. "It's the people that have the power to control it. Bastien thought the people you've been working with have plans to do evil."

Cadenza dropped her head and a single tear rolled down her cheek. "He was right . . . about everything."

Neil slowly clapped his hands. "Nice performance. Now let's get to the truth."

CHAPTER 36

"**Y**ou got another offer didn't you?"

"How did you know about that?" Cadenza asked.

"You just confirmed it," Neil said with a satisfied smile. "Two days before his death, your father made a trip to the center where he not only deleted files from your computer, but he also took the additional step of changing the password, leaving you locked out. He also deleted files off the main server and took physical files."

Cadenza's fists tightened into white-knuckled balls, her anger evident by the intensity of her glare at Neil. "Some technicians are about to face termination for their role in leaking confidential information."

"When you found out, you angrily stormed out of your office and out of the center," Neil continued. "Just to confirm, you managed to grab those crucial files from the house, before the fire broke out, right?"

Her face turned a vibrant shade of red. Every muscle in her body screamed with tension. "He maliciously sabotaged my future," she spit out in a fit of rage.

"Why would he do that?" Neil's question hung in the air, waiting for a response.

"A week after a technology journal published my paper, I received a call from a man who called himself Marc Smyth. He said he was the director of an NGO called BioVax that was working with the UN, providing vaccines to developing nations with critical health emergencies."

"Let's just call it was it is, Vaccineops with new branding," said Neil. "They came back."

"There are multiple agencies, working with the same aim: to save lives," said Cadenza. "Mr. Smyth said he was going to be in Montreal. He wanted to see my developments and to meet with the 'eminent Dr. Beaulieu' about his newly developed nano lipid delivery system."

"And you agreed?" Neil asked.

Cadenza nodded. "I told him that I would need permission from the director of the center. He said that was not a problem, he had already received permission because the NGO is funded by the same primary donor as the center."

"You mean the Elrod Foundation?"

"Yes, I assumed that to be the case."

"Go on."

"The prospect excited me, but Dad declined to meet with them. He said that he knew a journalist and asked her to investigate their NGO."

"Her?" asked Neil. "Who did he connect with?"

"I didn't ask. I was angry because he was being so stubborn." In frustration, Cadenza's clenched fist struck the arm of the chair. "The day before the meeting, he told me that the NGO was a shell company for another organization."

"I take it the organization was Loder and the NGO was Vaccineops?"

"Yes."

"They didn't seem suspicious to you?"

"No, why should they? Loder generously supports the foundation, which in turn funds the Center. Why wouldn't they offer financial support for worldwide vaccines?" Cadenza looked down at her hands.

"That must have put you in a tough spot," Octavia said sympathetically as she leaned forward with her elbows on her knees and her fingers entwined. "I wonder why he didn't confront them face-to-face."

"It was like he felt he would be contaminated by being in the same room with them. The day of the tour, Dad didn't show up. The director was not happy with him, but Mr. Smyth was attentive to my presentation."

"What did this Mr. Smyth look like?" asked Neil.

"He was lean, muscular. There was an energy about him—intense attention and focus. He wore tinted glasses. Funny, it was more like I had a sense of his eyes, though I couldn't see them. I remember his smile. It was warm and sincere. It put you at ease. His dark hair was slicked back, and he had smooth skin."

"So, he was a smooth operator," said Neil. "Continue."

"The next day, Mr. Smyth called and asked me to meet with him that afternoon, and he asked me to invite Dad to the meeting. He hinted that this was a test."

"A test? What kind of test?" asked Octavia.

"A test to see if I had the skill to negotiate with adversaries and turn them into willing collaborators. I called Dad, but he didn't answer his phone. I left multiple messages."

"But he didn't show," said Neil.

Cadenza shook her head. "The director of the center told me that our funder was not happy about the lack of cooperation and was threatening to pull our funding."

"So, what did you do?"

"I called Mr. Smyth and told him Dad was . . . unavailable. 'That's unfortunate,' he said."

"It was a package deal," said Octavia.

Cadenza dropped her head and nodded. "My chance was over. I was so angry at Dad. I asked them..."

"You asked them what?" Octavia prompted.

"I asked them if they would still consider me as a candidate if I could bring dad's research with me."

"So that's why Bastien made sure you couldn't get your hands on it," said Neil.

"I never thought..."

"That your actions would lead to your father's death?" Neil stood up. "I don't believe you. You knew Marc Smyth was involved in something much darker than he claimed. Your father wouldn't have acted the way he did, unless he had reason to."

"I tried to warn him they might come to the house," Cadenza said, defending herself. "But he didn't return my calls. It was pointless to leave voice messages or texts. He never checked them. I emailed, and I received the notification that it had been opened, so he knew what had happened."

"When did you decide to go to his house?"

"The day before he...died."

"What took place when you got to the house?"

"I was angry that he had stolen secured files. Files the center owned."

"You were planning to do the same thing, weren't you?"

"Files I had every right to have access to," she sputtered. "I could have negotiated a deal with the donor's backing." Cadenza took a breath and calmed herself. "He was on the verge of being fired. I didn't want him taking me down with him."

Octavia remained silent. Neil continued to probe.

"No wonder you disappointed him. What was the last thing he said to you?" Neil thought her words would be filled with venom. Instead, they came with remorse.

"He said he loved me and that he would protect me with his life."

"I have one more question. Who was in the house with you yesterday?"

"No one."

"Why was your car still parked behind your parents' house?"

She tried to choke out words.

"Whose van did you take?"

"I didn't kill her. I didn't start the fire. It wasn't me!"

"Who was she?"

"The housekeeper from the agency."

"What happened?"

"I don't know! She was alive the last time I saw her. I told her that my dad was dead and I was clearing out his work papers. She offered to help me with the boxes. There were too many to fit in my car, so she said we could put them in her van and she'd follow me to the Center and deliver them. She started the van—" Cadenza shook her head. "She was going to call the trip into the agency but realized she had forgotten her phone in Dad's office. She still had a key to the house, so she went inside..."

Cadenza took off her glasses and wiped her eyes with the sleeve of her bathrobe.

"The next thing I knew, smoke was pouring out of the house. I panicked. I wasn't supposed to be in the house, and all of Dad's files were in the van. I drove off. It was like a dream. The next thing I knew, I was on the other side of the city."

Neil and Octavia exchanged looks.

"You didn't try to get her out?" Octavia asked, her eyes widening in horror. "You didn't call the fire department?"

"I didn't kill her! I didn't start the fire!" Cadenza began gasping for air. She stood up. "I—have to—go outside! I—need—air."

Octavia guided her to the balcony. Neil went to the kitchen and brought out a brown artisan bread bag.

"Put this over your mouth and nose." Neil kept his hand on her back and spoke in a calm voice. "Breathe in... and out. Slow down. Slow down. Breathe in...breathe out."

With Neil's coaching, she began to control her breathing and shivered from the freezing air. Octavia walked her back into the living room. Neil shut the balcony door and went into the kitchen to open another bottle of wine. He brought a glass of merlot to Cadenza and instructed her to drink it.

She took a deep shuddering breath and looked up at Neil. She saw judgment.

The doorbell rang.

CHAPTER 37

"That will be McGregor. I look forward to introducing him to you."

Cadenza grabbed Neil's arm. "No, please! I'll tell you everything I know." Then she turned to Octavia. "Please don't let him turn me in."

The doorbell rang again. Neil and Octavia exchanged looks.

"Come with me," said Octavia as she grabbed her phone and began texting.

Cadenza released Neil's arm and followed her to the bedroom. Neil went to the door.

"It's about time." McGregor shivered as he entered. "It's freezing out there. The roads are hazardous."

He took off his coat. Neil grabbed the dripping coat and swiftly hung it up in the bathroom to dry.

"Would you like some wine?" asked Neil.

"No, I better not. I'm here on official business." McGregor sat at the table. "Evidently, someone in an Escalade tried to crash through the main gate. Security is on high alert."

"Should we be concerned?"

"I don't know. Should you be?" With a casual glance at the wineglasses, McGregor spotted a couple of broken slivers of glass that caught the light and sparkled on the tabletop. "I thought I heard arguing when I was out there. Are you and Ms. Clarke getting along?"

Neil picked up the glasses, wiped the table with a napkin, and went to the kitchen. "We were having a heated discussion about the quality of the wine we sampled. A silly thing to argue over, but things have been tense, you know—house fires and murder. Little things turn into big things." He began washing the glasses. "You said you had some news for me when you called."

"First, both you and Ms. Clarke are officially out of quarantine. But you will still need to have daily tests over the next week."

Neil stepped out of the kitchen, drying his hands. "That's good news. Now maybe we will make progress on the case."

"That means I will let you tag along on this case as a favor to Athena. You could offer me a hot cup of tea."

"Pardon my bad manners. I'm not used to playing the host. I'll put on the kettle." Neil went back into the kitchen. "How do you know Athena?"

"Her husband and I were friends. He was a good man."

"What do you think happened to him?" Neil asked.

"I don't know. No one knows. He's just gone. He was doing security on a peacekeeping mission in Indonesia. It had to have gone sour, or he would have been back long ago. There are agents still working on the case."

Neil stepped out of the kitchen. "Agents? What agents?"

The electric kettle began to boil and clicked off.

"We have a variety of teas. What would you like?"

"My dad always said Earl Grey was the best choice." McGregor grinned. "But Mom won me over to green tea."

"Green tea then?"

"Yes, please."

"Anything in it?"

"No. Are you going to join me?"

Neil arrived with a cup of tea and a fresh wineglass. "I'm going to finish the merlot." He sat across from McGregor and poured the remaining wine into his glass.

McGregor carefully sipped his tea and eyed Neil. "So, are you going to tell me?"

"Tell you what?"

"Who's here besides you and Ms. Clarke."

"Ahh. Well, that would be indiscreet of me."

"Indiscreet?"

Neil leaned forward and whispered, "Octavia has a guest."

"A guest?"

"Yes, a guest."

"I see." McGregor took a sip of his tea. "So, all three of you were arguing about the quality of the wines?"

"Yes."

"Where are they now?"

"That is really none of your business."

Octavia abruptly opened the bedroom door. She was wearing a dark green silk bathrobe, her hair was disheveled, and she was holding an empty wine bottle. "You were wrong about this wine, Neil. It is fabulous!" She laughed and walked to the kitchen, slightly limping in her bare feet. She'd left the bedroom door partially open. "Please tell me we have more. Oh, hello, McGregor. Excuse me, I'll be out of here in a snap. Neil, is there more of this?" She held the empty bottle out to show the label.

Neil looked at it and nodded. "We have one more bottle. Hold on, I'll get it." He took the empty bottle and went into the kitchen.

Octavia grinned at McGregor. "Have you found out who the dead woman—who is not my sister and *not* Michelle Perusse—is?"

"Yes, we have a pretty good idea," McGregor replied. "I hope you are not revealing any details of the case to outsiders." He glanced toward the bedroom.

Octavia frowned. "You're sounding judgmental, and I don't like that. I'm not a mindless idiot. I've had a rough week, and I need to talk to someone other than Neil, who can be incredibly insensitive and oblivious to feelings."

Neil cocked an eyebrow. "I'd say that was an unkind thing to say about me—if I cared about that sort of thing."

"So, who is being sensitive and attentive to your feelings?"

"That's none of your business."

"This is serious, Ms. Clarke." McGregor stood up. "We're talking national security. I need to know who you've been talking to."

He walked toward the bedroom door. Neil moved to intercede.

"I'm the insensitive and oblivious one, and even I know this is too humiliating for Octavia. I won't allow you to intrude on her life this way. And...you need a search warrant if you're going to be searching rooms."

McGregor stopped, suspicious of the scene playing out. "Get out of my way, Ames, or you will force me to arrest you for impeding a national security investigation."

"That won't be necessary." Octavia devilishly smiled and turned her head slightly over her shoulder. "I need you. Please come out."

Neil's right eyebrow arched, and a sly grin crossed his lips when he heard, "Yes, madam."

The door opened wide, and out stepped James, buttoning his crisp white shirt.

"Mr. Fenmore. What a surprise." McGregor looked at Octavia and Neil, then back at James. "I didn't see your car when I pulled up."

"I asked him to be discreet." Octavia took control of the scenario. "And he is discreet in all situations. He has passed intense security screening in a variety of countries and Yuu International Holdings, which, as you probably know, is stricter than most nations. I have complete confidence in him. More than I have in you or the Montreal police department."

Neil marveled at her confidence and authority. Standing in the room, barefoot, hair wild, wearing nothing but a bathrobe, Octavia exuded incredible power from within.

How the hell did she get James in here? And where is Cadenza?

The townhouse was silent except for the sleet falling on the roof and the balcony. James calmly fastened his shirt and tucked it in. He waited for any further instructions from Octavia. She continued to glare at McGregor, who was still looking suspicious.

Neil moved away from the door and stood next to Octavia. He had to defuse the situation and get the information that McGregor had come to tell him. There was also Cadenza to deal with. "Let's all calm down. This is ridiculous and unnecessary."

"You're absolutely right." Octavia turned her laser focus on Neil. "You should have told me you called McGregor. I have a right to know these things." She turned on McGregor. "And you owe me an apology."

McGregor's gaze zeroed in on Neil and James, his focus unwavering. "What's really going on here?"

Neither of them responded. Neil sipped his wine, and James adjusted his tie and cuffs.

McGregor redirected his attention towards Octavia. "I apologize for causing any embarrassment and for my intrusion into your personal life. I should have handled the situation better. Please forgive me. My mind is fixed on protecting Canada's national security. I think you can appreciate that."

Neil saw the look on Octavia's face and it wasn't good.

What's going on with her? What does she know?

Octavia confronted McGregor. "Why did you go to his house the day before he was murdered?"

"Who's house."

"Bastien's."

"Who told you I was at his house?"

"I did."

The voice had come from the bedroom.

James stood aside, and Cadenza entered the room.

"I saw you. I was there."

"This is certainly an interesting development. Cadenza Beaulieu, I believe. Just how many people do you have in your bedroom, Ms. Clarke?"

"Why were you at my father's house the day before he died?" Octavia demanded.

"Aumont is right. You two are incapable of being respectful of Canadian authority," said McGregor. "Cadenza Beaulieu, we've been looking for you. We found the missing van. I wonder how you got here?"

She glanced at Octavia but said nothing.

"I'm taking you in for questioning regarding the murder of Bastien Beaulieu and Molly Obote, the murder victim at the home of Bastien Beaulieu, and your actions involving a threat to national security."

"You can't do this!" Cadenza was still in her bathrobe. She glared at Octavia. "You did this. You set me up."

"Yes," said Neil, "but that's not entirely correct. I set you up, not Octavia."

"Neil, I can't believe you did that. You betrayed my trust. That's unforgivable." Octavia was incensed.

I hope she knows I'm making this up as I go along.

She turned on McGregor. "I'm not sure my sister is safe in your hands. How can we trust you when you weren't straight with us? You said nothing about going to the house. Why were you there? How do we know you were not involved with his murder?"

"You are close to getting yourself deported, Ms. Clarke," McGregor countered. "As for you, Neil Ames, our collaboration is at an end."

He pulled out his phone and was about to push a button, but a voice stopped him.

"I need to talk to you—privately."

CHAPTER 38

All eyes shifted to James. He stood there, exuding an air of elegance and sophistication with his four-in-hand knot with dimple silk tie that was done to perfection and impeccably tailored suit.

Octavia couldn't help herself. Her face glowed with heat.

"I'll talk to you after I make this call," said McGregor. "And don't think about helping anyone escape."

"What are you playing at?" Neil asked James.

"Yes, what is going on?" asked Octavia.

"You need to listen to me before you complete that call," James told McGregor.

Before McGregor could respond, a muffled voice answered his call.

Neil's gaze remained fixed on Cadenza, who stood on the verge of bolting, her bathrobe clutched tightly against her body. James kept his attention on McGregor, who requested a unit. McGregor listened closely and watched the four people in front of him.

"Right. Let me know." He ended the call. "It looks like we are going to enjoy each other's company for a while. Weather is hampering response times." He looked at James. "You want to talk to me privately? I'm intrigued. But I'm not letting anyone, especially Cadenza Beaulieu, out of my sight, so a private conversation will not happen."

James reached into his breast pocket.

"Easy with your hands," McGregor instructed him. "Whatever you are pulling out of your pocket, do it slowly."

James drew a small notepad with a gold pen attached. He wrote a single line and handed it to McGregor.

"I have a feeling that the true nature of James Fenmore is about to be revealed," said Neil. "Based on your posture and that impeccable tie, your background is military—the Royal Marines? You were likely engaged in counter-piracy, counter-narcotics, and counter-terrorism operations. Also, you're on perpetual standby to deploy anywhere in the world to *drive*, or is it to keep Octavia under *surveillance*?"

"What are you talking about? Why would he be spying on me?" Octavia frowned. "Did Yuu International hire you to monitor me?"

"Yuu International hired me to protect you," said James, "but that is not the reason I am here. At the present time, that is all I can say."

"Speaking of revelations," said Neil, "McGregor, how about revealing what you were doing at Bastien's house the day before he was murdered?"

"That is none of your concern, Ames. You are officially out of the information loop."

"I know you got your feelings hurt because I didn't tell you directly about our contact with Cadenza, but I did call and ask you to come here, and you came to tell me the second victim was Molly Obote, the housekeeper?"

"How did you find that out?"

"Bastien's house was immaculate when we toured through it with Aumont. It was obvious that a housekeeper or cleaning service was being used."

"You should get dressed," McGregor told Cadenza. "You'll be leaving soon."

"Her clothes aren't dry yet," Octavia said.

"You two look to be the same size. Do you have something she can wear?"

She motioned to Cadenza. "Come with me. I need to get dressed, too."

"No. I don't trust the two of you together. You bring the clothes out, and she can dress in the bathroom."

While McGregor checked out the bathroom, Neil whispered to James.

"What was on the note?"

"Europol."

"Really. Europol? Why are you working for Yuu International?"

"I can't answer that question."

Neil nodded Octavia's direction. "I don't think she's thrilled with you right now."

Octavia came out of the bedroom wearing a cream-colored cashmere sweater, skinny jeans, and her black ankle boots. She was carrying a black sweater, black socks, yoga pants, and Cadenza's damp sneakers. McGregor stopped her.

"Given your habit of defying rules, I cannot let the clothes be passed on to her without first conducting a thorough check."

"Are you referring to her clothes or mine?"

McGregor was not the blushing type, quite the opposite, and his appreciative examination of how her clothes enhanced her body prompted James and Neil to exchange amused glances.

"What are you two smiling about?" Octavia shot them an angry glance, as she handed clothes to McGregor. "I'm not happy with either of you."

McGregor examined the garments and shoes before passing them to Cadenza. "Don't be too long," he said as the bathroom door shut.

He turned and gave the trio a hard look. "I can't trust any of you. Ames, you are a rogue. Ms. Clarke, you are as bad as he is. And you,"—he pointed at James—"I don't know what you are yet."

"All I want is to find out who killed my father and why. I want to trust my sister, but I can't. And the people I trust the most have not been entirely candid with me," said Octavia.

"Now you know how I feel," said McGregor.

James pulled McGregor to the side and whispered. They would occasionally look at Octavia and turn back to their conversation.

"Talk to me." Octavia huddled near Neil. "We've got to come together on this."

"Agreed. Michelle Perusse is the only one on our side. She wants a story, and I want to know why McGregor went to Bastien's house."

James's phone buzzed. He turned away from McGregor and nodded as he read the text. McGregor sighed and shook his head as he approached Neil.

"You better not make me regret this." McGregor stood with his hands on his hips. "Bastien Beaulieu met with one of our agents in the Montreal office. He was troubled about a project Cadenza had agreed to lead and be funded by Elrod. He suspected that the project could be a major threat to national and international security. He was anxious about the safety of both of his daughters."

"Dr. Beaulieu had dealt with an organization like this in the past," said James. "It may be a variant of that same organization."

"Is that why Europol is involved?" asked Neil.

"Europol?" Octavia's eyes widened. "My god, James, are you Europol? I need more wine," she declared.

"Europol and ASEANAPOL have been closely monitoring the activities of problematic corporations with ties to criminal networks for many years," McGregor explained. "Both the FBI and RMCP have been engaged in a collaborative effort with their investigations."

"ASEANAPOL, what is that?" asked Octavia.

"The Association of Southeast Asian Nations Chiefs of National Police. It's the Asian equivalent to Europol," Neil replied.

"This criminal network doesn't just cross borders, it's global," said McGregor. Major corporations and governments have been monitoring Dr. Beaulieu's work since he published his first research paper. Now criminal networks and terrorist groups have created channels and joined forces to acquire his research as well."

"So, we're dealing with the next generation," said Neil.

"Yes." James slipped his phone in his pocket. "I have to check in at the campus security office. I don't think I'm needed here. Do you have any more questions for me?"

"No," said McGregor, "but don't leave the city."

James nodded. "I'm leaving, madam. Call me if you need me."

There was no response from Octavia. James left. McGregor continued.

"I contacted Dr. Beaulieu and went to his house. But when I got there, he was a little off. He kept quoting Thomas Merton. He said he had a proof—a math proof. But he said it wasn't safe for anyone to have it, that his daughter had the key. We made arrangements for the handoff of incriminating evidence against Loder the next day, but he never showed."

Octavia came back with a glass of wine in her hand. "No, because he was murdered," she said. "Cadenza has the proof?"

"*A* proof," said Neil.

"I don't know if she does or not," said McGregor.

They heard the toilet flush.

"How was the housekeeper misidentified as two different people?"

"The body was badly burned. Assumptions were made. Of course, when we saw the picture snapped by a traffic camera, we knew better."

"How did the identification become Michelle Perusse?"

"There was paper melted into the pocket of the victim's polyester jacket. The ME technician softened and detached it. It was a business card with Michelle's name on it."

"A faulty second assumption. Unbelievable!" Neil shook his head.

"When you told me Michelle was alive and well, I called in an RCMP medical examiner. Dental records gave us the true identification—Molly Obote. Knowing Michelle, she probably contacted the housekeeper and made arrangements to meet her at the Beaulieu home."

"This is all so horrible." Octavia finished her wine. "What the hell has Cadenza gotten herself into?"

"Speaking of Cadenza . . ." McGregor went to the bathroom door. "Dr. Beaulieu? You need to come out." There was no response. He knocked on the door. "Dr. Beaulieu?" Still no response. He tried the doorknob. It was locked. He pounded on the door. "Cadenza Beaulieu, open the door!" There was no response. "I'm coming in!" McGregor called out.

He kicked the door. It split, and he peered through the crack, then gave the door one more kick. It finally broke free, and he rushed in. The window was open, and the bathroom was freezing. Cadenza's bathrobe was on the floor, and his coat was gone.

Cadenza had vanished.

Chapter 39

Montreal was paralyzed by the freezing rain and icy streets. McGregor's team pounded on the door thirty minutes after Cadenza was discovered missing.

"Sit at the table, where I can keep an eye on you two," McGregor ordered. "and don't say a word, unless you're asked a question, and you're both under caution."

Neil and Octavia exchanged tense glances. Octavia's face was etched with worry as she poured wine in her glass.

An hour later, McGregor ordered them to vacate the townhouse and not return. "Don't try to help Cadenza in any way. If she tries to contact you, you are to notify me immediately." Every word he spoke dripped with an icy coldness matching the weather outside. "Let me make it clear, if you cross me in any way, there will be consequences."

Under the watchful eye of the agents, Neil packed his backpack while Octavia packed her bags and finished the bottle of wine. James arrived at the townhouse at 11 o'clock with the executive director of AZZ Productions. Octavia spoke briefly with the director and thanked him for arranging accommodations at the Ritz-Carlton hotel.

"Madam, I'm driving the director to his office, and I will be back to pick you up."

Octavia gave a silent nod of approval, avoiding any direct gaze towards James.

When James returned, Neil helped him load the luggage, a slippery and miserable task.

"I need you to take Octavia to the hotel. I'm going to stay here for a while."

"Of course, sir."

"And James . . ."

"Yes, sir?"

"First, you can cut the sir crap."

James grinned slightly.

"I don't believe you are really Europol," Neil continued. "You're an independent contractor, aren't you?"

"Yes," replied James. "Just like you, I work with an assortment of agencies, corporations, and individuals on a variety of cases, many of which overlap."

"Someone tried to intercept you on the way here, but you got the gate open before they could stop you."

"We had three Escalades after us. I transmitted a code to security for quick entry."

"They had the gate open?"

"Barely. The gate slid open seconds before we reached it."

"No one else got through?"

"Two vehicles collided, and the other swerved to avoid the gate. I didn't see it. I heard it hit something. My focus was safely delivering madam and the package."

"After you dropped Cadenza, you headed out, but you didn't leave the grounds?"

"I went to talk to the head of security." James said, closing the trunk. "He has footage, including the license numbers."

"A little too easy if we're dealing with professionals," said Neil. "The plates are probably fake. I want to take a look at the footage before the police get to it."

"That won't be a problem," James assured him.

Neil went back inside to look after Octavia. Her exhaustion and wine left her looking dazed. He helped her into her coat.

"Where is my work tote?" she asked. "Where are we going?"

"James is taking you to the Ritz-Carlton. Your tote is in the car. I will be there soon."

Neil helped her into the Audi, and Octavia looked up at him.

"Neil?"

"Yes?"

"I don't know where my sister is."

"I know."

"She might die in this cold."

"She isn't going to die."

"How do you know? You don't think she killed anyone, do you?"

"You've got to go now. James will take care of you."

Neil got in the car next to Octavia, and James slowly drove down the icy lane.

The head of security, McCain, was waiting outside the entrance to the security offices. Neil squeezed Octavia's hand before getting out of the Audi and watched James drive away.

"James Fenmore said you'd like to see the footage from tonight's incident," McCain said as they entered the building, "My superiors at Yuu International said to give you full access. I've got it set up for you,"

Neil sat at the monitor, eyes glued to the paused footage at 7:02 p.m.; McCain hit play.

The Audi approached. A large black SUV, an Escalade, emerged, tailing it aggressively. James accelerated. The SUV kept pace, its headlights piercing through the night.

Two more SUVs, also Escalades, roared onto the lane from both sides, engines growling. They tried to box James in, one swerving perilously close.

James swerved right, narrowly avoiding a collision; the Audi's tires struggling for grip on the icy road. He expertly countered the skid, regaining control just in time to dodge the second SUV.

The first SUV surged ahead, attempting to cut him off. The Audi darting forward. The third Escalade aimed for a head-on collision, but James veered left, skimming past by mere inches.

The second SUV, struggling on the icy pavement, fishtailed wildly. James took advantage, swerving right and threading the needle between the vehicles.

He corrected the skid with precision, the Audi spinning 180 degrees and rocketing forward as the SUVs collided behind it. The third Escalade, unable to stop in time, slid into a concrete barrier. The Audi sped off unscathed through the gate, which had opened just seconds before.

"Pause the video," Neil said, his voice filled with heightened excitement.

The video froze the two SUVs just before they plowed into each other.

"Can you boost the audio?"

McCain clicked on the volume bar.

"Let's move forward, half speed." Neil closed his eyes and let his ears take over the observation. The sliding thud sound of the SUVs colliding.

Shouts, multiple voices, digital voices in both vehicles. A cell phone conversation. Who's at the other end? What are they saying? Too much noise. "Target. Stay on target." Is that what they're saying?

"Do you hear that?" he asked.

"Hear what?"

"Headphones, I need headphones," Neil demanded.

McCain handed a set to Neil, then plugged in his own set to listen.

"Now back it up and listen to this sequence," said Neil.

They listened together. "Pause it," said Neil.

"Yeah, I hear it," said McCain. "Stay on target."

"Let's move forward," said Neil.

He watched as the first Escalade slid into the barrier that protected the underground power access. The security team divided into two groups: one heading toward the two SUVs that had collided and the other heading toward the SUV pressed against the barrier.

"Pause it!" Neil stared at the frozen image. "Now slowly forward the action."

McCain searched the screen as he leaned on the table beside Neil. "What do you see?" he asked.

Neil focused on the slow-motion video. The slowed-down voices of the security crew sounded grotesque, otherworldly.

There it is, just as I expected. The shadow and the sound.

"Pause it. Back it up about ten seconds."

"What is it?"

"Look at the window on the driver's side of the Escalade that slid into the barrier."

Neil examined the image, carefully observing each detail as it gradually unveiled the scene. "Here, a shadow on the other side of the driver. There was a second person seated on the passenger side."

As the scene continued to slowly unfold, a faint pinging sound began to emerge through the chaos of the security team's activities.

"The passenger opened their door," said McCain.

"Yes," said Neil. "Everyone was focused on the other cars and the driver, and..." Neil grabbed the mouse and paused the video, "Here," he moved the pointer to the top left of the video, "the gate is slightly open.

There's a chance that someone managed to slip by them without being seen."

"So we may have an intruder on the grounds who helped the woman escape," said McCain.

"Let's keep looking at the video and see what happens," said Neil.

On one camera, the two SUVs involved in the collision were seen reversing, narrowly missing a security crew member who jumped out of their way. The only thing that could be seen through the sleet were the glinting taillights as they roared down the lane toward the main road. When they turned on the road, the taillights were swallowed by the sleet and the night.

A second camera showed the driver of the SUV by the security station, shouting obscenities out of his window while gunning his engine. He slammed his Escalade into reverse and did a one-eighty, scattering the security crew in all directions. He headed down the lane, passing the second security team, and disappeared into the distance. The brake lights came on briefly, then the headlights and taillights disappeared.

"Well, that was enlightening." Neil stood up and headed for the door, then stopped and pivoted. "Let's watch that vehicle as it makes its move to get away. The portion when it is spinning around."

McCain reversed the video.

"The driver has his window open, and there is no one else in the vehicle," said Neil.

McCain grinned. "I was wondering if you would notice."

"You knew you had an intruder on your grounds."

"Someone tampered with our emergency back-up systems," said McCain. "The alarms monitoring the doors and windows throughout the whole AZZ complex continue to malfunction."

"Which is why, she was able to escape through the window unnoticed," said Neil. "And someone must have guided her out of the complex."

"We are still searching along with the RMCP and will continue to monitor the grounds over the next twenty-four hours," said McCain. "One more thing. We've been watching those SUVs since Ms. Clarke left late this afternoon. They were parked off campus, but close to the entrance. One of them lit up and followed Ms. Clarke's car when it left the complex."

"One followed her to see if she met up with her sister," said Neil, "and the others waited for her to return."

"And another thing," said McCain, "We had an anomaly this evening seventeen minutes before Cadenza Beaulieu was reported missing."

"An anomaly?"

"Yes. All of our cameras, movement monitors, and audio equipment monitoring the townhouse went offline."

Neil tousled his hair until it stuck out in every direction, then reclined in his seat and shut his eyes, lost in thought. "That one SUV stopped at the end of the lane and the lights disappeared immediately. Isn't that odd?" asked Neil. "We saw the headlights briefly as the first two Escalades turned onto the road. Maybe...Do you have cameras at the entrance of the lane from the road? Let's look at what they can show us."

They watched the video of the two SUVs entering the roadway and heading down the road. At two minutes, the third SUV left the lane, stopped, turned off the lights, and rolled a few feet away from the cameras before stopping again. However, instead of continuing down the road, it stayed parked. McCain paused the footage. "Look at that. It's just sitting there."

"Let's see how long it sits there," said Neil.

An hour passes, there are occasional black outs due to the weather or the tampering. Another half an hour passes, McGregor's vehicle appears and turns onto the entrance lane toward the complex. Forty-seven minutes later, McCain paused the camera, the lens covered with fractured ice from the sleet, giving it a surreal perspective. "Bingo!" he said. "The interior lights came on. Someone got into the Escalade."

"There's something even more interesting," said Neil. "Look at this second camera that's pointed the opposite direction. There's a car pulling up just before the entrance to the complex," said Neil. "Zoom in on that car."

McCain clicked on the keyboard. "Yeah, there it is"

"Can we zoom in?" Neil asked.

With a few keystrokes, the sedan image became clearer, yet still pixelated and fragmented like the first camera.

"Two figures are approaching from the grounds," said Neil. "One heads toward the Escalade and the other enters the car."

"The interior lights in the sedan didn't come on," said McCain. We can't get a clear image of the driver or the passenger; the sleet is interfering with our visuals at that distance and angle, You think that's your girl?"

"I do." Neil sat back in his chair and pondered.

"What was she wearing?" McCain asked.

"A black hoodie, yoga pants, and McGregor's coat—wait," said Neil. "The figure getting into the car wasn't wearing a coat."

"I have something to show you," said McCain, "Follow me."

Neil could see the flashing lights of the Montreal police units at the townhouse. Weather had delayed them. Despite icy pathway, he forged his way back to the townhouse.

McGregor and his unit drove by him. Neil watched as they came to a halt in front of the security office. At the bottom of the townhouse steps,

Aumont stood waiting for him, his arms crossed in a confrontational stance.

"So you helped Cadenza Beaulieu escape."

"I'm sure McGregor would have taken me into custody if he thought the same way," said Neil. "Someone helped her escape, but it wasn't me."

"You were harboring a suspect."

"That's not exactly true. I called McGregor."

"But you didn't tell him she was there with you."

"No, but he shortly discovered her and contributed to her escape."

"Are you trying to say McGregor helped her get away?"

"Well, she left with his coat."

"Stop trying to deflect your culpability. You and Ms. Clarke have flaunted the rules from the moment you arrived. You two should be arrested for abetting a suspect in not one, but two murders."

"I agree this was an inside job, but it wasn't us," said Neil, "This was a well-planned escape; and someone who knew the security protocols and key locations of power sources was involved. It was coordinated with multiple players, well beyond our capabilities."

"Nothing is beyond your capabilities," declared Aumont.

"So you finally recognize that, how nice," said Neil. "But, you shouldn't rule out McGregor, he was briefed on all the security measures before we arrived. You heard there was an incident earlier this evening?"

"Yes, I heard how Ms. Clarke and her driver secretly transported that same murder suspect past security."

"That's one way of putting it. However, they were pursued by three Escalades and security cameras show that there was an intruder on the complex. Before Cadenza escaped, someone tampered with the security monitoring system. When she opened the window, no alarm went off. Fifteen minutes after she was discovered missing, two individuals made their way across the complex to the main road, where one escaped in one of the Escalades and the other in a car that had been waiting for them."

"You think her escape was planned in advance?"

"Yes."

"You think McGregor helped her escape? That is ridiculous!"

"I think it is more likely that he *wanted* her to escape."

"Why would he want her to escape?"

"Because it's not Cadenza Beaulieu he wants—it's the criminal network he's after, and he thinks she will lead him to them. There's one problem: he placed a tracker in his coat, thinking she would take it when she tried to escape, but guess what the security team found halfway between here and the main road?"

"McGregor's coat."

Neil nodded. "With her phone and the tracker still in the pocket."

His phone pinged. *James.*

MADAM IS SAFE. HOTEL & YUU INTERNATIONAL SECURITY TEAMS IN PLACE. DEMANDING TO SEE YOU.

Neil texted back.

STILL WITH AUMONT.

Neil grinned at Aumont. "I need a ride to the Ritz-Carlton."

"I have a shorter ride in mind," said Aumont.

———

Neil sketched the evening's events while sitting in the AZZ security break room. He occasionally looked through the window to check the status of McCain's revelations to Aumont and chuckled at Aumont's explosive reactions and outbursts of French expletives, which usually ended with "*Ames!*"

He entered when McCain, clicking through graphs and spreadsheets, was recounting the timeline of the evening's activities. Aumont took notes and did not acknowledge Neil's entrance.

"That's what we know based on the data we've collected during the past twenty-four hours," McCain said as he minimized the screens. "The only missing information and surveillance video occurred when all of our systems went down approximately seventeen minutes before they alerted us that Cadenza Beaulieu went missing."

Aumont put his notebook and pen into his suit pocket. He sighed deeply and rubbed his face. He swiveled around to face Neil.

"Where is she? Don't bother lying to me. I know you had something to do with her disappearance."

"I don't know, and neither does Octavia."

"I'd like to believe you, because you are not the type to say you don't know something, but you can understand my skepticism."

"You have the same information I do. I'm sure you can come to the same conclusion I have."

Aumont scowled and shook his head. "I have worked with McGregor and I trust him. You are wrong, Ames."

"I hope so. But let's get back on point. This was a premeditated action."

"But Cadenza Beaulieu didn't contact her sister until later this evening. How did they know she would be here?"

"How did they know? They set it up," said Neil.

"Why?"

"Because their target wasn't Cadenza."

"Who was it?"

"It was Octavia, and I believe Cadenza knowingly tried to lure Octavia into a trap."

"Why would they want Ms. Clarke?"

"Because she has something they want."

"Why didn't they attempt to grab her when they met in the park?"

"Because James was with her. He's more than a driver. He's with Europol."

"Europol? Why is he Ms. Clarke's driver?"

"That is an excellent question," said Neil.

"He works for Yuu International, so he would be well versed in their security protocols, would he not?" Aumont asked McCain.

"Yes, he knows entrance and security codes for their headquarters and complexes such as AZZ," said McCain.

"But why do they want Ms. Clarke?" Aumont asked Neil.

"Because they need both sisters to break Bastien's code. Cadenza is allied with the wrong side, and Octavia would never join forces with them, so they have three choices: eliminate her, abduct her and leverage the information we possess for ransom, or inflict pain on her to extract the information."

"She is in grave danger," said Aumont.

"My purpose here is to protect Octavia," said Neil, "Bastien Beaulieu and his research mean nothing to me. Unfortunately, she insists on staying until she uncovers the killer, rescues her sister, and safeguards Bastien's precious code. I need a ride to the Ritz-Carlton."

CHAPTER 40

Three days had passed since Neil and Octavia left the town-house.

Once the story reached the popular press, they wasted no time in exploiting it to the fullest. In the accounts, Cadenza was implicated in the gruesome murders of Bastien Beaulieu and Molly Obote, leaving behind a trail of horror and chaos. She then executed a daring and audacious escape from the tight grip of the RCMP.

The headlines spiked internet sales of The Four-Bar Progression's vintage recordings, now selling for up to a thousand dollars for pristine vinyl records. Public demand brought requests for rights to produce digital versions.

Octavia received a call from Bernard Cachemaille, who reached out to offer his assistance and handle any requests for music rights. He suggested they should make an appointment to discuss what would happen to Cadenza's portion of the inheritance if she were convicted of Bastien's murder.

"I can't think about that now," Octavia retorted. "I don't believe she murdered anyone."

"You have no idea where she might be?" Cachemaille asked.

"No, I don't."

"Is there anything I can do?"

"Yes, I need to work. I want to work on the rights to my father's music."

They spent the day brainstorming strategies and carefully crafting contracts for leasing the rights to Bastien's music. It turned out that they worked well together, and Octavia found the time she spent with him a great relief.

That evening, she received two calls. One was from her brother, who had read the news about Bastien's death and the newly discovered sister's escape from custody. It was big news in New Orleans, where Bastien was remembered for his music, not his science. It felt good to talk to her brother, someone who knew the whole family story.

"I'm so sorry I haven't been a good sister to you," Octavia confessed." I've been self-preoccupied, self-centered, self-obsessed, selfish—"

"Yeah, that pretty much sums it up," said Micheal. "But you know what, sis? I still love you, and I always will. I know that if I ever needed you, you'd come flying over in that fancy private jet of yours."

They ended the call laughing.

The second call was from Michelle Perusse. The world's largest multimedia news agency had offered her good money to write the story of Cadenza's work and the events leading to her escape. Michelle had accepted the offer on the condition that she would not submit it until all the facts were known. They upped the offer when she indicated she would give them the first chance at a series on criminal hacking of nanotechnology and the death of Dr. Bastien Beaulieu.

"I trust you will do a good job," said Octavia, "but I'm not ready to talk about Cadenza other than to say I don't believe she killed anybody. She's frightened and doesn't know who to trust."

"That's something. I know you wouldn't say that if you didn't think it. I do want to get the details on what happened that night. How did she get in touch with you?"

Octavia was silent.

"All right, I get it. Look, I have good news—Charlie Allen got back to me."

"Who?"

"Charlie Allen. You remember he was one of the band members and the co-owner of the Deep Red Jazz Club?"

"Yes, I remember him now. Sorry, it's been a crazy few days."

"Totally understandable," Michelle reassured her. "He says he's willing to help in any way he can. He remembers you as the young woman who helped produce and market their most successful album. He said it shocked him when he read you are Bastien's daughter."

"No one is more shocked than me about . . . everything that has happened over the last two weeks."

"I've also located the band's drummer, Butch Bennett. He fell on hard times, according to Charlie. He was living in the States, but three months ago, he came back to reconnect with the band members. He hasn't been working, but he rehearsed with them, and he's been living in a small house in one of our less desirable areas."

"That's too bad," was Octavia's only response.

"Your father paid six months' rent in advance for him. Charlie says they seemed really close, which surprised him because Butch and Bastien got into a big argument over money several years ago and hadn't spoken to each other since, or at least until Butch's recent return."

"Everything is so damn complicated," said Octavia.

"I don't think Charlie knows anything, but I've got a feeling Butch may disappear soon. The rent on his place will be up at the end of the month. The thing is, the last time he spoke with Charlie, he told him he was going to move into a nice place. Charlie was bewildered because Butch didn't seem to have any steady source of income."

Octavia said nothing. Michelle continued to push.

"Look, I know this is a rough time for you. But Neil told me when we first met that you are an incredibly strong and smart woman who can charm the truth out of anyone. I know how to get people to confide in me, but I am not gifted with the skill you have to charm them into revealing things they hadn't intended to disclose. If we are to find out the truth behind your father's murder, we have to strike now."

There was a long silence.

"Okay," said Octavia. "Set something up with Charlie tomorrow. But I think I'll let Neil handle Butch. I agree, it sounds suspicious that he has recently come up with money for a better place."

"*Merveilleuse!* I'll text you after I arrange a time with Charlie, and we should probably talk to the owner of the Noir Jazz Bar. That was the last bar in the four-bar rotation gigs they played. I'll give Neil a call about Butch. I'm sorry you're going through this. It's like you've been hit with an emotional pandemic. Tu passeras à travers ça. Au revoir, mon ami. Je te verrai demain."

Octavia hung up and called Bernard Cachemaille. It went to voicemail. At the beep, She left a message and hung up.

She went into the bathroom and gasped at her reflection in the mirror. She began laughing and couldn't stop. Tears ran down her face, her nose was running, and she had to gulp for air. She finally calmed her breathing and wiped her nose.

Oh my god. I haven't looked this bad since I was in the hospital. I can't believe I worked all morning looking like this.

The last few days had taken their toll on her mental health. She hadn't done her skincare routine or makeup in three days. Her hair was a mess, and so was her state of mind. Her body hurt, and her balance was off because she had not done her prescribed physical therapy stretches and workouts.

She stood in front of the mirror and, gazing into her own eyes, she said out loud, "Today is the day I will be reborn. I will be strong and energetic. I will face the problems I want to run away from, and I will overcome them."

She washed her face and applied serums and creams to bring her skin to life. She brushed her hair and tamed the frizz until it fell in line perfectly. She took off her pajamas and stared at her naked body in the full-length mirror.

I'm not twenty years old; I'm a forty-five-year-old woman whose body is changing despite my stretches and workouts. Things are shifting.

She selected pink silk panties and a matching bra and made a mental note to seek better engineering for her bra.

I need to structure my underpinnings like an architect designs the bones of a skyscraper to remain upright and strong, with the ability to sway ever so slightly to accommodate the winds of time and events.

Octavia went back to the mirror after dressing in a slim-cut black pantsuit. She put on her bracelet and her black Japanese artisan sneakers. They were her trademark, part of her branding. Her hip and leg were hurting. Tonight, she would soak in the tub and do a thirty-minute yoga stretch program. As she looked in the mirror, she struck her power pose.

"This is who I am. I am strong. I am smart. I am beautiful."

She paused and took a deep breath.

"I am alive."

"You certainly are." Neil was standing in the doorway, smiling. "Welcome back."

She checked her phone.

Still no message from Cachemaille.

"I'm not back all the way, but at least I'm dressed. Where have you been?"

"I spent the day with Aumont. We presented our evidence to McGregor, who technically is in charge of the case."

"But you didn't tell him everything."

"No." replied Neil, "I didn't tell him that I know he let her escape, hoping she would lead him to the criminal network and the actual murderer. And Aumont, so far, has not revealed my suspicions about McGregor's handling of the case."

"How did they know she would be at the townhouse?"

"Octavia, they weren't after her."

She sat on her bed. "I see." Her poker face was on. "Do you think she's okay?"

Her phone chimed. "It's Cachemaille. I've been waiting for him to call me back."

Neil stepped out of the bedroom. He checked his phone. There was a text from Aumont.

APPROVED TO ENTER BEAULIEU HOME TOMORROW. PICK YOU UP AT 8.

A second text appeared, this one from Michelle Perusse.

CALL ME. WE NEED TO MEET.

He was about to call when Octavia entered the room.

"Thank you so much. I'll see you soon." Octavia hung up. "Bernard is on his way."

"I'm about to call Michelle Perusse. She texted me to call her."

"Yes, well, I can tell you something about that. Tomorrow, Michelle and I are going to meet with another band member, Charlie Allen. But . . ."

Octavia walked toward Neil. He could see that her balance was off and that she was in pain. She put her hand on his chest.

"I really need you to be the one to go talk to Butch Bennett."

"The drummer?"

"Yes. I don't have the energy to deal with him, and someone has to talk to him soon because he may disappear."

"Disappear?"

Octavia patted his chest and stepped back. "Michelle will fill you in on the details. Right now, I need coffee and something to eat before Cachemaille gets here."

"Why is he coming here?"

"They're reopening one of the clubs to have an impromptu memorial service for Bastien," Octavia said. "I'm going with Bernard."

"I'll call room service," said Neil. "What do you want to eat?"

"I desperately need salad. A large salad. Find out what their specialty is. Whatever it is, I'll eat it. I can't wait for coffee, so I'll make it here."

Neil ordered Octavia's salad and a roast beef sandwich for himself. He called the concierge and asked him to deliver a bottle each of Montrachet and Meursault wine.

He smiled at Octavia when she arched her eyebrow at his order. "One for tonight and one for tomorrow. We need to relax tonight. We'll get through this and be back home soon."

"I wonder," Octavia said under her breath as she brought the French press to the table. After the food was delivered, they talked as they ate. They talked about anything that didn't have to do with the past two weeks.

Her phone buzzed. Octavia answered it. "Are you here?...I understand... No, that's not a problem. Six is fine. I'll see you then. Goodbye." She hung up. "Cachemaille is running late." She looked at her watch. "It's only three. I'm going to do some stretches and take a nap."

Neil refilled his cup and stood up. "I need to prepare for tomorrow. Aumont is getting permission to enter the Beaulieu house. Do you want to come?"

"No. I'll give you the key I found, I know it fit the trombone case, but I have a feeling there's more to it than that."

"I agree," said Neil. "He went through a great deal of effort to conceal the key for a trombone case."

"Don't forget to call Michelle," Octavia reminded him as she handed him the key.

"I won't."

"I wonder what you'll find," she said. "I wonder where Cadenza is."

"We'll know soon."

"How do you know?"

"Because she has a keen sense of self-preservation, and though I don't trust him, McGregor wants to find her, too. I'm more concerned about your safety. I'd feel better if James were driving you. If anything happens that feels off, call me or James."

Octavia opened her mouth to argue. Neil stopped her.

"I mean it. No excuses."

"I was going to say that I will call you, but not him. I don't trust him anymore. Who is he? Who does he work for, really?"

"He is an independent contractor, and I don't know who he ultimately works for, but I believe he will always come when you call."

Octavia said nothing and went to her bedroom.

Neil went to his room and took off his shoes. He wanted to meditate, but felt a little too full. He realized he had forgotten his coffee on the table and went back to retrieve it. He glanced at the turntable.

"Octavia, do you mind if I listen to the Four-Bar album?"

"What?"

"The Four-Bar Progression album. Do you mind if I listen to it?"

She opened her door. "Use the headset. I would prefer not to hear it today."

He slid the album out of the sleeve, blew on it to remove any lint or dust, put it on the turntable, and turned it on. He placed the stylus gently on the first cut, put the headset on, and listened intently while finishing his coffee. He cranked up the volume when the tone of the album changed to a cacophony of bits and pieces of bars played throughout the album, but in a way that didn't work. He pulled the headset off.

Neil knocked, and Octavia opened her door.

"I have a question about that segment you talked about on the album."

"Hold on." She came out to the living room. "So much for taking a nap."

"Is there anything else you can tell me about the conversation you had with Bastien?"

"It's strange," she said as she walked to the window overlooking the cityscape of Montreal. "I knew I had fond memories of the experience, but I'd forgotten most of them. Now they're all crashing in on me." She sat in the chair next to the window.

"I knew we would not make any more progress that day, so I canceled the evening session."

"That was the day when you talked about the Four-Bar Progression composition?" Neil asked.

"Bastien invited me to dinner so that we could talk business. I thought he was hitting on me, but I said okay because I wanted to make sure he went along with the changes I requested."

"This was before you decided to go along with it?"

She nodded. "He asked about my background, how I got into music production, my plans for the future."

"The questions a father would ask."

"An absent father, yes." Octavia looked down at the floor. "He pulled the original composition out of his messenger bag. It was a simple composition that inspired improvisation, except for that one section. It was exacting. He put it in front of me and said, 'Look at this section again and tell me what you see.' "

"And what did you see?"

"I saw various bars, separate yet connected. He'd designed the music like an architectural schematic."

"Did you tell him what you saw?"

"Yes. He said, 'Now you see why this must stay? It's a map for the mind. It's a map of the future.' So, here it is. On this album, exactly how he wanted it."

"Thanks."

"I'm going to try for that nap, again," she said as she walked to the bedroom.

Neil grabbed his sketch pad and put the headphones back on. He sketched as the music progressed. He immediately identified the section Octavia had described. Her words "designed" and "architectural" were spot-on. Then he heard it—the sequence of notes mirroring the notes on Octavia's bracelet.

He played the album through twice, then slipped the record back into the album sleeve. Octavia came out of the bedroom.

"Amazing what a twenty-minute nap and some yoga stretches can do," she said.

"Remember what Cadenza said?" Neil asked.

"She said a lot. What would I choose?"

" 'Dad used to tell me that DNA is the record and the music is the genes.' Remember?"

"Yes, I remember your eyes lit up, and you got excited about it."

"The record holds the music, which is created with symbols."

"Yes, that's what you said."

"When you saw the original composition, you said it was designed and architectural."

"You think it has something to do with the nano–delivery system?"

"We need to see those files in your father's music room. The original composition may be in there." Neil paced around the room. "Be careful. Say nothing about this to Cachemaille. I think you shouldn't go alone. Always go as a pair. Get James to be your backup."

Before he could say anything more, his phone chimed.

"Hello, Neil. How would you like to go on a date?" The sound of traffic filled the sound around Michelle's voice. "Did Octavia tell you about Butch Bennett?"

"Yes, she thinks he might take a hike," said Neil.

"So do I...I think we should pay him a visit, today. Are you up for it?"

"Of course. What time?"

"5? The sun will be down. I like talking to people with the dark closing in."

"You are an odd woman."

"You're one to talk. I'll text when I get to the hotel."

"Someone might be watching the hotel. I'll slip out and catch a bus. I don't know where I'll end up, but I'll text you when I get there. Might be later than five."

"You think the world is at your beck and call, don't you?" said Michelle. "I have a life, you know. A schedule to keep."

"I don't believe that," said Neil. "You don't like being predictable."

"Don't keep me waiting too long, or I'll go by myself. *Au revoir, mon ami.*"

Neil put on his shoes and coat and wrapped a scarf around his neck. Octavia was on the phone with her staff in Japan. He pulled out the bottle of Meursault and set it on the coffee table with two glasses. He jotted a note and tore it out of his pocket notebook.

I'm meeting Michelle. We're going to track down Butch Bennett. If I'm not back by nine, start without me. Don't leave without backup.

CHAPTER 41

There were so many photographers and reporters trying to reach Octavia that the police had to create a press zone away from the hotel entrance. The area was under surveillance by both uniformed officers and private security.

The concierge arranged a bus pass for Neil and an escort through the back of the hotel, which had a bus stop half a block away. Neil waited about twenty minutes and got on the first bus to arrive. He didn't look to see where it was going, and it didn't matter. He needed time to think, and he would have Michelle meet him wherever the last stop was.

Neil sat toward the back by a window. The route was lengthy, with multiple stops. It followed the waterways, but Neil spent the time sketching in the small sketchbook he always carried with him. He would occasionally glance up at the driver or passengers entering or exiting the bus. All the passengers on the bus—three men and an older woman who chatted with a young woman sitting across the aisle—wore masks, holdovers from pandemic days. Neil sketched them to clear his head.

The light was fading. The interior lights of the bus popped on. Neil could see the dark images of the passengers reflected in the windows. Two men had gotten on the bus after Neil. One had an open book, but Neil noted he hadn't turned a page for several stops. The other man had earbuds in, and occasionally bobbed his head and looked out his window when Neil glanced his way.

The bus was approaching an industrial area where a few working-class bars and cafes were open; most offered only takeout options, but one offered limiting seating. Neil decided this was the spot he would get off. He waited until the young woman passenger rang the bell. She stood and waited for the bus to stop. Neil waited for her to step out before getting up and exiting through the door. The bus door closed, and the bus pulled away. Neil noted that the man with the earbuds and the man reading the book both watched him through the windows. Earbuds Man spoke into his phone. Neil headed into the doorway of a closed bar and waited until the bus was out of sight, then changed locations to the cafe offering limited seating.

The place was empty. He sat toward the back, facing the entrance. The server quickly appeared, wearing a baseball cap with the cafe logo printed on it. Neil ordered in French after glancing at the menu—an Americano and the special, a massive sandwich featuring, according to the menu, large thick slabs of smoked brisket seasoned to perfection piled high on rye slathered with yellow mustard.

He texted Michelle. The server brought his Americano in a to-go cup. His phone pinged.

TWENTY MINUTES AWAY.

He opened his downloaded copy of "A Scandal in Bohemia." There was an inexplicable allure to it, yet he continued to resist reading it. The server brought the sandwich. True to its claims, it was massive. Neil cut it into four pieces and carefully worked his way through it.

He glanced outside as he finished the last of his Americano. A vehicle slowed and parked across the street. It wasn't Michelle's. It was barely light outside. He could see the driver's window was cracked open. A cigarette butt burned bright briefly, and smoke was drifting out the window.

Neil slipped his phone into his pocket and motioned the server over. She brought his meal ticket to the table, her pen poised in case he was going to order anything else.

"N'importe quoi d'autre, chéri?"

"No, I want to pay my bill," he replied in French.

"Comment était votre nourriture?"

"Le pain et la poitrine fumée étaient excellents, mais une moutarde plus épicée aurait rehaussé les saveurs."

"Donc, vous êtes un homme épicée." She smiled and handed him the ticket.

Neil appreciated her attempt at flirtation and gave her a sizable tip. He put on his coat and texted Michelle.

SOON? I THINK I'M BEING WATCHED.

He went outside and stood in front of the doorway. It was cold and completely dark except for the streetlights and lights shining from the interior of the cafe. The server was cleaning and sweeping the floor.

Neil took the direct approach and stared at the vehicle across the street. If they were watching him, he would watch them. There was no sign of the lit cigarette. The headlights were off, but the interior lights of the dashboard were bright, showing the silhouettes of two darkened figures inside. He heard vehicles approaching from a distance. Though he could not yet see headlights, he could distinguish the sound of a container truck and a compact sedan.

The interior lights popped on when both the passenger and driver doors opened. Neil could see headlights in the distance. The two figures dressed in black hoodies walked toward him. The situation jolted a visceral memory of five heavily armed Taliban fighters encircling him, the day he and his contact were brutally captured. "This was nothing like that," Neil whispered to himself, his voice barely audible. "This I can handle easily."

After encountering and surviving the worst, everything after that was easy. Leaning against the streetlamp, he stood casually, a hint of a smile playing on his lips.

They're not here for a friendly chat—hands out just in case. Stay calm, project confidence; predators smell fear. Left guy has a limp, favoring his right leg; potential weak spot if things go south. No visible weapons, but that doesn't mean they aren't armed. Industrial docks at night—a perfect place for things to disappear, including me.

He slipped his hand into his breast pocket.

Amazing invention, the pen, Neil thought. *You can take it any-where. You can puncture, rip, immobilize, or blind an assailant. You may kill someone if the puncture reaches a major artery or passes into the temple of the forehead. No need for that.*

The two men walked casually across one lane and had almost crossed over to the second lane when a car roared up and skidded to a stop in front of Neil. The passenger window was down.

"Get in!" Michelle Perusse shouted.

The two figures dashed toward the car. She gunned the engine and took off before Neil shut his door, pulling recklessly out in front of the container truck behind her. The truck driver honked his horn, and the two figures leaped out of his way.

"I don't know which is more hazardous to my health," said Neil, "unknown assailants or you."

"I can drop you off here if you're scared. Your choice. You can deal with them or take your chances with me." She grinned as she glanced up at her rearview mirror. The truck driver was flashing his lights. "I don't think he's thrilled with me."

She swerved to the left and turned down an alley, away from the waterfront. The curve in the road hid her actions, and they soon felt confident that no one was following them.

"We're going to be driving for quite a while. How about spending the time filling me in on what has happened over the last few days?"

Neil filled her in on all the events that had happened since she and Octavia had parted following their interview at the club. Michelle had followed the press reports but knew it was a shadow of the true story.

"Wow! Wow!" was her only response as Neil revealed the story.

Michelle worked her way through the city, making a detour occasionally to make sure they weren't being followed. It was clear that she was no stranger to evading danger. Neil felt a twist in his gut. Memories of navigating treacherous war zones flashed through his mind.

"You seem adept at eluding mysterious vehicles."

She smiled. "This kind of thing happens to me all the time. It's part of my job."

"How did you decide to become an investigative reporter?"

"I'm a very curious and adventurous person. I'm on a quest."

"A quest?"

"Yes."

"Like Don Quixote?"

"I am on a quest to tell comfortable Western countries true stories about the reality of the world and make them think."

"So, you're on a hopeless quest."

"I am disgusted by the constant whining of people because they have to stay at home to save their lives. There are millions in the world who never know where their next meal will come from; what bomb has dropped on their house, their school, their street; whether this is the morning a sniper will shoot them on the way to work. All that along with a world of pandemics, famine, fires, and floods. So, I challenge windmills and shout into the wind."

Michelle turned into a low-income residential neighborhood with blocks of apartment buildings and duplexes.

"We'll be at Butch's place in a few minutes."

"Octavia told me you would fill me in on his story."

"Butch Bennet is a talented drummer, or he used to be. He got the chance to play with an up-and-coming rock band in the States, so he moved there and did a short world tour. But he has a demon: gambling. He'd be riding high one week and broke the next."

"I imagine that led to some issues with the band."

Michelle nodded. "He was constantly asking for more money, so the band's management let him go. They gave him a five hundred dollars and paid for a plane ticket to Montreal."

"And he gambled away his money."

"He built up a lot of gambling debt. Charlie and Cliff let him stay with them for a while, but he's not the most pleasant person to be around, according to Charlie, and they basically kicked him out."

"When did he get in contact with Bastien?"

"When he got desperate. They hadn't gotten along for years. Before Butch went to the States, some shady characters harassed the band. Charlie said that the only time Bastien and Butch spoke was while they were onstage, and only about the music."

"So, what does this all lead to? Why are we going to talk to him?"

"Because almost six months ago, Bastien signed a six-month lease on the place where Butch is currently living. That lease is ending. Here's the kicker. Butch bragged he had 'a sweet deal' that was going to get him into a nicer place and his gambling debt taken care of."

"What was the deal?"

"That's what we're going to ask Butch."

CHAPTER 42

Rolling down a dark lane with no streetlights, they reached their destination - an unkempt duplex. The peeling paint and overgrown weeds hinted at years of neglect. Behind the closed blinds, a dim lamp cast a soft glow.

"Do you think he had anything to do with Bastien's death?" Michelle asked as she removed the key from the ignition.

"If he did, he's probably the next target," said Neil as he got out of the car.

As they approached the porch, they heard music playing inside. Neil banged on the door. There was no sound of movement. He pressed against the door. It popped open. Michelle brushed past him and into the living room.

There was a drum set, a recliner with the dim lamp, and an empty soup can filled with cigarette butts sitting on a small table beside it. The house smelled strongly of cigarette smoke; the walls were dingy and smoke stained.

"Hello? Butch? Are you here? I'm Michelle Perusse, the reporter that's been calling you? I'd like to speak to you. Hello?"

The music abruptly ceased and was replaced by the crackle of a needle seeking a groove on a vinyl record. The vintage sixties portable record player sat atop a worn Formica kitchen table. On the side of the player was The Four-Bar Progression album cover.

"Hello? Butch? Are you here?" Michelle called out. No response. She lifted the tonearm of the stranded needle from the record and set it on its cradle.

"Something isn't right," she said, "Maybe he ran out when he heard the knock on the door."

Neil looked into the kitchen. "Odd."

"What's odd?"

"Look at the two rooms," he said. "Compared to the living room, the kitchen is spotless. The dishes are washed and stacked in the dish tray. No pots on the stove. The coffee pot is clean and the floor has been mopped within the last twenty minutes."

"How can you tell that?"

"There is a faint odor of disinfectant cleaner," he sniffed, "misguidedly labeled as mango and hibiscus scent, and it's coming from...over here." Neil walked towards a folding door and pulled it aside, revealing a tiny pantry with a mop in a bucket. "It's been rinsed out and the mop is still damp."

Spotting wire shelves leaning against a 1970s fridge, he went to it and opened the door. Inside was the crumpled body of Butch Bennett.

"Oh my god! Is he dead?" Michelle pulled out her phone and called 911.

Neil examined Butch. "There's some color lingering on the skin." He pressed two fingers against the side of Butch's throat. "He's cold to the touch, but there's a faint heartbeat, and he's breathing, *barely*."

Neil pulled Butch out and laid him on the floor. "There's no sign of blood."

"Right." Michelle hung up. "They're on the way. The 911 operator said to cover him with blankets and try to warm him up." She found the bedroom and returned with a blanket.

A raspy sound came from Butch's mouth. His lips moved, but the words were not discernable.

"Butch, what did you say? Who did this to you?" Michelle asked as she tucked the blanket around him.

Butch Bennett's eyes moved behind his eyelids. He took a shallow breath and his blue lips moved slightly.

"Drumstick."

"What?" asked Neil, moving his ear closer to the blue lips.

"Drums k-killed . . . Bastien."

He took in one more raspy breath but said nothing more. Sirens sounded in the distance.

"Hold on, Butch." Michelle rubbed his hands. "Help is almost here. Hold on."

Flashing lights bounced across the closed blinds. Neil opened the door just as two paramedics hit the steps with police officers behind them. He pointed them to the kitchen and remained in the living room.

Michelle was talking to a police officer. She glanced towards Neil, who slightly tilted his head toward the drum set. She caught on and pivoted slightly, a movement the officer mimicked, turning his back to Neil.

The other officer stepped onto the porch, chatting on his radio. Another set of paramedics came into the house rolling a gurney. Neil casually walked around the drums and sat on the stool.

Drumstick. Drums. Killed Bastien. What was he trying to say?

He rubbed his fingers across the skin of each drum. He took the lamp from the side table and examined them. As he was about to move around the set, an unusual mark on the bass drum caught his attention. He pulled out his phone, clicked on his camera, and zoomed in.

A logo?

He spotted drumsticks under the same drum. They were in a V shape.

It looks like they're pointing at the logo—no, it's not a logo. It's a symbol.

As Neil leaned down to take a picture, he bumped the drumsticks. They rolled slightly.

Damn, there're two more symbols. One on each stick. There's something odd about one of them.

The officer entered from the porch. Spotting Neil, he approached him but paused when the paramedics wheeled the gurney towards the door in the living room. Butch's face was obscured by an oxygen mask. His eyes were closed and his lips were blue, but he was still alive, encased in a warming blanket.

Michelle followed, still talking to the officer. She saw Neil at the drums with his foot on the drumsticks. Once again, she diverted the attention in her direction.

"Can I ride in the ambulance with him?" she asked.

"I'm afraid that's not possible," the officer replied.

She persisted, arguing all the way out the door and down the sidewalk, pulling everyone's attention away from Neil. He did not squander his opportunity. He grabbed both drumsticks and inspected them.

There's a ring or a groove around the top of this one, and it's heavier than the other one. I wonder if I twist or pull on it—

The top pulled off. Inside was a note with a symbol on it wrapped around a small vial. Neil took the note off the vial and saw it had a handwritten label. There were symbols around the top. He slipped the vial into his coat pocket and took a quick look at the note.

Keep this safe. Bring to the Noir Jazz Bar. We'll play the song.

Neil took a picture of the note and placed it back in the drumstick. He texted Aumont.

CHECK POLICE REPORT ON BUTCH BENNETT. SOMEONE TRIED TO KILL HIM.

Michelle walked in with the police. They questioned Neil. He and Michelle both agreed to go to the police station to make formal statements and got into her car. His phone pinged. Aumont replying to his earlier text.

BUTCH BENNETT? THE DRUMMER?

Neil realized that Michelle had been talking to him. "Sorry," he said. "Where are we going?"

"Montreal General," she replied. "Weren't you listening to me?"

Neil texted Aumont.

Meet me at Montreal General.

Neil added one more text.

He knows who killed Bastien Beaulieu.

CHAPTER 43

Michelle Perusse could've had a second career as a stunt driver. She weaved in and out of traffic and careened down alleyways until she caught up with the paramedics transporting Butch Bennett.

"The siren's still blaring and the lights are flashing. He's still alive," she said, "or at least not officially dead—yet."

Michelle screeched to a stop as the gurney was being wheeled into the ER. Neil leaped out of the car and caught up with the paramedics who continued working on Butch until the doctors and nurses took over in one movement. The ER doc rushed to the double doors and listened to the paramedic's report.

Neil took advantage of the shift of personnel and fully embraced the role of a distressed family member. "Hold on, Uncle Butch! Oh my god. Oh my god. Is he going to be all right? Please save him. Please save—" Neil broke down into tears.

The act worked. He was approached by a nurse wearing a mask who took him aside to soothe him. "We're going to do the best we can for him. Are you a family member?" she asked.

Neil nodded and went into full on blubbering. The nurse grabbed a face cloth and handed it to him. He worked himself into an ugly cry. His cheeks were wet with tears, and significant mucus streamed from his nose, soaking through the cloth.

Neil's anguish act showed no signs of subsiding as he sobbed between each sentence he uttered. "Someone broke into his house, and they hurt him. Why would they do that? Is he going to be okay? My girlfriend went to park the car. I don't know where she is."

As if on cue with Neil's performance, the doors to the emergency room parted, allowing Michelle to enter. Neil rushed over, wrapping his arms tightly around her. Her eyes went wide as he buried his soggy face into her hair.

"He doesn't look good. Oh my god!" Neil cried in a high-pitched voice, "What if he dies? What will I do without . . . Uncle Butch?"

Michelle patted Neil's back. "It'll be all right. They'll take care of him . . . babe."

"We're going to do our best," the nurse reassured Michelle.

The two police officers who had been at Butch's home arrived.

"Time for act two," Neil whispered in Michelle's ear.

Michelle patted his back and whispered, "If any of that snot gets in my hair, I'm going to—" Neil pivoted her around so that she could see the police walking toward them.

"Thank you, nurse," she said, "I'll take it from here."

"What are you two doing here?" asked the lead officer, "You need to go to the police station."

"What do you mean?" Michelle was nailing her part in the act. "I thought we were supposed to go in tomorrow morning. I thought—I thought someone told us that."

Neil turned and looked at them.

"Hey, guy, you look terrible." The second officer sounded concerned.

"I'm an empathic person." Neil put his hand on his chest and gasped, "I feel Uncle Butch's pain." Tears ran down his face and his words came out in a squeak. "I'm very sensitive. Oh no—I think I'm going to be sick." Neil gagged and threw up on the officer's shoes.

"Nurse!" Michelle shouted.

The nurse called out for an environmental services technician to clean the floor, as she slipped on disposable gloves and approached with an orderly pushing a wheelchair.

The concerned officer now looked a little sick himself. "Man, look at my shoes. Really? Did you have to puke on my shoes?"

Neil, still in character, widened his eyes. "I'm sorry, Officer. I just get really anxious around authority figures."

With careful precision, the orderly positioned Neil in the wheelchair, then placed absorbent paper towels over the vomit. The nurse wiped Neil's face with the washcloth, went over it again with a wet wipe, then handed him a vomit bag. "Sir, do you feel like you're going to be sick again? Do you feel lightheaded or dizzy?"

Neil shook his head. "Water. I need water."

"We'll get you some. If you feel sick, use the bag. Stay in the wheelchair; don't try getting up."

The environmental services tech arrived and handed the nurse a clear bag with the words 'environmental hazard' printed in red. He gave the officer paper towels to clean his shoes and directed him to the restroom. The officer's complaints mingled with the laughter of the other officer who followed close behind, slipping slightly on the wet floor and catching himself on the wall.

The nurse dropped the washcloth inside the bag and sent the orderly to get a bottle of water. She took Neil's vitals as the tech began cleaning the mess and put a 'caution wet floor' cone near the spot.

"Thank you, nurse. What's your name?" Michelle asked.

"Rose."

"Thank you, Rose." Michelle smiled and turned to Neil. "You're going to be okay, babe. Rose is taking care of you."

"Have you had any shortness of breath, dry cough, or any congestion over the past few days?" Rose asked. "Have you had a test for—"

Neil nodded. "Several."

"How about dry mouth, headaches?"

He shook his head. "No."

The orderly returned with a bottle of water.

"Take a sip of this," Rose said. "Take small sips, nice and slow."

"I'm upset about Uncle Butch." Neil took a sip of water. "I'm sorry. I'm not usually like this."

"Actually, he's frequently like this," Michelle whispered to the nurse. "He's an artist."

"Your vitals are okay. You don't have a fever. Your blood pressure is a little elevated, but not too bad." Rose turned her attention to Michelle. "You can stay here for a few minutes, so you can keep an eye on him, but then both of you will have to go to the waiting room."

"What about Uncle Butch?" Neil asked. Michelle put her arm around him. "You need to calm down, babe."

"We'll keep you informed of his condition," said Rose. She instructed the orderly to wheel Neil out of the way.

The orderly positioned Neil next to a wall with a perfect view of the double doors that Butch had been rolled through and put a chair next to him. They were out of sight and out of mind, and that was exactly what Neil and Michelle wanted.

"What made you look so miserable?" Michelle asked. "I thought you were really sick."

"Acting classes, years ago. I was proficient at looking sick and anxious."

"Why doesn't this surprise me?" She chuckled.

It was dinnertime. Staff switched out for meals. Michelle began clicking notes into her phone, looking up whenever staff came in and out of the double doors. Neil took out his pocket sketchbook and began to capture the intricate details of the crime scene at Butch Bennett's house.

More than an hour later, the doctor treating Butch emerged from the double doors, his face etched with exhaustion, but a mask of calm professionalism appeared when he saw Michelle approaching him. Neil was close behind until his attention was caught by the sight of Aumont and McGregor entering the ER. He pivoted and walked towards them.

———

"What's going on?" asked McGregor.

"Butch Bennett was attacked, and we don't know if he's going to survive. He has the answers we need." Neil revealed the few words Butch had managed to say, "Killed Bastien."

Michelle and the doctor headed toward them. Neil made eye contact with her. She slowed their approach and maneuvered the doctor around, his back turned from them.

"He killed Bastien?" asked Aumont.

"Not exactly, or perhaps exactly," replied Neil.

"What do you mean by that? Did he, or didn't he?" demanded Aumont.

"He was there when Bastien died. He knows who killed Bastien, and he tried to blackmail them. That's why they went after him."

McGregor's brows knitted, and he cleared his throat. "You are no longer a part of this investigation and you should not be here. How did you find out about Butch Bennett?" Then he caught sight of Michelle talking to the doctor.

"Why is Michelle here?" McGregor asked.

"Because she was with me when we found him stuffed in the refrigerator at his house."

McGregor left Aumont to talk to the officers and headed toward her. Neil followed him. As they got closer, Michelle turned the doctor towards them.

"Here are the police in charge now," she said.

McGregor introduced himself and flashed his badge. He made no reference to Neil, and Neil didn't identify himself; assumptions are made through association.

"I'm in charge of a murder investigation which has national security implications," said McGregor. "The man you're treating may have vital information."

"I'm Dr. Mayank Varshney. I'm afraid Mr. Bennett is in critical condition. We are trying to stabilize him. He is having seizures. We gave him medications to minimize them. Our scans indicate that parts of his brain are shutting down. I've asked for a neurologist to examine him. Bruising has appeared all over his body, and every time we move him, multiple fractures occur. I've seen nothing like it."

Neil was clicking away on his phone and paused. "You got the updated report from the ME's office."

"Yes," said McGregor.

"It proved my theory, didn't it?"

McGregor didn't answer him, but continued to talk to the doctor. "Is there a quiet place nearby where we can speak more confidentially?"

"There's a supply room down the hall to the right. What's going on?" Dr. Varshney asked.

"I'd like to bring in our medical examiner to assist you. I know it's unusual, but it will be useful for you and us."

Dr. Varshney nodded and called Rose over.

"I'm going to have a private conversation with these men. We'll be in the supply room if you need me."

"The supply closet?" Rose looked quizzically at Neil and McGregor.

While Dr. Varshney took her to the side, McGregor made a call to the ME, requesting he come immediately to Montreal General's emergency room. He motioned Aumont over.

"You need to hear this. Come with us."

Michelle walked over to Neil and whispered, "What's going on?"

"I think we're about to find out I was right—Bastien was poisoned with a nano robotic delivery system, and it sounds like the same thing has happened to Butch."

"Hey, let's go," said McGregor. "And 'let's' doesn't apply to you," he said pointedly to Michelle.

Neil followed McGregor and Aumont to the supply room. "Just so we're clear," said McGregor, "you're here only to tell me what you saw and found at Butch Bennett's home and anything that Cadenza Beaulieu mentioned about her research. You're not to reveal anything you hear to Michelle Perusse."

Once the supply room door closed, McGregor revealed the medical examiner's report.

"The results are still pending," McGregor said, "however, the injuries sustained by our murder victim closely resemble those of your patient. The damage was massive. His entire neural network was severed."

"Severed?" asked Dr. Varshney. "His neural network? How is that possible?"

"This is how the medical examiner explained it to me. Simply put, it is like a blizzard of miniature razors that systematically attacks the extracellular matrix—"

"But how?" The doctor asked.

Neil stopped typing on his phone and looked at the group. "I think I know how."

His phone pinged. Neil began scrolling through the message.

"Enough with the dramatic pause, Ames," McGregor exclaimed. "What do you know?"

Neil quickly responded to the text before answering.

"Butch's apartment was . . . untidy, but the kitchen was spotless. All the dishes were drying on a towel on the counter. The tray under the dish rack was still wet, which means we arrived shortly after the assailant left and that they were trying to destroy any trace of the nanorobotics that were used."

"Or we're dealing with a fastidious and precise assailant," said McGregor.

"No," Neil shook his head.

"Yes," said McGregor.

"What are you two arguing about? My patient is dying. I need answers now," said Dr. Varshney

"I'm right," insisted Neil.

"No, you're not right, but...also...yes," replied McGregor.

"Wait, I'm confused. Can you repeat that?" Aumont asked, with a bewildered tone.

"Oh," Neil exclaimed, a spark of arousal lighting up his eyes. "Oh..." he repeated, his voice filled with newfound realization. "Your ME found the nano robots, didn't he? But they were inert. They hadn't been activated." Neil couldn't contain his excitement, causing him to pace back and forth with quick, agitated steps.

McGregor continued speaking to Dr. Varshney. "Our ME is probably your best resource of information."

"Based on the effects of the attacks," Neil pronounced, "it appears that both Bastien and Butch were targeted by an assassin skilled in taijutsu, specifically aiming to disrupt their chakra network."

McGregor groaned. "Athena warned me he was a Sherlock Holmes freak."

Neil's persistent pacing filled the room, like a charge of electricity. "A more advanced technique exists, where multiple chakra points are struck in quick succession, effectively severing the entire neural network."

There was a knock on the door. Dr. Varshney stepped out. McGregor's phone buzzed. He answered it and went out into the hallway.

"Aumont, don't you see it's all connected?" said Neil. "International corporations, criminal networks, professional killers…It's connected to Emily."

Aumont kept an eye on the door as he moved closer to Neil. "Emily? Who's Emily?" he asked. "What's wrong with you?"

Neil continued to pace.

"Stop with this ridiculous talk of ninja assassins," Aumont snapped, his frustration evident in his voice. "I agree with you that McGregor knows more than he's letting on. I don't know what it is, but it feels like he's hiding something. Stop pacing and look at me!"

Neil's footsteps halted, his focus now fully directed towards Aumont. "You do not know the world I have traveled through." Neil stepped towards him. "Why?"

"Why, what?" asked Aumont.

"Why," Neil repeated, "are you suddenly willing to work with me?"

"I want to solve this case. I have permission from the fire marshal to go into the Beaulieu home tomorrow morning. If there hasn't been too much damage, we may find something."

"I suggest we go tonight," said Neil. He slipped the phone into his pocket. His fingers touched the vial.

"Something is bothering me, Ames," said Aumont. "Why aren't you more concerned about Cadenza Beaulieu?"

"I don't believe she's in danger. I'm sure we will hear something soon."

"I'm not concerned about her safety," said Aumont, "I'm concerned that she may kill again."

"No," said Neil, "someone else is doing the killing."

McGregor cracked the door open. "The medical examiner is here."

Neil and Aumont followed him back to the ER. Dr. Varshney and the medical examiner were speaking in hushed tones as they walked through the double doors. Neil spotted Michelle. She smiled as he approached. McGregor grabbed his arm.

"I know you two are thick as thieves, but I do not want you telling Michelle *anything*. I don't trust her with this. You understand?"

"Of course I understand," Neil said as he walked toward Michelle. He paused and turned back to McGregor. "By the way, she doesn't trust you either. It puts me in a difficult position."

"Athena trusts me enough to ask that I help you," said McGregor, "but I don't trust *you*. I shouldn't let you go to the house with Aumont."

"There's trust, and there's *trust*," said Neil, "It's been my experience that the ones you trust are the ones who can twist the knife in your back without hesitation."

"I should put you in custody and have you deported."

Aumont walked between the two men. "Don't worry, I'll watch him like a hawk, and I will drive him back to his hotel."

Neil turned and continued toward Michelle.

"Making friends and influencing people, *babe*?" she asked.

"We're dismissed, but I'm going with Aumont," said Neil. "Let's meet tomorrow at the hotel after you and Octavia have your meeting. I think we will have all the pieces of music we need to break this case."

"Pieces of music?" Michelle arched her right eyebrow.

"Butch is a goner, but he may rouse to say something. If he does, find a way to visit him."

"Did I tell you I look quite fetching in scrubs, protective clothing, and masks?" She grinned and waved him off.

As Neil exited the ER with Aumont, he texted Octavia.

BUTCH BENNETT ATTACKED. CRITICAL CONDITION. A & I GOING TO BASTIEN'S HOUSE. HAVE J DRIVE U BACK.

Chapter 44

It was nine when Neil and Aumont pulled up to the Beaulieu house.

Neil smiled when he saw the blind crack open and Agnes Abercrombie peer through her window. He waved as he stepped out of the police vehicle. The blind snapped closed.

Despite the recent freezing rainstorm, the smell of charred wood and smoke still infused the air as he and Aumont walked up to the front door, which had crime tape crisscrossing the entrance. Aumont pulled aside the tape, and they stepped in.

Aumont had a flashlight, and Neil used his phone to light the way. The house, which had been inviting the first time they'd arrived, now looked derelict and sad, stained with smoke and water damage. Its occupants were dead, and a stranger had died here. It was a house in mourning soon to meet its own end.

Neil checked his phone. Still no message from Octavia.

Neil sent a text.

James, are you with Octavia?

Aumont worked his way through the kitchen into the hallway. "Let's go inspect the damage upstairs."

He climbed the creaky stairs. Neil followed. The acrid smoky odor became more intense as they climbed.

"We need to go into Bastien's office first," said Neil. "There is something I need to check out."

"What?"

"I'll know when I see it or don't see it."

Aumont shook his head. "You're so obtuse."

"There's a first time for everything."

"What do you mean?"

"I've never been called obtuse before."

"Not to your face," Aumont uttered.

They carefully walked through the otherworldly scene. Aumont's flashlight beam darted around the space. They looked inside the music room.

"There's some smoke damage, but it's not too bad." Neil's phone chimed. "It's James." He answered it. "Where is she?"

"I don't know, sir. I haven't heard from her. I'm persona non grata. She sent me a text two days ago, letting me know that my services were no longer needed, though I am still technically on Yuu International's payroll at Mr. Yuu's insistence."

"Damn it."

"Is there a problem, sir?"

"Stop calling me sir."

"Yes, Neil."

Neil could sense his grin, and it inexplicably irritated him.

"She hasn't returned my texts. The last time I saw her, she was planning to meet the attorney, Bernard Cachemaille. They were going to—" Neil thought, replaying their conversation in his mind. "She didn't say the name of the club, but she said it was the last club Bastien played in."

"Cachemaille? He's a sly one," said James.

"You know something about him?"

"Nothing dangerous, just irregular."

"Yes, His name has shown up in some interesting places," said Neil. "I'm uneasy about Octavia being alone with him. I'll text the name of the club, and I want you to find her. If she objects, too bad."

"Yes, sir."

Neil hung up and called Michelle. She answered on the second ring.

"He's still critical," she said.

"I'm not calling about Butch. What were your plans with Octavia tomorrow?"

"We're going to talk to Charlie Allen. He owns the Deep Red Jazz Club, which is closed. The other club is also closed, but we were going to contact them. Why?"

"Do you know the name Cachemaille?"

"I've heard of him. He's a...shrewd operator."

"He's Bastien's lawyer. Octavia is with him. She said they were going to a private memorial service for Bastien and that it was at the last club he played."

"That would be the Noir Jazz Bar."

"Thanks."

"What's going on?"

Neil hung up and called James.

"Yes?"

"Try the Noir Jazz Bar. If she isn't there, try the Deep Red Jazz Club."

"Yes, sir." James hung up.

"Are you worried about Ms. Clarke?" Aumont asked. "Should we leave and come back tomorrow?"

"No. The key to everything is here."

They went into Bastien's blackened office. Smoke and charcoal hung on the charred walls like drapery. The room was haunted by the acrid scent of a burned body, a chilling reminder of the tragedy that had occurred. But Neil's attention was on the desk, now water-soaked and melted.

On the desk, there sat a pile of charred books resembling a stack of burnt toast. On top was a melted framed cover of a business magazine. It was the one with Octavia smiling brilliantly, but the only remnant of Octavia that remained was the section around her smiling mouth.

Beneath that was a misshapen blob that had once been a frame. It was the picture of Bastien and Cadenza smiling as she held her PhD. However, what Neil was truly searching for lay beneath that: three Thomas Merton books that had been sheltered from the flames by the melted frames. Two collections of his writings and a paperback copy of *The Seven Storey Mountain*.

Neil carefully thumbed through them.

"What are you looking for?" Aumont asked and flashed his flashlight around the desk.

"These books were important to him. According to Cadenza, they obsessed him. He was going to a conference to present a blistering rebuke of the nanotechnology world to come."

"That sounds biblical."

"Prophetic."

"What's the difference?"

"The prophets cautioned the mainstream that if they didn't take care and continued living the way they are, great calamity would befall them."

"And that's what he planned to do?"

"Yes, and that probably got him killed." Neil continued to go through the books, occasionally taking pictures of pages. "Bastien dog-eared pages, underlined sentences, and highlighted words. See here? He wrote brief notes in the margins. He particularly focused on the concept that the evil in the world is all of our own making."

Neil went through the second book of collections. "Here, he's underlined and put symbols next to a paragraph about mathematical evolutions being hierarchical rights devised by shamans without belief. He wrote something here: *Scientists engineer our worst nightmares*."

"I get the picture."

"There is one section that is highlighted, underlined, and starred. He's written in the margin. *Technology has its own set of ethics*. And farther down the page he's written, *Technology's ethics conflict with human ethics.*"

Neil turned to another section so revealing it caught his breath. "He was fighting a war in his mind about what he had been doing and how what he'd created was becoming twisted."

Neil turned more pages. "This is the last notation. It's a single word. I've seen this before." Neil took a picture of the page and went back through the book. "There it is. On the flyleaf."

Aumont came to his side to see what Bastien had written on the page.

In capital letters was the word "SIMULACRA." A series of symbols surrounded the underlined and boxed word.

"Simulacra. What does that mean?" Aumont asked.

"It refers to ideas and conceptions that look good but aren't. Ideals that claim to be humane but in action are callous, cruel, cynical, and usually criminal."

"What are those symbols?"

"They are like the symbols on the trombone and Octavia's bracelet."

"Is it a code?"

"Yes, and no. It's a keyword."

"A keyword? For what?"

"To the code. A method of deciphering the code, or it might be a password," Neil tapped on the melted keys of Bastien's computer. "I doubt we can retrieve anything from this."

"I have a question," said Aumont, "it's been bothering me since the night Cadenza Beaulieu escaped. Why do you trust James Fenmore?"

"That's the wrong question," said Neil as he pulled out the key. "Let's go to the music room."

CHAPTER 45

The Mercedes-Benz made Octavia feel hermetically sealed in a sensory deprivation tank.

Or a spaceship. I'm gliding through space with a strange man. His driver is like an automaton—perfect posture, immaculately groomed, clipped responses, a hear nothing, see nothing manner. Why am I so uneasy? I have worked with Cachemaille and was perfectly at ease with him, but in person, there is something that is triggering me. What is it? Say something. Get him talking. Smile. Be charming.

"Thank you for inviting me, Bernard. I have to admit, I'm a little nervous. Maybe I'm being too self-conscious. Who put the memorial service together? I want to make sure I thank them personally."

"You have nothing to be anxious about," Cachemaille reassured her, "they will be as charmed by you as I am. Would you like something to drink? We have a small but excellent selection."

He pushed a button and revealed a selection of small bottles of aged bourbons, vodka, and brandy. There was another section with club soda and a variety of fresh squeezed juices. The compartment above held a pair of Baccarat Crystal Louxor tumblers monogrammed with the letters BC.

"Beautiful glassware. BC. Before Christ?" Octavia smiled and brushed her hair behind her ear.

Cachemaille smiled back. "My initials are a small vanity. Might I suggest—"

"A Pappy Van Winkle 23?" she suggested.

"I have to say, I am impressed, you have excellent taste." He poured a shot into each glass and offered a toast before they drank. "Aux souvenirs persistants."

Octavia sipped and savored the refined oakiness from the years it had matured in the barrel. She closed her eyes and relished the heat as it ran through her body. "This is glorious."

"I think you are now feeling more relaxed, yes?"

She smiled and nodded. "Yes."

Octavia looked at the elegant man with silver hair, a charcoal Tom Ford three-piece tailored suit, a white silk shirt, and gold monogrammed Cartier cufflinks. He was a man of prestige. He radiated confidence.

There is an edge to him. I'm sure he can be quite a formidable adversary. He said Bastien was a good friend, but it seems an odd pairing.

"I'm afraid I'll be too formal for a jazz club. Do you mind if I take my tie off?" he asked.

"No, not at all."

Cachemaille loosened the knot and slid the tie into his suit pocket. Octavia's phone pinged. She looked at it and slipped it into her pocket.

"I should have invited your friend, Mr. Ames, to join us," he said.

"I'm sure he would have liked to come, but he has other plans for the evening."

The Bose speakers filled the air with a soothing ambient tone as the driver's voice announced that they would reach their destination in five minutes. They finished their drinks and Cachemaille inserted their glasses in a custom-built compartment.

Octavia used her cane to shift her position carefully. Her hip and leg were still bothering her. She grimaced.

"That is a beautifully crafted cane. I don't think I have ever seen one quite like it."

"Neil calls it my scepter. You have your monogrammed crystal, I have a customized instrument of mobility that was designed by the Yuu International futurist division. Fuji Yuu named it the Equipoise Scepter. It is brilliantly designed, but if I don't do my part with my physical therapy exercises, it's just a walking stick."

"We have arrived at our destination," the driver announced.

Octavia's door popped open before she realized they had stopped. The driver helped her out of the car, and Cachemaille was at her side instantly. The entrance to the Deep Red Jazz Club was ablaze with light, and the sound of the music of The Four-Bar Progression pulsed in the building. Octavia looked around the parking lot. There were only three parked vehicles, including Cachemaille's Mercedes.

"It's an intimate affair, but we are early, so more will probably arrive soon," Cachemaille assured her.

The club door opened, and Cliff Squire greeted them warmly.

"Octavia and Monsieur Cachemaille! Welcome. Thank you for coming."

"Cliff, it is good to see you again. Is Michelle here?" Octavia asked. "Michelle Perusse. She was with me the other day? She's a huge fan of the band."

"No, I'm sorry. I should have invited her. My brain, well, I haven't been thinking straight since Bastien died. But there is one person I'd like to introduce you to. You met him a long time ago. Do you remember Charlie Allen? Charlie, look who's here. Could you turn down the music?"

The volume dropped, and a large bald man wearing thick glasses and a mask approached them. The last time Octavia had seen him, he'd been a slight man who always had a cigarette dangling from his lips and a full head of hair that fell into his eyes. The only thing that remained the same was the thick glasses.

"Hello, Charlie! It is nice to see you. It has been a long time." She reached out to shake his hand, but he did not reciprocate.

"His immune system is weak, making him an easy target for viruses." Cliff grinned at him, but Charlie's gaze remained fixed on Octavia.

"So, this is your club? Do you mind if I look around?" she asked.

"It was my club," Charlie answered in a raspy voice. He glanced at Cachemaille. "I had to take on a co-owner to keep the place going."

"That sounds like a sound business strategy," Octavia said.

"A sound business strategy," echoed Cachemaille.

"Please, come sit." Cliff pulled out a chair for Octavia.

"I'd like to look around first." She looked at Charlie, who coughed as he sat in the chair that Cliff had pulled out for her.

"You can look around as much as you want," said Cachemaille. "I would like to have a drink, Cliff. What do you have?"

They went to the bar. Octavia walked to the stage and climbed the steps. She turned to look at the audience of empty tables and chairs. She stood where she imagined Bastien had stood with his trombone. She breathed in the air and felt the warmth of the lights. Charlie had a nice place. He was watching her. She looked at him.

"I heard you were ill," she said, concern evident in her voice.

"I was going to the States for treatment, but the border closed before I got across." He coughed and wheezed. "I wish I had made it. Things might be different."

"What things?"

"It sure is good to see you standing on that stage." Cliff clapped his hands. "You know exactly where Bastien stood."

"You're his girl, for sure," rasped Charlie.

Octavia stepped down from the stage and sat at one of the tables.

"Would you like a drink?" Cliff asked.

"Bernard spoiled me with exquisite bourbon on the way here, but club soda sounds good to me."

"Sure thing." Cliff poured the soda.

No one spoke. Octavia could feel the tension in the air. Something is off. Cliff and Charlie are cautious, and Cachemaille is too comfortable.

Cliff brought the soda to her.

"Thanks," she said and took a sip. " How many people are you expecting tonight?"

Cliff stuttered and stepped back. "We, uh—" He sighed. "It was the only way we could talk to you."

She took another sip of her club soda. "So, no one else is expected?"

"Well, yes. Uh, Butch, you remember Butch? He's supposed to be here. He's late."

Octavia took another sip and began typing on her phone, which was in her coat pocket. She had played the game with Neil countless times, texting each other with one hand without looking at the keys.

Neil always said it would come in handy.

She looked at Cachemaille. He leaned casually against the bar.

So, he's in on it too.

"Why don't you start the conversation while we wait for him?" she asked.

Cliff looked around the room—first at Charlie, then to Cachemaille. Charlie wiped his forehead with a napkin. Cachemaille sipped his drink, his eyes on Octavia. Charlie went into a coughing fit, covering his mouth with the napkin. As he gasped for air, he blurted, "Oh, for God's sake, tell her."

"Tell me what?"

Cliff sat at the table across from Octavia. "We want the rights to Bastien's compositions. We know he left them to you. But we're the ones who did the work. We did our share of work on those pieces; we deserve the rights and the money that can come our way. We need the money. We need it more than you do. Our clubs are folding. If Bastien knew how dire things are, I'm sure he would have changed his will or would have planned to assure that we would get a portion from the leases."

"You could have just asked me." Octavia finished her soda and stood up. "Is this why my father was murdered? So you could get your hands on the rights?"

"What? No. No. We would never," exclaimed Cliff. "We're not murderers. We loved Bastien. We were all like brothers. I'm heartbroken that he is never coming back through that door."

"It's him who is forcing us to do this," Charlie panted.

"Who?" she asked.

"You know who can explain all of this?" Cliff interjected. "Butch. He and Bastien were close. He's supposed to be here. Where is he? He can explain everything."

"That's too bad," said Octavia, "because he isn't coming tonight."

"What do you mean?" Cliff asked. "How do you know? Did he already make a deal with you?"

"No. I'm afraid Butch cannot explain anything. He's in critical condition and not expected to survive."

The color drained out of Cliff's face. "What? How do you know that? What happened?"

"A friend sent me a text on the way here. I don't have details. He was attacked, that's all I know." Octavia fixed her piercing gaze on the attorney, her eyes narrowing as she took a step closer. "Did you know, Bernard?"

Cachemaille put his glass on the bar and turned toward her. "I take it Mr. Ames was the one who texted you?"

"Him." Cliff pointed at Cachemaille. "He's the one who forced Charlie to make him a co-owner. He's the one who bought out the Noir Jazz Bar. He's the one who told us we should go after the music rights."

Octavia's lips pressed into a thin line, barely containing her simmering anger.

"You know, I wondered how Bastien came to hire you to handle his will and help me manage affairs. Your clientele list includes billion-dollar corporations, not people like my father. So, you were behind the scheme to steal my father's music rights," she said, her voice steady but filled with icy determination. "The money from the rights would barely cover the fuel costs for your Mercedes."

"You're right." Cachemaille smiled as he approached her. "I couldn't care less about the music rights or these pathetic jazz clubs. I am much more interested in his scientific work."

"You're after his nanotechnology research project."

"Your father thought he had found a sympathetic partner who held his same philosophies and concerns about the future of the world and the place of technology in it."

"But you were playing him."

"Like a trombone. Unfortunately, he didn't trust me with his secret work. That secret he left to you. I knew what to look for—that's why I helped you. But the secret he left to you is in code."

Octavia squared her shoulders, planted her cane in front of her, and leaned forward. "Did he find out what your actual intentions were? Is that why you murdered him?"

"You should ask your sister."

"What do you mean?"

"She could see the true value of his work. She has the potential to be one of the most celebrated and wealthy scientists of our time. After the reading of the will, she contacted me. She's quite angry about your existence, and, well, she has significant daddy issues. She offered a generous reward if I helped her get her father's project notes."

"You son of a bitch." Charlie stood up. His bloated face looked like it would explode. "Are you the one who fingered Butch? Is he dying because of you?"

Cachemaille ignored him and continued to focus on Octavia. "Do you want to see your sister?"

"You know where she is?"

"She asked for my help. I know where she's hiding. I can take you to her."

Octavia looked at Cliff and Charlie.

"They will not be of any help to you. They've got too much to lose. Shall we go?"

CHAPTER 46

Despite the fire, Bastien's music room remained untouched by the flames and only suffered minor water damage.

Neil went back to the desk. The composition was in the same position Octavia had left it. The symbols and notes were familiar to him now. He paid particular attention to the folds and matching notches that Octavia had connected to read the map to the key.

What was it that Octavia said about his composition?

Neil closed his eyes. When he opened them, he saw it. A poster framed on the wall across from the desk.

"He'd designed the music like an architectural schematic."

Neil concentrated on the composition in front of him and the configuration of the various shapes that existed.

Think like an architect or an engineer. I can construct his music as a 3D object. One on top of the other. Time and space. Watch for the chaos.

Neil took out his notebook and began sketching, one page of composition on top of another. *Symbols connect. What draws them to one another? What is the catalyst that causes the attraction?*

Aumont came back into the room. "If there're any files in his office, I can't get to them. The heat warped the cabinets shut. What are you doing?"

"I'm using DNA origami."

"What?"

"I'm drafting a structure using Bastien's composition."

"What are you really doing?"

Neil said nothing as he continued to sketch. He abruptly stopped and spun his sketch towards Aumont. "What do you see?"

Aumont frowned as he squinted at the sketch. He sighed and threw up his arms. "What am I looking at?"

"Stop looking so closely. Just make connections."

"What I see is that you are no Monet."

"Exactly. It isn't a Monet. It's Robert Delaunay."

"Who?"

"He was a cubist painter in the 1920s. He did a series of abstract compositional dissections of the Eiffel Tower. There's a framed poster of one of those paintings on the wall over there. Octavia told me that Bastien designed his music like an architectural schematic. His method is like DNA origami used to create nanorobots. Using symbols in this, Bastien created abstract, compositional dissections. Using those, I drew a schematic that shows us what this key opens."

Neil connected the dots. "If you place them together and reorganize them, you get . . . this."

"A car?"

"A 1968 Charger."

"The key you have isn't a car key."

"No, but whatever this key opens is in that car."

"Did he perchance compose the location of this car? The only vehicles known to have been on this property were Cadenza Beaulieu's and the utility van."

"Did anyone check to see if he had a car registered under his name?"

"Yes. He'd parked his Prius blocks from where they found his body. I'll have registrations checked tomorrow morning."

"I have a faster way of finding out. Let's wake up the Abercrombies."

———

"Husband, wake up!"

"Go back to bed, woman. Get that flashlight out of my eyes. Leave me alone."

"Je suis désolé, Monsieur Abercrombie, but we need your help." Aumont flashed his badge.

"Get that thing out of my face. Woman, why did you let him in?"

"He's the police, dear. Stop being so grumpy. He and that good-looking friend of Octavia's need our help."

"You help them. I'm going back to sleep."

"We need access to your garage," said Aumont.

"Why the hell do you want in my garage? What time is it?"

"It's a little past ten, dear," said Agnes. "Now get up and put your warm robe on. They want to see your car."

"Fine, it's in the driveway. Leave me alone."

"Not that car—the other car. The one in the garage. You know, the one Dr. Beaulieu gave to you."

"Damn it."

"Get up. This is important to the murder case. Isn't it exciting?" Agnes squealed. "Let's go. Octavia's friend is outside looking in the windows."

"Trespassing. I want him arrested. Call the police."

"I am the police," said Aumont, "and if I have to, I'll get a search warrant. This is part of an official murder investigation."

"All right!"

Grumbling all the way, Mr. Abercrombie stomped out to the garage in his pajamas and bathrobe, with the key in hand and his gardening boots on. Agnes was striding gleefully step for step at his side like two steam engines prodding through the night, their breath visible in the chilly air.

"Well, shine the light on the lock. I'm half blind without my glasses."

She pointed her flashlight at the padlock. He unlocked it and slid it off the latch. Neil and Aumont swung open the wide double doors. It was dark inside. Agnes pointed her flashlight around the space, as did Neil and Aumont. They could see the outline of a car wrapped in a black car cover.

"I'm going inside. You fools can stay out here all you want. Don't bother me anymore." Mr. Abercrombie turned and headed back to the house, the way lit dimly by the porch light.

"Do you have a key to unlock the car?" called Neil.

The old man kept walking. "It's unlocked," he said over his shoulder.

After he climbed the steps up to the porch, he turned and saw the beams from the flashlights occasionally escaping out of the garage windows into the yard. He shook his head and called out, "You know there's a light switch in there."

He tripped over something as he walked through the doorway into the house. There was a screech.

"Damn cat."

———

"My husband always admired this car, and one day Dr. Beaulieu gave it to him."

The garage and the '68 Dodge Charger were spotless. After removing the covering, Neil and Aumont searched the vehicle for any crevice that may have been hiding a lock for the newly discovered key. Agnes followed them and chatted as she peered through the car windows.

"During the spring and summer, Dr. Beaulieu would take his wife and daughter for a Sunday drive in this car. They were so happy back then. Mrs. Beaulieu would make up a picnic basket. Dr. Beaulieu had it custom made by a local basket weaver. It was an odd design; it had a leather strap on top with strange drawings on it. Very Avant Garde. It had a fancy key attached to it. I don't know what it was for. Who would lock up a picnic basket?"

"That's a good question, Agnes," said Neil. "What else do you remember?"

"When Dr. Beaulieu washed his car, my husband's face would light up and he'd go over there to help him. They'd talk for hours, discussing cars and Dr. Beaulieu's work. I think my husband really misses him."

Neil popped out of the car. "Agnes, do you know where that picnic basket is?"

"I don't know. Seeing the car made me think of it."

"Did the key look like this?" Neil held up the key.

Agnes moved closer and squinted at it. "It's a fancy key. That might be it."

Neil and Aumont exchanged looks.

"We're going to need the car key so that we can open the trunk. Would you—"

Agnes was already heading out the door.

CHAPTER 47

S myth's eyes were hidden by transitional lenses. His expression was composed, and his posture was perfect.

He was a human being designed for efficiency, a performance machine, the counterpart to the Mercedes. When standing at attention while Octavia entered the rear passenger seat, his body countered hers naturally to block any attempt of escape.

The doors locked with a humming sound when Cachemaille joined her in the back seat. The feeling of being sealed in engulfed Octavia, but this time it was worse. This time, she had a predator sealed with her.

She refused Cachemaille's offer of a shot of Pappy Van Winkle 23.

"You're trying to keep your head clear—I understand," he said. "My head is perfectly clear, so I shall indulge myself."

Smug bastard. Don't think about him. Stay calm. I'm too tense. Relax my grip on the cane. Remember, they designed the scepter to be a defense weapon.

Octavia nervously tapped her fingers along the customized Japanese Maki-e lacquer cane. Pictures of the mythical bonsai tree her grandfather had left her, Japanese guardian spirits, and the symbols on her bracelet created an exquisite design on the lacquerware, which was sprinkled and set with gold powder on the surface.

"That is a striking piece of artwork."

"Yes, I am fortunate to have many powerful, talented, resourceful friends and business associates."

Cachemaille smiled. "So do I."

"How long have you been plotting this abduction scheme?" asked Octavia.

"What abduction? You came with me willingly. I know where your sister is, and you want to see her."

"You two must have gotten chummy over the past few days."

"We've been *chummy* since your father died."

"So the reading of the will and her reaction were—"

"All an act."

"She already knew what was in the will?"

"Yes, of course."

"You saw Bastien's video?"

The speaker chime activated. "We are arriving at your destination."

Cachemaille smiled. "Shall we?"

Smyth held the door open, and Cachemaille extended his hand to assist her. She ignored it and defiantly stepped out. He gripped Octavia's arm and guided her towards an unlit building. The exterior sign of Noir Jazz Bar was faintly illuminated by a streetlight.

Octavia felt like someone had injected dread into her veins.

Neil Ames, where the hell are you?

CHAPTER 48

Agnes burst into the house, where she found her husband already back in bed. "Husband, I need you to tell me where the car keys are," she said softly, standing at the foot of the bed. "We need the trunk key."

"Leave me alone, woman. I'm trying to sleep," he muttered, pulling the covers over his head.

Agnes took a deep breath. "Do you remember when you and Dr. Beaulieu would spend hours talking about that car? He trusted you with his pride and joy. We need to honor his memory by helping Neil and the police find who killed him."

"Do they really believe they'll find the murderer hiding in the trunk of my car?"

"Please, it would mean so much to me, husband, and I know it would mean a lot to Dr. Beaulieu, too."

He sat up and sighed. "Fine. For Dr. Beaulieu, I'll get the damn key. I'll take it to them just to make sure they don't mess up the car."

He wrapped himself in his bathrobe, stopped long enough to reach into an empty vintage Texaco motor oil can to pull out a keyring with two keys, then stormed out the backdoor towards the garage, with Agnes and the cat following close behind.

"Here we are," Agnes called out.

"Merci, Monsieur Abercrombie," said Aumont. "Would you please open your trunk for us?"

"I don't know what you think you'll find in there," he grumbled. "There's just a spare, a jack, a lug wrench, and ..." He popped the trunk open, "a picnic basket. I guess he forgot to take it out."

Neil and Aumont stared at it.

"It looks like an ant's nest," said Aumont.

"That's the way he designed it," said Mr. Abercrombie. "Dr. Beaulieu said he was inspired by what he saw in nature, when he and his family went on picnics. I'll show you." He reached in to pull it out of the trunk.

"Wait," said Neil and Aumont in unison. Neil took out his magnifying glass and examined the leather handle at the top, then he took a picture of the basket and the strap.

"What's the importance of the handle?" asked Aumont.

"Bastien used to wear it as a bracelet," said Neil. "It's designed the same way as Octavia's, but the symbols are different. Why did he choose an ant's nest for the design?"

"Tell them what he told you," Agnes urged her husband. "My husband is a retired mechanical engineer, and they talked a lot about engineering."

"Woman, they don't want to hear about that."

"Quite the contrary," said Neil. "What did Bastien say he was researching?"

"Nano robotics and delivery systems."

"Nano robotics and delivery systems are an interesting topic to delve into," said Neil.

"We discussed different ways to fuel nanotechnology, such as utilizing biological mechanisms or tapping into magnetic fields."

"Fascinating," said Neil. "And you discussed nano robotics?"

"Nanobots," corrected Abercrombie. "We talked about the difficulty of developing methods so those little guys can communicate with each other."

"Those little guys meaning the nanobots?" asked Neil.

Abercrombie nodded and dropped his head then glanced at Agnes. "He wanted to find a way to treat people who had the same illness as his wife."

"He was so sad when she died," said Agnes.

"Go on, Mr. Abercrombie," Neil said. "Did you find the topic interesting?"

"Of course, I did. We were talking engineer to engineer. Just because I have white hair doesn't mean my brain isn't sharp."

"I have no doubt of that; I'm hoping you can give me some insights."

Abercrombie's eyes lit up. "Check out this basket, it's a perfect example."

Anxious to get to the point, Aumont asked, "Are we going somewhere with this conversation?"

Both Neil and Abercrombie ignored his question.

"Swarming behavior," said Abercrombie.

"Swarming behavior?" Neil repeated. "Ahh...I see it. Developing algorithms that allow nanobots to work together in swarms to perform complex tasks. Like ants building and supporting a nest. Collective behavior. Swarms of insects, schools of fish."

"Yes! You're smarter than you, look." Abercrombie grinned for the first time. "Now look at this." With a careful rearrangement of the sticks in the ant's nest design, and releasing the leather handle, he opened the basket.

"Cohesion and alignment," said Neil. The nanobots continuously coordinate to stay close together. By aligning with the average direction of nearby nanobots, they synchronize their movement."

"Exactly," said the old man with exuberance.

"But how are they controlled?" Neil asked.

"There is no central controller. That's what is wonderful and frightening about them."

Filled with a mix of awe and trepidation, Abercrombie's voice grew louder and more animated.

"Each bot makes decisions based on local information and interactions. Depending on task requirements and environmental conditions, they have the ability to change roles. And just like ants that leave pheromone trails, nanobots can deposit and detect markers to coordinate movement and task completions."

"The absence of a central controller allows for a decentralized decision-making process," said Neil.

"Imagine that in the wrong hands," exclaimed Aumont.

"Husband, you are so brilliant!" Agnes beamed with pride.

"Now, let's open this up," said Abercrombie. The top unfolded to reveal a flock of birds on the underside of the ant's nest exterior. "This represents the Boids Algorithm," he explained, "simulating flocking behavior. The things you talked about earlier. In this case, cohesion, alignment, and separations are used to display silverware, napkins, condiments, wine opener, and utensils. Everything is coordinated."

"But Bastien always examined the reality of chaos," said Neil, "he explored it in his music. Normal order and functioning can break down, leading to widespread disruption and disorder."

"Yes," said Abercrombie. "It can both create and upset the norm. Which is a way to stop the forward movement of what is thought unstoppable."

"Mr. Abercrombie, you are a philosopher," said Neil.

"Not me." He blushed. "You should see the painting he gave to my wife."

"Yes, I'd like to see it," said Neil.

"Follow me," said Agnes and she trotted out of the garage.

The cat, who had been curiously exploring the garage, leaped into the car trunk and purred softly as it rubbed against the basket.

"Get out of there, you damned cat," Abercrombie growled and started to close the trunk of the Charger."

"I need to take this basket in as potential evidence," said Aumont.

"Like hell you will."

As Neil and Agnes walked into the house, they could hear the argument escalating.

Agnes led Neil through her house to a bedroom that had been turned into a library filled with books about artists and art history.

"Impressive library," he said.

"I earned master's degrees in both education and art history before teaching at Dawson College for thirty years. Here it is." She pointed to a painting hanging on the north wall. "I keep it away from the light, to preserve its vibrancy."

Agnes looked at it fondly. "I think that's why he gave it to me. He knew it would be in safe hands. He and my husband talked about engineering. Adrienne and I talked about art. She won national awards for her landscapes from British Columbia to Nova Scotia. Here's the catalogue of her last exhibition." Agnes pointed to a large, glossy hardcover book.

But Neil was transfixed by the painting in front of him. Agnes followed his eyes. "It's called *Dynamic Harmony*. It was her last work and unlike anything else she had created. It was her wedding anniversary present to Bastien."

"That makes sense from what I am looking at," said Neil. He pulled out his pocket magnifying glass and examined the painting. "It looks like two unique artists created it, but it is her brushwork throughout the complete work."

"You have an eye," said Agnes.

"I was a dual major in college," said Neil, "art and theatre."

"So you see the world differently from most people. What do you see in this painting?" she asked.

"It's parallel worlds," he said, "yet the same world seen through fresh eyes."

"Yes," she said. "One sees the romantic impressionist beauty of the world, much in the style of Manet, but with the saturated color of Renoir and a hint of Cassatt using intimate domestic scenes, especially when she includes her daughter."

"But it transitions into the world of Robert Delaunay," said Neil.

"Yes, I see it, too," said Agnes. She pointed at different areas of the painting. "Here, it is a bold, unified structure using geometric shapes, circles, triangles, and rectangles. But the colors are harmonious and balanced. Shades of blue and green."

"But here," said Neil, "the original shapes begin to transform, varying in size and orientation and more shapes appear. Wait."

Neil pressed his hands together, as if in prayer, and closed his eyes. He remained silent.

"What is it?" Agnes whispered.

He opened his eyes. "Improvisation."

"What?"

"Overlapping shapes symbolize the complexity and interplay of the musicians' interpretations. The colors become more vibrant. There are contrasting colors, like reds and oranges." Neil was on the verge of being ecstatic.

"Adrienne often said she believed color could be used in the same way a composer uses notes to create harmonies," said Agnes. "Every sound had its own tone and hue."

"See, here," said Neil, "the shapes take on a more dynamic interaction. Larger shapes are contrasted with smaller, responsive shapes. The layout suggests a conversation. A call and response. One is leading and the others are following."

"Using alternating warm and cool colors to differentiate between the leaders and the followers, a rhythmic pattern is created visually," said Agnes.

"And look," said Neil, "there are distinct motifs—musical notations and mathematical equations."

"Yes," Agnes exclaimed with child-like excitement. "Using bright yellows and purples for emphasis."

"It combines *The Four-Bar Progression* with her unique perspective on the world," he said, "I think she and Bastien collaborated on this. Thus, the title: *Dynamic Harmony*. It's combining art and jazz."

"Thus." Agnes grinned. "Hardly anyone uses words like that anymore. Thus, I like that word."

Neil continued to stare at the painting. Then he tilted his head to one side and squinted at the center section. "You said, Adrienne often put her daughter in her paintings."

"Yes,"

"Look at the center section, there are two children."

Agnes squinted at the painting. "Yes, funny, I hadn't noticed the second child before. The one in the landscape is clearly Cadenza and her hair is the only dark spot in that section, but the second one is abstract and the hair is bright, like the sun against the red in the large triangle."

"That's Octavia," said Neil.

Agnes was about to respond when Neil's phone pinged, and pinged, and pinged again. The first from Octavia's phone.

GPS Security Alert

CHAPTER 49

A Honda Civic rolled to a stop in the Deep Red Jazz Club parking lot. The lights were on, and two cars were parked close to the building. A figure got out and ran to the entrance. The door was locked.

The figure pounded on the door, then stepped away. Just as they were about to pound again, the door flew open and light spilled out.

"Hello, Cliff. I heard there was a memorial party going on here for Bastien Beaulieu. My invitation must have gotten lost in the mail." Michelle Perusse pushed past him.

"Octavia?" she called out. "Are you in here? Neil is worried about you."

"Octavia isn't here," said Cliff. "Cachemaille has her."

"The attorney? What do you mean by 'he has her'?"

As Cliff blurted out his story, the tension in the room grew, and Charlie's breathing became labored.

"He needs help!" Cliff stood by his side. "He's never been this bad before."

Michelle called 911.

Overwhelmed by the stress of the evening, Charlie's final words came out as a gasp. "I think they're going to kill Bastien's girl."

"I think they're going to kill *us*," blurted Cliff.

Charlie Allen's heart gave out, he stopped breathing. Michelle started CPR. Minutes passed. Cliff was frantic. "When are they going to get here? Charlie, don't you die on me. Come back, buddy."

At last, the sound of sirens grew louder as they approached. The paramedics rushed in, with McGregor behind them. As the paramedics worked, McGregor questioned Michelle.

"Michelle Perusse, what are you doing here?"

"I came to Bastien Beaulieu's wake," she said.

"Don't be cute," growled McGregor. "What's really going on?"

"I think you already know what's going on, otherwise why would you be here?" Michelle countered. "Unless you've taken to chasing ambulances?"

"We've had this place under surveillance since Bastien's death."

"Why?" asked Michelle, "It's been closed for months."

"I'm asking the questions. What's going on?"

"Cachemaille has taken Octavia. He's been working with Cadenza to get the music rights, but I think you know what they are really after."

"Where is he taking her?"

"That guy knows." Michelle pointed at Cliff. "I was about to find out when Charlie collapsed."

As McGregor approached Cliff, the room seemed to shrink and every inch of him demanded an answer. "Where is she?"

Cliff's voice quivered. "Cachemaille told her Cadenza was hiding, and they're going to the club he bought."

"You idiot, he's going to kill her!" Michelle snarled and turned to McGregor. "They're going to the Noir Jazz Bar."

Cliff tossed back the rest of his whisky. "Cachemaille isn't going to kill her. He'll probably have that driver do it."

"What driver?" McGregor asked.

"He calls him Mr. Smyth."

"Mr. Smyth," echoed Michelle. She looked at McGregor. "Well, it looks like you have a chance to make up for Africa." She rushed out to her car and texted Neil.

Cachemaille has Octavia. Grave Danger. Noir Jazz Bar

James sent Neil a text.

Madam's security alert activated. Tracking GPS. En route.

The Audi sped through the dark, rain-slicked streets, the GPS alerts pulsing with Octavia's location. A woman's taunting voice came from the back seat.

"So, the great James Fenmore, always at Octavia's side. Her loyal lap-dog. Does she give you a pat on the head for your troubles?"

James's eyes never left the road. "My assignment is to protect both of you. That includes dragging you along to save your sister."

Cadenza sat with her arms crossed, a look of disdain etched on her face. "Protect me?" She snorted. "From what, exactly?"

"You've been playing a dangerous game, Cadenza. Betraying your sister, aligning with her enemies...killing your father," James said, his voice cold.

"I didn't kill my father. And I went along with your game, didn't I? You told me to call Cachemaille to let him know I was hiding out. He calls me back and here we are." Cadenza leaned forward, her eyes glinting with malice. "Wait until she learns you helped me escape," she whispered. "And just who is it that hired you to protect me?"

James's jaw tightened. "Like I said, my assignment is to protect both of you. Whether you like it or not, you're a package deal."

She let out a derisive laugh. "You're always referring to me as a package. Who is it exactly that you're protecting me from?"

James's voice dropped, low and dangerous. "From yourself. From whatever twisted game you think you're playing. You've betrayed your sister, but I won't let you jeopardize her life."

Cadenza's eyes narrowed. "And what if I don't want to be rescued?"

James looked in the rearview mirror, meeting her gaze with an intensity that made her flinch. "You don't get a choice. Not this time. Because this time, I'm watching you. Every move you make, I'll be there. And if you try anything, anything at all, you'll regret it."

A text notification appeared on the dashboard screen. It was Neil.

Aumont & I en route. Noir Jazz Bar. Killer has her. I have what he wants.

James retrieved a burner phone from the console and passed it to Cadenza. "Call Cachemaille, tell him you're on your way."

CHAPTER 50

Cachemaille received a text. "Good news, Ms. Clarke. Your sister will arrive shortly."

Octavia leaned on her scepter, fingering the base of the handle. "You won't get away with this."

"You have great faith in your friend, Mr. Ames. People who are thought to be trustworthy are so often a disappointment."

"Yes, I find you quite disappointing," she replied.

Cachemaille smiled. "I regret to inform you that you have more disappointments on the way."

His phone pinged. He glanced at the text and walked toward the front entrance. Octavia stepped back, closer to the fire exit. She twisted the ring at the base of the scepter handle, shifted her balance, and waited.

Cachemaille entered the code numbers on the security pad. The door buzzed and opened.

"I'm here. Where's my dear, sweet sister?" Cadenza smiled broadly "I have a watchdog," she said, "my sister's lapdog."

James entered the room behind her.

"James, I'm very glad to see you," said Octavia, "even if you are a deceiver."

Octavia walked toward her sister, grabbed her and hugged her close. Cadenza tried to pull away, but Octavia hugged her closer and whispered in her ear, "Stay close to me. We're getting out of here."

"But will *you* get out of here *alive*?" Cadenza whispered. She pulled away. "All we want is your bracelet. You're the skilled negotiator. Your life for the bracelet."

"What happened to you? Where have you been?"

"It seems I have a rescuer," Cadenza smiled and looked at James. "Don't worry about me."

"You helped her escape? Are you in on all this?" Octavia's anger burned hotter than her surprise.

"They don't want me dead," said Cadenza. "The man with Bernard is Mr. Smyth."

"The NGO guy. I see, he works for Cachemaille. When did you get so friendly with Cachemaille to call him Bernard?" Octavia asked.

Cadenza snickered. "Smyth doesn't work for Bernard. Bernard works for him. My deal is with Smyth, not Cachemaille. Smyth wants my brain, my creativity, my brilliance. All he wants from you is the bracelet. Unfortunately, it is the key to advancing the research. Give them the bracelet." Cadenza's lips curled up, revealing a sinister grin.

Octavia laughed. "You think you've played me, don't you? Well, I'd consider it—" She pulled up her jacket sleeve displaying a naked wrist. "If I had it."

Cadenza's smile turned into a scowl. "What do you mean? You wear it every day. You showed it to me. You told me you consider it your lucky charm."

"Considered. Past tense. It's not a lucky charm. It's a curse. I gave it to Neil."

"Bitch!" Cadenza shoved Octavia, her fists clenched and her features contorted. Octavia realized she was seeing her sister's true face—a face of jealous hate.

James went for Cadenza.

"You're a dead man if you don't stop, Mr. Fenmore," warned Smyth, his voice dripping with menace as he pointed his gun at James "Dr. Beaulieu, back off and search him for weapons."

"She's given the bracelet to Ames," Cadenza snarled.

"Do as I say," Smyth ordered.

Cadenza patted down James. "Nice," she said as she placed her hands in his pants pocket. She pulled out his phone and Audi key fob. "No weapons," said Cadenza. "He talks big, but he's harmless."

"Hand those to me," said Smyth.

Cadenza handed them over and stood cozily next to Smyth. He slipped both into his pocket.

"You gave your bracelet to Mr. Ames. That is both unfortunate and fortunate," said Cachemaille as he walked toward Octavia. "You see, Ms. Clarke, you have no purpose for us without the bracelet, and if Mr. Ames has surrendered your bracelet to the police, there is no reason to, shall we say, keep company with you, and since you know too much, we can't let you . . . live."

"No matter what I do, or don't do, doesn't change a thing...you intend to kill me, and that is unfortunate for *you*," said Octavia, standing boldly before Cachemaille, her eyes locked with his, unwavering. "Beware of the consequences if you decide to eliminate me, Neil will relentlessly hunt you and your organization."

"That's something he's been trying to do for nearly twenty years, and failed." Smyth smirked.

"What do you mean?"

"You wouldn't be the first woman in his life to be . . . *dispatched*."

"The first one of you to lay a finger on her is a dead man," said James.

"You said unfortunate and fortunate," said Octavia, "What's the fortunate part?"

Cachemaille turned and walked back to Smyth. "If Mr. Ames is still in possession of the bracelet, he will exchange it for you,"

"He won't do that." Octavia stood defiantly.

"Oh, if given enough motivation, I think he will." Smyth grinned at James. "You said the first one of us to lay a finger on her is a dead man." Smyth handed his gun to Cadenza. "Here's your opportunity."

Cadenza stepped back. "What do you mean?"

"Take it," said Smyth, "I hate guns, they're so easy, there's no fun killing with a gun." He took the safety off and shoved it toward her.

Cadenza cautiously reached out and took the gun that was offered to her, her fingers trembling slightly as she held it.

"You don't have to kill her," he whispered, "just wound her... for now. I don't know why you're so hesitant, you've killed before."

"That is not true. It wasn't intentional. She went back into the house. I didn't know you'd—"

"So, you're the one who set the fire," Octavia said to Smyth. With a sharp shift of her gaze, she directed her glare at Cadenza. "And you destroyed the home your mother loved."

"You destroyed that long before I did!" Cadenza spat out.

"I hate working with amateurs, don't you Fenmore?" said Smyth. "They're so dramatic. I mean the woman died of smoke inhalation; she didn't burn to death."

"You are despicable," said Octavia. "Cadenza can't you see who you're in bed with? Is this really the life you dreamed of? Because what you are walking into is a nightmare."

"Shoot her," said Smyth, "You know you want to. Don't you want to see her in pain, just like your father?"

Cadenza's voice trembled as she choked out the words, "I never thought you would do what you did."

Smyth laughed. "Whatever gets you through the night. You told Cachemaille that your father was handing over his research and information on Loder International's, what should we call it?...interest in the research to the RMCP. Of course, your poor daddy found out too late that Cachemaille was a liar and his daughter was a traitor."

"I thought you would threaten him...and get the research so I could use it."

"I would have," Smyth said reassuringly, "Unfortunately, he didn't have the research on him and he swallowed the specimen, but I got the proof he had against Loder after I immobilized him. It turns out your information is rarely reliable. You said he had the research papers, he didn't. You said you sister had the bracelet, she doesn't. But, his terror was exquisite. I'm very good at fracturing every good intention a soul has. I recorded it on my phone to share with the others. Would you like to see it?"

"You're a monster!" Octavia rushed toward him, knocking Cachemaille out of the way.

The handle of her cane released and became a dagger, which she thrust toward Smyth's throat. Cadenza pushed Smyth out of the way, knocking him down, and landing on top of him, covering him like a shield. The gun in her hand went off and hit James in the shoulder as he threw himself between the two sisters. Octavia countered to avoid stabbing James and Cadenza, lost her balance, and fell.

Smyth pushed Cadenza aside. He stood up and, moving with lightning speed, struck James with a precise blow to his wounded shoulder, targeting a vital point that sent waves of pain through his body. James staggered, but managed a solid punch to the stomach. Smyth followed up with a series of rapid strikes, targeting nerve points. James limbs went numb, and an agonizing paralysis spread through his body. He collapsed to the floor, helpless.

Smyth looked down at Octavia sprawled on the floor against an overturned chair, her hand still clasped around the dagger. He leaned down and grabbed the dagger out of her hand, slicing across her palm. She struggled to stand, clutching her bleeding hand. "You won't get away with this," she gasped, her voice filled with determination.

Smyth laughed. "I already have." His cold eyes scanned her body. Then he struck her one weak point, her leg, the one she had almost lost in the accident so many years before. With a swift series of strikes, he fractured the bones in her leg.

As she cried out in pain, she locked eyes with James, laying on the floor, struggling to breathe. Despite the pain, there was a silent understanding between them. This wasn't the end. Not yet.

"You're an abomination!" she screamed in both agony and accusation.

"You call *me* an abomination? What do you call your sister? I'll tell you what I call her—a murderous mad scientist. She knew what she was designing, and so did your father. Aren't you proud to be a member of such a bloodline?"

A phone chimed. The absurdity of the chime struck Smyth as hilarious. He laughed hard. Octavia managed a defiant grin from her gritted teeth.

"That's Neil. He's calling me."

"You idiot! Didn't you take her phone away?" Smyth growled at Cachemaille in disgust. "Dr. Beaulieu, get her phone and give it to Cachemaille."

Cadenza's expression shifted from abhorrence to amusement as she fished Octavia's phone out of her pocket. With a sly grin, she passed it over to Cachemaille. He answered it.

"Mr. Ames, how nice of you to call! Would you like to join our party? I'm afraid Ms. Clarke is not enjoying herself. She would feel much better if you were here. I'm sure you know the address. Oh, and it's customary to bring a gift for the host. Perhaps a bracelet?" Cachemaille looked at the phone. "That's rude. He hung up without saying a word."

"You fool!" said Smyth, "He's already here."

McGregor and his unit arrived shortly after Cachemaille and Octavia. They had observed James and Cadenza's arrival. Listening devices had been set in place, and the club was surrounded.

Michelle Perusse arrived next. She watched from her car until she saw Aumont pull up. Neil jumped out of the car and pulled out a two-by-three-foot rectangular object from the back seat. It was wrapped in a rose-colored fleece blanket.

Aumont went directly to McGregor. "I've dispatched police units to secure an eight-block radius. What's the plan?"

"We need to stop Ames from doing anything stupid," said McGregor as he headed toward Neil, who was on his phone.

Aumont caught up with him. "He's not a stupid man."

McGregor cocked his eyebrow. "I can't believe I heard those words come out of your mouth. I would agree with you if Ms. Clarke were not in harm's way."

Neil slipped his phone into his pocket as Michelle Perusse caught up with him. They spoke briefly until McGregor and Aumont approached. She turned to confront them.

"What are you doing here?" said McGregor. "Leave now, or I will arrest you under suspicion of being involved in the abduction of Octavia Clarke."

"I have every right to be here," she shot back, "and believe me there will be hell to pay if you try to arrest me,"

"I can have you escorted away from the area, which I'm going to do right now."

"Don't bother. I have everything I need," Michelle said. She glanced at Neil as she turned to go. He didn't acknowledge her, keeping his focus on the club.

"What's he got in his hands?" McGregor asked.

Before Aumont replied, they were standing next to Neil.

"My team has surrounded the club," said McGregor. "Did you know James Fenmore had Cadenza Beaulieu?"

"What?" Aumont's anger flared. "You knew he had Cadenza all this time?" He growled at Neil. "You told me you thought it was McGregor, who helped her escape."

"Me?" said McGregor. "Why would I help her escape?"

"To get where we are now," said Neil.

"Well, evidently, your Mr. Fenmore pulled a fast one," said McGregor.

"Both he and Octavia sent texts to me. Cachemaille is working with a man called Smyth. They have Octavia's phone and I've heard nothing from James. He's hurt or—"

"He's one of them," said McGregor. "Smyth and I have crossed paths before, on multiple occasions." His jaw tightened. "He's stealthy, quick, and lethal. He's used taijutsu on past victims, which puts him at the top of the list as Bastien Beaulieu's killer and the one that tried to kill Butch Bennett, it's not like him to leave his target alive."

"My only concern is getting Octavia out alive," said Neil.

"You won't do her much good if you're dead. He's a deadly snake. There is no hesitation," said McGregor.

"We shouldn't let you do this," said Aumont. "Don't screw up."

"Yeah, thanks for the advice," Neil said sarcastically.

The RCMP SWAT Team Leader approached McGregor and gave him a report. He quickly returned.

"Things are going bad in there, we need to move now. Once you get Ms. Clarke secured, we're coming in. Remember that Cadenza Beaulieu and Smyth are both a danger to national security," said McGregor. "Do you understand me?"

"I'm here to save Octavia," said Neil. "It's up to you to save the world."

"You don't have the bracelet. What's your plan?" Aumont asked.

"I don't need the bracelet," said Neil, "I've got this." He headed for the entrance.

"What does he have?" asked McGregor.

"A painting," replied Aumont.

"A painting? A painting of what?"

———

Cachemaille answered Octavia's phone. "Mr. Ames, you're unarmed, I'm sure. We wouldn't want a gun to go off accidentally and hit Ms. Clarke."

"I'm unarmed. Open the door."

Smyth took the gun and motioned to Cadenza to open the door.

"I distinctly remember you mentioning that you didn't believe in the necessity of a firearm," Cachemaille said, with a hint of sophisticated irony in his voice.

"A gun," Smyth said coolly, "is simply a tool to grab people's attention."

Cadenza entered the security code. The door buzzed and popped open. Neil carefully entered with the painting.

"What's this?" Smyth asked. "Where's the bracelet?"

"With the police."

Neil put the canvas on a chair. He scanned the room. The dim lighting made every corner a threat. Octavia was leaning against a chair in the center of the floor, her face pale and twisted in pain and her hand bloody. Her cane laid inches out of reach. James was lying next to her, immobile and in pain. Cachemaille stood nervously by, a coward, but still dangerous in his own way.

Cadenza stood next to Smyth, glaring at Octavia with a mixture of hatred and triumph. Neil headed toward Octavia. Smyth shot a bullet into the chair inches above Octavia's head. Then handed the gun to Cadenza.

"If he moves any closer, shoot her."

"If she dies, I will kill all of you," said Neil.

"If she dies, it will be your fault because you didn't bring what you were told to bring."

Neil continued to coolly assess the situation. Cadenza with a gun in her hand was a wildcard. But Smyth is a sadistic killer and now he loomed over Octavia, a cruel smile on his lips. He needed to act fast.

"I've brought what you asked for." Neil pointed toward the blanket covered package.

"Nice try, Mr. Ames, but it isn't the bracelet," said Smyth. He stepped closer to Octavia and poised to strike her throat.

"You need to see this, Cadenza. It has the answers to all your questions." Neil's voice carried a sense of urgency, yet remained remarkably calm.

"Wait," Cadenza said to Smyth. "I want to see what he has. We might need more information from him."

"All right, show us what you've got, Mr. Ames. Move very slowly. Dr. Beaulieu, step back and keep your gun on him," he warned. "I'll just stay close to your sister."

Neil went to the painting, removed the fleece blanket, and revealed it to Cadenza.

Cadenza's mouth fell open and her eyes widened. "This is the last painting my mother was working on. It was going to be an anniversary present for my dad. It was only partially complete the last time I saw it. There's the Abercrombie house. But the rest of this is nothing like anything she painted before. Why did you bring this?"

"Because your father put this in safe keeping. It holds the answer to everything."

Cachemaille chuckled. "A hidden object that conveniently solves the mystery, how nice."

Neil turned to Cadenza. "Come closer and tell me what you see."

She looked at Smyth. He nodded. As she closed the distance between them, she maintained a steady grip on the gun, her eyes locked on Neil. But her eyes were drawn to the painting, and she couldn't help but be captivated.

"It's the painting my mother was working on, the last time I saw her."

"Don't get too close to him. I'd hate to have both of you die," said Smyth.

"Look closer," said Neil. "Look at the signature on the painting."

"If you're trying to buy time for the police to arrive," Cachemaille said as he approached the painting, "you're wasting precious minutes to save your . . . friend."

Cadenza caught her breath. "Simulacra."

"What's that?" Smyth asked, but kept his focus on Cadenza.

"It was the title of the paper Dad was going to present at an upcoming conference in San Francisco. It was a conference on international medical research ethics."

"So, is that important to us?" Cachemaille asked.

She continued to scan the frame and the painting. "There's something etched along the edges. I need better light."

Cachemaille turned on the full bank of lights. Cadenza adjusted her glasses and moved her fingers along the edges. "There are mathematical equations etched into the painting. These are my dad's proofs. I've seen them before. He wanted me to collaborate with him on this project, and look, here's my equation, the one I created on the paper towel—no. It's similar, but different."

"What project?" Smyth asked.

Cadenza pushed up her glasses. "It's still in early stages, but it's a nanorobot killer."

Cachemaille's eyes widened with excitement. "A killer robot. That man was a genius. I hope you will be up to the task and expand on his work. This is good news."

"It's not a killer robot." Neil smirked and shook his head. "You have a rather one-track mind. Unfortunately, it's on the wrong track."

"You are in no position to be a smart-ass." Smyth's eyes grew cold and focused.

"Ask your resident scientist," Neil suggested. "Tell them how it works, theoretically."

"I don't know exactly. He didn't just want to turn them off. He wanted them to self-destruct," said Cadenza. "But, what's puzzling me is this abstract interruption in her landscape painting. This has to mean something. I need time with this. Look at this. I don't understand."

"Unfortunately, we don't have time for you to understand," said Smyth as he walked away from Octavia and headed toward Neil. "And you, Mr. Ames, have no time at all."

Neil's muscles tensed. Smyth moved first, his maneuver almost a blur. He aimed a precise strike at Neil's neck, intending to disable him quickly. Neil anticipated the move, raising his arm to block. The impact sent a shockwave through his body, but he held firm.

Smyth's eyes narrowed, and he immediately followed up with a rapid series of strikes aimed at Neil's vital points. Neil parried and dodged, each movement fluid and efficient. His training had taught him to turn defense into offense. He countered with a swift elbow strike to Smyth's ribs, causing the assassin to grunt in pain.

Smyth recovered quickly, his hands a blur as he attempted to hit specific points on Neil's body. Neil felt a sharp pain as Smyth's fingers jabbed into his forearm, causing it to go numb momentarily. He grit his teeth, ignoring the pain, and retaliated with a knee to Smyth's midsection.

The room had erupted into chaos. The two men circled each other, eyes locked in a deadly dance. Cadenza saw her chance. She grabbed the painting and scrambled toward the door, then realized the gun was still in her hand. She stopped and turned. Once again, her face contorted with pure hatred. She walked toward Octavia and raised her gun. Neil's voice rang out. "Cadenza, don't!"

Smyth smirked, his eyes gleaming with sadistic pleasure. Neil turned and lunged toward Cadenza. She hesitated. Smyth pursued him, aiming a lethal strike at Neil's spine. Neil twisted his body, feeling the brush of Smyth's fingers as they missed their mark and hit Cadenza in the base of her skull. Her eyes grew wide, her body froze, and she collapsed, causing the gun to discharge. The bullet missed its mark, embedding itself in the floor between Octavia and James.

Cachemaille tried to sneak away. The cane that had been kicked aside was now within reach of Octavia. Summoning her last reserves of strength, she grabbed the cane. "Not so fast," she muttered through gritted teeth, and swung it at Cachemaille's legs, sending him crashing to the floor.

Neil took a deep breath, focusing his energy, he feigned a punch, then suddenly dropped low, sweeping Smyth's legs out from under him. Smyth hit the ground hard and grunted out words that stopped Neil's crushing stomp aimed at his head.

"If you kill me, you'll never know."

"Know what?" Neil demanded.

"What really happened to Emily."

The lights went out, plunging the room into darkness. The front entrance and emergency exits flew open. The unmistakable sound of heavy boots and shouted commands of the SWAT team filled the air. Flashlights pierced the darkness, illuminating the chaotic scene. Smyth was pulled from Neil's grasp. The lights popped on. A dazed Cachemaille was crouched on the floor with his arms covering his head. Cadenza was motionless on the floor, her mother's painting beneath her.

"Damn it! Where's Smyth?" McGregor shouted orders to search the entire building. He called in more motor and drone units. Paramedics entered the scene after the police gave them the all clear.

The paramedics attended Cadenza and James first.

Neil rushed to Octavia's side. "It's over, Octavia. You're safe now."

She managed a weak smile, her voice barely above a whisper. "You always come through."

Neil's eyes filled with a fierce protectiveness. "I always will."

The paramedics took over and she was on her way to the hospital.

Neil stood in the room watching the forensics team take pictures, string measuring tapes, and mark bullet holes. The rush of adrenaline from the fight was slowly dissipating, replaced by a heavy wave of fatigue.

His muscles tensed and his senses heightened, ready to detect any signs of an impending flashback. But none showed up. He cautiously allowed himself to feel a sense of relief. The fight was over. He had won, but the danger was far from gone. He knew Smyth would come for him to finish the fight, but then realized that it was he that would seek Smyth.

'If you kill me, you will never know—what really happened to Emily.'

Neil walked towards the center of the floor and found the Abercrombie landscape painting—marred by a boot print in the middle.

"Agnes is going to be so mad at me."

CHAPTER 52

Seven days passed and Neil spent his time at the hotel. Yuu International hired him to submit a report to their security division. The hotel stay was on their dime.

He spent his evenings drinking wine and listening to The Four-Bar Progression while walking the circles of sketches. On the seventh day, Neil's phone rang.

"Hello?"

"I'm on my way to your room."

"Right."

Neil opened the door. McGregor looked haggard.

"Come in."

McGregor entered. The circles of sketches caught his attention. He walked around them without saying a word, then stopped at the circle with the sketches of Smyth and another man at the center. "Who is he?" he asked.

"Smyth said he knew what happened to Emily, and *this man*," Neil pointed to a sketch in the circle—"killed my fiancée twenty years ago."

"That was the Emily Smyth mentioned?"

Neil nodded.

McGregor picked up the sketch. "And this man?"

"He murdered her and got away with it."

"Smyth murdered Beaulieu and got away with it." McGregor's voice was filled with self-recrimination.

"For now," said Neil.

"For now," McGregor agreed.

"You were determined to capture him, yet he escaped. How was he able to do that?"

"He stole Fenmore's Audi. Ms. Clarke told us Cadenza gave Smyth the keys. The next day, we found the Audi abandoned near a private airfield. He's gone."

"You'll get him."

"Yes." McGregor placed the sketch back in the circle.

"I planned to place Fenmore under arrest for sheltering a murder suspect, which I should do to you and Ms. Clarke, but evidently he does have connections to Europol and he was freelancing for them. Yuu International is pulling strings for you two. So you're all getting away with it. I have to say I will be very happy when you all board the Yuu International jet and leave Canada." McGregor grinned. "Good riddance."

"What happened to Butch Bennett?" Neil asked.

"He survived, but he's still in bad shape. He says Cachemaille tried to bribe him to give a vial to him by paying off Bennett's gambling debts. He refused, when he found out about Ms. Clarke inheritance, he thought he could get a better deal from her. Smyth got impatient and went after him."

McGregor crossed his arms and narrowed his eyes. "Bennett said Bastien gave him a vial to hide and he hid it in a set of drumsticks. You wouldn't know anything about the vial he was talking about, would you?" McGregor asked suspiciously.

"A vial?" responded Neil. "What was in it?"

"Bennett didn't know."

"And Cachemaille?" asked Neil.

"He's trying to make a deal."

They stood in silence, their eyes locked as they assessed one another.

McGregor offered his hand. Neil took it, and they shook.

"Got any hand sanitizer?" McGregor asked with a grin as he went out the door. "Tell Athena she's called in all her chips."

———

The days turned into a month and then another. Octavia, Cadenza, and James were still in the hospital. Day after day, Neil would come to visit them.

Cadenza was still in a coma in the dimly lit Neuro-ICU. She was on a ventilator and an intracranial pressure monitor, surrounded by monitors and IV stands with central lines running to her arms.

Smyth's strike was continuing its work. Every movement stimulated multiple hairline fractures across her skull that could spread to her neck and travel down her spine. There was also extensive brain damage, but scans showed her brain was active, not just active, but hyper-active.

A rigid cervical collar encircled her neck; her head aligned with the rest of her body, supported by the collar, preventing any movement, and there was a spinal immobilization device under her body. Despite the swelling and bruising visible on her face, she appeared peaceful, her eyes closed, and a relaxed expression.

James was on a neurology ward recovering from Smyth's multiple strikes that caused temporary paralysis. The first week, he was in a full body brace. Along with other treatments, he underwent electrical stimulation to activate his muscles, to regain control over his hands and arms. He had progressed to wearing ankle braces during his physical therapy sessions on the parallel bars.

The paralysis had a similar impact to a stroke, prompting James to undergo daily speech therapy in order to improve his clarity of speech.

"Hel' uh way t' get a spa tree'ment," James had said to Neil with a lop-sided grin, during one of his hydrotherapy sessions.

"You're lucky," said Neil. "Smyth could have killed you. I wonder why he didn't."

James gave his head a wobbly non-committal shake.

"You were assigned to protect both Octavia and Cadenza. By whom?"

James gave him a sideways glance and said nothing.

A slight smile crossed Neil's lips. "Don't bother answering, I know who. It was the same organization that wanted you to provide a method of escape for Smyth. It's all quite obvious and you've always been open about who your employer is."

James's expression turned pensive. "He'z ah psy...cho...path. Smyth. Who...ever he works...for...not my employ...er."

"Which means your employer was under pressure or doing someone a favor." Neil turned to leave. "You know what will happen if anything happens to Octavia."

James nodded.

"Good," said Neil. "We have an understanding."

Chapter 53

Octavia was on the orthopedic surgical ward. She had gone through three surgeries to repair the fractures in her leg.

The cut across her palm had healed, but a scar remained. She was still in a traction device with external fixators and was in the early stages of physical therapy, which included a continuous passive motion machine.

Her room was brightly lit by natural light from a window overlooking Mount Royal Park. She'd organized the room into a Yuu International communication center. A new laptop with mega security was delivered, and daily video meetings with Fuji and a board executive committee were scheduled at her insistence. Despite the occasional brain fog left over from the anesthesia and pain meds, Octavia was a woman on a mission with three targets requiring a bull's-eye.

"Fuji, I need your help with this. I understand that it's a considerable favor, but I have the means to facilitate the acquisition of various major scientific advancements and the music rights to the compositions and recordings of The Four-Bar Progression for Yuu International. I want Yuu's legal team to sort through the Cachemaille contracts and items he may have hidden regarding Dr. Bastien Beaulieu's work. It's going to be a quagmire because Canada is going to claim national security is at stake."

"I'm sure our team will consider it fun." Fuji smiled and leaned closer to the camera. "But I am more concerned about your well-being and safety. This international criminal network has been troublesome for us for decades. My father dealt with them just as your grandfather did. They are not to be taken lightly, and from what I have been told, they hold grudges. You may still be in danger."

"I'm not the one they will go after."

"I understand. You are concerned about the safety of Mr. Ames."

"And my sister, which is the second favor."

"You want us to intercede on behalf of your sister?"

"She is quite brilliant, or was. I am optimistic for her recovery and she is of more value to Yuu research and development than going mad in a top-security federal prison when she wakes up. She could make Yuu International the premier futurist development company in the world, possibly beyond."

"I'm told she is already quite mad."

"She is brilliant and hyper-focused when it comes to her work. She is *mad* with jealousy and resentment toward me."

"What exactly is it you want us to do?"

"We are known for our technological prowess and intrusive security measures," said Octavia. "Our system is more advanced than any government's, including China."

"*We* are *finessed* in our interpretation of *personal privacy*," said Fuji. "I am happy to hear you include yourself as a contributing partner at Yuu International. I've always thought of you as a family member, but you've always held yourself as separate from the company. What has brought about this change in attitude?"

"If I have been hesitant to fully embrace the philosophy of the company, it might be because of my initial lethal introduction to it."

This was the first time Octavia had spoken directly about Fuji's sister's attempt to have her killed. It was a maneuver she had never intended to employ. Fuji sat back in his chair, looked off to the side of the screen, and typed on his silent keyboard.

Octavia smiled. She knew others were listening in.

Fuji stopped typing, and his eyes scanned a responding message. He leaned forward and put on a forced smile.

"Fuji, I'm sorry I spoke so directly. I apologize," said Octavia.

"There is no need to apologize. You have gone through a series of traumatic events. You may always speak freely to me."

A nurse walked into Octavia's room. "I have your medications, Ms. Clarke."

"I'm sorry, Fuji. Could you excuse me for a moment?"

"Of course. Shall we reconnect in five minutes?"

She nodded, and the screen paused.

"Damn," Octavia said under her breath.

"I'm sorry. This won't take long," said the nurse.

"No, it isn't you, I just have an exacting meeting coming up. Could you hand me my makeup bag? I need to look good for the director of the company."

"Well, I have some news that should put a smile on your face," said the nurse as she handed her the bag. "The doctor is going to be in to see you soon, and it looks like he's going to discharge you next week, once your rehab is set up in Japan."

"That is the best news I've heard in ages," Octavia said with a big grin.

"With a smile like that, you don't need makeup, but I know a bit of lipstick can cure the spirits like magic."

Octavia fixed her makeup, took a deep breath and looked at her reflection in the mirror.

"You can do this. You will do this."

The screen lit up, and Fuji was sitting back, sipping tea from a beautiful ceramic cup with delicately painted cherry blossoms.

"I'll be so happy to be back home and sipping tea," said Octavia. "It looks like I'll be back next week."

He put the cup on his desk and smiled. "I'm glad you consider Japan your home."

"I feel I have a stake in the future of Yuu International, and I have an audacious proposal that, if properly executed, will make our company the most progressive and powerful business entity in the world."

Fuji's smile turned into a broad grin, which burst into laughter.

"Octavia, what are you proposing?"

"I want Yuu International to provide medical treatment and legal representation for Dr. Cadenza Beaulieu, and that's not all. Is Murakami in on this conversation? If he is, I'd like to speak to him directly."

Murakami, Fuji's elder brother, had replaced his father, who had retired as head of Yuu International Holdings. Fuji was the creative side. Murakami was the numbers guy, and all his decisions were based on the bottom line.

Octavia was counting on this trait and smiled when he appeared on the screen. His appearance had transformed. He was no longer trying to look youthful or chic. Now he looked mature, more comfortable in his skin, a tailored designer suit and tie.

"Ms. Clarke, I hope you are recovering well from your injuries. Your presence is missed here."

Octavia did not miss the underlying message. *You've been gone too long, and you've been derelict in your duties.*

"I am fortunate to have such an efficient team under my direction," she said. "They have successfully completed every project I assigned them in a timely and professional manner. They are also eagerly awaiting my return."

"I understand that your sister, Dr. Beaulieu, is in critical condition."

"That's true. I am quite concerned."

"Family comes first, however complicated the relationship."

"Yes. Unfortunately, my presence would probably cause her more pain than good."

"I understand you want Yuu International to offer medical and legal assistance," said Murakami, "That may not be necessary if she continues to fail."

"This much I know," said Octavia, "Cadenza is a fierce fighter. I have confidence that she will recover. That is why I am eager to present my proposal to you, because if we don't do this, a variety of intelligence organizations are going to use her work to develop secret weapons. If we move fast and negotiate a deal with the Canadian government, Yuu International will have access not only to her mind, but to the research and development materials Bastien Beaulieu left me in his will."

She paused and waited for a response.

"What are you proposing?" asked Murakami.

"We will offer to construct a secure R & D complex in Canada, where she will lead a team of the best scientists in nanotechnology and DNA origami. The discoveries will impact every aspect of human existence, all to be patented by Yuu International."

Octavia continued, her voice resonating with confidence and authority. "Cadenza's status as a security risk means she must be housed in a secure facility. No one excels the security protocols of Yuu International. She won't be free, but at least she will be comfortable."

"A beautiful prison." Murakami's face was implacable.

A faint, controlled smile played at the corners of her lips as she maintained a steady gaze at the screen. *I've got him.* "There's more. It's not just intelligence agencies that will want her. There's Loder. They are going to claim ownership of Bastien's and Cadenza's work."

Murakami grunted, his equivalent to a chuckle. "We are not afraid of Loder."

"There's something else. If we are successful and move forward, the final work my father created was a method of shutting down all nanorobots if things get out of hand. The funding and quality of research and development must be at the same level as all the other nanotechnology

R & D work. If something happens, Yuu International will be the hero that saves the world."

Octavia paused. Murakami's facial expression did not change. His breathing was steady.

Reel him in.

"One more thing. Cadenza is not to work on any aspect of this defense part of the research. We will need someone brilliant to break the code of mathematics and musical notation to fully comprehend Bastien Beaulieu's solution.

"Neil Ames has already tackled beginning aspects of the decoding process, I suspect his mind works similarly to my father's, connecting dots and seeing patterns that others might miss. I can help with the musical notations, but I want no connection to the center or my sister. Her needs are to be handled by a neutral party."

Octavia leaned back and relaxed. Her wound was healing, but her hand still ached. She realized she had been holding all her tension there.

"There is one more stipulation," she said.

"Ms. Clarke, there is a limit to how accommodating we could be," said Murakami.

"This is a non-negotiable," she responded. "There is to be no animal testing of any kind used for research and development of any nanotechnology project."

Murakami's face remained stoic, his eyes fixed and unmoving. Octavia sat gracefully, emanating an atmosphere of confidence and tranquility, as she waited.

Murakami finally broke the silence with his soft-spoken words.

"You have an intriguing proposal. I will consider it, and if I decide to accept it, it will have to go before the executive board for approval."

Octavia leaned closer to the web camera; her eyes so intense they gave the impression that they pierced the screen. "I know whatever you recommend, they will approve."

CHAPTER 54

Six days later, Neil went to the hospital to see his friend. Tomorrow they would be going home.

As soon as she saw him, a radiant smile spread across her face. Octavia was back. The months of stress, grief, and terror were over.

Neil pulled up a chair and sat next to her. "How are you doing?"

"I've got my makeup on, and my hair is washed and combed. Now, if you would bring something over for me to wear on the plane, I could get out of this place."

"I had your clothes packed, but I had them leave a few things out for you to choose from." He pulled out his phone and pulled up pictures. "Here, take your pick. Remember, it's supposed to snow today."

"Snow," said Octavia. "When we first got here, the leaves were just starting to fall. It feels like a lifetime ago."

With a look of sheer pleasure, she carefully selected a cozy shearling coat, a cream-colored oversized textured sweater, and a flowing Altuzarra Lemna maxi skirt. "I've got to deal with this." She pulled aside the blanket to reveal a cast that encased the heel of her foot all the way up to the top of her thigh. "I'm hoping the treatment and technology at the rehab center I'm going to in Tokyo will have me downsizing this thing soon." She grinned. "And I've ordered a plain replacement cane. My broken scepter is going back home with me."

She covered her leg and sighed. "As is Bastien's urn. He left no specific instructions on where he wanted to be buried, there is a family plot, but when this whole—" she pointed at her cast, "ends, I'm taking him back to New Orleans, where he can have a real send-off, and I'll place him and his trombone beside my mother."

"What are you going to do about Bastien's house?" Neil asked.

"I'm having it bulldozed. I plan to have the property turned into a pocket park, someplace people can sit and sketch or paint, and a house that fits in with the neighborhood that will display Adrienne Beaulieu's paintings and feature other Canadian artists. Maybe offer artist retreat weekends. It's going to be named the Dynamic Harmony Arts Center. I've hired a landscape architect and building contractor. I've asked Agnes Abercrombie to form a citizen's committee to approve the plans and be the project manager. I'm hoping she'll consider being the center's executive director and curator. Of course, I wouldn't dream of impeding on her Professional Nosy Neighbor enterprise.

"She has a nose for the business," said Neil.

"I can't believe it. I don't think I've ever heard you make a joke. By the way, Agnes is not happy about what happened to her painting. The footprint can be removed, but you put those symbols on it, didn't you?"

"I copied some ciphers and sketched them onto the painting."

"You should go see her. She's probably thrilled it helped solve the case."

"I will, today. What's the news on Cadenza?"

"She's still in intensive, but she's held on this long. The nurses tell me that's positive. I've done what I can for her. I presented my proposal to Yuu International. The lawyers are working on my inheritance issues, and while going through Cachemaille's files they discovered Loder has been dancing around the tax laws, in effect laundering money through the foundation. The Yuu attorneys turned the files over to the Canada Revenue Agency. The foundation is under investigation. They froze the funding to the Elrod Nanotechnology Center. It's amazing how quickly governments can move when taxation is involved."

When will you hear about the board's decision?" Neil asked.

"There's going to be a meeting of the Yuu board this evening. All I can do is wait."

Neil put his phone back in his pocket. "Have you heard from your aunts and your brother?"

"They want me to stay with them, but I'm going back to Japan."

"What about The Pinnacle?"

Octavia dropped her head and thought for a moment. "We moving forward with the re-opening. This whole nightmare has reminded me how much I miss the music business and—home. I'm thinking of buying Old City Hall and turning it into a music studio and production facility."

"You already own the top two floors. The city isn't going to give you any problems. Are you getting Wood Groves involved?"

"Of course. You've got to play the cards you're dealt."

They sat quietly together.

"What's going on with you, Neil? You've been abnormally attentive to things you usually dismiss."

"Nothing. I'm glad we're leaving. I want to get back to the city. I need a break."

"You'll be home in time for Thanksgiving.""Thanksgiving?"

"Yes, it's next week."

"We've been here a long time."

Octavia reached out and touched Neil's hand. "Are you all right?"

There was a knock on her door. Sitting in the doorway in a wheelchair was James Fenmore with a bag on his lap.

"Am I interrupting, madam? I've brought food and wine for our last day here. I also have a message for you from Mr. Fuji Yuu."

She waved him in. "It's good to see you."

Neil stood up and moved his chair. "I see you've got a new set of wheels and your speech has significantly improved."

James smiled. "The clock is ticking, and in fourteen days, I'll be all set for action."

"What did Fuji have to say?" Octavia asked as James pulled out plates, glasses, and cutlery, roast beef sandwiches, and a large salad, followed by a bottle of red wine, and a corkscrew.

"He was checking on our travel plans, and he asked me to tell you the board meeting was rescheduled for an earlier time. It's happening within the hour."

Neil uncorked the bottle of wine and poured it into the glasses. Octavia offered a toast.

"Here's to the friends who never left my side and to embracing life with renewed strength and happiness. And also to a positive response to my proposal."

CHAPTER 55

Neil slept in the next morning, When his phone buzzed at 10 a.m. he smiled and answered.

"You leave a girl to cover your ass at the hospital, you walk into a hostage situation, and then you never call her?"

"Hello, Michelle."

"You owe me a story. I hear they're discharging Octavia."

"Yes, we're flying back to the States at 4 this afternoon."

"So, I have to do all the work in this relationship? Lunch it is. I'm bringing the best burgers and chips in town. You provide the drinks. I'll see you at noon. Bye, honey."

She hung up.

Neil made coffee, showered, dressed, and checked the time. As he poured his coffee, the thought of visiting his old friend Sherlock Holmes crossed his mind, and he realized it had been quite some time since their last meeting.

What to read? Collected stories. "The Adventure of the Speckled Band"? "A Case of Identity"? "A Scandal in Bohemia"—"A Scandal in Bohemia." Why am I so drawn to this one? I've read it too many times over the past few weeks. I could recite it. I'm not reading it again.

His phone pinged. He glanced at the message.

Daniel Upton? I haven't heard from him since, what, over a year ago?

Prosecuting attorney Upton was still riding the wave of positive public opinion since convicting the murderer of retired investigative journalist Katherine Sterling, a complicated case solved by Neil.

Neil read the text.

Call me. Important.

There was a rapid knocking on his door. When he opened it, Michelle Perusse swiftly darted past him, carrying a messenger bag brimming with mouthwatering burgers and crispy chips.

"How did you get by security?"

"You have security?" She pulled the bag off her shoulder and unloaded the food on the coffee table. "I don't think they're watching you anymore."

"Shame, I got used to having them around."

"I'm starved," she said. "Where're the drinks? And I don't mean sodas." Michelle grinned and shrugged off her pink biker jacket.

"You've cut your hair."

"Yes, I'm going to be traveling, and I needed something easier to handle."

"You're wearing makeup."

"Thanks for noticing. The drinks?"

"I have beer and a funky natural Beaujolais that would go well with the burgers."

"I'm a beer kind of girl, but I won't turn down a funky natural Beaujolais." Michelle spread out the food and sat on the floor. "So, you're leaving today. I bet you're glad to get out of this city." She took a bite of her food.

"You said you are going to be traveling. Where are you going?"

Michelle chewed and swallowed. "No," she shook her head. "I need the second half of the story...spill."

"You covered most of it in your last article. It got you a lot of face time on the nationals."

"But it won't get me a Pulitzer unless I get the rest of the story," she grinned."Come on, what's the aftermath?"

"There are some things I won't be able to tell you."

"Oh, *paleeze*." Michelle rolled her eyes.

"Octavia has delicate negotiations going on, so there is only so much I can say at this time..."

"Excellent, she's hot copy. I'll catch-up with her."Michelle pulled out her phone and clicked the record button. "Everything you say from this point forward will be on record."

Neil sat back with his glass of wine. "How much do *you* know?"

"I know about Butch and the nanorobots."

"Nanobots," Neil corrected.

"Nanobots. Okay. I could get in to see him until they found out I wasn't related. He's still not in good shape. He whispered Cachemaille's name and 'gambling debts.' He said a man with dark hair showed up, trying to get a vial Bastien had given him."

She downed her glass of wine and held it up for more. Neil filled her glass.

"I know they have arrested Cachemaille as an accomplice to the murders of Bastien Beaulieu and Molly Obote. And Smyth is somehow connected with Loder."

"I can confirm all you've said."

"You know, I've run across him before—Smyth, in Africa. So, spill it. What was that symbology with Octavia's bracelet? What's going on with Cadenza?"

"How much do you know about Thomas Merton?"

"Thomas Merton? The mystic?" Michelle looked confused. "He was concerned about technology stealing men's souls or something like that."

"That's not exactly correct, but close. Look into 'simulacra.' Bastien was going to present on the topic at a conference in San Francisco. He connected with you to see what you could find out about Loder. He was ready to reveal something at that conference."

"Like, what?"

"Like a way to neutralize nanotechnology before it destroys humanity."

"Ah," she said, 'the post-human civilization'."

"Exactly."

"Hmm, I wonder if that presentation is around to print?" Michelle hinted.

Neil bit into his burger. "This is good," he said, and sipped his wine.

"And Octavia's bracelet?" Michelle prompted him.

"The symbols on Octavia's bracelet is a primer for understanding his coding. He created other symbols as his work progressed. He added more to a bracelet he wore, on his trombone, on a basket and a painting. But primarily in variations of his composition of The Four-Bar Progression. That was the basis for what he was going to present at the conference."

"That made him dangerous. Did you find something to link Loder to Bastien's death?"

"Not enough to bring them down, but they were pulling strings behind the scenes. Cachemaille may be the key, as long as an unforeseen accident doesn't happen to him. As far as Cadenza and her involvement in all this, talk to Octavia. You know Cadenza may never wake up."

Michelle finished her wine and turned off the recorder.

"Now it's your turn," said Neil, "Where are you headed?" With a satisfying crunch, he popped a chip into his mouth.

"My chances of entering a hot spot region rely on whichever contact can pull a few strings. She sighed as she munched on her burger. "I want to go to Ukraine. The criminal networks are probably deeply invested in the war with Russia. You were there recently, yes?"

"Recently, I've only been here. Before that…not Ukraine specifically, but I spent five days in Kazakhstan. But, yes, you're right, there was a major gathering of the networks going on."

They continued to talk about the state of the world, conflict zones that Michelle had traveled to and reported on until the burgers were gone and only a few sips of Beaujolais remained.

Neil stood up and walked over to the circle of sketches he still had not gathered from the floor. Michelle followed him. "These are great sketches. Character studies. That one—" she pointed at a sketch in the center of the circle. "Yeah, that's Smyth. Like I said, I've seen him before. These guys were with him?"

"I suspect they are part of the same organization. This one killed my fiancée years ago and got away with it."

Michelle examined the sketch. "I feel like I've seen his face before, too." She went back to the couch and picked up her biker jacket. "Too bad you weren't able to catch Smyth."

"McGregor is upset. He seems resolved to catch him. Evidently, he's crossed paths with Smyth before."

"McGregor is upset, huh? That's funny."

"Why is that funny?"

"I told you I don't trust McGregor?"

"Yes. You said you thought he was the reason one of your sources was killed."

"Not just my source, but his whole family. When I was in Africa, the name Mr. Smyth came up in interrogations by investigators and interviews I did with one of the few survivors of the slaughter of an entire village. Slaughter because it was a virus that was purposely introduced into the village as an experiment—an experiment of extermination. Smyth was in charge of that atrocity."

Michelle exhaled loudly and ran her fingers through her hair as if to keep it from flying away.

"McGregor said his unit would capture Smyth. He said he was determined to take this guy down. But guess what?"

"Smyth was tipped off."

"My guess is that it was McGregor."

"It could have been anyone attached to the unit or a civilian who worked for them."

"I thought you were smart. Please don't disappoint me."

"Maybe I don't have all the information."

"All right." Michelle slipped on her jacket and put her phone in a pocket. "I saw them together when I was *involved* with McGregor."

"What do you mean you saw them together?"

"They were talking across the street from the bar I was sitting in. They were arguing, but—this is the weird part—before they parted ways, McGregor *hugged* him."

"That's unusual between a federal officer and a major criminal network player."

"That's what I thought, so I asked him about it."

"What did he say?"

"Let's say that it was an unsatisfactory answer, and we broke up. But—"

"You couldn't let it go. What did you find out?"

"McGregor's father was RCMP during the time there was an influx of Chinese from Hong Kong immigrating to Canada. He married a Chinese immigrant, McGregor's mother."

"Ah, the great Earl Grey versus green tea debate."

"What?"

"Never mind. Continue."

"They had two children: Matthew and Marc."

"Marc, as in *Marc Smyth*?"

"Look at that. You catch on quick."

"Do you have proof?"

"Not yet, but hear me out. Matthew followed in his father's footsteps, but his brother had a completely different mindset. He was much more intrigued by his mother and her family. He learned Chinese and went to university in Taiwan, majoring in chemistry. He went on to get an advanced degree in biochemistry at Tsinghua University in Beijing. He never came home, not even when his mother died. He occasionally contacts his mother's family and sends them money. They think he lives in Hong Kong."

"So if McGregor hadn't seen his brother in a long time," said Neil. "He might have given him a hug when he saw him."

"Depends on the brother." Michelle smiled at Neil and slipped on the messenger bag. "It's been fun. Let's do it again sometime."

Neil opened the door.

"Maybe I'll go to Hong Kong," she said. "Or maybe Scandinavia, with Sweden and Finland joining forces with NATO, it might be interesting to see the rise of the Vikings in a faceoff with Russia. So long, *honey*."

She walked out the door, and Neil picked up his phone.

"Aumont, I've called to say goodbye."

"What do you want?"

"I wanted to tell you how much I'll miss you," said Neil.

"I'd rather hear that from Ms. Clarke. How is she?"

"She's leaving the hospital today. She's eager to get back to Japan."

"And leave her sister behind?"

"Yes, but not forgotten. I have a question for you."

"I knew it. What is it?"

"I was thinking about the events of that evening, trying to work out how Smyth escaped."

"There it is. That's the reason you called me. You want to make it my fault that he escaped?"

"No, no, no…Was it?"

"Bon débarras, espèce d'abruti arrogant!"

The phone went dead.

CHAPTER 56

N eil and Octavia left a snowy Montreal. They were heading for the cool and damp of Seattle. James joined them on the flight. There was going to be a brief layover in Seattle to refuel and drop off Neil, then James and Octavia would continue on to Tokyo.

Octavia wore sunglasses. She hadn't slept. The board meeting, vote, and Fuji's call ran through her head. Her desperate plan to save her sister had worked. Now it was up to Yuu International and Cadenza.

They drank, ate, and occasionally laughed. Then they went quiet. There was nothing else to say. Octavia closed her eyes and dozed. Neil scrolled through his phone.

The Return of Sherlock Holmes caught his attention. Holmes returned to London and explained his great hiatus. Neil was several pages in when an attendant roused Octavia to notify her they were about to land in Seattle.

She rubbed her eyes and groaned as she struggled to get up. Neil steadied her. His backpack was slung over his shoulder. Octavia smiled and hugged him, her head pressed against his chest. "Thank you, Neil."

"I have something for you." Neil pulled out the vial he had taken from Butch Bennett's drumstick and a folder. "I found the presentation Bastien put together to give at the medical ethics conference. He planned to hand over this vial to a trusted researcher who was going to be at the conference. All the information is in the folder. No one knows about this. Do with it what you will."

He held her and whispered in her ear, "Keep an eye on Yuu International. They are not knights in shining armor."

"I know that." She put her palm over Neil's heart.

He handed the folder and vial to her then left the plane.

Neil had arranged for an Uber pickup. His test results were examined, and his passport was stamped. He jumped into the waiting Uber and they were on the road, heading to the city.

The reddish-brown smoke had been replaced by heavy rain clouds, and the air was breathable again. Neil's phone rang. *Upton.* He answered.

"Ames, when are you getting back here?"

"I just landed, I'll be back in town in a half an hour or so, depending on traffic."

There were sounds of children playing in the background of the Upton home. "Hold on, I have to get to a quieter spot." Daniel Upton's breathing changed as he climbed stairs. The children's laughter faded in the distance and went quiet as a door clicked shut. "Sorry about that. I'm taking the week off for Thanksgiving. How are things on your end?"

"It's a long story. I saw your text. What's up?"

"There's no easy way to say this."

"Say what?"

"Detective Sergeant John Wallace is dead."

"Dead? What happened?"

"He died by suicide."

There was a long pause.

"Ames? Are you still there?"

"John would never do that," said Neil.

"He left an envelope with a note inside. It's addressed to you."

"I would be the last person in the world he'd send a note to."

"Evidently, you were."

THE END

About the Author

Swinton Woolfe is an adventurer at heart with an insatiable curiosity which has led her through eclectic careers as a social worker, radio news editor, public affairs broadcaster, actor, director, and artistic director of a Shakespearean theater company. A lifelong resident of the Pacific Northwest, she is currently based in the idyllic San Juan Islands of Washington State, Swinton can often be found walking her dog, Sherlock, while plotting the next thrilling twist for the Neil Ames, PI Mystery Series. www.swintonwoolfe.com